To Su

WITH THE

DEVIL

Melanie V Taylor

ISBN-13: 978-1503332164
ISBN-10: 1503332160

Cover photographs © & courtesy of Rachel Groom
www.rachelgroomphotography.co.uk

For

Kristina

Acknowledgements

Anyone who has ever written a book will know that it is impossible to do it all on your own. I owe a huge thank you to Kay and Hannah, the two Dr Pat's for their ecological and botanical advice, Hilary for her guidance regarding environmental legislation, Annette for her advice on environmental pollution and Helen for her wise and generous advice on all sorts of things and to Rachel for the cover image and the countless numbers of cups of coffee when my muse took a rest and decided not to talk to me.

ABOUT THE AUTHOR

Melanie Taylor was born in England, but grew up on the Channel Island of Jersey. She was educated at The Jersey College for Girls.

Studying The History of Art, Architecture & Design part-time as a mature student at Kingston University, then completing a Master of Arts degree in Medieval and Early Modern Studies at the University of Kent as a full-time student at Canterbury, has allowed her to share her knowledge of art and medieval history with adult students. Currently, she is teaching Workers' Education Association groups in Harrow, Ruislip and Epsom. Local art groups have engaged her to critique their work and, in addition, she gives talks about the Tudor miniature portrait painter, Nicholas Hilliard and various aspects of art history.

Melanie writes a regular column on 16th century art for the subscription e-zine **www.tudorsociety.com** and has had two novels published by Made Global Publishing **www.madeglobal.com** who specialise in historical books.

This is her first foray into a novel set in modern times.

DE BRAOSE FAMILY TREE COMMENCES 11TH CENTURY.

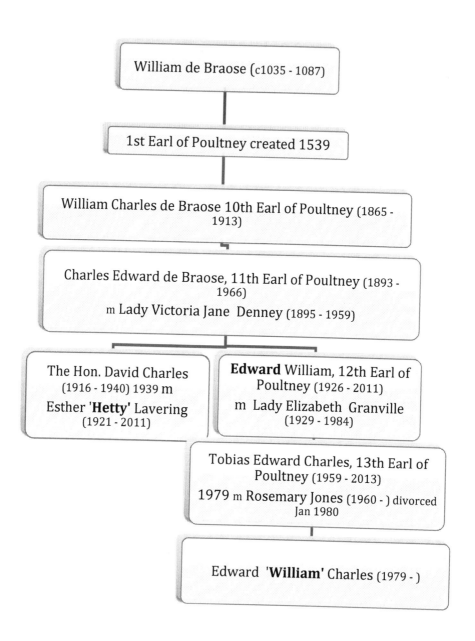

William de Braose (c1035 - 1087)

1st Earl of Poultney created 1539

William Charles de Braose 10th Earl of Poultney (1865 - 1913)

Charles Edward de Braose, 11th Earl of Poultney (1893 - 1966)
m Lady Victoria Jane Denney (1895 - 1959)

The Hon. David Charles (1916 - 1940) 1939 m
Esther 'Hetty' Lavering (1921 - 2011)

Edward William, 12th Earl of Poultney (1926 - 2011)
m Lady Elizabeth Granville (1929 - 1984)

Tobias Edward Charles, 13th Earl of Poultney (1959 - 2013)
1979 m Rosemary Jones (1960 -) divorced Jan 1980

Edward 'William' Charles (1979 -)

THE LAVERING FAMILY TREE

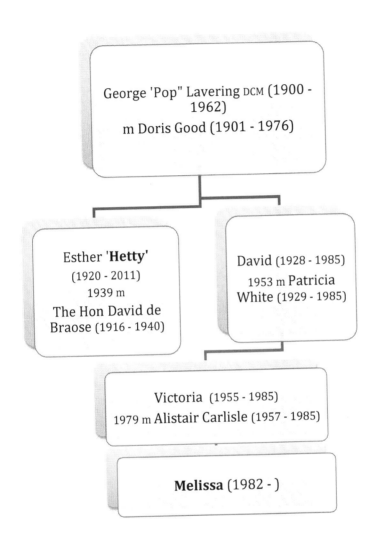

George 'Pop" Lavering DCM (1900 - 1962)
m Doris Good (1901 - 1976)

Esther **'Hetty'** (1920 - 2011)
1939 m
The Hon David de Braose (1916 - 1940)

David (1928 - 1985)
1953 m Patricia White (1929 - 1985)

Victoria (1955 - 1985)
1979 m Alistair Carlisle (1957 - 1985)

Melissa (1982 -)

THE WHITE FAMILY TREE

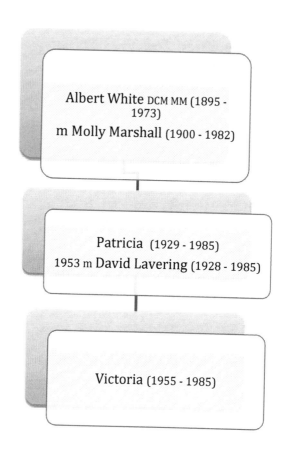

Albert White DCM MM (1895 - 1973)
m Molly Marshall (1900 - 1982)

Patricia (1929 - 1985)
1953 m David Lavering (1928 - 1985)

Victoria (1955 - 1985)

CARLISLE FAMILY TREE

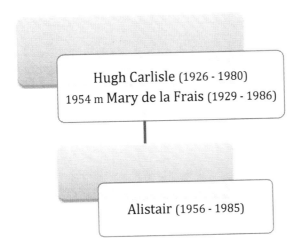

Hugh Carlisle (1926 - 1980)

1954 m Mary de la Frais (1929 - 1986)

Alistair (1956 - 1985)

2011

THE OLD MANOR

Melissa Carlisle stood on the doorstep of the ancient cottage. The heavy studded oak door, black with age, had to be opened, but opening it would acknowledge that Great Aunt Hetty was dead; the last link with her parents severed. Melissa sighed and remained standing outside silently willing the door to open, for Hetty to appear and throw her arms around her: but the door remained steadfastly closed.

Brought up in this medieval manor house surrounded by rambling woods where, at sunset, deer came down to the pond to drink before bounding back into the safety of the wood. Where ducks stood and quacked from the safety of their island as if daring those on the banks to swim across; they knew they were safe so were bold in their taunting. Hedgehogs snuffled through the leaf litter lying under the branches of the old beeches and ancient oaks while squirrels bounded overhead and in autumn buried hoards of nuts in the soft earth of the woodland floor. Today the swifts flew high overhead; their shreep, shreep call reminding her it was early summer despite the chill in the air.

Melissa looked at the large old ornate iron key in her hand. Finally, taking a deep breath, she slipped it into the keyhole and turned it. The door handle was cold. She paused, then pushed. The small inner porch was as it had ever been, lined with gardening clogs, Wellington boots and sundry pairs of shoes; a random selection of coats were hanging from wooden pegs.

After another deep breath she opened the inner door. The high ceilinged room was bathed in the late afternoon sun, but felt empty despite the furniture.

A vase of fresh cut flowers stood on the table with a folded piece of crisp white paper propped against it.

"*Dear Melissa, I have put the basics in the fridge and a cake (your favourite) and some of your special chocolate biscuits are in their usual place. You know where we are if you want anything, but we understand if you want to be left alone, Mrs P. x*"

"How kind." Her eyes welled with tears. Standing at the sink and looking out of the window across the garden and parkland to

Chanctonbury Ring, Melissa saw nothing. It was ten days since Hetty's death and she had been in Rome rummaging away in museum archives. She had hoped there would be a letter from the lawyer telling her where she should go and what would happen tomorrow. She wanted some idea of how long she would have to sort out Hetty's cottage and studio before the de Braose estate took it back.

Lovely Great Aunt Hetty; devoted to her painting, her cats, dogs, pheasants, ducks, geese, hedgehogs, deer - and Melissa.

"Ahum."

Startled, Melissa spun round. A tall, elderly, silver haired man and a small dog stood silhouetted in the open doorway.

"My dear, I saw you come up the drive so Betty and I thought we would walk over and make sure you were all right."

"Lord Edward, how nice of you to drop in," Melissa smiled weakly in an effort to appear strong. "Would you like a cup of tea?"

Lord Edward de Braose, 12th Earl of Poultney, put his arm round her shoulders. His gentle understanding unravelled her hold on her emotions and she gave in to her overwhelming desire to cry.

"It's all right, Melissa. Hetty had a good innings." He handed her a clean handkerchief that smelled faintly of lavender. She wondered if all nice men were born carrying freshly pressed linen handkerchiefs to hand to women whenever they burst into tears.

A soft bark (sounding more like a cough) introduced the miniature wirehaired dachshund.

"Hello," Melissa bent to stroke Lord Edward's canine companion, grateful for the diversion. "Who are you?"

"Betty makes sure I get out of my chair everyday."

Betty rolled on to her back and waved her paws in the air. She cocked her head sideways and Melissa was sure the little dog smiled as she bent and scratched its tummy.

The first difficult few minutes of coming back into the cottage were over. She busied herself making them both a cup of tea.

Edward sat remembering when the skinny little girl with long red plaits had come to live in The Old Manor. That little three year old had grown into this tall slender young woman who, he was pleased to see, had never cut her hair short. He remembered how Hetty had worn her hair casually twisted up into a clip; long tendrils floating free, softening the outlines of her face as she concentrated on what she was painting.

Melissa handed her guest a bone china mug and made herself comfortable at the other end of the sofa. Hetty's armchair stood next to the fire like an empty pedestal waiting for its statue.

"Lord Edward," Melissa paused, not knowing quite how to ask the questions that were bothering her.

The elderly man put up his hand to stop her speaking.

"Please, don't call me Lord. I would much prefer you called me Edward. Calling me 'Lord' just feels wrong. It always has, but, for whatever reason, Hetty insisted so, please, no more Lord anything!"

Melissa considered this for a moment, wishing to show deference to his age and position while still acknowledging he had been part of her life since the very beginning.

Edward de Braose had no idea what was on her mind, but hazarded a guess it was to do with inheritance

"Uncle Edward," Melissa began hesitantly "where's the funeral going to be held?

"Do you mean to tell me no-one's told you?"

"No!" Melissa felt foolish having to ask such a fundamental question. "Not quite. It's my fault." She admitted. "I didn't, or rather I haven't, looked at any of the emails from the solicitors. It was so much easier to focus on my research than what was happening here." Melissa studied her mug of tea. "It was childish, I know. I sat in the car and tried to access my phone, but there's no signal up here!"

Edward smiled ruefully, amused by her generation's reliance on technology.

"Your aunt will be laid to rest in the de Braose family chapel tomorrow morning at 11 o'clock."

"Lord," she stopped, "sorry, Uncle, Edward that's incredibly generous of you, but Hetty wasn't a de Braose."

"Oh yes she was."

Melissa gawped at her visitor. She needed time to digest this new information. "Would you like another cup of tea? I believe Mrs Podger's left me one of her fruit cakes, it would be a shame if we didn't have it while it was fresh."

More questions tumbled round inside her head as she made a fresh pot of tea. If her aunt had been married, who was her uncle? As far as she knew Hetty had spent all her life hidden away deep in the woods on the estate. She took another deep breath; and where she too had lived for the past twenty-five years since . . . since when?

She was an historian, so why did she not want to acknowledge her own history? Why did she not know more about the lovely kind woman who had cared and cherished her after . . . after The Crash?

She put mugs of tea and a plate with biscuits and slices of fruitcake on the table. Melissa nibbled a biscuit, wondering why she did not know about this part of Hetty's life. Betty wuffed reminding Edward that she too was hungry. Edward broke off a small piece of cake and Betty swallowed it in a gulp.

"Hetty was married to my older brother, David, so you see, Melissa, I really am your great uncle." Edward continued. "You may not be a blood relative, but you were my sister-in-law's great niece. Do you remember how I used to come over for tea and we would collect the little snails to feed the ducks?" Edward was not surprised that Melissa did not know about Hetty's marriage. In his opinion, Hetty had had some strange ideas about child rearing and Edward regretted he had not insisted he be called 'Uncle'.

Melissa smiled at her memories of the many summer Sunday afternoons spent with him, rummaging around the borders of the garden collecting slugs and small snails from the damp, cool underside of leaves and various crannies in the old stone walls, all of which were fed to Hetty's ducks who had been very appreciative. They would waddle towards them quacking loudly whenever she and Edward had approached the pond carrying buckets. If she came without a bucket they ignored her completely.

"You taught me why we could only collect the small snails and why we had to leave the large ones."

"A yes, they are so large, half a dozen are more than enough for a meal!"

Melissa made a face.

"Have you never enjoyed escargots in garlic butter, or served in a delicious tomato and garlic sauce?

Melissa shook her head.

"Well, I would suggest we collect some and get Mrs Podger to cook them up, but if William ever learned we'd done that, he would be incredibly cross! However, talking of Mrs P, I came over to see if you would you like to come and have a kitchen supper at New Manor? She said she was doing a venison casserole."

"That would be wonderful. Thank you."

"Excellent, then I'll finish this slice of her excellent cake and take a gentle walk back to the house with Betty here. Shall we say 7 o'clock in the kitchen?"

Edward rose to take his leave and Melissa kissed the old man on his cheek; he smelled of citrus soap and old tweed jackets.

"Thank you," she hesitated, "Uncle Edward." Calling him Uncle Edward felt strange despite it being true.

Melissa was left pondering his strange revelation. Her curiosity overcame her grief and she started looking at the various paintings hung on the walls, in the hall, up the stairs and in the various bedrooms. They were all Hetty's work except for the portrait of herself, which hung on the chimneybreast of the living room. Melissa had always hated it because she could not believe this man really believed her ear sat on top of her head and her nose was screwed round in that silly way. It had been on the wall since 1995, but she had never looked at it with adult eyes. The man who painted it had always been Uncle Patrick, appearing occasionally for lunch and then not being seen again for months. He had never seemed to be anything other than an artistic colleague, but then she had been a child so would have been unaware of any other sort of relationship. Another mystery and another brick wrenched from the solid wall of the childhood she had thought so secure. Then Melissa remembered another portrait - in Hetty's bedroom, but she was not ready to go into that room just yet.

It was a ten-minute walk through the woods to New Manor. The trees were dressed in the beautiful fresh greens of late May. Cutting through the gate in the north wall of the kitchen garden she saw that the fruit trees trained against the north wall were still in bloom. The bees were buzzing in and out of the beehives and neat weed free rows of seedlings in the raised beds showed that Mr Podger, head gardener of the estate and husband to New Manor's housekeeper, had been busy.

Melissa knocked on the open kitchen door. One of the estate cats lay curled in a wicker basket surrounded by several very new kittens, all fast asleep.

"Melissa don't stand there like a door stop!" Short, plump Mrs Podger enfolded her in a warm hug. "Mr P's just making sure 'e's got all the mud off 'iself before we 'ave supper."

"Thank you for everything in my fridge, Mrs P. I completely forgot to get any supplies. Your fruitcake was absolutely the best. Please, how much do I owe you?"

"Wouldn't 'ear of it. You put your money away. Hetty would box my ears if you 'adn't 'ad some cake to welcome you home. It's the least I could do, in the circumstances."

Melissa was just about to ask what circumstances then realised Mrs Podger meant Hetty's death. Lord Edward appeared from the cellar nursing a bottle of wine in one arm as if it were a baby and gripping a couple of bottles with foil wrapped tops in the other.

"Ah, Melissa, perfect timing. Mrs P, what about a drop of Bordeaux to go with your excellent stew?"

"Mr Edward, it's a casserole!" Mrs Podger sounded quite indignant.

Edward winked at Melissa. "I thought we should crack open a bottle of Chateau Margaux,'81; the year you were born. I'll open it and give it time to breathe."

Melissa managed to stifle a giggle. It sounded as though the bottle was being given time to gasp its last. She was amused by how Mrs Podger was distinctly peeved by Edward's calling the delicious smelling casserole she had spent much time and effort preparing, a stew.

"Hello, Mr Podger." Mrs Podger's husband appeared looking very scrubbed.

"Melly, I'm glad you're back 'ome. It's just like when you were little and snitching me raspberries from under me nose!" His accent still had a broad Devon burr despite his having left that county some forty odd years previously. Mr Podger always called her Melly. Her name suggested she knew all about bees and he had told her he would never call her Melissa until she learned to be a beekeeper so, until then, she would always be Melly.

"Now, my dear, perhaps a glass of chilled Prosecco as an aperitivo?" Edward was in the process of peeling the foil from one of the bottles, giving Melissa little chance to say anything but:

"Thank you, Uncle Edward. That would be lovely."

"Mrs P, you too?"

"You know 'ows I like a drop of the bubbly, but I don't suppose Mr P would be too keen. I've got some cider chilling away in the larder, and you knows 'ow fond 'e is of that."

Edward popped the cork releasing a wisp of vapour from the bottle.

Melissa watched the bubbles rise in single lines to the surface of her glass. The camaraderie between these elderly people felt wonderfully solid and reassuring and she wondered how many evenings Hetty had spent in the warm embrace of this kitchen in the intervening years since she had left for university.

"You see, my dear, with only the three of us rattling round in this huge old house it doesn't make any sense to stand on ceremony so we always eat together in the kitchen."

"Mr Edward, that's not always the case ..." Mrs Podger folded her arms. "When Master Tobias comes down 'ere you both eat in the dining room."

"Quite so, Mrs P. Thank goodness that doesn't happen too often."

"I can't remember ever meeting anyone called Tobias."

"Ah, Melissa," Edward sighed "you came here long after my son had left home."

Mrs Podger had dismissed Tobias with a sniff and with Edward providing only basic information, Melissa wondered how she could learn more about the heir to the de Braose lands and title.

"Now, before we get too squiffy perhaps I should run through the form for tomorrow." Edward sipped his aperitif before continuing. "The local vicar will take the service, not that Hetty was too taken with religion, and she will lie next to David. Mrs P has been busy making sure that anyone who comes won't go away hungry. There's nothing worse than going to a funeral, leaving full of cheap sherry and having to stop for fish and chips on the way home! You and I will be chief mourners, so you take my arm as we follow the coffin into the chapel, then it all just follows the normal form."

Edward's simple delivery made the following day's arrangements was very matter of fact. Tears welled and she wiped them away with the handkerchief he had given her earlier, thankful that tonight she was among friends.

The 12th Earl of Poultney and Melissa walked slowly down the aisle of the ancient family chapel. Hetty had been approaching her ninetieth birthday and Melissa had assumed there would not be many people of her generation left, but the chapel was full and there had been several men and women standing outside waiting for the funeral cortege to enter before they squeezed themselves in at the back.

Edward let Melissa step into the de Braose pew ahead of him. The coffin bearers laid their burden on the trestles and stepped away.

"I am the Resurrection and the Life, says the Lord. Those who believe in Me, even though they die, will live; everyone who lives and believes in Me will never die." The vicar intoned.

Hetty's favourite flowers lay on top of the wicker coffin, the draping foliage hiding the casket and making it appear to be one huge flower arrangement. Melissa experienced another stab of guilt. These flowers were something else she should have thought about and organised, but, like everything else, others had done this for her.

She had little idea of who most of these people crowded into the de Braose chapel were, or how they fitted in to Hetty's story. As far as she could remember Hetty had always been painting in her studio. Sometimes visitors had come for lunch, or stayed for the weekend and they had all loved little Melissa. Some of them had played with her telling her all sorts of fantastic stories. Others had taught her how to peel away the hidden layers of meaning of a painting artfully created by long dead artists from a time when the visual message was far more complex than today.

There was the wonderful eccentric scholar, Gerald, who had ignited her passion for old documents. He had told her stories about how the Romans and how they had introduced dormice and the large snails found on the Estate solely so they could eat them. Together they had gone on snail hunts, crawling through the long grass in the early morning dew dressed in togas made out of Hetty's sheets. He taught her how to make special snail noises to encourage the large ones to jump into the bucket. The four year-old Melissa had very soon realised that snails do not make any noise let alone jump, but that had not mattered because it had been fun. She smiled at this memory, realising that she had not seen Gerald's face among the mourners, so perhaps he too was gone. She thought that if he had, then surely Hetty would have told her, but then again, it appeared there were certain things that Hetty had kept to herself, especially if it involved death.

Then there had been winter dormouse hunts organised by Lord Edward. She shook her head remembering that he really was her Great Uncle. They had made medieval style cloaks out of blankets and on crisp, silent, frosty winter mornings gone listening for hibernating dormice. Again it had involved creeping along the hedgerows, but this time very quietly because they had to listen for the gentle snore of the sleeping rodent. At first she had thought this was another silly fancy like Gerald's snail calls, but Uncle Edward had proved to be right and dormice really did snore. She sat picturing the hibernating rodents tucked up snugly in nests hidden deep within the hedgerows that reverberated to the gentle snore of their inhabitants.

"And the blessing of God Almighty, the Father, The Son and the Holy Ghost be among you and remain with you always." The service came to an end. Lost in nostalgic reminisces of her childhood Melissa had not noticed the coffin disappearing into the chapel floor. Hetty would sleep her eternal sleep beside her husband.

"My dear," Edward whispered softly. She felt Edward's hand on her back. "We have to lead everybody out. Come, take my arm."

Together they walked towards the chapel doorway passing the pews full of unknown people. Mr & Mrs Podger were nowhere to be seen. Melissa made to continue walking towards New Manor, but Edward held her back.

"Oh, Uncle Edward, sorry. Er, what do we do now?" She wanted to run away and hide.

"Don't worry, you're not expected to know everyone."

She recognised people from the village who offered their condolences and sympathies and kissed her on both cheeks. Then there were the people from the art world who were surprised to find Hetty had any living relatives. She shook hands with them humbled to find that not everyone knew of her existence.

Edward offered invitations to everyone to come back to New Manor to celebrate the life of a great friend and artist. Melissa took his arm again and together they walked down the rose lined path.

Mrs Podger had been busy: busy supervising the caterers who were providing a buffet lunch. The dining room opened on to the ballroom that was a Victorian extrusion at the side of the Georgian extension of the original Elizabethan house, which was built on the foundations of an Augustinian monastery bought from the Crown by William de Braose in 1539 after the Dissolution of the Monasteries. The long history of the house wrapped itself around her like a safety blanket.

A waitress walked through the crowd carrying a tray of drinks. Melissa took a glass and wondered how she was ever going to afford to repay Edward for this lavish hospitality. She knew enough about fizzy wine to know this was not Italian Prosecco, but real champagne.

The tall man, who had spoken to Edward on the way back from the Chapel, was heading in her direction. There was no escape.

"Melissa, we spoke briefly on the 'phone." She shook the proffered hand, recognising the voice as that of Hetty's solicitor, Douglas Lansbury.

"Mr Lansbury, how kind of you to come."

"We have much to discuss, but this is neither the time nor the place." He paused. "Rather than you coming up to London," he continued, "perhaps it would be more convenient for me to come to your cottage?"

"I do have to return to college at some point. When were you thinking of?"

"Tomorrow?"

The immediacy of his suggestion surprised her.

"Shall we say 10 a.m?" he continued.

Melissa nodded. "Thank you." Clearly the lawyers wanted the cottage back sooner rather than later. She wondered whether she should ask Edward if she could have a couple of months to sort out Hetty's things.

More faces passed in a blur of platitudes and sympathetic murmurs. Melissa smiled inanely, nibbled at a plate of smoked salmon and at the first opportunity escaped to the safety of Mrs Podger's kitchen where she slipped into the rocking chair and hid behind a copy of The Telegraph. The black and white tomcat wandered in and wove itself around her legs before making himself comfortable on her lap. Timmy was the scourge of the local mouse population, but today was too hot to chase mice. The two of them contemplated the newspaper, neither of them taking in what was printed on the page. Melissa had a headful of questions that had no immediate answers and the cat had found a comfortable place to wait out the time until someone decided to feed him.

"Melissa, Melissa, wake up."

"Oh, Mrs P, I'm so sorry, I've taken your chair!"

"Never mind that, my dear, I was worried where you'd got to. Mr Edward said to tell you 'e would see you tomorrow up at the cottage with that lawyer. 'e's found today very tiring so 'e's taken 'imself off to 'ave a little lie down."

"Oh Mrs Podger, here I am hiding away when it should have been me doing all the hard work."

"My dear, Mr Edward saw it as a privilege to give Hetty a good send off." The elderly housekeeper pulled one of the wooden dining chairs out from the table and sat down. "Ee, that's better. Me feet are killing me!"

"Mrs P, how long have you known Hetty?"

"I've been 'ere ever since Master Tobias was born in '59. Lady Elizabeth, Mr Edward's wife, wanted me to train up to replace Mrs Fairfax who was the old 'ousekeeper. It took me five years to learn everything from 'er. By then I'd met Mr Podger, 'im being a trainee gardener 'ere, and the rest, you might say, is 'istory. Hetty was part of the family then, her living in The Old Manor House."

Melissa hesitated. "Was Lord Edward's brother still alive then."

"No, but I think it's better 'e tell you than I get things wrong."

"What is Tobias like? I can't remember him at all."

Mrs Podger harrumphed in a disapproving way, but said nothing.

"I get the feeling that nobody likes him very much."

Mrs Podger gave something that was a cross between a snort and a laugh.

"Until you meet Mr Tobias, me telling you anything would be unfair to Mr Edward, I think it best 'e tells you 'imself."

"What about William? I haven't seen him for years."

"Ah, now young William – 'e's a bit older than you. 'e's the apple of Mr Edward's eye, 'e is. No side to Mr William; what you see is what you get and 'e doesn't demand dinner in the dining room, or that we 'know our places'."

Melissa wondered why the son was apparently so different from the father.

"I'm not one for gossip, my dear, but you do 'ave to wonder whether Mr Tobias was a changeling 'e's that different from 'is own father. William is much more like Mr Edward, but I mustn't rattle on. You're that tired I'll get Mr P to run you back to your cottage. You look as if you could do with a good night's sleep, but before 'e takes you home, I'll put som'at together for your supper."

Melissa tried to demur, but providing sustenance was Mrs Podger's way of showing she cared.

10TH MAY

Melissa had just finished plumping the cushions on the sofa when Betty ran into the cottage wuffing her strange coughing bark, followed by Edward and Douglas Lansbury.

"Good morning, my dear," Edward kissed her on both cheeks: his presence was comforting. Mr Lansbury shook her hand.

"Please, make yourselves comfortable gentleman. Can I get you some coffee or tea?"

Mr Lansbury seated himself at the head of the table and laid some documents in a neat pile on the table.

"Melissa, coffee would be lovely." Edward patted her shoulder then he too sat at the table.

Melissa poured the boiling water into the prepared cafetiére wondering what was coming next. Half of her wanted to know; the other wanted to run away. She was worried about the costs of yesterday's expensive lunch as well as having to pack up and leave the only home she could remember.

"Miss Carlisle, I understand you were unaware your great aunt had once been married."

"Lansbury, it's not your job to interrogate Melissa as to whether or not her Great Aunt had discussed her marriage." Edward intervened.

"It's OK Uncle Edward." Melissa placed the cafetiére on the table and sat down thinking Mr Lansbury must think her incredibly foolish. "Hetty took me in when I was little and I've been here ever since." She wondered who had told him about this. From Edward's reaction she did not think it would have been him.

"Quite so, Lord Edward." The lawyer addressed the 12th Earl. "It's only a matter of months since I joined Tewksbury, Graham & Mather. Unfortunately, I never had the privilege of meeting the late Lady de Braose." Lansbury turned back to Melissa. "I apologise if I've caused any offence. It's usual for someone of your great aunt's standing for a partner to attend these particular occasions, but I've only been assigned this case since Mr Perry retired."

"None taken, Mr Lansbury." She wondered why the lawyer thought Hetty's marriage was relevant and she found what appeared to be idle curiosity, irritating.

"Miss Carlisle, the cottage is, of course, yours."

Melissa gasped.

"In fact," Lansbury continued, "I see from the deeds, the cottage has been yours since you reached the age of eighteen."

"No!" She whispered.

"This is your signature?" Mr Lansbury passed her a document. Her signature was clear and the deed was dated 22nd February 1999, the day she had turned eighteen. She remembered Hetty asking her to sign something at the same time as she handed her a bacon sandwich. Later they had gone out to lunch at the local pub and Hetty had given her the keys to a brand new car.

"How? . . . or rather, why?" She looked at Edward for an explanation.

Mr Lansbury coughed. "Miss Carlisle, we come to the reading of the will."

"I'm sorry, Mr Lansbury, can you give me a moment." She got up, made another cafetiére of coffee and put down a bowl of water for Betty. The callousness of her ingratitude bore down on her. Hetty must have had her reasons, but why had she never said anything? From his own mouth, it was apparent Mr Lansbury had no knowledge of Hetty except from what was in the papers on the table. It was Edward who held the key to her questions and she needed time to formulate these, but not in front of this stranger.

"Mr Lansbury, I shan't waste anymore of your time. Please continue." She looked at Edward who smiled encouragement.

"Hetty de Braose left everything to you." Douglas Lansbury started to summarise the document in his hand. "The 1999 Deed of Transfer of the cottage to you includes the paintings and the contents. Since she rented the studio . . ."

"Mr Lansbury, that's gross. Who made my great aunt pay rent!" Melissa was horrified. This was so wrong! This was Hetty's home!

"Miss Carlisle, it was for tax purposes and I can assure you it was completely legal."

"Legality is not the issue." The cold way Lansbury was delivering Hetty's last wishes broke the last vestiges of Melissa's dwindling reserve. "The fact that Hetty paid rent for somewhere she'd lived all her life, is vile."

"Miss Carlisle, it was the most legally tax eff . . ."

"Lansbury, I DON'T WANT TO HEAR IT! DO NOT REDUCE HER TO A POUND SIGN ON A BALANCE SHEET!" She loved and cared for me and you've reduced that gift to nothing but a commodity. Melissa slammed her fists down on the table. "GET OUT!"

Melissa ran out of the cottage.

The key to Hetty's studio was in its usual place under the rock at the bottom of the two gnarled wisterias growing up and around the door. The scent of the long white and purple racemes filled the air. Hearing Lansbury deliver Hetty's last wishes in such a perfunctory manner had driven home the fact that she was the last member of her family left alive.

The studio still held the familiar smell of paint. Copies of da Vinci's notebooks, his anatomy drawings, books on his paintings and engineering works were stacked neatly on a shelf. Various pots held clean paint brushes; plan chests kept unframed prints and originals clean and flat; exhibition catalogues were stacked on the bookshelf behind the couch. An easel supported an unfinished landscape and a tea stain covered half the canvas. This piece had apparently not gone as planned.

Melissa sat in the battered armchair and Betty jumped up on her knee. Melissa hugged her close, stroking the dog's rough coat.

"Betty, until this morning life was so simple. In a minute I'll wake up and this will all have been a horrible dream." She sobbed into Betty's neck and the dog heaved a sigh, bearing Melissa's sobs with equanimity.

Finally Melissa stopped sobbing and putting Betty on the floor, she got up and took one of the exhibition catalogues off the shelf. The cover showed a painting that had hung over the fireplace in the Notting Hill flat she had rented from one of Hetty's friends. The next catalogue was for an exhibition in New York in 1955; another was for an exhibition at a gallery in Cork Street, London in 1957. Every catalogue was for solo exhibitions held in major galleries around the world in Sydney, New York, Boston, Washington DC, Los Angeles, Perth, Hong Kong, Paris and London from 1938 up until 1985. 1985. That was the year she had come to live at The Old Manor House. These statements of Hetty's professional life had been on the shelf all the time and she had never even looked at them.

Lovely Hetty, the woman who had devoted herself to making Melissa's childhood as magical as possible after her parents were killed.

Killed

Up until now Melissa had always thought about their dying as

The Crash

Surely, the Hetty she knew was the real Hetty?

Melissa held that thought close as Hetty's global reputation as an artist threatened to swamp her.

An inset detailing the prices for each of the paintings in fluttered out of the 1985 catalogue. £25,000, £15,000, £10,000. Melissa was stunned. These were phenomenal prices. There were canvasses stacked against the walls, all of which, she realised, now belonged to her. She preferred Hetty's watercolours on the walls of the cottage to the oils. Melissa had achieved a certain competence as a painter, but did not posses even a smidgin of the indefinable talent Hetty had possessed.

"Melissa" Edward had entered and been watching her as she examined the various catalogues. "I know Lansbury was a bit ham-fisted in the way he told you about her will, but you should not have shouted at him."

Melissa blushed. "Uncle Edward, I'm sorry, but he was turning Hetty into a pound sign. Is he still here?"

"No, and there's a lot more I need to tell you. Hetty was a canny old bird, and between us we've managed to ensure minimum death duties are due."

"What do you mean?" Her voice was small and pathetic.

"When your parents and grand parents were killed some twenty five years ago you became the sole heir to all their estates."

"What?" Melissa looked at him askance. She had never considered where any money had come from. "Why?"

"You and your parents lived on Jersey so, as an orphaned minor, under Jersey law you were subject to something called a Curatel, which is similar to the English Ward of Court. The members of your Curatel decided you should be brought up by your great aunt here in England."

Melissa knew about Chancery and the Court of Wards, but it had never occurred to her that she might have been any sort of ward herself.

"Hetty created a Trust as a way of saving death duties and ensuring your inheritance of her assets."

"Lansbury referred to Hetty as Lady de Braose!"

"As my older brother's widow, she sometimes called herself Lady de Braose whenever she wanted a table at a restaurant, or tickets to Covent Garden."

"But she signed herself Hetty Lavering."

"Quite so. I can't remember her ever using her married name where her art was concerned."

"Lansbury really has no idea of what she was really like at all, does he?"

"When someone of Hetty's standing dies it's usual for the partner in charge of their affairs to be the one who first deals with the family. The original partner knew Hetty very well, but Lansbury tells me Mr Perry is ill, which is why he wasn't here yesterday."

"Oh, poor man."

"Melissa, Hetty was determined you were going to have as normal a childhood as possible, which is why she probably never told you anything about any of the Trusts."

"You said Trusts in the plural. Are you telling me there's more than just Hetty's?" Melissa looked at him and frowned.

"Your great aunt didn't fancy the Government benefiting from all her hard work, so firstly there's her Trust, which devolves on you when you're thirty years old or on Hetty's death, which she believed would come much sooner than today."

"Oh!"

"Don't worry, you'll have the best advisors to guide you."

Melissa listened closely, still not absorbing everything Edward was telling her.

"Further, again when you reach the age of thirty, there are the Trusts in Jersey that also devolve on you, being the estates of your paternal and maternal grand parents and your own parents."

"Oh" Melissa's voice was a quiet squeak "No"

Melissa sat with her mouth open. "No! Why?" She felt sick. "How?"

Edward was not surprised by Melissa's complete ignorance of her financial position. For Hetty, money had been a tool and had found the whole industry around making it, managing it and making more money, incredibly boring. She had placed the responsibility for protecting the heir to the various estates from paying unnecessary taxes squarely on his shoulders, but the Trust set up was a complex structure. He decided that it was probably better to leave any explanation of these until another day.

"Would you like to know more about your Great Uncle?"

Melissa brightened considerably at the possibility of learning more about Hetty's husband.

"Uncle Edward, why do you think Hetty never said anything?"

"I have no idea. Perhaps she didn't want you to be saddened by constant references to tragedy."

"It's strange, but I don't remember either my parents or my grandparents."

"You were only four when they died my dear."

"It's not just that I don't remember them, it's as if my life was always here at the cottage. I've no memories of living anywhere else."

"At the time Hetty decided the best thing was for you to be as unaware of what had happened as possible. In retrospect, I'm not sure that was the right thing, but you have to remember that in that one accident she lost her brother, her sister-in-law, her niece and her nephew-in-law. It's more likely that, by not talking about it and focusing on you, she was able to cope with her own grief. I do not believe it was a deliberate attempt to eradicate any of your own memories."

"I hadn't thought of it like that. When I was little she just made everyday magic."

"Melissa, you became the focus of both our lives. My own son Tobias had divorced so you became a surrogate grand-daughter despite Hetty insisting you called me Lord Edward."

Melissa looked at the old man as if seeing him for the first time. To the outside world he appeared to have everything. Now she now realised there was a deep grief written into his face and his life had been riddled with sadness and loss. Melissa was suddenly acutely aware that the privilege and status enjoyed by Lord Edward de Braose did not bring anything like the happiness she had naively thought they might.

Back in the cottage Edward retrieved some old photograph albums from the bookshelves.

"I was the photographer at Hetty and my brother's wedding, which had been arranged in a great hurry."

"Why?"

"In 1939 it was very evident that the storm clouds of war were about to burst so my brother David asked Hetty to marry him before hostilities broke out and they were married on 25th August. He'd joined the RAF in 1938, much to my father's chagrin and was a fighter pilot."

"Was it a long engagement?"

"No. David asked Hetty in the June of '39 then telephoned our father to let him know that they were getting married. My parents and I appeared up here at The Old Manor together with a bottle of champagne."

"So Hetty was already living here."

"My parents had been at the private view of Hetty's first solo exhibition and at some point Hetty had said she was looking for something out of the way and quiet so she could paint and my father offered her The Old Manor House. It had been let, but the tenant had decided that Canada was probably going to be safer than remaining in England."

Edward paused and poured himself some more coffee. "She and my brother had known each other since they were children and my father gave them the cottage as a wedding present."

"Did they marry in the family chapel?"

Edward nodded, remembering the hot August day as if it were yesterday, when the chapel was full of everyone who had come to celebrate the wedding of the dashing de Braose heir to Hetty Lavering, the new darling of the London art world.

"War was declared on 3rd September and the country mobilised for war." Edward stated flatly. "Most of the men on the Estate were called up or volunteered, which left the estate without most of its workers. Hetty decided that as her contribution to the war effort, she would run the estate farm and managed the small army of land girls who came down here."

"How long were she and David married?"

"Exactly a year. David was shot down over Kent on 24th August, 1940."

Melissa caught her breath at the starkness of his statement. For Edward the memory was still as raw as the day the telegram had arrived informing the family of David's death.

"Uncle Edward, do you think Hetty giving me the cottage on my eighteenth was a bit like your father giving them the cottage as a wedding present."

Edward nodded. He turned the page of the album. A handsome RAF officer, his cap tilted at a raffish angle, had his arm round the waist of an exquisitely beautiful woman.

"This is David with our mother."

"You can see the family likeness."

Melissa turned the page and a young Hetty, dressed in a long cream lace dress, stood next to a beaming gentleman wearing top hat and tails.

"Hetty was beautiful, too." Melissa ran her fingers over the photograph in a gesture of remembrance.

"You are a lot like her, Melissa."

"Many a time she thought she'd lost her favourite paintbrush, forgetting she'd stuck it through her bun."

Edward smiled remembering how Hetty's paintbrushes had often stuck out at odd angles from her bun. Until he had lost his beloved Elizabeth he had not fully appreciated the extent of Hetty's grief at losing her husband. He had adored his older brother, but losing your life partner was different to losing a sibling. When he had lost Elizabeth he had felt as if his life had come to an end, but Hetty had propped him up. Then there had been the crash and little Melissa had come to stay. Both of their lives had taken on a new meaning; someone had to look after this little girl. Like everything else Hetty did, she had got on with it. Despite the events of the past couple of weeks he almost believed she would appear through the French windows and offer him tea and cake.

"She was a very special person, Melissa."

"How old were you when they got married?"

"Oh, I was ten years younger than David."

Melissa wondered why there had been such a big gap between the brothers.

"My father was involved in Whitehall in some way, but he never talked about it, and my mother preferred to live in the country rather than London."

"It must have been quite a daunting thing to be best man so young?"

"It was, plus I was also tasked with taking the photographs."

"Were there lots of people there?" She wanted to know all the details.

20

"Much against your paternal great-grandmother's wishes there were only thirty guests in the chapel followed by a slap up sit-down lunch in the dining room at New Manor."

"Did great grandmother want a big bash then?"

Edward nodded. "Mrs Lavering had wanted the big society wedding with photos in the society review of The Tatler, but Miss Hetty Lavering thought otherwise."

"That sounds like Hetty. Was she anything like her mother?"

"In some respects. Your great grandmother was a determined woman. She had eloped with your great grandfather, 'Pop', in 1919 and got married at Gretna Green much to her father's horror. Your great grandfather then took ship to Canada telling her he would send her a ticket when he'd saved enough money."

"And did he?"

"Well, your great, great grandfather was absolutely convinced Pop had gone for good. Luckily, the letter from Canada with a ticket for her to take ship from Liverpool to join him in Montreal arrived the same day she found out she was pregnant."

"So Hetty was born in Canada?"

Edward nodded. "Pop made a lot of money there and after four years they returned to England, then in 1928 your grandfather, also called David, came along."

"Is he the other boy in these photographs?" A solemn lanky boy stood awkwardly in the wedding line up. There was a strong family resemblance between him and his father and between him, Hetty and their mother, but Hetty's nose was less prominent.

"I wonder where Hetty and I get the red hair from?"

"I remember 'Pop' saying he thought they were descended from Viking marauders."

"Well that could explain the red hair. My great grandfather seems quite short, but I can't tell what colour his hair is in these black and white photos. Can you remember?"

"He was a strawberry blonde and your great grandmother had deep chestnut hair."

"Do you know where they met?"

"I believe Pop was home having been demobbed and your great grandmother was serving in her father's pub. Pop always said it was love at first sight."

"Why was my great, great grandfather so against them marrying?"

"They had only met about five times and were both only nineteen. It shocked the town. Somewhere in Hetty's albums are the news cuttings from the local paper that ran the story of their elopement on their front page."

"How did he meet your father?"

"They'd been together in the Somme."

"But Pop must have only been 16!"

"Quite so. He lied about his age. At the beginning of World War One recruiting officers didn't turn anyone away who volunteered, despite how young they looked."

"I knew that, but when it's your own family it brings it home rather sharply. But you haven't said how your father and my great grand father met?"

"Your great grandfather saved my father's life."

Melissa sat stunned.

"I believe Pop heard groaning coming from no-man's land and he crawled out under the barbed wire, across the mud and literally dragged my wounded father back into the trenches."

"Were they under fire?"

"I don't know because neither of them ever talked about it, but Pop was awarded the Distinguished Conduct Medal."

"Why do you think Hetty never told me?"

"I have no idea, Melissa." He paused, remembering. "I suppose you know nothing about your other great grandparents either?"

Melissa shook her head. "Did you know them too?"

"Hetty's parents were theatre people and they all met in 1946."

She rummaged in the back of a cupboard and brought out some more old photo albums. The album marked 1946 had photos of a more grown up version of the lanky youth and the other people in the wedding photos.

"Was this my grandfather?" Melissa pointed to the youth.

"Sorry, Melissa, I was miles away." Edward bent forward and looked at the photograph. "Yes, that's your grandfather, David. He was about to go up to Oxford to study medicine."

"Which college?"

"Magdalen"

Melissa gasped. "How weird! That's mine."

"I thought you'd chosen Magdalen because of your family links."

"I chose it because the professors were the ones I wanted to study under. I'd no idea that anyone of the family had studied there. But that doesn't tell me how my grandfather met my grandmother?"

"'Pop" and Doris Lavering had taken Hetty and David for a week's break at the Imperial Hotel, Torbay and your grandfather started chatting to this young woman who eventually became your grandmother."

"But who was she?"

"Patricia White, only child of Alfred & Margaret White. With the help of his two brothers, Alfred ran Lichen Entertainment that had variety theatres and cinemas the length and breadth of the Britain."

Melissa was beginning to feel angry because she had been denied this knowledge. History had become an obsession and academic success a safe haven from the school bullies who had mocked and jeered her for living with her great aunt because she apparently had no family of her own,.

Edward's history lesson continued.

"Your mother was born in 1955 and married your father in 1979. Then you came along in 1982."

"How come they lived in Jersey?"

"Your grandfather David had hoped to specialise in lung diseases, but antibiotics had come along making many of these diseases easily curable, so he became a GP."

"But why Jersey?"

"He'd seen an advert in one of the medical publications saying the island needed doctors, so he married your grandmother and then set up his practice on the island in 1954."

"Did you go to my mother's wedding too?"

Edward nodded.

"Where did my maternal great grand-parents live?"

"They moved to Jersey in 1965."

"Why?"

"When Labour got into power in the '60s, income tax went through the roof so your great grandfather and his brothers sold up Lichen Entertainment and he moved to Jersey where tax was low."

"I don't understand why Hetty never told me any of this."

"Well, young lady, I cannot answer that, but I know you had two very brave great grandfathers and two gutsy great grandmothers."

"You said two brave great grandfathers."

"Alfred White was in Mesopotamia during the 14 - 18 war and was awarded both the DCM and the Military Medal." Melissa's jaw dropped in amazement. Edward continued. "Like Pop, he was awarded the Military Medal for rescuing his commanding officer and was wounded in the process, but I don't know how he earned the DCM."

"Did Alfred lie about his age too?"

"No, he was a bit older than Pop."

Melissa shook her head: it was a lot to take in.

"Melissa, perhaps we should take a walk back to Mrs Podger and let her ply us with some of her excellent cake."

"Uncle Edward, my family seems to have been smashed apart by that crash. However, you have a family you can trace back to the time of William the Conqueror."

"That's true, and thankfully the name will carry on through William."

"I remember him coming here quite a bit when I was doing my GCSE's."

Edward smiled. "Dear boy, determined to save the world from exploitation by those whose god is Mammon." He wondered why he always thought of William's father as belonging to someone else, coming to the conclusion that it was because, deep down, he rather hoped he did.

"Didn't William read law at Cambridge?"

"He did. How long is it since you last saw him?"

"It must be more than ten years ago. I was revising and he was about to go up."

"I'm very proud of him, but I never know when he will appear."

"Uncle Edward," Melissa's paused, not quite knowing how to ask the question.

"Spit it out, my dear."

"The papers Lansbury left behind." She paused again.

"Yes." Edward sensed she was trying to wriggle out of addressing the subject of her aunt's estate.

"Can they really wait until after my viva?"

"That depends on when that is."

"Can't I just sign them?"

"You should never sign anything without reading it first!"

"Oh, yes, of course." She blushed remembering the document that had made her the owner of the cottage.

"Hetty made you an executor for a reason."

"I thought the executor was going to be Lansbury."

"She appointed two Executors and you are one of them."

"Oh – but I don't know anything about wills and probate."

"When is your viva?"

"Er, next Friday and, before you ask, I'm not going to defer. I've worked for a very long time and I want to graduate this summer. Hetty would never forgive me if I didn't finish and I'm not sure I could if I put it off."

Edward silently cursed his sister-in-law for being so molly coddling.

"Edward, can't I just not be an executor?"

"Melissa, Hetty has given you that appointment for a reason. Ring Lansbury and tell him you'll see him after your viva." Edward picked up the telephone "Damn it . . . do you have Hetty's address book handy, Melissa? I can't remember if T, G, & M's number ends in 28 or 82!"

"Lansbury left a business card" Melissa dialled the mobile number.

"Mr Lansbury, I'm sorry I shouted." Melissa's apology came as a surprise to the solicitor: she continued; "I would like to be involved in the winding up of my great aunt's affairs. However, I've got my viva on Friday and hope a delay of a week won't be too much to ask."

"Miss Carlisle, sorry, I didn't quite catch that; your what?"

"After next Friday, I'm all yours." Melissa continued.

"Well, Miss Carlisle, I suggest we meet the Friday after. Shall we say at my offices at 11?"

"Thank you. I'll be there." Melissa stuck her tongue out at the telephone.

"Now, Uncle Edward – by dealing with Lansbury today, I can concentrate on my viva."

"Hetty would often stand just like you are now, her hands on hips, head on one side and switch subjects just like you especially if it was something she found distasteful."

"I have different priorities Uncle Edward. While I could postpone the last hurdle to my DPhil on grounds of family bereavement, I feel I'd be letting Hetty down if I did."

Edward nodded. "Are you sure you'll be in the right frame of mind?"

"Lansbury can wait. He is just a lawyer with a piece of paper."

"In that case, Mr Podger can drive us up to Oxford and I'll book us a couple of rooms at the Randolph, or do you still have college rooms?"

"No, I gave up my lodgings in Oxford because I was mostly in Europe, so if ever I was in college I stayed in a local B&B."

"Have you spoken to your tutor since . . ." Edward let the words "Hetty's death" remain unsaid.

"Yes, we were together in Rome when I got the call." The old man shuffled in his seat. "Oh – Uncle Edward, you look shocked." Melissa giggled.

"No, no." Edward blushed.

"**She** was visiting her in-laws, so I took the opportunity of meeting up with her and her husband."

"I apologise. It was unworthy of me to have had such thoughts. Have you been asked to lunch?"

"Yes. It's going to be a long day so please don't worry about driving me down."

Edward beamed. "Melissa, Hetty will come back and box my ears if I'm not with you, and besides, I haven't been to Oxford for many years. It will do me good to have an outing especially for such an important occasion."

Melissa thought for a moment. If it all went wrong and she failed, then Edward would be the best shoulder to cry on.

"In which case I will accept the Professors' invitation to bring a guest to lunch."

Melissa sat twiddling her thumbs. It was too late now: her viva was over. The door opened.

"Melissa, come in. Please come back in."

Melissa was again seated before the four Professors who had grilled her earlier that morning.

"Well my dear, that was an impressive and thorough piece of research. Congratulations **Dr** Carlisle."

Her hands flew up to her face. Her relief was so intense she burst into tears.

"Under the circumstances we wouldn't have minded if you'd deferred until later in the year. Now, let us progress to luncheon."

Her tutor handed her a tissue. It was not the first time a doctoral candidate had burst into tears when told they had achieved the required standard, nor would it be the last.

Mr Podger picked Edward and Melissa up outside Magdalen College.

"Doctor Melissa Carlisle. Your Aunt 'etty will be jumping for joy up there in 'eaven. Mr Edward, don't you think so?" Mr Podger was grinning so widely his face looked as if it were going to split in two.

"Mr Podger, I doubt Hetty would want to be in heaven, she wouldn't know anyone." Edward was trying hard to look serious.

Laughing, Melissa threw her arms round Mr Podger's neck and gave him a big hug: it was the first and probably the only time Mr Podger would call her Melissa. She was not sure what she felt. Elation perhaps, with an underlying feeling of trepidation?

"Uncle Edward, why did you ask if they'd asked me to lunch?"

"You mean to say you haven't worked it out yet?"

"No!"

"Well, they wouldn't have asked you to lunch if they weren't going to award you your bonnet."

"Oh!" It was so simple she wondered why she had not realised it herself.

"Get in Melly. Mrs P's cooking a special supper tonight." Mr Podger held open the rear door of the Bentley.

"That's good, Mr P, because madam here hardly ate anything." Edward had thoroughly enjoyed his lunch even though Melissa had picked at hers.

"Uncle Edward, I hate poached salmon!"

The Bentley purred along eating up the miles and within two hours they were turning into the mile long drive to the estate. Mr Podger stopped the car in the stable yard.

"Come, Doctor Carlisle," Edward proffered his arm. "Mrs P awaits."

They walked through the kitchen garden bathed in the late afternoon sun where Timmy the cat lay dreaming in a patch of sunlight and the swifts flew high catching insects to feed their young hidden in the nests tucked up under the south facing eaves of the stables.

"Doctor Melissa, come 'ere, my darling." Melissa was engulfed in Mrs Podger's enthusiastic embrace. "I'm that proud of you. Now is it tea, or champagne?"

"Tea, please Mrs P. I'll end up completely squiffy if I have champagne."

"Our Doctor Carlisle isn't fond of fish Mrs P and lunch was a particularly fine poached salmon." Edward explained.

"Well, tea it is and a slice of newly baked chocolate chilli cake to keep you going 'til suppertime."

"Mrs P," Edward thought it about time someone thought of indulging him. "I'm just going up to change out of this suit, but I'd like a cup of tea and perhaps some of your fruit cake?"

"Oh my, Mr Edward, but of course. In your study, or 'ere in the kitchen?"

"I will be down in about ten minutes, so perhaps in my study." He looked wistfully at Melissa, reminded of how like she was to both her mother and Hetty. "Young lady, I have something for you."

Mrs Podger busied herself with the kettle and the tins containing the cakes. A vague whiff of alcohol soaked fruit came from the Quality Street tin in the same way that the blue Danish shortbread tin always smelled of chocolate. Anyone who was familiar with Mrs Podger's kitchen knew what tin contained which flavour cake, just as they knew that the square tartan tin with Scottish Shortbread printed on the lid actually contained oatcakes.

"Melissa," Mrs Podger smiled "you've made him so proud. 'E might not show it, but Mr Edward is as proud as a peacock.'

"But what about his grandson?"

"Oh William, 'e's proud of him too, but 'e didn't 'ave the contact with 'im whilst 'e was growing up, not like 'e 'ad with you."

"Why?"

"That'll take time, and it's not the right time now, but suffice it to say William's father and 'is mother were divorced when William were only a year old.

"So William was brought up by his mother?"

"Mr Edward would invite Mrs Tobias and William down for the weekend or longer and it would be great fun. When William went to boarding school 'e would come and stay in the 'olidays and when William was a teenager, in the summer 'e and Mr Edward would go up to Scotland."

"It's a long time since I saw William."

"'e's thirty two this November. Now Melissa, the choice is yours: would you like a grand celebratory dinner in the dining room?"

A bell on the ancient Victorian bell rack tinkled. Edward had arrived in his study.

"The kitchen please, Mrs P. I'll take Uncle Edward his tea."

Melissa wheeled the loaded trolley down the corridor. The study doors were open on to the terrace. Edward was seated in a winged leather armchair. Melissa poured the tea.

"It's been a long day."

"Yes my dear, days as historic as this are to be savoured."

Melissa handed him his cup.

"Thank you."

The chilli in the chocolate cake had the delicious effect of making the chocolate filling seem to flow like lava. Edward savoured every morsel of the rich fruitcake. The fruit had been soaked in a mixture of Earl Grey tea and sherry so the raisins and currants were fat and juicy. Mrs Podger only ever used butter and eggs from the estate farm. Her favourite saying was 'rubbish in equals rubbish out' and did not tolerate margarine, or any other ingredient she considered sub-standard.

"Melissa," Edward picked up a little parcel from the table next to him and handed it to her, "this is a small token to celebrate your attaining your bonnet."

"Oh, Uncle Edward . . ."

Melissa took the small tissue wrapped gift held together with red silk ribbon. A small envelope with the words "Dr Melissa Carlisle" written in Edward's elegant hand was tucked under the bow.

Melissa opened the card:

'On the occasion of your being awarded your DPhil, Much love, Uncle Edward'.

Gently pulling one end of the ribbons the bow unravelled. Melissa slid her fingernail under the tape and unwrapped a small, ancient leather bound book held closed by jewelled clasps.

"Oh Uncle Edward." She slipped open the clasps and revealed the opening page of a 16th century illuminated Book of Hours. "This is exquisite."

"You will appreciate it far more than either my son or William. Tobias will only sell it and William wouldn't even be aware of its existence. If you have it I know it will be safe and what's more, appreciated."

"How long has it been in the family?"

"As far as I am aware, since the early 1500s."

Melissa turned the vellum pages of the exquisitely illuminated book. Each month of the zodiac calendar was illuminated. A painted dragonfly stretched its wings and the edge just broke into the margin for the page for June.

"Do you have a hand lens, Uncle Edward?"

Edward handed her a magnifying glass. As far as he knew, the de Braose Book of Hours had been commissioned from one of the leading families of Flemish illuminators. The old accounts told how his ancestor had paid a small fortune, but that detail was for Melissa to discover for herself if she wanted to examine the extensive de Braose family archives.

"If I'm not mistaken this is from the Bening workshop, one or two of the illuminations might be by another hand, but most of them appear to be by either Simon or his father, Alexander." Melissa looked up. "Did you say early 1500s?"

Edward nodded and waited. He had found the book hidden away on the top shelf of the library several years previously. He knew she would enjoy taking the journey through the de Braose archives and since her ability to read the handwriting from that time greatly exceeded his own, she would read these documents in a fraction of the time it had taken him.

"It's absolutely beautiful, but I can't accept it."

"Why not?"

"Because it's part of the de Braose heritage. It would be a travesty to give it out of the family."

"Melissa, as I said, Tobias will only sell it when I go."

Melissa frowned. She was developing an intense dislike for the de Braose heir. It was difficult to be objective about a man whom everyone avoided mentioning and when they did, they said as few words as possible. Melissa had no memory of Hetty ever mentioning him. That was classic Hetty; if she was unable to say anything nice she said nothing at all.

"My dear, I'm aware of its value, but that's nothing if it's not appreciated. You live and breathe illuminated manuscripts. Hetty knew of my intentions and thoroughly approved, and since she was my sister-in-law thus making you my great niece by marriage, giving it to you means it's not going out of the family." The grandfather clock in the hall chimed seven. "Now my dear, a glass of celebratory bubbles is called for." Edward levered himself out of his chair, "and we had better take the tea trolley back to the kitchen."

"Mrs P, that was delicious." Melissa placed her knife and fork together on her empty plate. The beef had been perfectly pink and the Yorkshire puddings had risen heavenwards. Freshly grown new season runner beans, some early baby carrots, roast potatoes and purple sprouting from Mr Podger's garden had complimented the organic rolled rib of beef from the De Braose farm.

"Is there any left for me?" a voice came from the doorway.

"William!" Edward rose to greet the young man entering the open kitchen door. "Dear boy come in, come in. Mrs P, William needs a plate and a glass."

"Don't rush me, Mr Edward."

Mr Podger was as pleased by William's unannounced arrival as Lord Edward. He had taught William all he knew about the rhythms of the garden. Like Melissa, the raspberry canes had been William's favourite.

William embraced his grandfather, giving Melissa time to appreciate the family likeness. Where Edward was tall and silver haired, William was tall and his hair dark and unruly. Both had striking blue eyes and a strong jaw line.

"This is a delightful surprise and you come at exactly the right moment to toast Melissa's success."

William took a glass of champagne from Mrs Podger and raised it.

"Wha's like us," he said, raising his glass; to which Edward replied "Damn few" and together they chorused " and they're all deed!"

Melissa recognised the toast.

"Perhaps I should more rightly say, they're all in this room!" William added.

"Today, our Melissa has become Doctor Carlisle, having gained her DPhil for her research into the illuminated manuscripts by the Bening family." Mrs Podger delivered her oration with undisguised pride.

William bowed to Melissa. "That's truly something to celebrate. Can you read all that funny writing?"

Melissa giggled nervously.

"Yes, but it's easy once you get used to the hand." She paused, not used to being the focus of a good-looking man. "You read law at Cambridge, I believe? Torte, probate, criminology, litigation are all as complex as deciphering ancient documents."

"Melissa that's extremely kind of you to say so, but I haven't reached the heady heights of a doctorate."

Mrs Podger placed a full plate in front of William. "Now Master William, you look 'alf starved as usual."

"William is more than capable of looking after himself, Mrs P." Edward stated.

"Not like this I'm not" came William's mumbled response.

Melissa hoped that whatever had brought William to New Manor it was not going to upset the old man.

William finally leaned back, replete.

"Melissa, the last time I saw you, you had long plaits and every time anyone spoke to you, you vanished."

"That was nearly fourteen years ago." She said softly.

"No, it can't be that long, Master William!" Mrs Podger was horrified. "Time can't 'ave gone that fast, surely not!"

"Yes, Mrs P. I was taking my GCSEs and William was about to go up."

"If you think that time is speeding up, then my dears, it's a sign of age, and I hate to say this, but I'm pooped! It's been a long day." Edward turned to his grandson "William, will you forgive me if I retire; I'm sure you've lots to tell me, but I'm afraid it'll have to wait until tomorrow."

He turned to Melissa. "Melissa, well done." He brushed her cheek with his hand, which felt dry and leathery. "William will you see Melissa home?"

William got up and gave his grandfather a hug. "No problem, Gramps."

Melissa was about to say she was quite capable of finding her own way home, but Mrs P gave her such a look she said nothing.

"Come on, you two, you can 'elp me clear the table before you see Miss Melissa home."

VERY MUCH LATER

"I'm sorry I couldn't be at Hetty's funeral." William and Melissa were walking along the lakeshore. "I came to know her really well more recently." William continued.

"How?"

"She was a shareholder in the farm."

"Oh" Here was another unknown piece of the Hetty jigsaw puzzle.

"Gramps made me a director when I was 25 and gave me 50% of his shares, which made Hetty the majority shareholder."

"Ah" Melissa realised her Oh and Ah responses were sounding silly. "William, I've been so focussed on my viva I've not given a thought to anything else. A Mr Lansbury came down last week, but I was not in the right frame of mind to see him so I told him I would see him next Monday in London so I haven't got much of a clue as to what Hetty's will contains."

"She was very much involved in the farm."

She paused, thinking.

"When you say very much involved, do you mean everyday?"

William nodded. "Perhaps she felt she needed something to fill her days."

Another "ah" slipped out before Melissa had time to stop it. The idea her absence leaving a void in Hetty's life was unpleasant.

"When you were doing your degree did you come back to see her?" He asked.

"At first, but as I got to grips with my subject I was usually in the library at weekends and so only came home in the vac. Later, I was either in London or in Europe."

"Where?"

"Ghent, Bruges, Venice and Rome."

"That's quite an international forum. Do you speak Italian?" Melissa nodded.

"As well as ancient Latin and Greek?" he asked.

She nodded again.

"Hmm, impressive!"

"And Modern Greek, French and Spanish." She added.

"Do you want a job as a translator?"

"William, I'm an historian. What would I know about being a translator?"

"I need someone I can trust and my Greek is rubbish. You don't have any Russian as well do you?"

Melissa realised he was serious.

"My Russian is minimal so I don't think I would be of very much use to you."

"Hetty often wondered why you hadn't done languages."

"Did she?" She blushed discovering she had been the subject of their discussions. "William, it seems you know far more about me than I do you."

"That's typical Hetty. I don't suppose she told you I came to visit her."

"No, there's lots she didn't tell me."

"Perhaps she didn't think it was worth mentioning."

"I'm beginning to feel I never really knew her, despite living with her since I was three."

A silver pathway of reflected moonlight lay across the lake to the trees on the other side.

"Melissa, she adored you. She talked about you to everyone; she was tremendously proud of you. Giving you the freedom to do what you wanted was the greatest gift she could have given you."

34

"I don't see it that way." Melissa replied. "It's as if she didn't want to share her life with me."

"Look" William pointed to a spot on the other side of the lake. "

A deer appeared out of the wood and came down to the lake to drink. This one was soon followed by several more.

"They look so delicate." She whispered.

"They're part of the park herd."

"What sort are they?"

"I can't be for sure in this light. The park has a mixture of red and fallow deer. From their size, I think they're red. Look, over to the right – in the gap between the trees."

Melissa could not see where William was pointing.

"Look straight down my arm."

She looked at the gap in the trees.

"What am I looking at?"

"Badgers!" He whispered. Suddenly the deer skittered back to the safety of the trees "Bother, something's spooked them! Come on, let's get you home. Next time I'll bring some night sights."

"Night sights?"

"They're special binoculars so you can see stuff in the dark."

"Do you do this as part of your job?"

"You mean scooting round in the dark spying on things? No, I'm usually in offices making sure companies comply with environmental law. Sometimes I need to do field trips, but not often enough."

"Did you come and see Hetty with your father?"

"Good God no! Hetty and he couldn't stand each other. Apart from Gramps, he and I don't have anything in common."

They reached the cottage door.

"Would you like a coffee?"

"Thank you." William paused, looking at her. "You look just like her."

Surrounded by Hetty's photo albums, the two of them identified the young Edward, Hetty, her husband David, Hetty's parents and brother David, Edward's parents and a small child they thought was probably Tobias. A later album showed another set of elderly people who had to be Melissa's other great-grandparents, the Whites. Melissa identified the young woman holding a baby as their daughter, Patricia. It was strange looking at the woman who was her grandmother and she had never seen before. The date was 1955, so the baby had to be her own mother, Victoria. The album for 1979 had photos of a big wedding in a country church. Hetty had written "*St Brelade: 12th May 1979. Victoria & Alistair's wedding*" in gold ink on the inside cover.

"Hetty doesn't seem to have any photos of your mother and father's wedding."

"No, his wedding was in a registry office."

"Why?"

William hesitated and Melissa thought she had overstepped the mark with this question.

"My father was born in 1957 when Gramps and my grandmother had virtually given up hope of having any children, so you can imagine the arrival of a son and heir was heralded with much celebration. Gramps had suffered from TB as a child so was declared unfit for the Forces, which was why he was able to go to university in '43 and never did National Service."

"I know I should know, but I don't, so this is not such a silly question, what was his subject?"

"Physics. He ended up with the British nuclear team during the '50s and was out in Los Alamos with the Yanks."

"Was Tobias born in the US?"

William nodded. "My great-grandfather, another William, was still alive, and when my great grandmother died in 1959, Gramps was summoned home to learn how to run the Estate. Luckily, great grandfather lived longer than seven years otherwise most of the Estate would have been sold to pay the death duties."

"Why seven years?"

"Broadly speaking, if you gift something of value to someone then you have to live another seven years for there to be no estate duty payable on that gifted asset."

"What about Trusts?"

"Is this to do with Hetty's Estate?"

Melissa nodded.

"You'll have to ask Gramps because it was probably him that dreamed up anything to do with trusts. I've only been involved with the farm side of things, but after Gramps was summoned home he decided to do a law degree."

"But you must be able to give me some idea of Trusts."

"Each one is individual to the situation. Who's the lawyer?"

"Someone called Lansbury."

"Douglas Lansbury?"

Melissa nodded again. "Do you know him?"

"Not personally. My mother knew a Douglas Lansbury who was in the same year as Tobias."

"What did your father read?"

"History."

"Do you think it's the same Lansbury?"

"Possibly. It could be a coincidence, but I'm not a believer in coincidence. I'll ask her about him for you if you want."

A blackbird began to sing.

"Grief, Lissie, it's nearly dawn. You should get some sleep. I've got to talk some stuff over with Gramps tomorrow, no wrong, this morning. Ring the house when you wake up, but if you're not up by noon then I'll ring you."

Melissa yawned, suddenly aware she was incredibly tired.

William let himself out.

Melissa fell into bed and was instantly asleep.

"Good morning William." Edward spoke from behind his copy of The Times. "You were late back last night."

"Sorry, Gramps. Did I wake you?" William helped himself to the bacon, tomatoes and mushrooms keeping warm on the Aga.

"No, dear boy, I was awake with the dawn chorus."

"Gramps have you met this Lansbury?"

"Who?"

"The solicitor in charge of Hetty's estate."

"He was at the funeral."

"Gramps I've got a niggle and I don't like it. Has Melissa inherited the farm shares?"

"When Lansbury wanted to discuss Hetty's will she threw a tantrum and threw him out of the cottage."

"Melissa doesn't seem to know anything about her parents or grand parents at all."

"Hetty was wrong in that."

"She's got nothing she can call family memory except for life with Hetty and that seems to have been incredibly sheltered."

"William, Hetty did what she thought was right, but I agree, Melissa does seem to have very few ancestral references to draw upon. Perhaps we can help fill in some of the gaps."

"That's going to have to be down to you and perhaps Mrs P, but I can start with a tour round the farm. If she's inherited Hetty's shares perhaps we could invite her on to the Board?"

"William, she might not even be interested so let's wait and see if she thinks the same way we do before making her a director of anything."

"Quite so, Gramps, I wasn't meaning we should offer the invitation today."

"Anyway, William, what was it you wanted to discuss?"

"Did Lansbury leave a copy of Hetty's will?"

"He left Melissa a load of papers which she said she was going to leave until after her viva, but I doubt she's even aware of where she's put them."

Edward could not have been more wrong. Melissa was sitting at her dining table with three sets of documents in front of her. The one right in front of her was Hetty's will; to the right, a share certificate, a

Trust Deed sewn with red ribbon and a notepad. To her left was a document torn in two.

There was a short written list of questions she wanted to ask the one person she trusted absolutely.

Melissa picked up the will and read it again.

"As to my personal possessions within the cottage, these I give and bequeath absolutely to my great niece, Melissa Victoria Carlisle, daughter of Alistair and Victoria (née Lavering) Carlisle the one exception being the oil painting of my late husband The Honourable David De Braose in his RAF uniform which I leave to my brother-in-law Sir Edward de Braose unless he predeceases me, in which case, this portrait is to be given to his grandson William.

I leave the entire contents of my studio to my great niece, Melissa Victoria Carlisle, aforesaid, absolutely.

Melissa had read enough ancient wills to know this was a very simple document. However, the Trust Deed needed more consideration.

Betty rushed in and coughed/barked, followed moments later by the two men.

"Did you sleep well, Uncle Edward?" she asked, kissing his cheek.

"Like a log, my dear. I gather you were quite late?"

"We watched the deer by the lake so it was well after midnight wasn't it, William."

William smiled, but said nothing.

"However, Uncle Edward," Melissa continued "I've been reading the papers that Lansbury left and I've a couple of questions."

"Melissa, I hope you're not going to let Lansbury do all the work." William asked.

"On the contrary." Melissa picked up the two pieces of the torn document and tossed them across the table.

William picked them up, pieced them together and read what was a Power of Attorney giving Douglas Lansbury full authority to act as he thought fit regarding any aspect of the late Hetty Lavering's will as well as for and behalf of all of Melissa Carlisle's financial affairs. William handed it to his grandfather.

"Gramps, perhaps we should have a look at all the documents Lansbury's left if that's OK with you, Melissa. I think he's after the farm shares."

"Why would he want those?" Melissa asked.

"Hetty owned 50% of the farm company, William has 25% and I have the other 25%." This time it was Edward who replied.

"Melissa, any chance of some coffee?" William asked, stifling a yawn. "The farm is over two thousand acres, plus there are a whole load of cottages let to various tenants, the farm shop and the saw-mill, plus the majority of the woodland and the whole of the lake, all of which makes up the land owned by De Braose Farm Ltd."

Edward picked up the Trust Deed and flipped to the Schedule of Assets.

"Melissa, the farm shares form part of the Trust and there's a list of assets you might like to look at." He folded the Deed at the list and passed it over.

500 Ordinary £1 shares in De Braose Farm Ltd.

The freehold of the property known as 28 Notting Hill Gate, London.

The freehold of the properties known as 17-25 Randolph Road, Oxford

20 Randolph Road was where she had chosen to live with three other graduates and they had all paid rent to a management company.

28 Notting Hill Gate was the address where Melissa had 'borrowed' a garden flat from a 'friend of Hetty's'. Because much of the research for her doctorate had to be done in London Hetty had said she would pay the rent until such time as she qualified. Melissa did not know whether to be cross with Hetty for not telling her any of this, or happy because her life had appeared to be the same as any other student. William was leafing through the bundle of papers.

"Here, William, is this what you're looking for?" Edward handed his grandson a draft set of farm accounts. "Melissa, this Trust was set up years ago. Hetty had owned the Notting Hill property since the late fifties and converted the house into flats, keeping the garden flat for herself and renting out the others. This Trust was set up to protect both of you from death duties. It bought the Oxford properties and the rent from these paid your fees and your allowance."

"But, Uncle Edward, when Lansbury was here, you mentioned something about Trusts in Jersey."

"You'll have to visit the Trustees in Jersey for the up to date details as the professionals who administer these are in St Helier. I've not been involved for many years except as an ear when Hetty moaned about the fees they were charging. You'll probably find the files in her study."

Melissa had been sitting cross-legged on the sofa; she unfolded herself and took herself off to Hetty's study.

"William," she called. She stood in front of the closed door hesitating.

"You OK, Lissie?"

"William, I'm scared I'm not going to like what I find."

"There're no ghosties and ghoulies in there – spiders maybe, but probably only books and stuff!"

"Stop it. This was Hetty's private study."

"OK, I understand. I'll go first."

The door opened onto a sunlit room filled with neat bookshelves groaning with books. Two shelves above the desk had files marked *Melissa* and *Melissa – Jersey Trusts* in date order from 1985 onwards up to the present day.

"See, no hobgoblins hiding behind the fireplace!"

"No, only ones on the bookshelves."

William reached up and took down the earliest file marked *Melissa – Jersey Trusts*. The top sheet listed the contents: Members of the Curatel; the individual wills of David & Patricia (née White) Lavering, Alistair and Victoria (née Lavering) Carlisle: the Trust Deeds for the Estates of Mr & Mrs Alistair Carlisle, Mr & Mrs George Lavering, Mr & Mrs Alfred White and Mrs Hugh Carlisle.

William then took down the latest file, which contained the last combined set of accounts for all four Trusts and handed the open file to Melissa.

"No!" Melissa squeaked. "No!"

Edward was standing in the doorway. Melissa handed him the file. "Oh, yes my dear that's what I thought they might be worth."

"But eighty million!" Melissa sat down feeling sick. "How?"

Edward flicked through the file. "Property mainly."

"If I'd signed that power of attorney would Lansbury have been able to do what he wanted with all of this?"

"Yes, I think a Power of Attorney would extend to the Channel Islands if it were registered with the Jersey lawyers. He would certainly have had authority over Hetty's estate."

"But why would I want to give someone I don't know that sort authority?"

"Perhaps you should ask Lansbury on Friday."

Melissa presented herself at the offices of Messrs Tewksbury, Grange & Mather and was shown up to Douglas Lansbury's office on the fourth floor.

After the initial shock at the audacity of Lansbury's ruse she had got extremely angry. She had wanted to report him to the Law Society immediately, but both Edward and William suggested she try and find out more of what he was up to.

Lansbury's office had wood panelling and bookcases lined with leather bound legal yearbooks.

He stood and proffered his hand. "Miss Carlisle"

"Mr Lansbury, thank you for taking the time out of your busy day."

Lansbury settled back into his chair. Melissa sat down and crossed her legs. His secretary brought in a tray of coffee and biscuits. The middle-aged woman smiled at Melissa and left. "Coffee, Melissa?"

"No thank you and it's Doctor Carlisle." Melissa re-crossed her legs – the only sign she was extremely nervous. "Mr Lansbury, it is Mr Perry who was appointed Executor as well as myself."

"Quite so," Lansbury paused very slightly before adding, "Dr Carlisle. "However, when an Executor is a solicitor who has retired, the duties are undertaken by the firm where he was a partner." He sipped his coffee.

"Lansbury, I think I've examined enough wills from across the centuries to know the format. You and I know that if this were the case the address of these offices would have been cited instead of Mr Perry's private residence and I'm here to tell you that Mr Perry and I will be winding up Lady de Braose's Estate as per the executor clause in my late great aunt's will. Plus" she paused, "I am dismissing your firm for acting for me in any capacity whatsoever."

"Dr Carlisle, this is most unwarranted." Lansbury spluttered. "Our firm has acted for Lady de Braose all her life."

"Lansbury, just instruct your accounts department to send me a final invoice for any outstanding work, plus all the various files you have, both current and archived."

"But what about the Trust?"

Melissa's voice dropped to a whisper. "Under the terms of the Trust, the assets become mine on the death of my aunt or my thirtieth birthday, whichever comes first."

"Quite so, but there are things that need to happen!"

"Since the assets are not numerous, their transfer to me is nothing a local solicitor could not undertake."

"This is most irregular. I must insist I'm allowed to bring this Trust to its conclusion."

"NO! . . . On no account are **you** having anything more to do with either me, or my great aunt's affairs."

"Dr Carlisle, your tone is most displeasing."

"Various people are aware of your attempt to get me to sign a power of attorney." She paused. "Need I say more?" Her voice was barely a whisper.

Lansbury sat back wondering where the hysterical child he had met only a few days ago, had gone to.

"Your firm is no longer acting for me in any capacity. Your invoice will be paid as soon as it is presented and I expect all files to be couriered to me immediately."

"Dr Carlisle we never hand over files until the final invoice is settled." Lansbury tried to recover his position by falling back on company protocol.

"You have my word that your invoice will be settled as soon as it is presented." Melissa's voice was barely a whisper. "If you don't trust me, perhaps your accounts department would like to email it to me to speed the process."

Melissa got up and walked to the door where she turned.

"By the way, Lord Edward is having lunch with your senior partner today."

Lansbury watched the door close. He felt sick. He should never have allowed himself to be persuaded into getting her to sign a power of attorney. He reached for the phone.

Outside, Melissa hailed a cab.

"Where to, love?" The cheery cabby asked. Melissa thought for a minute.

"RAC Pall Mall, please."

"Luverly day, Miss, ain it. Seems as if Lon'on's got 'er summer dress on."

"Quite so. I've not really taken much notice recently."

"Been away?"

"Sort of." Melissa's last memory of weather had been in Rome. Since the funeral each day had just happened, except for the day in Oxford when she had been aware Edward's immense joy at being with her and how the sun had shone. Was that really only three days ago? The cab stopped at traffic lights.

"Are you having a holiday this year, cabbie?" She asked, wanting to talk about anything banal than actually know his plans.

"Yep. Taking the wife and kiddies to Malaga – two weeks of sun and fun I thought, 'specially after this last winter. Now the bloomin' weather decides to be 'otter than Spain! Might as well 'ave saved me money and stayed at 'ome! With this sort of 'eat we could 'ave gone to Brighton or Bournemouth and got just as brown as being in Spain!"

The cab sped round Trafalgar Square and through Admiralty Arch.

"I'm sure you'll have a lovely time when you get there."

"Well, it's one of them Mark Warner 'olidays, so it's a bit on the expensive side up front, but everything's included and there's lots for the kids to do."

"How many children?"

"Four – 'ere we are love." The cab came to a halt outside the RAC. Melissa handed him a ten-pound note and waved away the change.

A highly polished vintage car was on display in the foyer. Melissa enquired at the reception desk whether Lord de Braose had arrived and was told he was in the Long Bar.

"Shall I have you escorted, Madam?"

"That won't be necessary." A deep brown voice spoke from behind her.

"William, I had no idea you were included in this lunch."

"I wasn't. Come," he took her arm and linked it through his; "I too remembered Gramps is having lunch with the senior partner of T, M & G. How did this morning go?"

"I've just sacked Lansbury."

"That wasn't on the plan!"

"I know, but he tried to tell me that the firm had been appointed as executor and Mr Perry's name was just a formality. Knowing that wasn't the case I found myself telling him his services were no longer required."

"Bloody hell . . ."

"I thought it only fair to come and tell Edward and Mrs Tewksbury after the Trustees' meeting this morning, but they'd already left the office."

"So they have no idea?"

Melissa shook her head. "I don't think so." They paused at the top of the stairs scanning the bar for Edward. "William, he's over there in the corner."

"Well, old Tewksbury's in for a bit of a shock when he gets back to the office."

"William," Melissa paused. "Would your firm act for me?"

"I'm sure they'd be delighted. By the way, you can't do business on Club premises so I wouldn't mention sacking Lansbury until Tewksbury's left."

Edward and Mr Tewksbury rose as the two young people got to their table. "My dears, how lovely. Tewkers, this is my great niece, Doctor Melissa Carlisle and you remember my grandson, William."

"Doctor Carlisle, I believe congratulations are in order. Edward tells me he was with you when you were awarded your bonnet."

Melissa blushed. "I've yet to graduate, but yes, I've reached the level of DPhil." She shook the elderly solicitor's hand.

"William, it's good to see you again. Are you still immersed in environmental law?"

"Mr Tewksbury, indeed I am. Someone has to save the planet."

A waiter pulled out the chair for her to sit down.

"Uncle Edward, did you have a successful meeting?"

"Indeed we did and the assets can now be transferred into the Jersey Trust of your choosing. Can't see any problems, can you Tewkers?"

"Indeed, we've signed all the relevant documents, you just need to countersign them."

"What's your area of expertise?" Melissa liked the older man.

"Trusts, my dear. I've known Edward ever since he and I did our articles together in the early 70s. I was fresh out of university and he'd decided to have a change of career. More to the point, what's your area of research?"

"Illuminated manuscripts of the late 15th and early 16th century, by various 'Masters of' from Bruges and Ghent."

"Ah, so very highly specialised. Perhaps we should have champagne to celebrate?"

"I would very much prefer some fizzy water with some orange juice, if you wouldn't mind."

"Of course; anything you like."

Melissa hoped her actions were not going to spoil their longstanding friendship. William nudged her foot gently. He was finding everything highly amusing.

By mid-afternoon they were all standing in the foyer and Mr Tewksbury declared he would walk back to his office.

"Now you two. How come you decided to gate crash my lunch?" Edward asked as Mr Tewksbury walked away eastwards along Pall Mall.

"Well," Melissa groped for some form of explanation, "I just wasn't in the mood to go shopping and I didn't think you'd mind since Mr Tewksbury was one of my Trustees."

"Melissa's phone was turned off and I thought she might come to the Club to meet you. But there's something I want to show her right now, so I'm going to whisk her off." William took her hand. "Come on Lissie, this won't wait."

Edward opened his mouth to speak.

"Sorry, Gramps. I'll tell you when we get back to the country."

"Go on, Melissa." Edward waved his hand. "Mr P and I will go back home on our own."

William had hailed a black cab and was giving instructions to take them to Cockspur Street as fast as possible.

"Get in, Lissie. We have to get to Tewksbury first and tell him what Lansbury's been doing. He clearly hadn't a clue about what happened with you and Lansbury this morning and we need to know what Lansbury's been telling his partners."

"William, couldn't we do this on the phone?"

"We could, but face to face is always better when you're accusing a partner of a major law firm of attempted fraud."

"How do we know if Mr T's going straight back to his offices."

"Didn't you hear him tell Gramps that he had a partners' meeting this afternoon?"

"No, well, sort of. I haven't actually accused Lansbury in so many words, just made him realise he couldn't treat me like an idiot and then sacked him as my solicitor."

William snorted in amazement at her naivety.

"'Ere you are, guvnor." The cabbie stopped and William shoved a couple of ten pounds notes into his hand.

"Come on, Lissie." He took her hand and half dragged her down the street to where they could see Mr Tewksbury very nearly at the office building.

"William, I can't keep up wearing these heels!"

"Catch me up!" William sprinted the fifty yards down the cul-de-sac and disappeared through the doorway seconds after Mr Tewksbury.

Melissa hobbled after him in her fashionable, but impractical, high heels and minutes later caught up with him just inside the building, gabbling to the bemused solicitor.

"Lissie, perhaps you should tell Mr Tewksbury why you really busted his lunch appointment!"

"Come upstairs. My office is a much better place for confidences."

The receptionist was trying hard to get her senior partner's attention, but Mr Tewksbury ignored her. The lift swept them to the top floor.

Mr Tewksbury's office reflected his position within the firm and they made themselves comfortable in the leather armchairs on the client side of his desk facing his legal throne, which was framed by a plate glass window that gave a view across a secluded park on the Embankment where London's traffic flowed alongside the River Thames.

"Rebecca, can we have tea for three." The lawyer spoke into an intercom.

Melissa looked at William, who was looking smug.

"Now you two. What's so important that you've dashed here to ambush me as soon as I get through the door?"

William looked at Melissa and raised his eyebrows indicating she should relate the morning's events.

"Er, actually it's me, Mr Tewksbury." Melissa paused. Mr Tewksbury waited for her to continue. "I had a meeting with Mr Lansbury this morning about Hetty's will."

Mr Tewksbury looked puzzled. "Mr Perry may have retired, but when he learned of Hetty's demise he was most insistent he undertake his duties as Executor; they were close friends so I don't understand. What's this got to do with Lansbury?"

"I take it then that Mr Lansbury was never going to be in charge of winding up her Estate?"

"Certainly not. He's new to the firm and has nothing to do with the De Braose affairs."

William and Melissa exchanged glances.

"Mr Perry isn't ill then?"

"Good grief, no. He's as fit as any overweight, elderly solicitor can be. Who told you he was ill?"

"The day after Hetty's funeral, Lansbury came to The Old Manor House and told me he was representing your firm, then read me Hetty's will. Since he came from your firm, neither I, or Uncle Edward, had any reason to question him. It seemed as if all she was to him was a line in a balance sheet. It upset me and I threw a hissy fit and stormed off to the studio. Edward told me that Lansbury had left a bundle of papers, which I decided could wait until after my viva, and Lansbury agreed we could meet this morning. It wasn't until this weekend I went through the bundle and read his hand written instructions of what to sign and where and one of these was a general Power of Attorney."

"What!" This shook Mr Tewksbury out of his post lunch lethargy.

Melissa held up her hand. "This morning I came to tell him I wanted to take up my duties as Executor, but ended up sacking him and telling him to courier all the files to me."

"Do you have the Power of Attorney?"

Melissa opened her handbag and handed him the two pieces of the unsigned document.

"Did Edward know about this?"

Melissa nodded. "He knew I was going to tell Lansbury that he was not going to be winding up Hetty's affairs, but he had no idea I was going to sack him."

Mr Tewksbury flipped the intercom to his secretary. "Rebecca, is Douglas Lansbury still in the building?" There was a knock on the door. Rebecca entered carrying a tray with tea for three and laid it on the corner of the desk. She handed a white envelope to Mr Tewksbury, who slit it open with a paper knife.

Rebecca poured them all tea.

"Do you know what this is, Rebecca?" Mr Tewksbury held the sheet of paper in front of him.

"No, it came in the internal post."

"Lansbury has resigned with immediate effect." Mr Tewksbury passed it over to Melissa.

The secretary gasped.

"Rebecca, could you talk to his p.a. and see if she knows anything and, if you hear anything outrageous write me a note and bring it into the partners' meeting."

Rebecca nodded and withdrew.

"Well, Melissa, it appears Lansbury is condemned by his actions. I can only apologise on behalf of all the partners and say that we will be calling in the fraud squad and undertaking a full internal investigation."

"Oh, gosh. Mr Tewksbury!" Melissa looked bewildered. "Why?"

"I can think of a whole Trust full of reasons, my dear, but I'm not sure why he targeted you?"

"You said Lansbury had only been with the firm for a couple of months." William asked.

"Yes William, we wanted to expand our area of expertise and Lansbury was recommended to us because of his expertise in international corporate law so we created a partner's position for him."

"But, if Mr Perry isn't at death's door, why didn't he come to Hetty's funeral?" Melisa asked.

"He was having the batteries in his pacemaker renewed." Mr Tewksbury replied. "I too tried to shift a meeting but couldn't. I had no idea that Lansbury had even been to New Manor."

"Did he buy in?" William's asked. Melissa wondered why this would be relevant.

They were interrupted by a quiet knock on the door and Tewksbury's secretary poked her head around the door: "The partners are all in the Board Room."

"Well, Melissa, would you like to tell them your story, or would you rather I did?" Mr Tewksbury looked questioningly at her.

Melissa looked at William, who gave the faintest nod of encouragement.

"Perhaps it would be best coming straight from the horse's mouth." She replied.

"Gramps, I believe this is the same Lansbury who was at University with my father. Mum never had a good word to say about any of father's university friends and, according to her, he and Lansbury were close and apparently, are still in touch." William was bringing Edward up to date.

"You have proof of this?"

"She saw them having lunch in Simpson's."

Edward looked at his grandson questioningly. "And this gives you a reason for concern?"

"It does."

"Why do you think this meeting would have anything to do with Melissa? Your father may be a genuine client of Lansbury's."

"Well, his behaviour after Melissa left his office, for one. He clearly panicked. Plus it was after Monday's episode he was seen with Tobias." William paused, waiting for Edward to make a comment, but the old man remained silent. "Tewksbury told us that Lansbury had been recommended for his expertise in international corporate law."

"Did Tewkers say who recommended him?"

"No."

"This is all just circumstantial evidence. Just because he had lunch with your father doesn't make him a fraudster. And how come you just happened to be at Pall Mall on Monday lunchtime?"

" I disagree, it's all **too** circumstantial. As for being at the RAC, when I couldn't get Melissa on her phone, I thought she might come to tell you about what had with Lansbury, so I waylaid her in the club foyer."

"Why didn't she tell us both at lunch?"

William looked sheepish. "On the way to the Long Bar I told her there was a club rule about no business discussions on the premises."

Edward raised his eyebrow. "There's more business done in the Long Bar than you've had hot dinners and you know that! What was your real reason for stopping Melissa telling us her story? Are you suggesting Tewksbury may be involved?"

"It was possible. Hetty's Trust is not inconsiderable."

"I have known Tewkers for forty years and he was with me all morning. I don't like the implication that you think he is capable of fraud!"

"You have to consider what could have happened if Melissa had signed that Power of Attorney and not called Lansbury out?"

Edward still could not see how the friendship between Lansbury and Tobias had anything to do with Melissa.

"Gramps, my father will be furious when he learns the details of Hetty's will." William continued.

"If you're thinking about the 50% share of the farm, he's never shown the slightest interest in it."

William pushed his chair back and went to look out of the window. It was drizzling.

"When was the last time you saw him?"

Edward picked up the paper and re-immersed himself in the sports pages. Tobias was a wealthy man in his own right, so there was no reason for him to be involved in attempted fraud.

"Why do you want to know?"

"Because I don't want to see you hurt."

"He can't hurt me anymore than he's already done, but that doesn't stop the fact that he will be the next Lord De Braose, nor that he's your father. You are making some serious allegations. Lansbury could quite easily come after you for defamation."

"I doubt that!" William snorted. "The man's up to his neck in shit. I know he is."

"With all due respect you should get hard evidence before making allegations like that."

"Gramps, Melissa's had a phone call from Mr Tewksbury. Evidently Lansbury got his secretary to photocopy all Hetty's files and when he did a runner she thought someone ought to know."

"William, Melissa is the one with the grievance and, whilst I admire your championing her cause, you should be advising caution." Edward stood up. "Now it's late and I've had a busy week. I'll see you in the morning." He looked down at the dachshund snoring on her tartan cushion.

"Come, Betty. Time for bed!"

5TH JUNE

Melissa gave up trying to sleep. Why had Lansbury bolted? William kept saying he had a theory, but so far had not offered any further explanation. She wondered what would happen to her relationship with Edward if Tobias really were involved in some way.

The drizzle had stopped and the garden was studded with diamond dewdrops. The sun was only just above the horizon, but the day was already warm. It was so peaceful she took her cup of tea out to where she could sit and appreciate the delicious early morning scent of roses and honeysuckle. A rabbit hopped into the undergrowth and a blackbird trilled his early morning tribute to Phoebus just as the first rays of dawn touched the terrace.

Melissa sat wondering how often Hetty had sat doing just what she was doing now. Hetty had always been up and about as soon as the sky began to lighten. Light had been so important to her. In the long dark nights, after the clocks went back, the curtains were drawn at sunset to forbid the dark ghosts of winter entry except when it snowed then the curtains were flung back and the strange, pure light reflected from nature's white blanket flooded the rooms. Reflected moonlight from white snow was a unique light and Hetty had captured this in some of the paintings that hung in the house. The turning of the seasons were key to her landscapes with the different lights of spring, summer, autumn and winter all needing a different treatment. Inside the house the scatter cushion covers were changed when spring arrived. Lime greens, blues and soft greys for spring and summer, but hot reds, gold and oranges gave the sofas a warmer feel for autumn and winter.

The cottage and its ten acres of woodland and pasture merged into the de Braose estate with no boundary fences to mar the view and the only sound to be heard was the dawn chorus greeting another day. Now The Old Manor had passed into her stewardship.

"Oh Hetty, thank you so much." She spoke the words softly. Hetty's body might be gone, but Melissa felt as if she were watching. "Did you and David sit here as I'm doing now?" A blackbird sang as if in reply. "I hope that blackbird singing is you telling me you did. I promise I'll look after it for you; all of it."

"Talking to yourself is one of the first signs of madness."

"William, you gave me such a fright!"

"Couldn't you sleep either?" William sat down next to her.

Melissa shook her head. "The past couple of weeks have been mind boggling."

"Don't you graduate soon?" he asked as he sat down next to her. "As a doctoral graduate do you give a speech?"

"No, only the honorary docs do that. Who'd want to listen to me talk about illuminated manuscripts?"

"Do you have any idea what you're going to do next?"

"Are you're asking if I've got any idea of what I'm going to do with the rest of my life?"

"You've got a lot to think about."

"I haven't thought that far, William. I'm still trying to get to grips with how everything has been completely turned upside down. I haven't the first clue what to do next."

"I heard you say you would look after all of this."

"Don't mock!"

"I'm not. Hetty was very involved in the Farm so it's not just The Old Manor you have to think about."

"I thought you had a manager."

"We do now, but in the early days it was all Hetty."

"Edward told me about her farm work during the war, but I hadn't realised it had continued."

"Oh yes. She's the reason the farm was one of the first fully organic farms in the country. Back in the '50s it was Hetty who insisted we didn't grub up all the hedgerows to make huge fields. I found that in the Minutes. After the war, my great grandfather had appointed a new manager who wanted to strip out all the ancient hedgerows and create massive fields so it was easier to get the new big combine harvesters into the fields."

"Why?"

"The thinking was that larger fields meant greater production. Hetty pointed out that this could end up with the wind stripping off the soil because there wasn't any protection."

"So the hedgerows stayed."

"No. They split the farm in two and the manager farmed one half his way and Hetty farmed the other her way."

"What happened?"

"After five years we reinstated the hedgerows and the manager left. She was way ahead of her time. I think it was just when Gramps had returned from the US."

"I'm beginning to realise she really didn't like change, so perhaps that was why she wanted the hedges kept."

"I don't buy that," replied William "the Hetty I knew was more concerned with keeping things in balance. She was the one who persuaded Gramps to install the latest biomass boiler to heat the New Manor as a way of using the waste chips from the sawmill. He was pleased because it reduced the heating bill and Hetty was pleased because it was a sustainable use of sawmill waste. She's also why we have the field margins as they are because she saw how this would benefit both the native wildlife and crop fertilisation."

"If I'm a shareholder then I'd better have a look at what we're talking about."

"I'll take you over later, if you want." William reached across and brushed a tendril of hair away from Melissa's face.

"That would be great. I've been going through some of her old diaries from the war and there are lots of entries about stuff to do with the farm. One in particular caught my eye, which was in her diary for 1941."

"Oh, what was that?" William looked mystified. "Go on."

"Evidently the fish stocks in the lake had never been good, and, what with the war on, she wanted to increase these so the Estate workers had a local source of protein that wasn't rationed. Various people told her she had no chance because the lake had a monster in it."

"Is this all in the diary?"

Melissa nodded. "Hetty decided that the monster myth should be exposed for what it was, which is weird because she was always making up stories about gnomes and elves who lived in the wildwood."

"Didn't she ever tell you about a monster in the lake?"

Melissa shook her head. "The diary states how everyone was of a mind that she was mad to anger the monster, but the lake was drained and, hang on . . ." Melissa got up and disappeared through the French doors into the study.

"Here's the entry." She handed him a small notebook, her thumb holding open the page. Neat copperplate handwriting filled the lines.

"31st March: So much for there being a monster in our lake! We have finally reached bottom, leaving a vast expanse of mud.

Right by the sluice was a huge catfish just under 7 feet long - a true monster indeed. Edward came down with his camera and took lots of pictures of the huge fish. I have to say that catfish is not good eating, but we shouldn't moan. We could be in London with the bombs falling round our ears."

"Does this diary tell us if the re-stocking was successful?" William flicked the pages until his eyes were caught by a reference to crayfish.

"15th April: Taught Edward how to set a crayfish trap in the streams feeding the lake, which is now nearly half full since the sluice was closed. With luck we will have a decent amount of crays for lunch. Need to restock the lake. Lady de Braose compares eating carp to eating mud-flavoured cotton wool full of pins, but I think any fish is better than nothing. Perhaps some of our local anglers will have some ideas. Trout would be nice."

"How old would Gramps have been in '40?"

"Fourteen. Edward told me he spent the war down here with his mother."

"Hmm, I gather my great grandfather did something in Whitehall, but no one has the faintest idea what it was, so it was my great grandmother and Hetty who looked after the Estate."

"I did some more digging." Melissa handed him another diary. "Take care with this one, some of the pages are loose."

"7th June. Churchill down this weekend with Harris, Dowding and various other senior Forces people. They were closeted for hours in the library."

"It seems as if your great grandfather was right at the centre of the War Cabinet."

"Bloody hell! I never knew that! Wasn't that just after the British troops were all evacuated from Dunkirk?"

"William, have you had breakfast? I'm going to have a bacon sandwich."

Melissa enjoyed making breakfast for the two of them.

"William, how big is the farm? I've forgotten what you said."

"1000 hectares, which includes pasture for the dairy herd and the rare breeds." William wiped tomato sauce from the corner of his mouth.

"William, I'd like a guided tour."

Melissa's red VW Golf meandered over the cart track as she tried to avoid the potholes on the way to the back entrance of the farm.

"Is this all open to the public?"

"Not this bit. Park over there." William pointed to a space next to a green Range Rover with 'de Braose Estates Ltd' in gold lettering on the front doors. "All this space is admin. We converted the old dairy into the farm shop and café, relocating the milking parlour down the road. We didn't want the public upsetting the cows."

"I thought that part of the ethos was to educate, not isolate Joe Public from the reality of the farmyard."

"There're all sorts of Health and Safety issues with the lambs, rabbits, kids and calves without adding to the chaos with idiots scaring the dairy herd. Can you imagine the headlines in the local paper if someone got injured!"

"I suppose so, but it's a shame."

"You wouldn't believe some of the things people ask about livestock."

"Go on – try me."

"You won't believe it, but we've been asked if a bull will eat someone if it caught them."

"Oh, come on. No-one's that stupid - are they?"

"Yep and quite a lot of them have no idea where milk comes from."

"William, I know the state education system fails some, but I've been through it and many of my colleagues at Oxford came through it too."

"You weren't educated in the hallowed halls of Cheltenham Ladies' College or Roedean then?"

"Grief, no – the local girls' school, which has a very good reputation for academic achievement. What about you?"

"What do you think?"

"Eton?"

William nodded. "My education is bit of a cliché really. Eton, Cambridge, followed by a job in the City."

"Yep, I'd say that's more than a bit of a cliché. Do you enjoy what you do?"

"Mostly."

Inside the farm shop there were piles of fresh vegetables, serried ranks of jars of pickled onions, marmalade, jams and local honey and other local produce. If you were interested in knowing where your food came from there were deep freezes full of frozen sausages, legs of pork, minced beef, venison, steak and ale pies, venison in red wine pies, cottage pie, shepherds pie, sausage rolls made with meat from the estate and other local farms and a chilled fresh meat counter. Everything was from local suppliers who were listed on the wall behind the counter. As well as a delicatessen with local cheeses, there were black and green olives either stuffed, pitted or with stones, sundried tomatoes, artichokes in oil with basil, anchovies and slivers of roasted red and green peppers.

"So olives and green peppers are local produce then?" The irony of a Mediterranean delicatessen counter in an English Farm Shop was not lost on Melissa.

"If the punters like it, we supply it and it's all certified organic. Come on, let's find my retail manager." William took her hand and led her into the café.

"'morning, Gill."

"William, how nice to see you."

"Any chance of a coffee, Gill? Is Neil around, or is he out on a tractor somewhere?"

"You'll find him in the office." Gill looked at Melissa and smiled. Melissa proffered her hand, "Hi, I'm Melissa, Hetty Lavering's great niece."

"Oh, I was that upset to hear of Hetty's death. She was always down here helping out. I shall really miss her."

"Thank you." Melissa liked the older woman immediately.

"Now, how do you take your coffee?"

"Any chance of a latte?"

"I'll have mine black, thanks." William interrupted.

"You two go up and see Neil and I'll bring them up to you."

At the top of the stairs were three offices marked 'Manager', 'Staff Loo' and 'Where The Real Work Is Done'. William knocked on the one marked Manager and opened the door. A man of about thirty was grappling with a printer.

"Bloody thing!" he tugged at a piece of paper that ripped. "Bugger!" He muttered softly to himself.

Melissa giggled.

"Sorry Miss. Hello William. You couldn't unjam this could you?"

"Sure, Neil." William lifted the top of the printer and fiddled inside. "How's it going?"

"Well, apart from the paperwork, we seem to be weathering storms, drought and plague."

Melissa coughed.

"Oh sorry. Neil this is Hetty's niece, Melissa."

Neil held out a hand calloused with hard manual work. He was clearly a man who preferred the outdoors to office work. William's hands, on the other hand, were soft and beautifully manicured. Melissa wondered why she had noticed William's hands, let alone was comparing them to those of a man she had just met.

"Glad to meet you. Hetty's going to be missed."

"Neil, I hope I can go some way to step into her shoes. It will be from a standing start as I know nothing about farming, but I'm willing to learn."

"Excellent. William here likes to think he's a farmer, but he's much better at the politics. He understands all the stuff that comes out of Brussels, which is a weight off my shoulders."

Melissa was amused by Neil's summing up of William's input.

"How many farm staff are there?" she asked.

"Me, a stock man, three full-time labourers and a part-time bee-keeper. Talking of bee-keeping, William, we've told the bees that Hetty's passed on, so hopefully they won't be swarming."

"Why would you do that?" Melissa asked.

"When someone dies, or you have any other major family news, you have to tell the bees because otherwise they leave."

"Isn't that an old wives tale?" William asked.

"Put it this way, William, we have one hundred and forty hives up through the orchard and on the field margins. Do you want to risk that lot swarming and losing the lot. If telling them it makes them happy, then why not? It doesn't take much of my time?"

"I take your point. Thanks, Neil." William turned to Melissa. "See, now Hetty would have known that."

"Now, if you aren't going to do something useful, I've got to get on." It was obvious Neil wanted to escape the confines of his office.

"Come on, William," Melissa fixed William with a stare, "let's get our coffee." If she was ever going to be able to fulfil her promise to Hetty it appeared she was going to have to learn medieval farming folklore in addition to everything else.

They intercepted Gill and took their coffees outside where they sat watching a steady stream of customers drive up and disappear into the shop.

"Not bad for so early on a weekday."

"William, I get the feeling Neil could step into the shoes of anyone on this side of the Estate. If he left, could you step into his?"

William looked at her. "Are you suggesting I couldn't do his job?"

"I'm asking in case anything happened to him."

"You're right, Neil hates the EU paperwork, but could do it if he really had to."

"Have you any experience at animal husbandry?"

"Sort of. I have a place in Scotland."

"Is it let?"

"It sort of runs itself. I'll be up there for New Year. Do you fancy coming?"

"It's only June – how can you think of New Year?" Melissa laughed. "I'll see if my diary's free and, if it is, I'd be delighted. But that doesn't answer my question of who could look after the farm if anything happened to Neil. What I've read of Hetty's diaries so far shows just how much she was involved on a day-to-day basis, even this year. The farm would be rudderless without Neil."

"Ok, so what do you suggest we do?"

"We – this is yours and Edward's farm."

"No – you have the majority shareholding."

"Oh! Tewksbury said something about that all the necessary paperwork was done, but I didn't really take much notice." She paused. "William, is there a signal here?"

"For your phone?"

Melissa nodded.

"Should be. We won't have masts situated on the farm as we think it could be a factor in bee colony collapse, which is why you can't always get a signal at The Old Manor, but you can here."

"How would that affect the bees?"

"Not sure, but there's recent research suggesting radio waves might upset their navigation. There're various reports of bees dying for no apparent reason. No disease, no mites, nothing so we aren't taking the chance of telephone masts being the culprit. Why?"

"I was only going to ask Tewksbury something."

"I'm a lawyer too, or had you forgotten."

"William," she paused considering her next words, "I have a horrible feeling your father may be behind all of this Lansbury stuff."

"Me to!"

Melissa was surprised by his answer. "All I have is a niggle. Why do you think so?"

"My father is a manipulating ponce and it would be typical of him to use his friendship with Lansbury to try and make a quick buck or two."

"The Trusts are more than a buck or two, but I don't understand is why they might have targeted me. Or rather I couldn't until . . ." her voice trailed off. "I've something in Hetty's diaries and I'm not going to say anything else until you've read it because I might just be being an idiot."

"I meant to ask you earlier, why have you got all those canvasses propped against the walls?"

They were sitting in Hetty's study.

"Edward's suggested the completed ones were safer up here and gave me strict instructions that the valuers only needed to see the inside of the studio as that is the only thing that forms part of Hetty's Estate. Why?"

William chuckled. "Canny old goat. Melissa, you do exactly what Gramps tells you."

"Edward said he would be here with me, holding my hand."

"Have you and Mr Perry spoken yet?"

Melissa nodded, "We agreed he would do the paperwork and I would do the running around. I'm reserving my right to be an Executor, or whatever you do when you don't swear the oath or sign the papers."

"What are his instructions?"

"He suggested I tidy up the studio making sure that any completed paintings were kept safe here. He also told me to keep the one of your great uncle David in his RAF uniform in the studio for now and to do whatever else Edward tells me to."

William roared with laughter.

"What's so funny?"

"Nothing, Lissie."

"Well, if it's nothing why're you cackling like an old hen."

William continued to chuckle. "Let these two old men play their games. But we didn't come back here to talk about probate valuations, what is it you want me to read."

Melissa handed him another of Hetty's diaries with pink piece of paper marking a page. Hetty's normally neat copperplate writing was all higgledy-piggledy as if she had written this entry in a hurry.

> *"14th July 1968: Caught young Tobias down at the lake torturing a fish. The boy is a spoilt brat, but I had no idea he was so vile. He said he was conducting an experiment to see how long it would take for the fish to die when it was out of water and was observing what it was experiencing. The toad is nearly ten years old and should know better. I threw the fish back into the lake. Tobias pulled out his penknife and jabbed me in the leg. I shouldn't have done it, but I lost my temper and grabbed him by the scruff of the neck, holding his head under the water for a few seconds. He screamed that he was going to tell his father, so I did it again! This time I held him under longer and told him I was conducting an experiment to see how long it was before he stopped thrashing about. Tobias got the message."*

William read the small entry several times.

"Do we know if she ever told my grandmother?"

"Hetty doesn't say any more about this incident until an entry in '79. She handed him another dairy, also marked with a piece of pink paper.

> *"29th December 1979: Elizabeth came to see me this afternoon to tell me Rosemary is leaving Tobias. Evidently he has turned into the sadist I always thought he might. He's moved on from fish and taken to tormenting people. Rosemary showed me the finger marks on her neck. He had tried to strangle her last Wednesday. Evidently this was the latest in a long line of assaults. She's worried he might hurt William. Elizabeth has told her about the fish incident and they want my advice about*

how to tell Edward. I don't have any ideas, but suggested R consult a solicitor asap and move out. I've given R key to the flat. They will be safe there. I'm worried what this will do to Elizabeth. She's not been feeling well and they can't seem to find anything wrong with her."

William read the entry twice.

"Melissa, can I use your phone?"

Melissa nodded. "Use the one in the study if you want." She offered. She put their lunch on the table and loaded a jug with ice cubes before filling it from the tap.

William picked up the phone on the kitchen counter, punched in a number and waited.

"Hi Mum." He paused whilst his mother spoke. "Mum, I'm down at Hetty de Braose's cottage and we've been going through a few of her diaries from the 70s." Another pause, longer this time. "Hang on, Mum, I need a notepad." William waved his hand miming he needed something to write on and with. Melissa gave him the biro and the notepad she had been using.

"OK." Pause. "That was when?" Longer pause, frantic scribbling, "Yes." Very long pause, much scribbling on to the next page. "No, but I think you're right, he's up to something, but we'll have difficulty trying to prove it." Pause "I promise I'll tell you everything."

William replaced the receiver and sighed. "Well, I think we have a possible motive for Lansbury's shenanigans."

Melissa looked puzzled. "But why would that include your father?"

"Do you still have the two pieces of the POA?"

Melissa shook her head. "I let Tewksbury have them."

William looked thoughtful. "I wonder if Gramps has Tewksbury's home phone number, because I need to know if it was Lansbury's name on that POA or if had been left blank."

"Oh it was definitely Lansbury's because I noted his middle name is Aloysius. I also have Tewksbury's phone number."

"Good girl. We need to know who it was who introduced Lansbury to T, G &M."

It turned out that Lansbury's introduction had come from the chairman of an investment bank and Tobias was on their board of directors.

Melissa had her ear pressed to the other side of the phone so she could hear what Tewksbury was saying.

"William, the Fraud Squad are now involved. Can you tell Melissa she's a very plucky girl; it's rumoured Lansbury has quite temper if he's crossed."

Melissa moved away not wanting to hear any more. Suddenly the cottage did not feel quite so safe any more.

William depressed the button ending the call and immediately dialled again. "Sorry to disturb you on the weekend, Mr Bailey. I've got a family crisis and I'm taking the next couple of weeks off." Again, a pause as the other person responded. "No, I can deal with that without having to be in the office, I just need the files." Pause "yes, no problem, there'll be someone here to take delivery." Pause "Well yes I am on my grandfather's estate, but I'm actually staying at The Old Manor, which is signposted to the right as you come up the main driveway." Pause "Fine, I'll see you in a couple of hours."

"William, what're you doing?"

"I'm staying here to make sure you're OK. I'm not happy about Lansbury being out and about and I think we need to go through Hetty's diaries very carefully."

Melissa's world was spinning out of control yet again. Everything was going black around the edges; her ears were buzzing and the black edges got closer and closer.

"Melissa, Melissa." The voice seemed miles away "Melissa . . . are you OK?"

"William, what happened?"

William lifted her off the floor.

"You fainted. Here, put your feet up." William laid her on the sofa and fussed over her, plumping cushions and putting them under her feet.

"I'm sorry. I'm being a wuss. I'll be fine. Give me a few moments."

"Lissie, Mother told me some stuff about her divorce and I gather Hetty was very involved in protecting her and me, against my father."

"She lent them her flat."

"Yes, but I think there's more than that." He paused, thinking about motive and implementation. "Perhaps he now wants to persecute you now that Hetty is no longer around."

Melissa closed her eyes, feeling sick.

"But I'm not going to let that happen." He continued.

William stood up.

"Hello Gramps."

Melissa groaned inwardly. How much had Edward heard or seen.

"Since you two have been so quiet today, I thought I'd come up and see what you were up to. I hope I've not intruded."

"Not at all, we've made some inroads, but we haven't had lunch yet and Melissa fainted."

Edward stood and looked at Melissa lying prone on the sofa. "What's the matter my dear?"

"Uncle Edward, I think it must be the heat."

"WUFF" Betty stood on her back legs demanding she be allowed up on the sofa.

"Come on, Betty." The little dachshund launched herself up on to the sofa.

"Gramps, join us for lunch."

"Thank you." Edward made himself comfortable at the table.

"I understand Lansbury's now the subject of a Fraud Squad investigation." Edward announced.

"News travels fast."

"Tewksbury telephoned me about twenty minutes ago with the news. He also told me he believes your father is implicated."

"We've come to the same conclusion."

Edward waited for his grandson to explain.

"Mum told me what happened when she left my father. However, Melissa had already discovered Hetty's diaries." William paused, giving his grandfather time to digest this information. "We've also discovered why Tobias and Hetty never spoke."

"Ah, the fish incident." Edward looked out of the window. His face was grim.

"We weren't sure you knew about it."

"I didn't until your mother left him and then your grandmother told me. Since then I've tried to pretend I didn't know about it." He stopped; his expression was sad. "Hetty once showed me the scar where Tobias stabbed her, so I know all about how she held his head under the water."

Edward poured himself a glass of water. "It appears Tobias is now determined to try and take everything Hetty had, for himself."

"Uncle Edward . . ."

Edward held up his hand. "Melissa, Tobias is a great disappointment to me, but it's probably my fault. We had waited so long for a child that when he came along we indulged him in everything. It was our fault he was a spoilt brat and boarding school didn't sort that out. What Tobias wanted, Tobias usually got. His teachers identified a ruthless streak in him, but unfortunately by the time he was at boarding school, his character was formed. Hetty was the only one who put boundaries on him and then, after the fish incident, she made sure she was never around when he was here. She took herself off to Jersey to paint, staying with your grandfather whenever Tobias came home for the summer holidays. It was the end of the first term of Tobias's final year at Cambridge when he came and told us we were grandparents and he'd married your mother."

"Is that how he told you, Gramps." William asked softly, putting his hand over the old man's. His touch brought a flicker of a sad smile to the old man's face.

Edward nodded. "Your grandmother was so terribly hurt. We first met your mother that December when he brought you both down to meet us. Your mother was beautiful, but oh so young, and you were only three months old." Edward's face turned grim. "I was horrified when I saw the bruises on your mother's throat."

William started to say something, but Edward held up his hand. "My photographs got her an instant divorce, Hetty lent her the flat in Notting Hill and until she married your stepfather, I gave her an allowance." William opened his mouth to speak. "Let me finish, William. Your father abrogated his responsibilities to you, his wife, as well as to his mother and me. Unfortunately I can't pass the title to you."

"Oh Uncle Edward." Melissa was beginning to understand why Hetty had tried to give her a 'normal' upbringing. She too could have ended up as a spoilt, indulged orphan. She had gone to a state school and was made to help around the house and garden. However, she had not had to take out a student loan for her university fees and Hetty had given her a generous allowance. Any extra costs for trips or foreign courses were paid for, but there was no indulging her every whim. How much of this had been done because of Hetty's observation of the results of

Edward and Elizabeth's indulgence of their only child, she would never know.

"Gramps, why did you give me Cremorne?" William was taking the opportunity of learning as much as he could whilst his grandfather was in this talkative frame of mind.

"Ah, your grandmother's inheritance." Edward paused. "Your grandmother's great grandfather had land, but no cash, so he married the daughter of a very rich American. It was a fair trade; the rich American was delighted his daughter had married a title and your ancestor got the cash injection he needed. Your grandmother ended up as their only heir and had decided the Scottish property should by-pass Tobias and be yours when you reached twenty-five. Unfortunately she died when you were still a baby so it passed to me so, in respect of her wishes, I gifted it to you."

Melissa was beginning to understand why Tobias might have more than one motive. Their mutual loathing was enough reason for Tobias to dream up a way of getting his hands on Hetty's assets. Now it was apparent he had been bypassed for some of the de Braose assets.

"William, would you mind taking an old man back home?" Edward looked careworn.

"Uncle Edward, I'll take you." Melissa offered.

"Are you sure, my dear?"

Melissa nodded. "Come on, Betty."

"Could you bring my stuff back, Lissie?"

Edward looked at William and raised his eyebrow.

"Gramps, I don't think Lissie should be here on her own so I'm sleeping on the sofa."

Edward nodded. He was too tired to argue that, in his opinion, Melissa might be better back at New Manor.

"Are you alright to drive, my dear?"

"I'm fine, Uncle Edward. To be honest, I think it was because I hadn't eaten." She lied.

The old man nodded. "Tobias was not an easy child and I will never forgive him for what he did to Rosemary or for stabbing Hetty. He's a wealthy man so it can't be that he's needing the money."

"There's no direct proof of that, Gramps."

"There will be. Lansbury doesn't have motive except greed and how would he know to target you? My son knows which firm of

68

solicitors the family have always used and with Hetty's death, you, Melissa, are a vulnerable target. Presumably he got Lansbury to front the whole POA thing with promises of sharing the eventual haul."

Melissa nodded. Edward's conclusion mirrored William's.

"Uncle Edward, can I ask a question?"

"Of course."

"Why have you insisted I put all the completed paintings from the studio in Hetty's study?"

Edward tapped the side of his nose. "Just humour me, my dear."

The evening terrace of The Old Manor was flooded with sunlight from mid afternoon until sunset. From here you could see across the large pond and down to the woods. Overhead swallows were vying with the swifts for the flying insects and on the lawn rabbits were grazing the clover and other sweet plants. A moth flew towards the open windows, attracted by the lights.

The shadows lengthened and the sky turned deep gold and apricot as the sun headed towards the horizon. Midges danced over the surface of the pond and ripples told how a fish had risen to grab a snack. Bailey had delivered the files and stayed for tea while William had given his boss a brief synopsis of what had happened to Melissa. The visiting solicitor had been sympathetic, murmuring that he had heard on the grapevine that someone at T, G &M had been arrested.

"It's been quite a day, Lissie. I'm not sure how I feel about all we've found out. What about you?"

Melissa sat contemplating the deep violets, pinks and golds of the fading sunset "I still don't understand why my world was such a sham."

"At least you don't have a heartless bastard as a father."

"No I don't. I don't have any father I can remember."

"Sorry, Lissie. I didn't think."

"Since I can't remember my parents, I don't know what it's like to have a father. However, we both have Uncle Edward."

"I feel guilty about raking up the past with Gramps, but we have to know."

"William, do you really think Lansbury would come up here?"

"No, but let's not take the chance." He looked at his watch. "It's late and I'm starving. What do we have in the fridge?"

"No idea. Mrs P gave me a box of goodies when I dropped Uncle Edward back and it's all in the fridge."

"Did she now. I think we need to explore the Podger fodder."

"William, don't you think we're rather indulged?" Melissa followed William into the kitchen and perched herself on the worktop.

"What do you mean?" William mumbled from inside the fridge and handed her two fillet steaks, fresh mushrooms, lettuce, tomatoes, cucumber and spring onions from the crisper and a bag of new potatoes, finally taking a bottle of white wine from the fridge door. "Where's the corkscrew?"

"William, it's a screw top!"

"Oh yes! So it is!" William poured her a glass. "You make the salad, I'll scrub the 'taters and do the steaks."

She twisted the tops off the tomatoes and concentrated on slicing them evenly; then sliced an onion and broke the slices into rings. The simple tasks gave her time to think about the strange feeling she felt whenever she heard William's voice. When he had first appeared at New Manor's kitchen door her stomach had done a strange flip. He had appeared so quietly and suddenly she had thought perhaps surprise had caused this strange sensation. However, every time Edward mentioned his name or she heard William's voice she had another frisson of something she could not explain. His presence was very reassuring, but she was not sure how to respond to him.

She thought how she had never really observed how couples responded to each other. She picked some of the leaves from basil plant on the windowsill, tore them up and scattered them over the tomatoes.

She was embarrassed to realise that, at twenty-nine, she was a sexual novice. In her first year at university she had seen fellow undergraduates make idiots of themselves. At one party she remembered how a very drunk man had tried to force his tongue down her throat. It had not been a pleasant experience so she had not bothered going to any more parties.

That memory made her slice the cucumber with more vigour than she had sliced the tomatoes.

As a result of her boycotting the Oxford undergraduate social scene she had focused on her studies and had achieved stunning academic results, but she had no close friends of her own age. Now she was in the presence of an attractive man who was causing all sorts of mental and physical reactions and was completely unable to interpret any signals he might be giving her.

"Where're the saucepans, Lissie?"

"Oh!" His question jolted her out of her self-analysis. "In that cupboard there. The frying pan's in there too."

"Here's tay us?" William handed her a glass of wine.

"Whar's like us" she replied.

"Dam few, an' they're all deed!" they chorused, clinking their glasses together.

Neither of them said anything for a few minutes as they reflected just who was like them. Yes, some were dead, others known only as references in Hetty's diaries. William was the first to break the silence.

"I've never told Gramps, but when I was seventeen my father insisted I had a DNA test."

"Why?"

"I think he wanted to prove he wasn't my father."

"What did your mother say?"

"She was all for it. When it came back proof positive that Tobias was my father we didn't hear from him for a whole year."

"What happened then?"

"Gramps and I had just got back from Scotland and Tobias appeared unannounced."

"I remember you coming down the day before my GCSE results."

"Yes, you were sitting by the pool with your head in a book."

"Did Tobias turn up here?"

"No, he turned up at New Manor, which was why I took refuge here."

"So you've no idea what his visit was all about."

William shook his head. "No. Every time Tobias has come into my life it's never been good." He stuck a knife into the potatoes bubbling away in their pan. "These are nearly done. How do you like your steak?"

"Rare – please."

William flung the meat into the hot pan.

"Sit down, I'll serve."

Melissa watched as he checked the potatoes again, turned the steaks and pressed them down. A knob of butter was dropped into the frying pan. Melissa continued to analyse what she was feeling. William drained the potatoes, placed the steaks on the plates and dribbled the pan juices over them.

"Voilá. Dinner is served."

"Thank you." Melissa stood, made a mock bow and sat down again.

"What're you working on?"

"My firm's advising a national body that's concerned about the new draft planning regulations the government are planning to bring in."

"Oh – have they been scrapped?"

"No, it's still being negotiated, but from what I've seen so far, the proposed National Planning Policy Framework is nothing better than a developers' charter."

"Why would the government want to change the building regulations?"

"The economy was left in such a mess by the last shower in power." William chuckled "I like that, the shower in power – I think I'll use that in my note to Bailey."

Melissa smiled. She had no liking for what years under the auspices of Blair and Brown had done for the country, but it appeared to her that the current coalition seemed no better and seemed to lurch from U-turn to U-turn as each piece of proposed legislation proved to be either badly written or ill thought through.

"Up until now I would have made some disparaging remark about Westminster being full of over fed fat cats with Trust Funds, but that would be hypocritical."

It was William's turn to smile. "Does the fact that you're an heiress make a difference to how you think?"

"Yes."

"How?"

"It's all right for you; you've been brought up with money and went to the same school as nearly everyone else on the Tory front bench."

"Does that make a difference?"

"Yes, because you know how they think."

"It doesn't mean I agree with them."

"No, that's not what I'm saying, but it should give you an insight into why they're doing it."

William snorted in derision. "Yes, but we'd need a team of super sleuths to get the evidence to prove what I think is behind that!"

Melissa looked at him quizzically.

"Lissie, I'm sure the NPPF was conceived with the very best of intentions. This country needs something to kick start the economic recovery, but the way these new regulations are drafted means developers will be able to drive a combine harvester through the so called protection of the Greenbelt and the countryside, not just a bus."

"Aren't the Conservative party supposed to be the stewards of the land?"

"Originally that might've been true, once; but our blinkered Chancellor believes the economic resurgence has to be construction led, which is why these new, less stringent regulations are being proposed."

"Who're the government consulting?"

"Oh, various bodies, but mainly the big development companies and industrialists. The intention is to make property development much easier than it is currently. There are, at present, over fifteen hundred pages of regulations and the proposal is for these regs to be reduced to about fifty or so."

Melissa raised her eyebrows in surprise. William continued.

"The regulations do need to be revamped and quite possibly some of the older concepts revisited, but I don't like what I'm seeing. They're asking the wrong people for advice. Bailey has to present our thoughts to our client on Monday. Can I use Hetty's computer?"

Melissa nodded. "The landline broadband link is fine. Hetty was not completely technophobic."

William sighed with relief. He was finding the lack of mobile phone connection irritating so was grateful to be able to access his email through the landline.

"William, I've made up the bed in my room, so you won't have to sleep on the sofa."

"It's OK Melissa, I'm fine with the sofa."

She blushed.

"Oh, I'm sorry William. I'm sleeping in Hetty's room, I didn't mean . . . er, oh gosh,"

It was William's turn to be embarrassed.

"Lissie, I'm sorry . . . it's getting late. Thank you, a bed would be considerably more preferable than the sofa."

William lay staring up at the vaulted ceiling thinking about his presumption. Had he become so used to girls throwing themselves at him that he had immediately assumed she wanted to climb into his bed? That had been the case at college and he had taken full advantage of these offers, but there had been no-one special. He was well aware his surname gave him a certain caché and had avoided the gold diggers, not wanting to embarrass either his mother or his grandfather. Now here was Melissa who had been on the periphery of his world for nearly twenty-five years. Why did he feel so determined to protect her?

Was it because his father appeared to be behind Lansbury's attempt to get her Power of Attorney?

Was he was jealous of his grandfather's interest in her? He thought about what Edward must have gone through in the 1980s. His beloved wife is diagnosed with advanced breast cancer and dies; his son is shown to be a sadist and then his sister-in-law's family tragedy that orphaned Melissa. Her coming to live at The Old Manor had provided the focus both his grandfather and Hetty had needed.

William imagined himself in Melissa's place. Just who had been around in 1985? Firstly, Hetty, who was there everyday and Edward, who lived just across the park and there were the Podgers. William felt a twinge of envy at how much time Melissa must have spent with all of them. His own examination of Hetty's diaries showed how meals at New Manor were a common occurrence.

He had stumbled into what was clearly a family celebration. He admitted he had been envious and realised this reaction was completely irrational. He treasured his own memories of being with Mr P helping him in the vegetable garden and of Mrs P's warm kitchen and how she would nurse his scraped knees, making him feel better with treats of fresh raspberries, meringues and cream. These summer memories were few and far between after his mother remarried, but treasured all the more because of their rarity.

From the box of goodies that had supplied their supper and his examination of the contents of the fridge he realised Mrs Podger had ensured they had something for breakfast. Whenever he had stayed with his grandfather in the past few years, Hetty had spent the evenings in the New Manor kitchen with all of them. So far Melissa's basic culinary talents showed she was a chip off the Hetty block.

He had never realised just how much Edward loved Melissa.

His thoughts turned to Melissa with the long red hair, who had been sitting outside under the roses watching the dawn. Why had he come up to the cottage at such an early hour? He had heard her promise to Hetty. The cranes embroidered on her kimono were symbols of fidelity and Melissa's promise seem to reflect her loyalty to the land.

He wanted to stroke that waterfall of red hair and wind it round his fingers. He wondered what it would be like to wrap his arms around her. Would she push him away? She did not appear to be at all interested in him, so he turned his thoughts to what his mother had told him.

Rosemary's telephone conversation had shocked him. Until he could confirm what she had said, he was not going to mention it to either Melissa or his grandfather, but if it were true, it would be yet another nail to pin Tobias to the wall of ignominy.

Melissa lay for a long time looking at the portrait hanging on the wall opposite her bed. The painting was signed HL, dated 1938 and Melissa had never given it any thought.

David de Braose was seated in a chair, his head slightly to one side as if listening to someone. He looked directly out of the painting and there was a hint of a smile playing round the corners of his mouth. His dark curly hair was just like William's. The casual shirt was open at the neck and the colour complimented his eyes, which were the same deep blue as William's. She noticed that David and William had the same generous shaped mouth.

Melissa continued gazing at the picture. Eventually Hetty entered carrying a tray of drinks. She was wearing the silk kimono with the cranes. David turned, smiled at his wife and took one of the glasses; Hetty sat herself at his feet; they chinked their glasses together and the scene faded.

"Good morning, my dear." Edward entered the studio followed by a short tubby man carrying a clipboard. "This is Mr Smith."

"Miss Carlisle, I gather this is everything your great aunt had in her studio."

"Yes, Mr Smith." Edward was pleased Melissa was not deviating from his instructions. "The portrait of my late aunt's husband over here is the one specified in my great aunt's will."

Mr Smith examined the portrait of David de Braose in his RAF uniform. Melissa thought about the painting in Hetty's bedroom and the extraordinary dream of the previous night.

"It is a wonderful portrait, Miss Carlisle."

"Mr Smith, my great niece is Dr Carlisle." Edward was still glowing with pride at Melissa's academic achievement.

"I'm so sorry Dr Carlisle."

Melissa blushed. "Mr Smith, I've only just achieved my doctorate."

"Congratulations then." Mr Smith beamed at her.

"I don't think this will take us long, will it Mr Smith?" Edward turned to Mr Smith.

"Indeed not, Lord Edward. Miss, sorry Dr, Carlisle, is this the only completed picture?"

"There is the one she was working on" Melissa pointed at the easel. "I think it wasn't quite going to plan as this tea stain demonstrates."

"Ah, that's a shame, but some would call that art in itself!"

"What about the two plan chests, Mr Smith?" she offered, ignoring Edward's raised eyebrow. Mr Smith opened the top drawer of the one closest to him. The drawer was full of sheets of sketches and studies.

"Are any of these signed?"

Melissa shook her head. Mr Smith nodded and counted the various sketches in the drawers of both chests then made some notes.

"I believe the building belongs to you?"

"It does."

Edward took down a book from the shelf, blowing the dust off the top. Mr Smith examined the catalogues of Hetty's various exhibitions.

"I see these end at 1985. Did Lady de Braose stop painting?"

"Yes, indeed. My great niece had been orphaned and Lady de Braose was her guardian. Dr Carlisle was only four in 1985 so looking after a little girl left little time to continue painting. She herself was approaching sixty-five so you can appreciate that having a young child to look after was a full-time occupation." Edward explained.

"I'm sorry, Dr Carlisle. I had no idea."

"My great aunt did sometimes paint for pleasure, but as you see from the tea stain, not always to her satisfaction."

"Quite so. Well, Lord Edward, Dr Carlisle, I think that's me done."

"Can I offer you some coffee, Mr Smith?" Melissa felt she owed it to her aunt to make some effort at hospitality despite Edward's instructions otherwise. She flipped the switch on the kettle and reached for three mugs.

"That's very kind of you, Dr Carlisle, but I'm afraid I have to get back."

"Thank you for coming. What happens next?"

"I shall send a copy of my inventory and valuation to Lady de Braose's solicitors, then it's all down to the Executors." Mr Smith smiled and shook her hand.

"Mr Smith, thank you for your time. I shall walk you to your car." Edward ushered the man out of the studio leaving Melissa alone.

Melissa looked at the space in the bookshelf left by Edward's removal of the book. Next to it was *The Complete Dictionary of Symbols in Myth, Art & Literature.*

"Cranes: This bird with long legs and a long neck and bill represented vigilance because it was thought that, while the rest of the flock slept with their heads under their wings, their leader kept watch with his neck stretched out. He signalled a warning by his cry. The bird's role in art as the personification of Vigilance may also go back to a description in the works of Aristotle wherein he describes how the Crane held a stone in its mouth so that it would wake if it dropped the stone in sleep.

In China, where a crane flying toward the sun symbolized social aspirations, the bird's white body represented purity, its red head the fire of life."

Melissa slipped the dictionary back into place, her curiosity satisfied. Hetty's deep love of the land and in particular, The Old Manor, was symbolised by the crane and she liked the cranes' red head being symbolic of the fire of life. Perhaps her red hair, like Hetty's, was just that.

"Has he gone?"

Melissa jumped.

"William, will you stop scaring me half to death."

"Sorry, Lissie." William stepped through the French-windows.

"Will you now explain all the cloak and dagger stuff about the finished canvasses and the stuff in the studio?" Melissa demanded.

"Perhaps we should talk to Edward." William grinned.

Back in The Old Manor Edward put the book from the studio on the table. "Do you realise this is a rare 16th century edition of Cennini's Il Libro dell'Arte?"

"Shouldn't we tell Mr Smith?" she asked.

"Melissa, it's something he didn't see, so no." Edward's tone was adamant.

"Ah, I get it, now the house is crammed with signed finished works by Hetty and you're telling me this book is a rare edition of Cennini's treatise on art that just happens to be here and not there, so somehow all this is not going to form part of her estate."

"Melissa, are you suggesting Gramps connived in your evading paying inheritance tax!"

"Yes." She paused. "What's the level inheritance tax kicks in?"

"Three hundred and twenty five thousand pounds."

"Do you really believe Hetty's completed canvasses will come to more than this?"

"Melissa, the art world will eventually decide the value of Hetty's work and value is determined by all sorts of oddities such as whether the artist is alive or dead, fashion, rarity, the stock market, etc."

"I can't see what this has to do with Hetty?"

"William, you saw a Hetty Lavering up for auction just last week. Do you know what it went for?"

"A hundred and fifty thousand."

"WHAT!"

"So you see my dear, even at probate value, your aunt's unknown signed finished works would push her estate well into inheritance tax."

Melissa sat and looked at Edward through horrified eyes. "What you're saying is I've a fortune in paintings stashed in this cottage?"

They both nodded.

"Do you want to put them back in the studio?" William asked.

"Yes, and perhaps they'd better go in the cellar under the big plan chest."

"What cellar?" the two men chorused.

William rolled up the large shabby rug on the studio floor revealing a hatch.

"The light switch is on the wall under the stairs." Melissa instructed. The cellar had more completed canvasses stacked against one wall. Shelving carried various odds and ends of rolls of canvas, brushes, boxes and other detritus Hetty had collected during her lifetime.

"There's about another fifty canvasses here, Lissie, but you'll either have to wait until I get back, or shift the ones in the cottage yourself because I've got to fly. There's something I've got to do in town, so I'll see you both later."

"It's quite dry so these'll be quite safe. I might not be able to paint like Hetty, but she did teach me a thing or two about storing paintings. I think there's enough space for the ones in the cottage, but they can stay there for now."

"What did you find down there?" Back in the cottage Edward was sitting in Hetty's armchair. Melissa told him and he smiled. "Typical Hetty, I bet they're of a much better quality than the ones we moved up here."

"How did you know that?" Melissa asked.

"She was just being one jump ahead of the tax man, but I don't think she realised just how popular her work would become. Now we have the studio inventory out of the way, what plans do you have for the next few days, Melissa?"

"I don't know. I had a letter from Jersey this morning." She fished an envelope out of the back pocket of her jeans. "I haven't read it yet."

"What does the letter say?"

"Give me a minute." Melissa rifled through the jars on the shelf looking for a clean palette knife, slit the envelope and unfolded the contents.

Dear Miss Carlisle,

Please accept my condolences. I was deeply saddened to hear of the etc.

On the 22nd February next year, you will reach the age of thirty, at which time the various Trusts of the estates of your great-grand parents, grand parents and parents will devolve on you and we will require your instructions.

If you wish to discuss any issues we would be very happy to do so at your convenience at our offices at a mutually convenient date and time. Yours sincerely, Peregrine Daghorne-Ffrench.

This sounds awfully official." Melissa handed the letter to Edward.

Edward was remembering the wily impresario from Newcastle-upon-Tyne who had been sensible enough to get out of the English tax system long before the November 1974 deadline.

"I think you should take a trip to Jersey?"

"When?"

"If it were me, then I'd want to know what this was all about as soon as possible and I think you and William should go and find out everything you can about the Jersey trusts."

"Why do you want William to come with me?"

"You should you take time to visit the places your grandparents and parents lived and I think you would have more fun doing it with him than me."

"I can't remember anything from before I lived here." Melissa frowned, contemplating exploring her past. Melissa thought about this for a moment longer. "Do you think the Jersey Trustees would be able to see me so soon?"

"Melissa, you are a very valued client. I'm sure they will see you whenever you want."

"What about getting there?"

"A minor detail, my dear."

"We can fly, or we could go by ferry. What do you reckon?" William was seated in front of the computer.

"If we went by ferry, which car would we take? Mine's in need of a service."

"So the options are we either fly and hire a car, or we go by ferry and take mine."

"What about accommodation?" she asked.

"How comfortable do you want to be?"

Melissa thought. "Comfortable."

Edward wondered about their relationship. Even Mrs Podger approved and hoped 'they got it together'.

"This sounds quite comfortable: *Longueville Manor Hotel. This hotel was once one of Jersey's manor houses and dates back to the 13th century when it was a nunnery. It is a family run hotel with a reputation for excellence . . .*"

"Sounds perfect. William, book it." said Edward.

How much?" Melissa asked.

"How long is it since you had a holiday?" William asked.

"I asked how much . . ."

"I'm not telling you."

"William, just book it!" Edward's tone was unexpectedly sharp.

"Excuse me, don't I have a say in any of this?"

"NO." William and Edward chorused. Melissa bridled at their chauvinism, but part of her liked the way William had taken the trouble to find a lovely sounding hotel.

"We could catch the 8 o'clock ferry from Portsmouth tomorrow morning, arriving late afternoon."

"Have you ever been to the island, William?" Edward asked.

William shook his head. "Lissie, I don't have to be back in the office for some time and Bailey can always get me on my phone if he needs me, so how about we stay for a week?"

"Oh, that would be great. We could go to France for the day, perhaps." Melissa was warming to the idea.

The phone rang and William answered it. "OK Mrs P. By the way, Lissie and I are off to Jersey tomorrow morning. Any chance we can come for supper?" Pause "Right oh." He replaced the phone on its cradle.

"Mrs P wants us at the table in half an hour, which will just give me time to book this lot." He took his wallet out of his back pocket.

Melissa rose and Edward put his hand out to stop her.

"My dear girl, he's a de Braose looking after de Braose. This is what we do, we look after our own."

"But Uncle Edward . . ."

"No 'buts', Melissa. You've been through a tough time and William is making sure that if there're any more nasties to come crawling out of the woodwork, you won't be on your own."

Melissa realised Edward was thinking about the letter and the invitation to meet her Jersey Trustees.

She was thinking about something completely different.

"I can't believe how calm that crossing was." Melissa buckled her seat belt. William pushed first one button, then another, then another! First his seat slid backwards, then the steering wheel rose up and moved out towards him. He pushed another button and the roof of his Mercedes started an intricate weave folding it away.

"What are you doing, William?"

"I'm trying to find the SatNav?"

One of the stevedores muttered something in Spanish. Melissa stifled a giggle.

"What did he say?" William asked.

"I don't think either you or I are supposed to have understood."

"Come on, Lissie, tell!"

She shook her head too embarrassed to translate. Engines were being turned on and cars were starting to move. The stevedore watched enviously as they rolled down the ramp towards the quayside.

Custom officials were stopping cars at random, but they were lucky enough to be waved through.

"It's a good thing I printed off the directions to the hotel." Melissa retrieved a sheet of paper from her bag.

"OK Cleverclogs, which way now?"

"Turn left, the at the second roundabout go right and then through a tunnel following the signs to Longueville."

"OK." William stopped at the red light that went straight from red to green. "Crikey, no warning amber! They don't have white stop lines either! I thought this was supposed to be part of Great Britain? How come they have different road markings?" William pulled up at the next set of lights. A few minutes later Melissa told him to slow down and turn left through a granite arch.

"Here we are at Longueville Manor Hotel. Now Mr de Braose, are you going to tell me why you don't know where your SatNav is?"

"This is the brand new Batmobile, Batwoman and I haven't a clue!"

Melissa raised her eyes heavenwards, relieved to know that even William was not perfect. "Just how long have you had this car?"

"Since yesterday!"

"Was this the incredibly important meeting?"

"I could hardly say I was going to pick up a new toy, could I?"

"Surely half the fun is finding out what a new toy does?"

"I agree, but I hadn't anticipated taking it to foreign parts quite so soon."

"How can I help you?" The perfectly manicured receptionist behind the desk smiled a welcome.

"The name is de Braose."

"A yes, Dr Melissa Carlisle and Mr William de Braose. If you would sign the register, please." The receptionist waved her hand and a porter appeared. She turned back to Melissa and William. "Dr Carlisle, I hope you enjoy The Tower Suite; Mr de Braose you are in Garden Room No 8. Enjoy your stay."

They followed the porter who pushed the brass luggage cart loaded with their luggage.

The Tower Suite consisted of a bedroom with a spacious ensuite bathroom and a separate sitting room. The bathroom was the latest in chic design with a stone bath and huge shower. The rooms were cool and quiet.

"I'll leave you to unpack, Dr Carlisle. Perhaps we could meet in half an hour?" William's sudden formality was shocking. Only a short time before he had been calling her Batwoman and making silly faces at her!

Melissa had read that the hotel liked their guests to dress more formally for dinner. She hung her dress in the bathroom and turned on the shower so it belched clouds of steam. The steam would sort out the creases of one of Hetty's original Chanel's. She had found it in the wardrobe, tried it on finding and it had fitted perfectly, so she had thrown it, and a further two classic Paris originals, into her suitcase. Wearing it felt as if Hetty had put her arms around her and was telling her everything was going to be all right.

Melissa did not hear William's first knock and jumped at the second. She opened the door.

"Dr Carlisle you look stunning."

"Thank you." She was overcome with shyness.

William offered her his arm.

"Is it my imagination or have you grown six inches in the past half hour?"

"Don't mock. These are my best shoes."

The maitre d'hôtel showed them to a quiet table near the window. The dining room looked out onto the hotel gardens and the swimming pool where the sunbeds were being stacked away for the night.

She looked at the menu and it was as if it were written in Chinese.

"Perhaps I could recommend the fish; we have lobster and halibut, both freshly caught in Jersey waters; or perhaps the rack of Welsh lamb." The waiter suggested in his lilting accented voice.

She chose the lamb, William chose a steak and ordered a bottle of claret.

"Please may I have some iced tap water?" She smiled awkwardly as the waiter inclined his head in acknowledgement.

They placed their napkins on their laps, both suddenly very aware of the other.

"What do you . . ." they both said together.

"Sorry, William – you first."

"No, Lissie. What were you going to say?"

"I was about to ask if you thought the Trustees will be able to see us at such short notice?"

Back on familiar territory the growing shyness between them eased.

"I can think of some eighty million reasons why they will see you the minute you click your fingers."

"Oh, er, yes, I suppose so."

"Lissie, you still haven't quite got it yet, have you?"

"Got what? The fact I'm suddenly filthy rich; or that I don't know who I am anymore."

"The fact that even if you don't understand why things are as they are at the moment, people were entrusted to look after your affairs until you reached a certain age."

"I don't feel twenty-nine. Aren't I supposed to be responsible and know what do to?"

"I don't suppose you've had much interaction with the world of commerce, but I'm sure there're many similarities to academia. How many old accounts have you studied, searching out the facts behind the various exchanges between patron and artists? There's no difference between then and now."

William's gentle explanation made it sound easy.

"Lissie," William put his hand over hers. "Lissie, you are not alone." Melissa turned her hand over and gripped William's. William lifted her hand and kissed it. Melissa looked up, startled by a kiss that was burning the skin on the back of her hand.

Melissa tossed and turned before finally falling into a troubled sleep. Dreams where her hand caught fire and was extinguished by Hetty throwing buckets of water over her; mountainous seas where she was on an invisible boat, with an invisible crew she could hear talking to each other about paintings and money. Her phone alarm went off at seven and saved her from being trapped in a cave by a giant octopus with 'Tobias' tattooed repeatedly along its tentacles.

She had just finished showering when there was a knock on the door:

"Can I come in?" William asked.

"You're up with the lark." Melissa said as she let him in.

"I wondered if you wanted breakfast?"

"I've ordered mine in here." Melissa was conscious she was only wearing the kimono.

"Would you mind if I joined you, or do you want to be alone?" he asked.

"No, no, please. I'm sure we can order another. I didn't mean . . oh hell, William. I'm sorry. I don't know what I'm doing."

"Then I suggest we have breakfast and make a plan of action." He rang room service and requested the order for the Tower Suite be increased to two continental breakfasts, with both tea and coffee.

"When in doubt, Lissie, make a list. We have to see your Trustees and, depending on what they tell you, we take it from there."

"Yes, you're right, so I'll phone them when their offices open and depending on when they can see us, the world is ours."

"That's my girl. So what's their phone number and address?"

"William, I don't know what to wear!"

"We haven't got the appointment yet, so that's irrelevant."

"OK, yes, you're right, but it's important! First impressions count."

"Lissie, one step at a time; what's their telephone number?"

"But it's only eight in the morning."

"Lissie, give me the number." She handed him the letter and he dialled. His call was answered on the second ring.

"Good morning. Is it possible to talk to Peregrine Daghorne-Ffrench?" William made a thumbs-up sign.

"Speaking. How can I help?" the male voice responded.

Melissa listened as William outlined how they were in the island and how Dr Carlisle hoped Mr Daghorne-Ffrench would be able to see her as per his letter.

"Mr Daghorne-Ffrench, what about if you come to the Longueville Manor Hotel." Pause "Excellent, Dr Carlisle and I will see you and your colleague here at 11."

William turned his phone off. "See Lissie, that's what I mean. The professionals will be falling over themselves to keep your business."

She nodded. The thought that she might want to change who looked after her money had not occurred to her.

Melissa stood watching the guests lounging round the pool from her sitting room window and wondered if she would be able to do the same as them later. William had suggested he meet Daghorne-Ffrench in reception. She took a deep breath and thought for a minute. This was purely a fact-finding mission; they were just making contact with the professionals who administered these Trusts.

William had explained that in the event of a mass incident such as the crash that had killed her family, where it was impossible to tell who had died first the law took the ages of the victims as being the order in which they died i.e. the eldest having died first and the youngest, last. In this case, her grandfather had been older by a year than her grandmother and her mother was older than her father.

The door opened and a waiter brought in a tray with cups, saucers, sugar, milk and coffee.

"Thank you," she smiled at the young man as he held the door for William and two young men to enter.

"Melissa, this is Mr Peregrine Daghorne-Ffrench and his colleague, Malcolm le Perrier." William introduced his two companions.

She shook hands, wondering if Mr le Perrier practised his wet fish handshake or if he were just incredibly shy.

Melissa made herself comfortable in an armchair.

"Gentleman, may I offer you coffee?" William asked. She sat, puzzled; she had been about to do that.

"Congratulations are in order, I believe, Dr Carlisle. I apologise for not having your correct title." Peregrine Daghorne-Ffrench made himself comfortable on the sofa; "I gather you've recently been awarded your doctorate?"

"Yes. Thank you." She was beginning to feel quite blasé about being congratulated.

"I understand Mr de Braose is here in an advisory capacity?"

"This is not my area of expertise, well not in this millennia anyway, so yes."

Mr Daghorne-Ffrench looked puzzled.

"I'm more familiar with documents of the 15th and 16th centuries. Unfortunately this all seems hugely complicated."

"Sometimes, Dr Carlisle, I wonder. At least these documents will be easier to read than the ones you're used to."

Mr le Perrier was producing papers and placing them in individual piles on the table. He sniffed and pushed his spectacles up his nose.

"Well Doctor Carlisle," Mr Daghorne-Ffrench continued, "the firm I represent has been looking after your Trusts for the past twenty-five years. Under the terms they will cease when you reach the age of thirty, so we will require your instructions by your next birthday."

"I'm not sure why you wanted to see me now? It's only the end of June so we have another eight months before then."

"In the case of a small Trust that might be the case, but much has changed since these Trusts were created and we thought you would like time to consider the various options open to you."

Malcolm le Perrier handed her one of the stacks of paper.

Melissa relaxed, glad for the confirmation that she was not going to have to make any instant decisions, but it appeared she being given lots to read.

"Mr Daghorne-Ffrench, what sort of value are we talking about?" William was seated in the other armchair.

Mr Daghorne-Ffrench looked at the top sheet of his set of papers, "Combined, the Jersey trusts total ninety-five million sterling at today's figures."

"Oh!" Melissa's hand flew to her mouth.

"Dr Carlisle, we are awaiting the latest valuations for the current year, but in my professional opinion you can safely say that the overall valuation will have grown by at least five per cent. The London property market has been especially strong. It may well be more"

"My great aunt had calculated that the assets would be in the region of perhaps eighty by the time I reached thirty. That was a big enough shock, but ninety-five million!" The suggestion that she might have expected more struck her as surreal.

"We have brought a set of draft accounts, of course subject to those awaited property valuations, together with the schedules of assets for you to study. Would you like Mr de Braose to have a set?" She nodded and Mr le Perrier passed it across to William.

William ran his eye over the figures. Melissa looked at the income figures and felt sick at the number of zeroes.

"Am I right in thinking you were born in the island?"

"Er, actually I don't know." She felt incredibly stupid not being able to answer such a simple question.

"Mr Daghorne-Ffrench," William interrupted "Presumably you're looking to the future regarding domicile?" Melissa had no idea what William was talking about.

Mr Daghorne-Ffrench nodded. "Yes. Our expertise is not only in Trust management, but also in ensuring minimal future exposure to tax." He turned to Melissa. "Dr Carlisle, if you, or your advisor, have any questions or if we can be of any help in any way, you only have to ask."

"Actually, do you know whether any of the properties belonged to my mother and father?"

Malcolm Le Perrier shuffled through his papers. "Here's the schedule of properties.

Melissa took the proffered sheets. The top two listed commercial and the third listed various Jersey and English residential addresses. None of the addresses brought a flicker of recognition.

Melissa looked at the front sheet of the other sets of papers: the White Family Trust and the Carlisle Family Trust. The complexity of it all was beginning to make her head ache.

In addition there were the assets of Hetty's Trust and she wondered what should be done with these. William was talking what appeared to be gibberish. Finally the meeting came to an end and the two men got up to leave.

"Thank you Mr Daghorne-Ffrench." She heard him say. "No doubt Dr Carlisle will be in touch."

William held the door open and she led the two bankers down the corridor. The men continued talking incomprehensible banking stuff as they all made their way to the hotel reception.

"Daghorne-Ffrench, what are you doing here?" An impeccably dressed man in his late fifties interrupted their conversation. He was accompanied by an equally well groomed, but plump woman of similar age.

"Mr Cliffe, may I introduce Dr Melissa Carlisle." Daghorne-Ffrench introduced her to the newcomer.

"How nice to meet you, Dr Carlisle. I knew your father and grandfather. Are you on holiday?" Mr Cliffe smiled, full of bonhomie.

"A combination, Mr Cliffe." She was conscious of William standing right behind her. "This is my cousin, William de Braose."

Mr Cliffe held out his hand. "de Braose, good to put a name to a face. Your grandfather is Lord Edward, is he not?"

"You too, Mr Cliffe. Yes, he is." William murmured as he shook the older man's hand.

Melissa, aware of Mrs Cliffe's scrutiny, realised she was being categorised and pigeon-holed by what she was wearing. She wished she had not worn one of Hetty's vintage dresses.

"Please don't hesitate to contact me should you need anything, and I mean anything." Mr Cliffe reached inside his pocket and handed her his card.

"Thank you, Mr Cliffe, that's very kind." She glanced at the card in her hand. Charles Cliffe, Managing Director.

"My dears, it's a pleasure to put faces to names, but if you'll excuse me, I'll leave you in the good hands of Daghorne-Ffrench here. Remember, we're all here to help." He beamed avuncular solidity before shepherding his wife towards the bar.

"So he's your boss?" Melissa looked at Peregrine Daghorne-Ffrench questioningly.

"He's been managing director of the company since he was thirty two and single-handedly created its global reputation."

They made their way outside to where Malcolm le Perrier was waiting.

"Damn, I didn't put the roof up last night!" William pointed his key and the lights on the Mercedes flashed.

"Nice motor." Daghorne-Ffrench's tone was of genuine admiration. "Our speed limit will be a bit inhibiting!"

William was amused by the other man's envy.

"Thank you for coming, Mr Daghorne-Ffrench, it's much appreciated. I'm sure Dr Carlisle will be in touch soon."

Daghorne-Ffrench had forgotten she was the client.

As they drove away he looked in the mirror and saw William put his arm around Melissa's shoulders and wondered just what sort of an advisor William de Braose was.

"William, I want some fresh air to clear my head."

"Get in and see if you can find the SatNav." He gave her the car keys. "I'll get my wallet."

It was ten minutes before he reappeared.

"Where to, Lissie?"

Melissa waved her hand. She did not care.

They had driven westwards through country lanes that twisted and turned around small fields enclosed by stone walls. In some, cows grazed contentedly, others were empty, but all made up a pastoral idyll that belied Jersey's reputation as an international financial centre. William stopped the car at the top of a hill so they could take in the view.

The vista before them showed a broad expanse of golden sands. A sharp bend took them past a concrete bunker – a relic of the German occupation of WW2. William followed the road round and down a steep hill. The land was now sand dunes with the odd sparse, wind-blown fir tree twisted by the prevailing south-westerly winds. Gone were the neat fields with their cows or serried ranks of the main potato crop. The coastal road was clear and it was tempting to push the Mercedes faster, but William resisted.

"This looks like an interesting place for lunch. What do you think, Lissie?"

Melissa nodded. William drove into the car park, quietly cursing the granite gravel that might flick up and chip the bodywork of his new toy.

"William, it's a beautiful island, but that drive didn't stir any memories at all."

"We've only driven through some country lanes, so it's not surprising."

"I don't know if I want all this."

"What do you mean?"

"I'm not equipped to manage what appears to be an empire! I felt a complete fool having to tell Daghorne-Ffrench I didn't know where I was born."

"I don't think you've got much option! As for where you were born, try looking in your passport. You must have had to fill this out when you renewed it!"

"Hetty did that for me, and I've never even looked at it. The photo's dreadful, that was enough."

William could not believe what he was hearing.

"So, are you going to look?"

"Oh, yes." Melissa rummaged in her handbag and flicked her through the pages until she got to Place of Birth.

"Why didn't I think of that?" Melissa said, more to herself than William.

"Hetty loved you very much, but it would have been better if she'd been less inclined to do everything for you."

Melissa got out of the car and half ran, half walked down the cobbled slipway towards the beach, fighting back the tears threatening to spill down her cheeks. William ran after her.

"Lissie," he grabbed her wrist and pulled her round into his chest.

"You must think I'm a complete idiot." Big sobs welled up from deep inside her. "I know where my parents were born; where my grand parents were born, even where my great grandparents were born. I know that Hetty was born in Canada; your father was born in the US, but I didn't know where I was born. Now I find my whole life has been a lie."

"Lissie, no-one's expecting you to know all about managing Trusts. That's why there are professionals like Daghorne-Ffrench and Cliffe. My god, they charge enough."

She leant against him: he felt so safe.

"Would you expect them to be able to understand what you do?"

"No," she sniffed again. "but I should at least know where I was born."

"Listen, you do now, so problem solved. We can tell Daghorne-Ffrench and he will be happy."

"OK, I hear you." Melissa sniffed. "He must think I'm a complete idiot."

William handed her a handkerchief. Unlike Edward's, this one was not freshly ironed, but at least it was clean. "Dry your eyes.

Daghorne-Ffrench can think what he likes. You're paying his salary so all he needs to know is facts. First, we need lunch."

Melissa let herself be led back to the café where William read out the menu from a blackboard that showed that Big Verne's soup of the day was homemade tomato & basil with freshly baked granary roll and butter. That would be more than enough for her. William ordered egg and chips.

"What do you suggest we do now?"

"When you're researching something, how do you go about it?"

Melissa thought for a while. "I'd establish provenance."

"Well, you've done that. Then what?"

"Analyse the document in front of me, identifying what it was about and the individuals involved." She was warming to the idea of transferring her skills. "If it were an illuminated document, I would try and identify the artist by style and comparing other known works by the artist or monastery, which might also give me an idea of where it had been created."

"Excellent. So how about if we look at the lists of the Jersey residential properties then drive past some of them. That might jog some memories for you." William suggested.

Melissa looked perplexed. "That's fine, but you can't get your SatNav working. Besides, I haven't a clue where to start."

"Lissie, I've got the list of residential properties Daghorne Ffrench brought this morning and I'm not going to be beaten by a piece of technology. After lunch I suggest we take a look at the manual and crack the SatNav problem."

"OK, it's worth a try. However, I have a small problem to be solved before then."

William was exasperated. What possible problem could she have now?

"I need a swimming costume. I forgot to pack one."

"For a minute I thought you were going to tell me something important."

"What a pretty cottage." Melissa said.

William slowed down so they could admire a cottage built into the crux of a mind boggling 180-degree corner of a steep narrow country lane. Looking across the bay, there was nothing to break the force of the winter gales as they whipped in from the Atlantic, which was why the few trees were permanently bent to the will of the prevailing wind.

"Continue up the hill" directed the mechanical female voice. It had taken only a few minutes to fathom out the Mercedes' navigation system and to punch in one of the addresses. William did as he was bid until they reached a crossroads.

Melissa sat forward as the voice told them to "Go straight across."

The road sign said Rue de Douet. William drove slowly down the little lane with its high grassy banks. A square Georgian style edifice dominated two Jersey granite farmhouses.

Melissa waved her hand "Keep going"; he continued slowly down the lane. "Stop!" she shouted.

"You have reached your destination" the disembodied voice announced.

William held his breath. Melissa did not get out, but sat looking intently at a white arch giving onto a courtyard.

"Yes." Melissa whispered to herself. "I remember a man picking me up and throwing me in the air."

William said nothing.

"He made me milkshakes with ice cream and fresh raspberries and taught me how to burp very loudly."

Melissa closed her eyes, embedding the resurrected memory of a time she had forgotten. "There were three naughty gnomes called Impe, Grympe and Grumpe who lived in the garden."

"Lissie, that's great."

She shook her head. "I always thought Hetty had made them up, but I think those stories were invented by my grandfather." She paused, "William, do you think it was her way of keeping the memory of him alive for both of us?"

"That's more than possible."

William's phone rang. "See who that is, Lissie, there's a tractor coming up behind us and I need to move."

"William de Braose's secretary. How may I help?"

William was pleased to hear her mood lifting.

"Dr Carlisle?"

"Yes." Melissa looked surprised.

"Daghorne-Ffrench here. I'm sorry to ring Mr De Braose's phone, but I don't have your mobile number."

"I didn't give it to you, Peregrine. How can I help?"

"Are you at the hotel?"

"No, we're lost somewhere in the wilds of the northwest of the island. Why?"

"We have some deed boxes in our strong room that I should have brought to you this morning. I can only apologise for this oversight. Would it be possible to drop them off later?"

"Yes, sure, what time were you thinking of?"

"Perhaps an hour from now?"

"OK, and Peregrine you know you asked me about my birthplace. It was Jersey."

Daghorne-Ffrench thanked her and noted this on her file. He would have liked to call her Melissa, but company protocol meant he could not even though she had called him Peregrine. He thought this unduly pedantic, but until he was a Director it was Mr This, or Mrs That and always Lady or Lord, or Your Grace.

"Can we have the instructions to get to the hotel from here?" William squeezed the car into a passing place and the tractor trundled past. Melissa punched in the address of the hotel and the voice told them to turn left in fifty yards, then immediately right and to continue onwards.

"Isn't that Daghorne-Ffrench parking his car?" Melissa asked.

William swung the Mercedes into a parking space next to the banker. "I think you're right. He's a bit early for 'see you in an hour'."

William got out and came round to help her out. She liked his old fashioned manners; she also liked the way he kept hold of her hand.

"That was well timed, Mr de Braose, Dr Carlisle." Peregrine opened the boot of his car.

"Indeed, it was." William looked at the deed boxes. "These are considerably larger than I'd imagined. I'll go and see if I can find a porter." William disappeared inside the hotel in search of the porter's trolley.

Melissa looked at four metal boxes wrapped in wire and sealed. She examined the seals, which were a bit battered, but still intact.

"Have they been in your vaults since 1985?" she asked.

"I believe the Executors of the Estates for the Lavering and Carlisle boxes deposited them with the bank in '86 and '87 and 1988 for the two White family boxes. Please accept our most sincere apologies for not bringing these this morning."

"Peregrine, if you knew how many archives that have hundreds of boxes just waiting for someone to open them up and list their contents, if you only have a few, you're doing well. Do you know what's inside them?"

Daghorne-Ffrench shook his head. "I don't. The solicitors who wound up the various Estates are either dead or retired."

"Don't worry; I can see the seals are intact."

William re-appeared with a porter who was directed to take the boxes to Melissa's suite.

"Would you join us for a drink?" Melissa asked.

"Thank you, but I'm afraid I still have work to do. Mr Cliffe asked me to give you these." He reached into the inside of his car door and produced two pristine white envelopes.

"Thank you. Do you know what they are?"

"Invitations to The Bankers' Ball on Friday and on Sunday Mrs Cliffe is hosting an At Home for all our major clients."

"That's very kind. Will you be going?"

Daghorne-Ffrench nodded. "I'll be there Friday night, but not on Sunday."

"Thank you for bringing the boxes." Melissa put the two envelopes into her handbag. William stood silently behind her.

"Nice to see you again, Mr de Braose." Daghorne-Ffrench shook William's hand before turning to Melissa, "and you too, Dr Carlisle."

They watched him drive away.

"See, Lissie, what did I tell you? Now you have invitations to a ball and Sunday lunch at the Managing Director's home."

"William, do we have to go?"

"Don't ask me, you're the one to decide if we're available."

Melissa flipped open the envelope and read the enclosed card. "Mr William de Braose & Dr Melissa Carlisle" was written across the top. "*Are cordially invited to the Annual Ball of the Jersey Federation of Finance Houses to be held at Longueville Manor Hotel on Friday 17th June: 7.30 pm. Dress: Dinner Jacket, Carriages at 1.30 a.m., RSVP.* Well that's easy, I don't have a dress and you don't have a dinner jacket."

"Oh, no Melissa! That's no excuse."

"Hang on William, there's another card in the envelope." Melissa read out "*Mr and Mrs Charles Cliffe request the pleasure of your company at a private reception to be held in the Bateman Room, Longueville Manor Hotel, at 6.30 – 7.30 pm on Friday 17th June. RSVP* etc."

"And the other envelope?"

"*Mrs Anne Cliffe requests the pleasure of your company At Home on Sunday 19th June from noon onwards.* Do we really have to go?"

"We do, but only if you want to retain Cliffe's firm as your financial advisors."

Melissa looked perplexed. "Can't I just tell them that?"

"Lissie, life isn't that simple. Come on. Let's go and have a look inside those boxes."

"I asked reception if they had any wire cutters."

"Stop, William." Willian was about to snip all the wires on all the boxes. "Let's not just open these randomly. I want to start with the Alistair & Victoria Carlisle box first." She lifted the smallest metal box onto the coffee table and he snipped away the wires.

Taking a deep breath she lifted the lid. It was full of envelopes and a red leather jewellery roll lay on the top. "Oh my. I suppose this was my mother's." She lifted out the red leather roll and put it to one side, then lifted the top envelope. This held her birth certificate, her baptism certificate, both her mother and father's birth, marriage and death certificates. The next envelope contained her parents' passports and driving licenses.

William picked up another envelope and shook out some photos picking up one of a little girl with two labradors. Melissa snatched the photo out of his hand.

"That's Baxter and Digby! What are they doing here?"

"Is that you?" William pointed to a little girl.

"Oh, yes, oh lordy, William; gosh I'm porky!"

"Aren't Baxter and Digby the . . .?"

"Yes, they were the labradors we had at The Old Manor." Melissa sat back and thought. "William, I must have blanked the memory of how they came to be at Hetty's." She picked up another photograph. "Look, here they are at that house we stopped at this afternoon, and here's me with Gampa." She shuffled through the rest of the photographs, picking up one where she was sat on another man's shoulders as they walked along a beach. It was the same beach they had been on this afternoon, recognisable by the white hut in the background.

"This is Daddy and me." Her voice was barely a whisper.

Another photo showed the same man holding her high above his head and the two black labradors were clearly jumping and barking. "Look William, there's that house again."

William was examining a photograph of Melissa's parents. Her mother had long red hair and a smattering of freckles. Melissa was very like her, but her eyes were those of Alistair Carlisle.

"William, do you think they would do us supper in here?"

"I'm sure they would. Anything in particular?"

"You order, but nothing fancy please"

"Are you going to tell Charles Cliffe we are going to the ball?"

"Are you saying these invitations are a complex way of asking me whether or not I'm going to retain his company's services?"

"Socialising is a way of cementing client relationships, as well as justifying exorbitant fees."

Melissa made a face. "Do you think I should I keep them on?"

"Yep." William was studying the room service menu.

"I get the feeling you're more than happy with Charles Cliffe and his team."

"I am."

"Are you going to tell me why?"

"Because he's someone I think you can trust."

"How do you know that? We've only just met him."

"Because he asked me if I were Lord Edward's grandson."

Melissa shook her head. "You're talking in riddles, William."

"If he'd said, so you are Tobias's son, I would be recommending you ditch the company and find someone else."

"I asked you to keep it simple, not answer me with another riddle."

"Lissie, he's my father's generation and the banking world at that level is very small, so by asking me if I was Edward's grandson he's letting me know he's not in Tobias's camp. I'll ring Gramps and see if he actually knows Cliffe. He also said he knew your parents and grandparents well, which was telling us that he wants to get to know you."

"What happened to simple language?"

William paced up and down waiting for the phone to connect. "Gramps," pause, "yes, fine. No problem. Listen, do you know a Charles Cliffe?" Pause, "Excellent," pause, "yes," pause, "No, she's fine. Ok, we'll see you next week."

"Gramps does know Charles Cliffe. Say's he's a top bloke." He handed her his phone "Ring Cliffe and say we'll be there."

The Cliffes were having dinner when the phone rang. Charles answered it.

"Delighted, my dear. That's wonderful, I look forward to seeing you and William on Friday evening."

"Who was that?" his wife asked.

"That was Dr Carlisle accepting my invitation to the Ball on Friday and lunch on Sunday."

"She doesn't look as if she's two brass farthings to rub together, so she's clearly after de Braose's money."

"I thought she was rather sweet."

"Oh Charles! You can almost take the straw from her hair!"

"Don't you find that rather refreshing? She's got a brain on her too."

"You don't actually believe she's a doctor, do you? Probably bought the qualification off the Internet."

"Anne, if you spent less time with your nose in the air and more time doing something useful, you might find there's more to life than spending my hard earned money!"

"Charles Cliffe! This house takes a lot of running and you're not the easiest man in the world. Not to mention this Sunday, with all your pompous clients and their nosey wives traipsing through my house seeing whether I can afford to change the curtains or not. These events take a lot of organising."

"Well, my dear, if it will ease your ire I'll ensure you're seated next to young de Braose on Friday."

"Well, I suppose that's some small satisfaction. I dread to think what she'll turn up wearing. I hope he takes her shopping."

"Put the claws away for now dear, even though I can't see why you've got this sudden attack of the green eye if she's so unattractive. You can tear her to shreds after Sunday if you have to, but until then - BE NICE."

"I've ordered us fish and chips and a jug of fresh orange juice."

"Oh, lovely." Melissa brightened considerably. "We can have a picnic. Thank you." Melissa stood up and kissed him on the cheek. "Thank you for everything. I feel I'm actually beginning to know who I really am."

There was a knock at the door and an oversized exotic flower arrangement, a large box of chocolates and a bottle of champagne in an ice bucket were delivered. Melissa looked at William questioningly.

"My money's on Cliffe." He said.

"Why?"

"His firm's South African and those are all South African flowers."

Melissa swam length after length. Swimming helped her think.

To survive in William's world, in addition to the necessary education in whatever profession or chosen career, it helped if you had been to the 'right' school and had the 'right' contacts. Whatever profession she had come into contact with recently, be it accountancy, law, stock-broking or banking, the common factor was money and education. Either the desire to make it, steal it, or manage it (and charge high fees) the men all seemed to have similar backgrounds. Nothing appeared to be what it was on the surface.

After William had gone to bed she had opened the deed box that had Lavering painted on the top, which held similar documents to those in the first box, including Hetty and David's original birth certificates. Hetty had been born in Vancouver in 1920 and her grandfather in Grimsby in 1928. Great-grandfather Lavering's citation for his DCM detailed how he had saved a senior office who she already knew was Edward's father. Hearing Edward tell the story had been as if she were listening to a fairy tale; reading the official words telling how this man's action had been above and beyond the call of duty brought her family history alive. She thought about the diaries in these boxes and decided these and the other documents would be better studied where she could refer to Hetty's diaries and the various files in the study at The Old Manor.

Today she had the more immediate problem of what to wear to The Bankers' Ball. All William had to do was hire a dinner jacket, but it was evident from the way Mrs Cliffe had looked at her that Melissa would be judged by who had designed and how much she had paid for what she wore tomorrow night. The memory of Anne Cliffe's searing glance made her swim faster: she felt as if she had been standing stark naked in front of the banker's wife. If she was going to avoid embarrassing William she was going to need help. Reaching the end of a length Melissa stopped to catch her breath.

Why did she want to avoid embarrassing William?

What about letting herself down?

Thanks to the care of a lot of people she had never met, she was a wealthy woman. Melissa decided to swim another five lengths before getting out; she had still not addressed the question of why she wanted to avoid embarrassing William.

Trying to imagine what it was like to have the same lack of family identification as Melissa was giving William a lot to think about. Negative identification of the sort he had with his father, was an identification of sorts. Many of his contemporaries at school had divorced parents.

Boarding school had given him a resilience Melissa did not possess. She appeared emotionally self-contained, but he realised she was happier lost in her subject than engaging with the world around her. Her reliance on Hetty to do the everyday things amazed him. He wondered whether she knew how to clean a pair of shoes, or had Hetty done that too? Mrs Podger was just as bad with her boxes of groceries and coming with her team of girls to clean The Old Manor every week while Mr P mowed the lawns and looked after the garden.

Not knowing where she had been born he found bizarre. He took it for granted that he came from nearly a thousand years of de Braoses, traceable back to when the original William de Braose had come across with the Duke of Normandy.

He wondered what Melissa's childhood had been like with just the two of them rattling around The Old Manor.

Sometimes he had felt jealous that his stepfather had a call on his mother's affections, but had learned from observing their relationship that you cherish those you care about. He wondered what it would have been like to be brought up without any male influence, or worse, if his mother had stayed married to his own father.

William was even more confused by his own responses. Why had he decided to spend a ludicrous amount of money on a five star hotel with a girl he was not sleeping with? Yes, he could more than afford it: so could she. Then again, Melissa Carlisle was unlike any girl he knew.

Was it because she wasn't interested in him? Girls were always flirting with him except, in this instance, he was doing all the running. She seemed interested in Daghorne-Ffrench, but had not picked up that Daghorne-Ffrench was not interested. If anything, Daghorne-Ffrench appeared more interested in him.

A tapping on his patio door brought him from his confused semi-conscious thoughts of girls past and present, Daghorne-Ffrench and Melissa. He was unsure whether the Melissa with the wet hair he thought was standing outside was a dream. The tapping came again.

"It's open." He waved for her to open the door.

"Come on William, the day's half over and you're still asleep." She perched on the edge of his bed.

"Hmm, what time is it?" he murmured.

"I've just had a lovely swim and there's absolutely no one about."

"It's early then," he mumbled into the pillow. "What's the rush?"

"Well, I've got a plan of action even if you haven't. I'm taking a taxi into St Helier and before I disappear I thought I'd come and let you know what I was doing."

"OK, so when do you think you'll be finished." He could feel himself drifting off to sleep again.

"Ring me, sleepy head. You're no use to anyone." She ruffled his hair and left him wrapped in the arms of Morpheus.

By the time she was dressed it was nearly half past eight. She had no idea where to get a suitable dress, but was sure the receptionists would be able to help. In many ways she thought today was a bit like the first day at University.

"Lissie, where are you?" William had a vague memory of having seen her with wet hair and wearing a bathrobe.

"Er, I think the store's called de Gruchy's."

"What are you doing?"

"Shopping! I haven't got anything to wear for this shindig you want us to go to, remember?"

"Did you come into my bedroom earlier?"

"Yes, Clunkhead, but you didn't want to get up; don't forget you need a DJ."

"OK, OK. Stay where you are."

Melissa giggled. This morning had been great fun. The two girls at the hotel had given her some very good advice about where to go for something really special. She had found the dress, which was now wrapped in tissue and packed in a very smart box, and she had found some evening shoes that were comfortable as well as exquisite. There were benefits to having money in the bank and being able to afford anything she wanted. By the time William found her she had added some rather chic lingerie to her purchases and was in the perfumery department.

"Lissie, have you finished shopping?"

"Yes, have you?"

"No, I haven't even started. Could you help?"

It had not occurred to her that he might want someone to give him the thumbs up on his sartorial purchases.

"William, you go and start looking. I'll be with you in five." Melissa turned back to the assistant.

"Your husband?"

"No, my cousin." Melissa smiled at the woman's presumption. "We have an unexpected invitation to a formal do, so he needs a dinner jacket."

"Is the aftershave for him?" The assorted perfume houses had gift boxes galore and Melissa had no idea what to choose. "

"Yes, he's been very kind to me and it's just a little something to say thank you. What do you suggest?"

The assistant smiled. "What about this one. High on the citrus notes, with a hint of sandalwood as an afterthought." She squirted a piece of paper and waved it dry. Melissa could not believe the hype of the sales pitch supposing it was another justification for the cost, just like the packaging. Her little shopping expedition was providing an insight into yet another world. "That's lovely. Thank you."

She found William standing admiring himself from all sides in a full-length mirror. Melissa wondered if this was what it was like to go shopping with a lover. That thought stopped her.

"Lissie, what do you think?"

"Are you going to wear it with that T shirt?" He made a face as if to say no, and asked to see a selection of dress shirts. Melissa sat waiting for him to finish adding all the other necessary items required to complete his outfit. "Do you think I should have a blue cummerbund, or a black one?"

"Blue." She replied, surprised that he really did want her approval.

"Are you ready for lunch?" He asked as he paid the bill.

Melissa wondered if he ever thought of anything other than his stomach, but admitted she was hungry. He wondered if Melissa would ever remember to eat unless prompted.

"Turn left in 50 yards". The SatNav prompted.

"Where are we going?"

"After yesterday's success, I programmed another of those postcodes into Mavis."

"William, it's a piece of technology, not a person!"

"OK, but she's got the most irritating voice on the planet, so I've called her Mavis."

He turned into a small private road. Melissa wondered who from her past had lived here. They crawled round the corner and the houses seemed piled on top of each other. A woman peered out from a kitchen window as they drove down to a tarmacked circle, turned round and drove away.

"Sorry, William, it's triggered nothing. These houses are incredibly close to each other."

"You're spoilt living in that house of yours."

"I think you'll find that you and I have lived in the same flat!"

"Really! Where?"

"The Garden Flat in Notting Hill."

"Of course, I didn't make the connection before."

"So don't accuse me of not knowing what it's like to live cheek by jowl. However, I admit I like the isolation of The Old Manor."

A few minutes later he parked the car.

"Here we are, The Oyster Box as recommended by the girls at reception."

"William, thank you for doing all of this. I know I couldn't have done this on my own." Melissa said as they walked up the path.

"Lissie, come here." He pulled her into a brotherly hug. Melissa put her arms round his waist. "Gramps's wants to see you happy before he goes."

"So he told you to do all this?" She tried to pull away.

"Not exactly." he was holding her fast. "What I wasn't aware of was just how much you didn't know about your early life."

"What do you mean?"

He chose his words with care. "I had no idea that anyone could live such a sheltered life."

Melissa looked away.

"You think I'm a child."

"No, on the contrary, what you've been through I wouldn't wish on anyone, but Hetty's protection has left some large gaps in your education." He lifted her chin so she had no choice but to look at him. "I'm here to make sure you don't get taken advantage of."

Melissa had the urge to tell him she had done very well without him, but knew she would not survive in his world of City high flyers.

"Charles Cliffe is a very clever man and he's the one you have to deal with. I can't make decisions for you, but I can guide you through the worst of the jargon and, whenever you feel it's all getting too much, we stop. Now, however, we deserve a slap up lunch."

The urge to tell him to take a hike disappeared. It was interesting how he used food as a means of thinking things through. She had never thought of meals as being anything other than a means of taking in sustenance, but William liked everything to do with food. The growing of it, the preparation and even the formal setting of tables covered in crisp white tablecloths, polished cutlery and glasses, all accompanied by waiters and fancy wines.

"Now Dr Carlisle, what about some fresh Jersey lobster? We are, after all, on holiday."

They were shown to a table where they could see the whole expanse of the beautiful St Brelade's Bay. William waved away the proffered menus, but looked at the wine list. "Plateau Royal and a bottle of 703, please."

"And some fizzy water." Melissa added.

"Pellegrino, Evian or Highland Spring, madam?"

Why was a simple request for some water fraught with a challenge of choices, but she chose Pellegrino because of her times in Italy.

"William, what's Plateau Royal?"

"Wait and see, but I believe there will a mixture of crevettes, chancre crab, Jersey oysters, maybe whelks, mussels and cockles and lobster."

"It's all crustacea then?"

"And it's all delicious. You'll enjoy it."

Melissa looked down at her lap.

"William, I'm allergic to shellfish."

William paled, shuffled in his seat then blushed deep red.

"Oh, Lissie, I should have asked."

She burst out laughing. "Oh William. You should have seen your face!"

"Lissie Carlisle, you are the most awful tease, but I shouldn't have assumed that's what you'd want." He paused. "Are you allergic to shellfish?"

"Not that I know of, and it all sounds very interesting. I've never had lobster, or oysters for that matter. What if I don't like them?"

"Then you can have something else and there'll be all the more for me!"

"How do you eat a lobster?"

"Look over there."

A couple seated at a nearby table had what looked like an oversized two layer cake stand in the middle of their table. The top layer had a selection of crevettes, clams, oysters, whelks and mussels; the bottom layer had lobster and dressed crabs. The woman turned over her crab shell and lifted out a mixture of brown and white crabmeat with her fork. The man took a lobster claw in one hand, a pick in the other and flipped out the flesh intact revealing an identical, but floppy, version of the shell claw.

"It seems a huge amount for two people."

"Lissie, the fruits of the sea are something to be savoured, so we will take our time and enjoy Neptune's bounty at our leisure."

"I've never thought of eating as a leisure activity. Hetty and I were always doing something else. If we did have people over, it was a collective event and everyone brought a dish. If it was just the two of us we'd go down and eat with Edward and Mr & Mrs P."

"Then Edward and the Podgers are far more your family than anyone you've discovered here." It was a stark observation. He loved his grandfather Edward deeply, but the majority of his very early memories were of his other grandparents. His maternal grandmother had been similar to Mrs P in that she had kept a spotless house and been a fantastic cook. His grandfather had kept an allotment and grown all his own vegetables. He had also kept chickens so there were always fresh eggs. This had been a hangover from the war when everything was rationed except if you grew your own. This grandfather had taught him the best way to compost and how to grow fruit and vegetables with the phases of the moon. The vegetables that grew down, such as parsnips, potatoes and carrots, were planted when the moon was on the wane: those that grew up towards the sun were planted when the moon was waxing.

108

Marigolds would be planted between the rows of carrots to keep off the carrot fly and various other forms of companion planting meant the garden pests were kept in balance. Nets kept the pigeons off the brassicas, but he was not keen on either cabbage or Brussels sprouts. The strawberries were bedded on to straw to protect the fruit and grown next to the cabbages under the net.

"William, a penny for them?"

"Sorry, Lissie."

"You were miles away."

"I was thinking of my grandparents – my other grandparents."

Melissa waited, wondering if he would share his thoughts. The waitress came and served the wine and water. William tried the Chablis and nodded. It was poured and Melissa sipped, thinking how decadent it was to be drinking wine at lunchtime.

"I was remembering how my other grandfather taught me how to grow veg by the old ways. He had an allotment and we used to spend time together just pottering."

"Where do they live?"

"My mother was brought up on a council estate in Nottingham, but those grandparents have both gone now."

"Oh, I'm sorry." She sipped her wine wondering what to say.

"My mother won a place at Cambridge in 1978, which was when my father was in his final year. I believe they met at a party and she got drunk and pregnant."

"Did she finish her degree?"

"Yes, but much later thanks to Edward. She didn't return to Cambridge after she'd had me."

"Where did she study?"

"UCL, which is where she met my stepfather."

"Is he the reason why Tobias wanted a DNA test?"

William turned to look out across the bay. "Lissie, my father's gay."

"Oh." She took time, considering the implications of this statement. "I take it Edward doesn't know?"

"No, I don't think so."

"Do you think your father was trying to prove you weren't his?"

William nodded. "However, the DNA test proved I was."

"What was his motive?"

"I'm not sure. I did wonder if he was making sure just in case Edward ever found out about his sexuality."

Melissa sat for a moment considering this piece of the jigsaw. Without William, the title would die. Fleetingly she considered whether it was possible that Tobias wanted to ensure the de Braose name continued. This thought did not fit with the person Hetty had described nor did it explain why Tobias would go to such lengths to get his hands on her inheritance.

"Do you think Lansbury's his lover?"

"Hey, where did that idea come from?"

"You've established Lansbury and he were at uni together. Plus Lansbury has an air about him." She paused "a bit like Daghorne-Ffrench. I'm just trying to work out why Lansbury targeted me, someone he doesn't even know, and how he came to be a partner at TG&M. It can't be a coincidence since Tobias is a director of the bank that recommended Lansbury to the partners of TG&M."

William traced patterns in the condensation forming on his wineglass.

"I'm suspicious, like you, but so far I've only got circumstantial evidence about my father and Lansbury." William paused, hearing his own conclusions voiced by Melissa had, for some reason, hurt. "I wasn't sure if you'd clocked that Daghorne-Ffrench was batting for the other side."

"Oh yes. He found it incredibly difficult to focus on me, his client, and was much more at ease talking to you. When the Cliffe's appeared, he barely acknowledged her and his body language towards his boss was positively sycophantic.

"Well, blow me Dr Carlisle, and there was I thinking you didn't pick up on these things."

"It comes from years of watching students make prats of themselves, especially those in their first year. When you're teaching you learn to identify those who might not be able to take the pressures that Oxford applies."

"You taught?"

"Oh yes, you'll find this ironic in the light of what we've discovered in the past few days, but Hetty said that if I wanted to continue at Oxford doing any post-grad qualifications I had to fund it myself, so for the past five years I've been teaching."

110

William laughed. "Yes, that is ironic. I've had all the opportunities that money can buy, while you, who could have been funded all the way through your university career, turn out to have been teaching for the past five years to pay the fees for post graduate qualifications."

"Hetty might have cosseted me when I was at home, but I had a very normal university career. I chose to rent a house rather than stay in college, and I shared it with three other post-grads. I gave that up last year so I would have more money to spend time in Rome while I finished my research. Now I find I was paying rent to myself."

"Did you have a job as an under-grad?"

"No. Hetty gave me an allowance so I wouldn't be distracted from my studies by having to wait on tables, or get a job as a checkout girl. She believed that under graduates should never have to work because it was a distraction from studying. However, as a post grad, it's different. Teaching is all very well and academia is fascinating, but academics are notoriously protective about their research. Bitchy isn't strong enough to describe some of the stuff that goes on. I didn't have a social life. I have acquaintances, but nobody I can, or particularly want, to ring up and have a night out with. If I did, we'd probably all end up in the Bodleian with our heads in books."

"That sounds fun - not."

"So, apart from dining at High Table now and again, I've not been to balls, or dinner dances."

"Didn't you do the usual beginning and end of year balls?"

Melissa shook her head. "And before you ask, I didn't have anyone to go punting with either so I sat on the river bank and watched everyone else from over the top of a book."

Two waitresses appeared, one bearing the tiered stand loaded with shellfish nestling in seaweed and crushed ice, the other a polished metal salver loaded with bowls of mayonnaise, finger bowls of water and lemon slices, plates and a metal stand with an empty bucket.

The contents of large polished metal salver were placed on the table, then the salver itself was placed in the middle of the table and the tiered fish stand placed on top.

"Bon appetit."

"William, there's enough here to feed a family of four for a week." She whispered.

"No there isn't . . . well, perhaps there is, but we're on holiday and holidays are a time for being indulgent, so let's indulge. Most if this is shell anyway." He was already tucking into the crevettes. "Try these, Lissie, they're so sweet."

"Don't you think this bay is a bit like the south of France?" she asked. She was looking across the beach while sipping her coffee.

"Yes, sort of. I suppose it's the pine trees on that headland that does it. When were you last in the south of France?"

"I drove along the Cote d'Azur on my way back from Rome."

"You drove from Rome?"

"Why are you so surprised? I was spending some time doing some more research into the Medici. I had gone to Italy by car, so yes, I drove back from Rome when I got the phone call. Hetty wouldn't have minded that I didn't come back straight away" she paused "and I didn't want to come back to the cottage until I really had to." She thought she might cry if she said anymore.

"Come on, Lissie, let's walk along the beach. I'll pay the bill and meet you at the bottom of those steps." William was intrigued by the contradictory parts of Melissa's abilities and chose not to answer her question.

"William, I was going through some of the certificates after you went to bed last night and, according to the certificates, that's the church where they were married and I was baptised." Melissa pointed to the church across from where they were standing.

"Well then, perhaps we'd better take a look." William put his arm around her shoulders and she slid her arm around his waist. Their strides matched each other as they walked through the wavelets of the oncoming tide.

The church was open and the guidebook told how the church dated from the 11th century, but the separate Fisherman's chapel was considerably older. The vicar was inside and Melissa asked if they could see the registers for the year 1955. He was most obliging and invited them back to the Vicarage where he kept various church registers from 1945 onwards. He explained that if they wanted to know anything from before the German Occupation they would have to consult the archives in St Helier.

They found the record of her parents wedding in August 1979; the register for 1955 recorded her mother's baptism and the 1982 register showed her own. They thanked him for his time and Melissa gave him £50 for the restoration fund.

"William, what was the address of that property we drove to this morning?"

"Les Mignonettes, Park Estate. Why?"

"It doesn't make sense."

"What doesn't make sense, Lissie?"

"Well, the property we found yesterday on Rue de Douet was the one shown on my grandparent's death certificate as well as being listed in the schedule of assets of the Lavering Trust, but the one we went to this morning didn't trigger any memories for me at all, but did feature on the list of Carlisle trust properties."

"Sounds like a good idea if we drive past the other properties to see if you recognise them, or not, as the case may be."

"I've got the postcode of another one in St Brelade."

"If you continue being this logical, you'll grow pointed ears. Did you look at the address on the death certificates of your parents?"

"Now why didn't I think of that?"

"Because you do history, not probate. Let's start with the one you've got."

'Mavis' gave them instructions of how to get to the postcode provided. "La Rue du Bocage" had another extreme bend.

"Stop! I remember this." William had slowed to a crawl and before he stopped Melissa jumped out and ran back to stand in the driveway.

"We lived behind that archway. I remember Daddy driving in and parking his car up on the left and the swallows nesting up under the arch. You can see the pigsties through there," she was jumping up and down with excitement. "That's where he said Digby and Baxter were going to live, but they were such tiny puppies I insisted they slept with me. Oh William, I remember! Thank you." She threw her arms around his neck and kissed him.

She stepped back, embarrassed.

"Oh, William, I shouldn't have done that. I'm sorry."

They had shared supper, watched some television and at midnight William had gone to his room. She had fallen fast asleep and dreamt of nothing for six hours. Now she had the hotel pool to herself.

As she ploughed her way up and down trying to sort out the tangled 'thought spaghetti' in her head she was vaguely aware of the attendant setting out the sun beds. Throwing her arms around William's neck had been a spontaneous splurge of delight. She had meant to kiss him on the cheek. Now she was confused and a little bit frightened as to what could, or might, happen next. She tumble turned and pushed off, dimly aware of another swimmer.

Tonight they would attend a reception and the ball. No doubt there would be a herd of women like Mrs Cliffe, with their withering looks and incredibly rich husbands. She winced remembering the amount she had spent yesterday.

She did another tumble turn.

It occurred to her that the Anne Cliffe's of this world were nothing but glorified Christmas trees, expensively decorated to show off their husband's wealth. It would be interesting to know how many would be wearing jewellery given as an apology for extra marital liaisons. She wondered if the way it worked was that the more frequent the straying, the larger the diamond. Knowing hers were inherited was very satisfying.

Five more lengths and she would get out; another tumble turn. Her thoughts turned to William.

William de Braose. His humble background was a turn up for the books.

Then there was Tobias. The revelation of the DNA test on top of what she had read in Hetty's diaries, only confirmed the man was as odious as she had first thought. William seemed quite sure that Mr Cliffe was on their side, but she wondered whether his method of deduction might be flawed. Then there was Daghorne-Ffrench who probably knew more about the details of her financial affairs than Cliffe and, if he was, as William so quaintly put it, 'batting for the other side", perhaps he knew Lansbury and Tobias.

Reading Hetty's diaries suggested that any motive had to be a combination of greed and spite and it was becoming apparent that banker Tobias was the key.

She did a last tumble turn and pushed off towards the shallow end.

"Melissa Carlisle, where do you get your energy?"

"William. I thought you'd still be asleep!"

They stood together at the shallow end.

"I decided to take a leaf out of your book and have an early morning dip, but I've only done five lengths and I'm exhausted."

"Well, if you do another forty five you can have breakfast. I'll order yours for eight thirty."

William rose to her challenge and pushed off doing a slow crawl to the other end. She watched him turn and start the return length before she left.

Melissa was right; swimming was good for thinking. He realised just how unfit he was and if he was to compete with her, he had better shape up. It appeared she had done fifty lengths without even breaking into a sweat. He liked her simple approach to life and it appeared his upbringing was not too dissimilar to hers, except perhaps for his public school education and that his grandfather was a Lord.

His mother had made him work off a debt he had run up in his first year at Cambridge. There had been wild undergraduate parties and late night poker games and by the end of his first year he had owed a Townie three thousand pounds who threatened to 'do him over' if he did not pay. She had paid off the Townie then made William work during the summer vacations to repay her. He had taken a job in a canning factory and every Friday she had taken his wages and given him ten pounds for the weekend. It had been gruelling work, but over two summers he had paid her back every penny and the experience had taught him a valuable lesson.

His mother had told her father - his other grandfather – and the dressing down he had received from him had scared him even more than his mother's reaction when he had told her. That grandfather had hated debt and had drilled it into him that just because his other grandfather was a Lord, William could not go round giving himself airs and graces. He would never forget how he had felt when the old man had said how disappointed he was by his behaviour and that he was ashamed William was his grandson.

Lissie had never done anything to blot her copybook and had had a spotless student career.

Today there was a sparkle to her eyes and she seemed to stand taller. Her spontaneous kiss had surprised and, he admitted, delighted him.

He wondered what she had bought to wear tonight. He hoped she would recognise any bitchy comment by Mrs Cliffe as being nothing more than jealousy.

Picking up his towel, he made his way to the Tower Suite. Lissie was studying documents.

"I bet you didn't manage forty five lengths in that time!"

"No, but I did manage twenty. You're quite a swimmer."

She nodded. "It's in the genes, so I've discovered. Here, look at this." She handed him a certificate. "Before you go sitting on that chair making it all wet, put this on it." She threw him a folded towel.

"Ok, bossy boots."

He unrolled a certificate that had been awarded to her great grandfather Lavering on the completion of his cross Channel swim from Calais to Dover on 22nd August, 1935, in the time of fourteen hours and thirty-eight minutes.

"That's quite a swim."

"These two boxes have been quite an eye opener and I'm sure there's more to come.

"I thought you were going to take them one at a time."

"I have. Anyhow, I'm going to lock them all away now because I can look at them when we are back home. I want to do things I can't do at home."

"Do you want to go to any of the other properties?"

"Not really, now that I've recognised where I lived with my parents what's the point, and you were right, the two addresses on the schedule of assets matched the ones on the other death certificates. I'm not bothered about the rest of the addresses, so why don't we just enjoy ourselves?"

"That's fine by me."

"Except we have to be back here by three because I've got a hair appointment." Lissie handed him a cup of coffee. "The receptionist was incredibly helpful and booked for someone to come to me here to do my hair and nails so Mrs Cliffe won't have any excuse to make any snide remarks."

"She's really got under your skin, hasn't she?"

116

Lissie nodded. "I don't know why . . ." she paused, "actually, I do. She stood and looked me up and down as if I were something she'd found on the bottom of her shoe."

"Lissie, she's jealous."

"Why should she be jealous of me?"

"You're some twenty plus years younger than her for starters and her husband clearly took a shine to you, for another."

"Rubbish! OK, perhaps she's the sort of woman who finds getting older difficult, but Mr Cliffe's just being polite."

"A man in his position has many temptations and I bet Mrs Cliffe's seen off a couple of contenders in her time."

"William, can you remember if the invitation said this ball is hosted by Cliffe's company or if it's a combined effort on behalf of all the finance houses?"

"I think it said something about the Jersey Federation of Bankers. Why do you want to know?"

"Like any good general I want to be aware of the facts before going into battle."

"I know it's a charity fundraiser so the raffle prizes are likely to be pretty amazing to get hard earned dosh out of the Jersey banking elite."

"Oh, should be we get some cash?"

"Not unless you want to walk around with great wads of notes in your purse, but we should get some cash out anyway. And I know you think I'm always focussing on the next meal, but take it from me, these do's are boozy and it would be a good thing if we had a solid lunch."

Melissa made a face at the thought of yet another meal.

"Lissie, how about you see if we can get on the special Garden Lunch while I get dressed. That way we get to have a guided tour of the walled garden and a potted history of the property itself.."

"What're you going to do while I'm having my hair done?"

"I'm going to lie by the pool and read a book."

The tour of the walled garden and the history lesson had been interesting and the lunch delicious, but not what William considered stomach lining. Now they were enjoying coffee.

Melissa reached into her handbag and placed a gift-wrapped box on the table. "It's a very small something to say thank you."

"I've got something for you too." William placed an identically wrapped box next to hers. They burst out laughing.

"OK, so who's going to open theirs first?"

"Are you sure you know which one is which?" He pretended to switch the position of the identical boxes.

"William, stop it – I put down the one on the right . . . didn't I?"

"We won't know until we open them: you take the one on the left."

Melissa took her time undoing the bow then slowly slitting the tape with her knife.

William watched, awed by her patience. "Don't you ever rip anything open?"

She sniffed the still wrapped box, her fingers keeping the paper in place. "I'm savouring the expectation of what's inside."

"Egads woman, hurry up. If you don't like it I've still got time to take it back."

"William, let's open them together."

He ripped the paper from the other boxed set. Hers contained bain moussant, shower gel, body lotion and eau de toilette, plus a large bottle of parfum by Chanel, his – a bottle of après rasage, shower gel, deodorant and eau de toilette by Givenchy.

"Thank you, William."

He smiled. "We're both going to smell delicious!"

LATER

"Mirror, mirror on the wall?"

The hairdresser and manicurist had been and gone. Somehow the reflection thought like Melissa, sounded like Melissa, but did not look like Melissa. Yes, she had the same red hair and the same figure, but this person looked sophisticated and demure.

The reflection looked as though she would not make any political comments and would try and keep off inflammatory subjects such as world poverty and the banking crisis. In view of her newly discovered wealth Melissa's opinion of the banking crisis would be difficult to justify.

She turned to look at herself sideways. Her stomach was completely flat, but so was her chest. No knicker line, thanks to the lingerie lady's suggestion she wear French knickers. They too were navy blue, trimmed with lace and exactly matched the colour of her dress. Her new shoes were not too high and had just the hint of glitter.

"OK, Cinders, you can go to the ball."

The reflection supressed the desire to wink.

"Lissie." William had let himself into her suite and wondered whether the closed bedroom door meant she had decided she did not want to go the ball after all. "It's 6.25: are you going to be much longer?"

Melissa put on her jacket, sprayed her hair with eau de toilette and dabbed perfume on the inside of her wrists. Finally, she slipped her mother's sapphire and diamond ring on to her right ring finger. Taking a deep breath she opened the door.

William was standing in front of the fireplace adjusting his bow tie in the mirror.

Melissa stopped. The man reflected in the mirror was the man in the portrait in Hetty's bedroom.

"Lissie," his voice croaked with surprise on seeing her, "for a minute I thought you were Hetty."

"I thought you were David."

"If Mrs Cliffe says just one word out of place, I'll . . . "

Melissa recovered her poise at the mention of Anne Cliffe.

"No you won't. You'll smile sweetly, whisk her round the dance floor and tell her how beautiful she looks."

"OK, I promise, but only if you promise me the first dance."

"I'll have to check my card, but I think I'm free."

"Mr William de Braose and Dr Melissa Carlisle" were announced into the Bateman Room where Charles and Anne Cliffe were greeting their guests.

"My, Charles! Where's our ugly duckling disappeared to?" Anne Cliffe murmured softly so only Charles could hear.

"Anne, keep those claws sheathed." He replied softly as they approached. "My dear, you look wonderful. William, great to see you again."

They shook hands with Charles before moving on to his wife.

"Melissa, it's so nice to see you again dear. I do hope you are both enjoying your stay?"

"Thank you, Mrs Cliffe, indeed we are."

"Please, call me Anne."

William took Anne Cliffe's hand and kissed it. "It's a pleasure to see you again, Anne."

"Oh William, how lovely old world charm hasn't completely disappeared."

William and Melissa moved on after the banal exchange of greetings.

"Now Lissie, that wasn't too bad, was it?"

"William, she's putty in your hands, but I don't think she's my best friend just yet."

"May I take your jacket?" the coats lady asked.

Melissa smiled, murmured "Thank you" and slipped the jacket off her shoulders.

William chuckled. He looked back at his hosts. Mrs Cliffe was dressed in what was clearly an expensive designer creation. The bouffant skirt all layers of net and tulle and the heavily embroidered boned satin bodice was tightly nipped in at the waist. Her décolletage was more than sufficient for a woman of her age and despite the obvious surgery to lift, tuck and hide the ravages of sun and time, she still looked several years over the wrong side of fifty.

Melissa's outfit was the essence of demure. From the front, long sleeves and a high neckline that cut straight across her collarbones, but she was standing with her back to him.

"Oh Lissie" he whispered. "She's going to hate you!"

"Do you think it's a bit too daring?"

William admired her back, bare to just below the waist, framed by what could only be described as a scoop of finely beaded navy strands that flowed from shoulder to shoulder. Melissa had knotted a long rope of pearls that hung down her back.

"Lissie, you look sensational." She was aware of him standing close behind her as they moved to the middle of the room. People were looking to see if they recognised the newcomers.

"Champagne, madam?" a waiter proffered the tray. Melissa took a glass and turned slowly to face her companion.

The level of conversation dipped slightly then rose again.

"Mr de Braose thank you, for everything."

They chinked glasses.

"Lissie, that was priceless," he whispered "I wouldn't mind betting that if Anne Cliffe could sink her claws between your shoulder blades, she would."

"Good, that evens up the odds a bit."

"What do you mean?"

"Don't tell me that you aren't aware that every woman has her eye on you. Given a chance I bet they're going to try and eat you for breakfast!"

"Lissie, look at me." She looked up.

"Charles Cliffe, you'd better keep your sticky paws off young Dr Carlisle or I'll sue you to the end of your bank account."

"Anne dear, I can't afford her, even if I wanted to."

"What do you mean?"

"She's the client, not de Braose. He's her cousin, or as Peregrine told me, her advisor."

"What?"

"Head Office would be extremely upset if we lost her business."

"Well I never. And I suppose you're going to tell me that kiss is because they're cousins!"

"Even if it were, it's none of our business."

"You thought he was gay - like his father."

"Rumours are, Tobias has been caught at some party trussed up like a chicken."

"Not the same party where that poor boy was found dead?"

"I believe so, but it's only rumours. I gather some high up Government official is involved, which is why, so far, it's been kept out of the Press."

"You don't suppose William knows, do you?"

"Ah, Anne you do so love to gossip." Charles sighed, wishing he had not mentioned the rumours sweeping the banking world. "I very much doubt it. It's well known father and son haven't spoken for years. As for William and Melissa, no, I think this is an old friendship that's only now just reaching a more, shall we say, adult level."

"Well, I think it's more likely he's after her money."

"Don't judge everyone by your own standards dear. Come now, we have guests to entertain."

"Ladies & Gentlemen, in accordance with tradition I'm making my speech at the beginning of the evening. Despite the problems the banking sector has suffered I hope you'll be as generous as in previous years."

Melissa wondered if any of these people had suffered anything more than indigestion during the past twelve months. Judging by the glittering jewellery and the latest expensive designer dresses, it did not appear that the Jersey finance fraternity were suffering unduly.

"The Princes' charity has a special interest in the work done to conserve and preserve African wildlife and the environment. To date, the charity has raised over £20 million for a wide range of projects across the continent earning a reputation for financial efficiency, with an average of 80% of the net funds raised reaching the field. Currently, there are fifty-seven field projects in eighteen African countries aiming to protect wildlife and alleviate poverty through sustainable development and education amongst rural communities who live alongside the wildlife. I know South Africa is far from home, but like Europe, as the ever-expanding human population and its demand for more land brings increasing conflict with wildlife, the charity's aim is to forge an inextricable link between the preservation of Africa's natural heritage and the future of its land, culture and people.

British Airways have donated two business class tickets and a two-week safari for two. The winners of this prize will be guests of my bank during their stay in South Africa and in addition to the safari, will have a guided tour of the wine provinces and travel on the prestigious Golden Train from Johannesburg to Cape Town. All in all, this prize is a month's holiday for two in beautiful South Africa.

The Jersey Diamond Company have generously donated a rare four carat solitaire Brazilian blue diamond together with a pair of matching two carat tear drop diamonds. Their own internationally acclaimed jewellery designer, Katherine Franworthy, will make them up to an agreed design as part of this prize."

Melissa had to admit Charles Cliffe was good.

"The star prize is a brand new AMG GT Mercedes, donated by our very own Mercedes agent." More applause. Men were bringing out their wallets in anticipation of purchasing a winning ticket. Charles let this die down before continuing. "Gentlemen, I'm sure your ladies are worth your generosity. After all, where else would you find a gathering of so many beauties?" There was murmured agreement and a ripple of applause. "Our raffle sellers will be coming to your table very shortly and are happy to accept either cash or cards."

On queue, accompanied by a rhythmical African drum beat, two teams of girls, each dressed in what Melissa assumed was the traditional dress of some of the fifty-seven African countries benefiting from this charity's largesse, appeared and began selling tickets from table to table.

"Well my dear, you look wonderful." Charles Cliffe said as he sat down.

"Thank you for inviting us."

"I know the offshore banking world has a slightly grubby reputation because of its various services, but we do try and do some good for those parts of the world less fortunate than ourselves. This year, it's the Princes' project in Africa."

"I must buy some tickets." Melissa reached for her evening bag.

"No, no, my dear, tonight it's only the men who buy the tickets. They're the ones who earn the big money so this is when they have to dig deep for a charity other than the one that begins at home."

Melissa smiled at his acceptance of the banking world's reputation. She looked down the table and saw William was punching in his pin number. He looked across and winked.

"Sorry, Charles, you were saying . . ."

"I'm sure William has bought you a lucky ticket." He patted her hand and she thought this might be a prelude to a grope on the dance floor.

The table decorations were of bright orange and blue 'birds of paradise' flowers that looked like fireworks bursting out of the top of their tall vases. Like dining at High Table, fine wines were served and were all South African. Melissa ordered a jug of iced water.

All through dinner a string quartet played classical music. Notes from Vivaldi, Mozart and Purcell all hung in the air; their volume was such that the music did not preclude conversation. While coffee and liqueurs were served there was a cabaret, then a brief pause while the ladies 'powdered their noses'.

The band struck up and Charles Cliffe and his wife led the couples on to the floor.

"Doctor Carlisle, may I have the pleasure?"

"Mr de Braose, I'd be delighted."

William led her out and they performed a passable quickstep. "Lissie, you're right, the woman's a first class nightmare and the most terrible gossip."

"I think Charles is leading up to a grapple and grope on the dance floor, but I don't think it will be anything I can't handle."

"Are you sure? I thought you said you were a novice at this sort of thing."

"He will be much the same as fighting off an over zealous professor, except Cliffe can't afford to lose my business whereas at college I couldn't afford to upset a professor who might have given me a crap grade if I'd been rude."

"You catch on quickly."

"Besides, dancing with her husband will upset the old bag."

"Melissa Carlisle, you're turning into quite a player."

"William de Braose, are you accusing me of indulging in mind games?"

"Would I do that?" He spun her round to the finale of the music. She was beginning to appreciate Hetty's insistence she learned to ballroom dance when she was at school. Dancing was a bit like riding a bicycle; once you had learned the basic movements, if you had a good partner you just relaxed and let him lead. It was very pleasurable to be led by William.

"Lissie, I think we're going to have to bite the bullet and dance with our hosts."

"Good luck with Anne."

"I'll just hold her close and push her about a bit."

Melissa gave him a sweet smile as she sat back at the table and William held out his hand to invite Anne Cliffe on to the dance floor.

"Are you prepared to brave your toes with an old man?" Charles asked.

"Charles, how could I possibly say no." she accepted, smiling her most charming smile.

Despite her worst fears, Charles Cliffe was not a groper and was very light on his feet. She could see William doing exactly as he had described and Anne was beaming.

"The raffle is to be drawn after the next dance." Her host announced as they glided past William and Anne for the third time.

"Did you raise what you expected?" she asked out of politeness, indifferent as to whether or not Jersey's wealthy bankers and their clients had sufficient sympathy to give up a day or so's pay.

"Indeed, the girls did well tonight so we're up twenty thousand on last year."

This figure made her blink and she wondered how many tickets William had bought.

"We've been selling tickets in the island for the past couple of months so it's quite possible the winners aren't even here." Charles continued.

"No one can resist the possibility of a big prize for a fraction of its value, can they Charles?"

"No my dear, but then that's what life's all about, one big gamble."

A breathless Anne was hanging on to William's arm as he delivered her back at the table.

"Now my dear, it's raffle time."

"Oh Charles, is it that time already." Anne turned to Melissa. "It's just one of those little duties one has to do when you're married to someone as important as Charles."

Melissa smiled at her statement, wondering what on earth the woman was talking about.

Anne thought Melissa a simpering idiot. William was clearly a man with a wandering eye. It was good to know she had not yet lost her touch.

"Dr Carlisle," William whispered softly in Melissa's ear, "I believe Anne Cliffe thinks she's made a conquest."

Anne was now standing on the stage, fanning herself with a dinner menu and smiling beatifically at any one who was watching.

"William, can we disappear?"

"Not until we know we haven't won anything. Do you know the price of those tickets?"

"Charles only told me that they were up twenty thousand on last year's ball."

"That's good! The one redeeming feature is that this charity is one of my favourites."

"And the winner of the matched set of Brazilian blue diamonds is ticket number 5609." Charles announced.

"Lissie, that's one of ours." William picked up one of the tickets lying on the table in front of him and gave it to her. "Go on, up you go."

"Why me? They're your tickets."

"Because it's the ladies who're claiming the prizes, not the men. Go on."

Reluctantly she made her way across the empty dance floor. Charles beamed his delight and insisted he kiss her on both cheeks. Every year The Jersey Diamond Company donated three exquisitely matched solitaires and every woman in the marquee had hoped their partner had that winning ticket. Melissa had no knowledge of any of this, but was conscious that every man in the room was watching her as she walked back across the dance floor, her eyes fixed on William.

"Nice one, Lissie," he murmured as he stood up and held her seat for her to sit down. He had heard the woman on the other side of him instructing her partner that 'blue stockings' were notoriously frigid. The reply had been rather crude. For a moment he wondered whether the woman was going to ask him if her partner were correct.

Official duties completed, Charles sat down and ordered himself a very large brandy. Anne was bouncing round the dance floor with a terrified looking Daghorne-Ffrench.

"Come on Lissie - up." William grabbed her hand and dragged her in amongst the dancers. "You're once, twice, three times a lady . . ." the singer crooned. She was conscious of William's hand in the small of her back. After another couple of dances he murmured in her ear: "I think we can make our getaway shortly without appearing rude."

Her feet were beginning to hurt as they finally made their way back to the table.

"Charles, would you mind if I took Melissa away. She was up at six and hasn't been sleeping well."

"Of course not dear boy. Wish I could do the same." He gave William a big wink. "Shall we see you on Sunday? I've got some paintings Melissa might like to see."

"Thank you Charles, we are looking forward to it, and thank you for a wonderful evening." Melissa stressed the 'we'.

"Melissa, my pleasure." Charles Cliffe emphasised the 'my'.

They made their way across lawns to the hotel.

"William, if having lots of money means having to spend my time doing this sort of social stuff then I'd rather be broke. I've got better things to do with my life than listen to a load of overstuffed peacocks tell each other how clever they are and what model of super car they're buying this year."

"Unfortunately you're going to have to make a decision about another invitation for tomorrow."

Melissa raised her eyebrows in disbelief. "Who and why?"

"Daghorne-Ffrench wants to know if we'd like a visit to the German Underground Hospital, evidently a relic of the Nazi occupation. Then he'll take us on to the Jersey Diamond Company."

Melissa groaned.   "What do you want to do, they're your diamonds."   She paused, bent down and removed her shoes.   "I'm sorry William.   You've been doing all the driving.   Yes, let's accept, but do we have to do the whole flash dining thing?   I'm wanting something really plain, like soup!"

"Good.   He's picking us up at 10.30."

"William de Braose, if I didn't know you better, I'd say you had an alternative agenda."

"Perhaps I have Lissie, perhaps I have, but you've been up since before sparrow fart so you should get some sleep."

"Goodnight, Lissie." They were outside her suite: he wished her sweet dreams, resisting a strong urge to try and find out if blue stockings really were frigid.

"Melissa Carlisle, I do believe you wanted William de Braose to do more than kiss you chastely on your cheek." The voice in her head sounded slightly shocked.   Now devoid of makeup and her hair tumbling round her shoulders, the old Melissa looked out of the mirror.

"And what would you have done if he had tried?" she asked herself.

Her dreams had been explicit and she lay staring at the ceiling wondering if her subconscious was teaching her what it was like to make love, or was it a memory of some trashy novel surfacing to tease her with what she might be missing. The image of the man who had tried to stick his tongue down her throat superimposed itself over William's face and she shuddered.

She valued William's friendship and wondered that if anything should happen and it all went wrong, could they still remain friends. She was not so naïve to expect their friendship could continue should he marry. A wife would ensure all his female friends from his single years would never be allowed to set foot in their house until they too were safely wedded to Mr Someone Else and even then their social paths would probably not cross often. Would she recognise the signs if William were interested in her?

"Ah well, Doctor Carlisle, for all your degrees and qualifications, you are rubbish when it comes to personal relationships." She said out loud.

"Time to try another form of study"

The voice was so clear Melissa got out of bed and looked to see if anyone was in her lounge. She sat back on the bed. Perhaps the voice was right, perhaps it was time to try dipping her toe in the unfathomed depths of romance. Her phone showed it was eight thirty, which meant there was no time to have a swim and have breakfast. She opted for the swim. She could raid the fruit bowl afterwards.

The pool area was devoid of people and she dived in the deep end. She might be sexually naïve, but she had read enough romantic stories to know the basics. Hetty had loved all Jane Austen books, but Melissa found Austen's novels irritating, all that female simpering and as for Mr Darcy! Yes, Colin Firth was incredibly attractive in his soggy shirt, but that had been a cheap visual device for television, it did not happen in real life. If Mrs Bennett had been her mother Melissa thought she might have strangled her, but admitted the woman had wanted the best for her daughters even if her social climbing was toe curling.

Better Austen's story lines than those of Charles Dickens's. Given her own history, she too might have lived a life similar to the plot of Bleak House with everyone waiting for the outcome of numerous challenges to a will. The only people who had come out of that story successfully were the lawyers. Thanks to very clear instructions left by people who had loved her, but she could barely remember or had never met, she was now fabulously wealthy.

William seemed to be completely at ease dealing with huge sums of money. Edward had given her a present of a Book of Hours that was, for her, priceless. Edward was right, someone, probably American, would pay millions to own such a piece of medieval history. In a way these Trusts were the same as Edward's gift to her. Last night had shown how the wealthy liked parading just how much they were worth by draping their partners in jewellery and expensive clothes. But were they happy? Perhaps the cost of the raffle tickets had eased their consciences. She had discovered the raffle tickets were £500 each. At £500 those diamonds were a bargain.

There was a splash as another person joined her. She kept swimming.

She hoped Daghorne-Ffrench's invitation was not part of his job description. Since he was picking them up it would mean that they would not have to rely on the irritating 'Mavis' for directions.

"Wear your jeans and flip-flops." The voice inside her head instructed. Perhaps not her cut off jeans, perhaps a sundress she thought. The voice in her head said nothing. If they were going to the diamond place then she wanted to look as if she could afford . . . No!

She readjusted her thinking. She wanted to look as if she were the one that William wanted to drape with glittering gems.

"And make up." Again the voice gave instructions inside her head. Yes, she would make wear make up.

"Thank you." Melissa blew the voice an imaginary kiss.

Melissa pulled herself up onto the side of the pool. William was sitting talking to Charles Cliffe. Melissa groaned inwardly. She could not get back into the water or walk off and not say good morning without appearing extremely rude. She was conscious of the older man's gaze, but managed to smile as she walked over to where they were sitting.

"Melissa, you set quite a pace. Do you swim every morning?" Charles Cliffe asked.

"Fifty lengths of the nearest pool."

"Fifteen hundred metres after a late night, is impressive. I managed ten lengths!" Cliffe turned to William. "Are you not braving the water, William?"

"Charles, I can't keep up with Lissie. She wasn't in her room, so I came to see if she was ready for breakfast. Daghorne-Ffrench has kindly offered to show us the island."

"Young Daghorne-Ffrench, eh. He's quite an expert on the Occupation. He'll go far, provided the local gossips don't take offence at his sexuality. Their tongues can cut a man dead at fifty paces. Get him to show you the Underground Hospital, Melissa. He'll value your thoughts on why the Nazis dug so many tunnels into our hillsides."

"I'm not a modernist, Charles, but I like listening to people who are passionate about their subject." She wrapped the towel around her body, wanting to shield herself from his eyes. "I had no idea you were staying overnight. Is Anne up yet?"

Charles chuckled. "After you two slunk away, the party really got going. Anne is nursing a cup of tea and a couple of Paracetamol."

"Oh, I'm sorry."

"Don't be, my dear, she brought it on herself; too much champagne and too little water." He had noted that Melissa had drunk little alcohol the previous evening. Anne and her collection of island cats had sharpened their claws and metaphorically sunk them deep into Dr Carlisle's back, ripping her to shreds even before last evening's reception was over. By the end of the ball he had heard three luridly different stories about Dr Carlisle and William de Braose, which, if they ever reached Melissa's ears, had the possibility of ending in a case for defamation.

"Well, I'd better go and brave Anne's moans and groans. We'll see you tomorrow at 12.30."

"We're looking forward to it, Charles." William stood as good manners dictated.

"Thank you for last night, I had a lovely time." Melissa shook his hand.

"I'm glad those diamonds didn't go to one of those overdressed society" he paused before choosing his next word, "ladies."

"Oh, thank you Charles. Er yes, we're planning on going up to the jewellers this afternoon, as a matter of fact." She wisely kept her thoughts about whose diamonds they were, to herself. Jersey was a very traditional patriarchal society; a rampant feminist 'blue stocking' was not how she wished to be remembered.

"Good. So, á demain." The older man left to re-join his petulant, hung-over wife.

"Oh dear, I bet Anne's tongue is particularly harsh this morning." Melissa felt sorry for the banker.

"At least she's got twenty four hours or so to get over it. Presumably she's got caterers so will be able to exorcise her hangover on them."

"William, are you hungry?"

"Yes, I came to see if you wanted breakfast. I've ordered coffee and croissant on my patio."

"Good, I'm ravenous, but won't we be late?"

"So what; we can ask if Peregrine wants to join us for coffee."

"Lissie, how old you think Daghorne-Ffrench is?" William ladled some Confiture d'Abricot on to his flaky croissant.

"Late thirties, possibly early forties, and before he appears, can we get sort the whole diamonds thing out. I'm aware Daghorne-Ffrench will report everything to Charles, which is why I think we have to get it sorted before he arrives." William let Melissa ramble on. "So, perhaps the best design would be a simple bar brooch. Daghorne-Ffrench can then report that the diamonds have been set and you can keep them safe for whoever you want to give them too, and everybody's happy."

"Fine, Lissie, if that's what you want."

"William, can we also discuss the costs of this week?"

"Why?"

"Because I want to pay my way."

"No."

"Why not?"

"Because I say so. Lissie, just because you want something, doesn't mean you're going to get it."

"Pass the jam."

He was amused by Melissa's ninety-degree change of subject avoidance tactic. "Please." He reminded her and passed her one of the little jars of apricot conserve.

Melissa spooned a generous dollop on to her plate. "I don't feel right with you paying for all of this."

"Are you enjoying yourself?"

"Yes, but . . ."

"Lissie, think of it as your cousin's belated twenty-first, or if you want, an early thirtieth birthday present."

"Thank you for reminding me that between now and next February I have to learn the equivalent of an MBA in order to understand a tenth of how to handle my Trusts."

"Think of yourself as the natural heir to the Medici."

"At least they were marginally better than the Borgias. However, our discussion about the diamonds is not yet over." She stood up, drank the last of her coffee and ate the last of her croissant. "I'm going to get dressed."

William poured himself another cup of coffee, buttered himself another croissant and read the paper.

"Dr Carlisle, Mr de Braose, good morning."

Daghorne-Ffrench was waiting for them in the hotel reception at exactly 10.30.

"This is very good of you to give up your Saturday for us."

"It's not often I have the opportunity to talk to a proper historian."

"Thank you for the compliment. I understand your particular interest is about four hundred years after my own."

"Jersey's not noted for its academic prowess, so when someone of your qualifications comes to town I try and grab the opportunity to talk them."

"I understand your special interest is the German Occupation."

Daghorne-Ffrench nodded.

Outside a man of about Daghorne-Ffrench's age was leaning against an Audi estate.

"My friend Scott volunteered to drive." Peregrine introduced them. Pleasantries were exchanged: William sat in the front and Melissa and Daghorne-Ffrench in the back seat. Scott drove through green country lanes until they arrived at the Jersey War Tunnels.

"You have to ask yourself what Hitler's motives were for this whole project. This is quite a feat of engineering." William said.

Despite this not being her period of history, Melissa was completely absorbed in what she was seeing.

"My thoughts exactly Mr de Braose." Daghorne-Ffrench replied.

William looked at the young banker.

"Don't you think we can cut the Mr stuff, Peregrine? If I'm calling your friend Scott and he's calling me William, it is a bit ridiculous for you to keep calling me Mr de Braose."

Daghorne-Ffrench opened his mouth to speak; William held up his hand to stop him. "Don't worry, I won't tell Cliffe and I can assure you Melissa won't either. She's not good with titles, most of all her own unless she takes a dislike to you then she wields it like a sword. She's well aware of the social niceties on Jersey."

"Peregrine . . ." Melissa called.

"See what I mean?" William said.

Scott laughed and Daghorne-Ffrench looked relieved.

"Yes, Dr. . . sorry Melissa?" Daghorne-Ffrench replied.

"What's the official version for the making of these tunnels?"

Daghorne-Ffrench led his little party down the slope into the side of the hill.

"I thought you should see it without either the official version, or my own theory, colouring your conclusions. The Tourist Board have created a tableau in the completed areas and the uncompleted tunnels are under the auspices of the War Graves Commission."

There was a steady flow of tourists exploring the starkly lit interior. Melissa stood in front of the opening on to the uncompleted tunnels.

"William," she sought his hand. It was reassuring to feel his warm grasp. "We're face to face with Hitler's evil fanaticism."

They could see how the rock face had been hewn away and a discarded shovel was propped against a pile of stones: its presence a lonely reminder of the people who had died here because of the insane logic of a psychopathic ego. The memorial stone told how forced labour had dug these tunnels; another plaque listed their nationalities.

The completed concrete lined barrel vaulted tunnel had what appeared to be steel railway tracks set about a metre apart in the concrete floor. Off to the right were wards that could be closed off by inches thick steel doors. To the left were administration offices and an operating theatre set out as if those who used it had just left. The effect was spooky. The railway track went into each ward and followed the main corridor round the corridor. Originally the track would have led out into the open air, but now it ended in a museum displaying artefacts such as ID cards, ration books, photos, and a crystal radio set. A whole wall of young faces identified those who had played any part in resisting their German oppressors.

Those who had been shipped off to the death camps were listed. Melissa read that a Peter Painter and his father Claude had been sentenced to deportation to Dachau for the possession of a crystal set (among other things). She was horrified that a young man had been sent to Germany just because he had a radio. He had never returned.

Further down the wall a vaguely familiar face looked out at her from a group of young men. The caption underneath described how this group had tried to escape the island in five canoes after the Allies had landed in Normandy in June 1944. Only one canoe had made it to mainland France. The names were listed starting with the two who had managed to escape, but Hugh Carlisle, was one of the unfortunates whose canoe had sunk and he and his fellow canoeist had swum back to shore to find the Germans waiting for them. Those who had tried to escape and failed had been imprisoned. No wonder the face was familiar, she had seen his photograph only the day before in the Carlisle deed box.

So her paternal grandfather had been in Jersey during the Occupation and been part of the local Resistance. She was overwhelmed with sadness that she had not known him as the same box had included his death certificate. He had died in 1981.

It was nearly two o'clock before they adjourned to a pub.

Scott and William put down the drinks on the table together a couple of menus.

"Presumably the Germans requisitioned all the big houses." William asked.

"Some. My great grand parents lived in a big house over on the other side of the island which some of the senior German officers decided was the type of comfort they preferred." Scott offered.

"Bet that went down like a lead balloon." William was trying to imagine what it would be like to be ousted from your house by an invading army.

"Evidently my great grandfather was well miffed because the Gerries drank his cellar, which, according to family legend, was the finest on the island."

"What did your great grandfather do?"

"He was a Jurat."

"Thanks Scott, but I meant what did he do when the Germans threw him out of his house. What happened to him?"

"After German law was imposed there was no requirement for a Jurat, so he took the family to live with his sister on her farm."

"Did this happen a lot?"

"No, there were lots of empty houses where people had gone to England, but I suppose the German officers had taken a liking to my grandfather's house. Recently there's been a big campaign to record as many memories as possible of those who lived through the Occupation." Scott explained.

"Many of the islanders stayed because they were convinced Churchill wouldn't let the islands fall, despite the various direct proclamations that he couldn't afford the troops to defend them." Peregrine continued. "Scott and I have been among the volunteers who've been collecting the stories and it has been fascinating."

"How long have you lived here, Peregrine?"

"Scott and I met at University and after we both did a stint in the City, Scott came back and I followed."

"Did you join Cliffe straight away?" William was curious to know more about Peregrine's career.

"I became Charles's assistant in 1996 when he became MD."

"And you, Scott, are you in finance too?" William asked.

"No, I'm with an international law firm linked with hedge funds. What about you?"

"Environmental law. It's a comparatively new area and I felt I might be doing something to help save the planet."

"It must be good to feel you can do something positive. It's all a bit of a farce over here and if I'm honest, I think we're on borrowed time."

"How so?" William wondered if Peregrine meant the planet or Jersey's finance industry in particular.

"Blair and Brown emptied the British coffers so we're sitting ducks for a Treasury raid on our tax haven status."

"Only if there's an international tax treaty and I doubt if Westminster will manage that. There would be an exodus of the seriously rich to whatever countries offered the best terms, so I doubt it will happen. What Britain really needs is a different mind set when it comes to tax. Perhaps more like the Scandinavians."

Peregrine laughed. "You'll never get that. Most of our clients are like dragons guarding their pots of gold."

"Was the islands' independent tax status granted for any specific reason?" William asked. The German occupation had shown just how difficult it was to defend the island.

"I think it was Charles II who said the island could be exempt from English tax, but they had to fund their own militia because the king recognised the islands were indefensible by a mainland English army." Peregrine explained.

"Clearly Hitler didn't share King Charles's view." William found the royal logic compelling.

"William, are you related to Tobias de Braose?" Scott asked. Melissa felt William stiffen.

"I'm his son. Do you know him?"

"I met him years ago."

"Was it business or pleasure?"

"It was in a club."

"Melissa, you're very quiet." Peregrine wanted to turn the conversation away from Tobias. Charles Cliffe had given him a very clear instruction there was to be no gossiping.

Melissa drank her lemonade. "It doesn't make any logical sense."

The three men looked at her.

"What doesn't?" Peregrine asked.

"All this concrete defence work across the west of the island and this underground hospital. It just doesn't make any sense at all."

"It's well established Hitler wasn't logical, Lissie." William wondered where she was going with her analysis. She chose to ignore him.

"Remember the model of the island with all the lights that showed the various defence works I assume were built by the slave workers from the Alderney POW camp." She rummaged in her bag and brought out a notebook and drew a rough map of the Channel Islands, the south coast of England and the Normandy peninsula. "Look. We know these islands are of no strategic importance to either side."

Peregrine nodded. "Yes, I agree, but the accepted thought is that Hitler thought that, by occupying part of the British Isles, it would be a morale booster to his troops and a demoraliser for the Brits." He relaxed now they were back discussing his favourite subject.

"But Churchill had said he would not defend them, because they were indefensible. So why do it?"

"To ensure that, at a later date, no-one would use them as a jumping off point to France?" William suggested.

"From the signing of Magna Carta until 1940 these islands have known mostly peace. War did not visit them even though there might have been the odd skirmish with France." Scott offered. "The last major invasion of any significance was the Vikings when they came and settled the Normandy peninsula."

"And the only two big defence statements, up until the twentieth century, are Gorey and Elizabeth Castles." Peregrine added. "Some of the island families, such as the de Carterets, can trace their lineage back to William, Duke of Normandy and a fair few of them at least five hundred years."

William was beginning to understand why the islanders had a reputation for being fiercely independent and wondered if any of his own forbears had passed through the islands.

"William Camden has the islands listed in his Brittanicus as being of a fair climate with Jersey sloping to the south and Guernsey sloping to the north. Evidently the Jersey people earned their living by fishing and farming the now extinct four horned sheep." Melissa added.

"I thought it had always been the cows." Peregrine looked surprised. "Was it Raleigh who introduced the potato?"

"No idea. He was governor at one point, which was, I believe, when Elizabeth Castle was built, but as for the potato, I can't answer that one." She pulled her bread roll apart and dipped it in her soup. "OK, Peregrine. How much of this island was actually given over to the recuperation of German soldiers who'd been injured at the front?" She asked.

Daghorne-Ffrench shook his head. "I don't think we've got any figures for that, because the hospital wasn't finished."

"So why put the operating theatre, admin offices etc as if their occupants have just left these rooms?" The three men looked at each other, but did not reply. "Are there any other tunnels like this?" Melissa asked and scribbled some notes.

"Yes, there are more at St Aubin's and elsewhere. Many of them were used as ammo dumps. Hitler poured concrete and defences into the islands even more so than up at Calais. Why did you ask about the tunnels?"

"I believe the defences weren't anything to do with demoralising the British. Yes, I think the defences are to keep people out of the island after the 'final victory'." She paused. "But I think this underground 'hospital' was a designed as a place of death."

Melissa's statement left a deep hole of silence.

"I totally agree," Peregrine replied eventually, "but how did you come to that conclusion?"

"This will need a lot more research, but my premise is drawn from the basic design and, without recourse to any of the documents or architectural drawings, I think the official version of it's being built as a hospital was a piece of German propaganda that has never been questioned. If it has, then perhaps those who drew similar conclusions to us have decided not to publicise them."

"Why not?" Scott asked.

"Fear? Détante? Personal reasons. Perhaps they couldn't face the horror of the reality?"

"OK, so expand your analysis." Scott was holding Peregrine's hand.

"Weren't the Nazis all for training their young men in the outdoors? Not only that; all the major religions refer to light. Christ is The Light of the World, the Greeks and Romans had the Sun God, the Egyptians had Ra etcetera, etcetera. All the religions refer to the sun as life giver, and medically, we need sunlight to produce Vitamin D. In England, the hospitals that were looking after the wounded all recommended fresh air and sun to aid their recovery."

The three men nodded agreement.

"Which is why it doesn't make sense to put a hospital underground." She paused to give the men time to consider what she had said. "What if it was nothing to do with health and healing, but something to do with Hitler's vision of creating a master race? What if this island, and possibly Guernsey too, were to be turned into vast death camps after the Nazis had conquered Europe. Perhaps the islands were to become inescapable prisons for all those the Nazis thought imperfect. In Nazi ideology, the existence of anyone who might affect the purity of the

138

German race or was against Hitler's vision had to be eradicated. Taking all this into consideration, then perhaps this 'hospital' was going to be something like Mengele's laboratory at Auschwitz, hence the operating theatre? Those massive defence works may well have been designed to deter nosiness from across the Atlantic when the victorious Nazis started to eradicate all and everyone they thought impure here in Europe."

There was complete silence as Melissa's appalling theory was considered.

"And you have concluded this just by looking at the architecture?" Scott asked.

"Yes. Why else would those wards have eight inch thick steel doors if they are tens of yards underground; plus they don't appear to have any form of ventilation shafts. The propaganda may well say they are blast doors to protect the injured, but the entry has a ninety-degree dogleg to the corridors so any blast at the entrance would be deflected. Not only that, if this valley were to be bombed, then the entrance is very well hidden and would require pinpoint accuracy of low flying aircraft to get an effective hit."

They three men nodded.

"But the clincher for me is the floor."

"I agree absolutely with everything you've said so far, but why do you think the floor is important." Peregrine asked.

"Have you ever seen a hospital with railway tracks set into the floor? They are contemporary with the construction of this place, aren't they?"

"We believe so." Peregrine replied.

William thought about what she was saying. She had a point. The problem of disposing of bodies had been the major problem at all the death camps. On the islands it would have been simple. The local problem would have been getting dead bodies out of the 'wards', which could explain the rail tracks. If the end use of the tunnels was for them to be a killing place, all the Germans would have had to do was to get the bodies to a disposal point and then tip them into the sea where the fishes would do the rest. Melissa's theory was too awful to contemplate.

"We thought we were the only ones who thought this." Peregrine voice was low. He seemed shocked hearing his theory being expanded by someone else.

"Do either of you speak German?"

The two men shook their heads. "Do you?" Scott asked.

Melissa nodded. "If you are serious about pursuing your theory, then I suggest get yourselves as fluent as you can, then go off to Germany and bury yourselves in the Nazi archives. There might be stuff locally providing it wasn't destroyed at the end of the war and even if it is still here, the files may still be closed."

"Melissa, thank you. We've both been convinced of this for some time."

William put his arm around her shoulders as if he were trying to protect her. He thought this theory was still too horrifying for the islanders, or even the world, to contemplate. It had shocked him.

"Can I suggest you publish anything under pseudonyms?" He suggested. "You might find your companies aren't too keen on having their employees being connected with anything to do with the Nazis."

A BIT LATER

"It's always so nice to meet the winner of the diamonds. I'm Jenny de la Roche." A smartly dressed blonde held out her hand. Peregrine introduced them.

"Dr Melissa Carlisle and Mr William de Braose."

Melissa had not argued about visiting the diamond company. After the atmosphere of the War Tunnels she needed something frivolous to distract her from the awfulness and sadness of the Tunnels.

William produced the box containing the diamonds from his jeans pocket. Melissa was shocked at how he was treating them as if they were of no real consequence. The three stones sparkled with amazing intensity under the showroom lights.

"Have you considered how you might like these set? A ring and earrings perhaps?"

"I thought perhaps a simple bar brooch." Melissa offered.

"Perhaps you would be kind enough to show us some of your designs." William suggested.

Peregrine and Scott were amused.

"A woman who hasn't got her eye on an exact design for those diamonds has to be a first." Scott murmured. "One thing's for sure, he's not like his father!"

Peregrine raised his eyebrows " I don't think William has the same taste as his father in a lot of things."

140

"I bet Anne was over him like a waterfall."

"But he wasn't playing ball. However, I can't quite get what his relationship is with Melissa. Look at them."

"I'd say they're a normal couple." Scott said.

"Do normal couples have separate rooms?"

"OK, so it's an old fashioned relationship."

"The Tower Suite is over eight hundred pounds a night. Come on, Scott, you'd expect to be getting your jollies for that sort of money. One thing's sure, Charles doesn't want to lose her business. Confidentially, she's worth over ninety-five million and that's just the Jersey Trusts. She's also inherited her great aunt's estate." Peregrine whispered.

"OK, that's a lot of reasons why William would be taking things slowly, but she's not at all interested in the diamonds! What woman in Jersey do you know who wouldn't have some idea of how she wanted them set. It's as if she doesn't even want them!"

"She's not any sort of woman. How many PhDs do you know with that sort of money?"

"Dr Carlisle, may I take your ring size?" Jenny slipped different sized ring measures over Melissa's left ring finger and noted the size.

"Oh Jenny, sorry, not that finger."

Jenny measured her right ring finger and noted that too.

"Well Lissie, I think that's a fair compromise to your dilemma."

"William, I don't have a dilemma. They're your diamonds, you choose how they're made up."

"Jenny, it looks as if my lady is still making up her mind, so it would great if you'd send us some designs and, when we finally agree, I'll have the diamonds couriered back to you." William handed over his business card.

Jenny returned the diamonds to their box and handed them back.

"Mr de Braose, I'll be in touch within the week."

"Peregrine, Scott, thank you for giving up your Saturday. Would you join us for a drink?" The four of them were outside the hotel entrance.

"William, many thanks, but we've got a long standing engagement we can't break." Peregrine turned to Melissa. "It's been a real pleasure to have the opportunity of talking with you."

"Peregrine, thank you for a really enlightening day," Melissa turned to Scott. "One word of warning; be prepared for your theory to be wrong and test your evidence, unless of course, you turn up the original blue prints, in which case, ring me immediately!"

They both kissed Melissa before shaking hands with William.

"Well Lissie Carlisle, I think I've now got a far better idea of what makes you tick." William murmured as they watched the two men drive away.

"Why didn't you leave the diamonds with the company?"

"And just when I thought you were quite bright!"

"What do you mean?"

"I didn't want them swapping the original stones for inferior ones. Fancy a swim?"

"Are you always this cynical?"

"Only when I'm walking around with about twenty grand's worth of rocks on me."

"This reminds me of Brittany." William pulled the car close to the side of the road to let an oncoming car pass. The hill was steep and the doors to the granite cottages opened straight on to the road. "What is it with this island. It seems to have more than its fair share of a hundred and eighty degree bends!" William was thankful for the light power-steering of the Mercedes.

"William, this must be it." Melissa looked at the bundle of purple/blue and orange balloons tied to an imposing wrought iron gate.

"It's all done in the best paassible taste!" William mocked. Melissa looked at him as if he were mad.

"Oh come on, Lissie. You must have heard of Cupid Stunt?"

She continued to look baffled.

"Well, Cupid was character Kenny Everett invented – all blue satin mini dress, fishnet tights and blonde wig i.e. him in drag, complete with beard, and a pair of huge false plastic tits." Melissa still had a serious expression. William stopped the car just inside the gates.

"And?" she asked.

"Well, whatever anyone was talking about, Cupid would interrupt and say how it was all done in the 'best paassible taste'," William looked crestfallen that his attempt at humour had fallen flat; "but it loses something in the translation!"

"Don't say anything else. I'm looking her up on YouTube."

William chuckled as Michael Parkinson interviewed Miss Stunt, remembering how, as a child he had never understood the *double entendres*, but had loved the funny bearded woman who behaved so outrageously.

"And you think Anne Cliffe would fit this role?"

William nodded.

Melissa chuckled. "I agree – Cupid is hilarious."

"Today would be much more amusing if Cupid were hosting it. We might finally get to meet people like Sid Snot and Marcel Wave."

"We still might – but they'll be disguised as the Jersey social elite."

"Lissie, behave!" William drove slowly down the wooded drive, chuckling as he imagined Anne Cliffe dressed as Miss Stunt.

"William, I'm fairly certain I've been here before." They parked in the gravel laid courtyard of an Edwardian house overlooking a rocky bay sheltered by a wooded headland.

"It's not listed on any of the property schedules."

"That doesn't mean I haven't been here."

"Anne, who's that divine young man talking to Charles?" Suzie Sampson watched Charles, William and Melissa walk past the kitchen window to join the other guests on the terrace.

"That, Suzie, is William de Braose – the 12th Earl of Poultney's grandson and he can dance divinely! You should have been with us on Friday. He was wonderful."

"He's much younger than Charles's usual clients."

"Oh, he's not the client." Anne paused. "She is. Plain little thing isn't she?"

"Anne, you're only jealous because you aren't that slim. Is she local?"

"No, they're staying at Longueville Manor and no, they're not sleeping together."

Suzie was impressed by Anne's knowledge. "Just how did you find out they're not a couple?"

"Chambermaids. Charles tells me he's her advisor! Personally, I think he's playing a long game. I'm sure he's in it for the money."

"What does William do?"

"I don't know, some sort of lawyer I think. Who's Who wasn't too forthcoming and she's not in it at all."

"What's her name?"

"Dr Melissa Carlisle, and not even a doctor of something useful. I think she just calls herself that. Oh look, Charles is doing his benign uncle bit. He said he wanted to show her his Hetty Lavering's. Now why would some blue stocking be interested in some of his daubs?"

"Did you say Carlisle?"

"Yes." Anne replied. "Why?" But Suzie had disappeared through the kitchen door.

"Mrs Cliffe?" Anne was distracted by one of the waitresses.

"Yes dear?"

"Would you mind moving out of the way."

"Here we are, Melissa." William and Melissa were standing in front of a portrait of a much younger Charles. "Hetty painted this in celebration of my first Board appointment."

"You knew my great aunt?"

"I didn't want to talk to you the other night because there were far too many ears, but yes, I knew her very well."

Several more of Hetty's paintings were spread through the ground floor of the house. Melissa found it strange seeing Hetty's work on someone else's wall.

"In fact, I knew all your family. Your mother and father and I grew up together."

Charles opened a door onto what was clearly a den.

"I had this extension built when the kids were teenagers. Now they have family of their own, when they're here it keeps the disturbance down to a minimum, plus it's somewhere the grandchildren and their friends can be without being under our feet."

A group portrait of a woman and three children, one sitting on a rocking horse, gazed at them from one of the walls.

"That's Caroline, my first wife. When Anne moved in, she banished this painting to here."

"Why?"

"Caroline is the children's mother; she died when my youngest was only three."

"Oh Charles, I'm sorry." Melissa answered sympathetically. He smiled sadly.

"Anne's been good with the children."

"When were you married?"

"To Caroline?" Charles asked. Melissa nodded, letting him tell his story, but desperate to ask him some questions of her own family.

"1985." He replied.

"Have you always lived here?"

"No, I inherited it from my father ten years ago."

"I know this sounds really silly, but was that rocking horse ever in the attic?" Melissa asked.

"Yes, that's where the nursery was. Why?"

"This is going to sound really strange, but I feel as if I know this house."

"That wouldn't be a surprise. Your parents and I were always in each other's houses and Dad was very fond of both Alistair and Victoria. It's quite likely you came here as a little girl. Dad hadn't done anything with the house since he'd inherited it and Nanny was still with us, so when any kids came to visit you'd have been put into her charge and played up in the nursery."

"Melissa Carlisle, the last time I saw you was Christmas 1984 when you were knee high to a grasshopper." Suzie Sampson exploded into the room. "Charles, you didn't tell me you'd invited Victoria and Alistair's daughter. Melissa, forgive me, I'm Suzie and your parents, Charles and me, we all did the same round of parties. Then your mother married the best looking man on the island and we all went into mourning."

"Melissa, may I introduce Suzie Sampson."

"Now Melissa, have you come back to the island to live?" Suzie asked, all the while holding Melissa's hand.

Melissa was completely overcome with the newcomer's rush of enthusiasm.

"No, Mrs Sampson, just visiting."

"Please, call me Suzie."

"Suzie, our Melissa has just gained her doctorate in early modern history from Oxford." Charles beamed in reflected glory.

"My dear, why am I not surprised? Your parents were both incredibly bright. Alistair was incredibly clever and the first thing he did when he'd finished his degree was to ask your mother to marry him before she got whisked off by any of the other various young men hovering around." Suzie looked meaningfully at Charles.

"No, Suzie, you are quite wrong. Victoria never had any eyes for anyone but Alistair, despite some of us doing our best to persuade her otherwise."

"Charles, I was wondering what on earth was keeping you?" Anne approached the group admiring the family portrait.

"Your mother and I were at school together." Suzie continued, ignoring Anne. "and we all had such fun. Your father and Charles went off to University, I got married and Victoria did a year's secretarial course, then followed Alistair to Cambridge and worked at one of the colleges whilst he finished his degree."

146

Despite the rather garbled reminiscences, Melissa felt a solid connection to her parents.

"Oh, their wedding was such a wonderful affair. Then you were born. Luckily Hetty came over otherwise I think Victoria and her mother might have come to blows!"

"Yes, I believe she lived with my grandparents for some time."

"Well, that was when she wasn't either looking after you or painting. I've got one of her landscapes of St Ouen's Bay, just when the sun is about to dip below the horizon. It's incredibly dramatic. Tell me, Melissa. How is Hetty?" Suzie asked.

"Oh Suzie, do shut up. How would **she** know your silly artist friend?" Anne was irritated by the fuss Charles and Suzie were making over Melissa.

There was a deadly hush.

Melissa and Anne looked at each other.

"Mrs Cliffe, thank you for your hospitality. You have a lovely house. It's a shame it's not the friendly place I remember it to be." Melissa turned to Charles and gave him a big hug.

"Charles, thank you for everything and especially for your memories of my parents. I'm sure your wife will be interested to learn who Hetty was." She heard Suzie gasp at the use of the past tense. She turned to William. "William, can we go . . . now."

William shook Charles's hand. "Charles, thank you. As you've probably gathered, there're large gaps in Melissa's childhood memories."

Charles murmured apologies for his wife's behaviour.

"Oh, Melissa, has Hetty gone?" Suzie took Melissa's hand. "I'm so sorry. I had no idea. Please forgive me."

Melissa smiled, fighting back tears. "Suzie, of course."

"Anne, my study, NOW." Charles hissed. Taking his wife's arm he marched her through the open French doors and across the lawn to his study.

Behind closed doors Charles turned to face his wife.

"When I say do not gossip, I mean just that. If you ever repeat today's performance you will find your bags on the street."

Charles held up his hand as Anne opened her mouth to speak.

"Don't try and defend yourself. Your behaviour towards de Braose on Friday was more than embarrassing. He's young enough to be your son."

"Charles Cliffe, how dare you accuse **me** of improper behaviour! What about you and the so-called Dr Carlisle? I bet you wouldn't mind her warming your bed on a cold winter's morning."

""Don't you ever accuse me of anything improper with her. Melissa Carlisle is the only child of my best friends who were killed in car crash." He hissed.

"What's all the fuss about this silly artist, then? Anyone would think she was someone famous!"

"If you spent less of my money on ridiculous fripperies and got yourself an education, you would know that Hetty Lavering is, or rather was, one of Britain's greatest artists."

"So what!"

"She was my friend and now she's dead."

"Well then, you should be happy that your collection will go up in value. I think they're dreadful daubs."

"Do you ever think of anything other than money?"

"Charles stop being such drama queen. So she's dead; it happens."

"Not only do you accuse me of improper behaviour; you then insult the paintings you know I treasure. I don't want to hear your voice again today: get out."

"Charles Cliffe, you're insane. What will our guests think?"

Charles smacked her face.

"GET OUT!"

Anne staggered back, nursing her cheek and trying hard to hold on to some shred of dignity.

It was the first time Charles had ever raised his fist to a woman.

Anne fled.

Charles sat at his desk overwhelmed by memories of his childhood friends.

"Well that was quite an exit!" William was manoeuvring the Mercedes through twisty country lanes.

"William, do you think we could find our way back to the first place we had lunch?"

148

"I thought you'd never ask. I'm starving."

Despite Anne Cliffe's callous comments, Melissa was happy.

They were enjoying walking across St Ouen's bay in the sun, killing time before a table at Big Verne's became free.

"William, thank you."

"What for?" William was surprised by her thanks.

"If I'd come over on my own, I wouldn't have gone to the ball and I don't think I'd have gone today."

"Mrs Cliffe might have been relieved by that!"

"Seriously William. I might never have known Charles was my father's best friend, nor met Suzie."

"She's a bit of a firework!"

Melissa nodded. "Yes she is. I've always had a void where other people had memories, but it's now gone."

William looked a bit puzzled. "Is it a bit like amnesia?"

"Never having had amnesia, I couldn't say."

"So when people at school were talking about trips to Granny, you couldn't identify with what they were saying."

Melissa nodded. "What's really funny is that walking into Charles's house today was like being in a recurring dream."

"What do you mean?"

"For years I've occasionally had the same dream about being in an attic sitting rocking on a rocking horse while a little old lady told me stories. The horse was painted chestnut, had a blonde mane and today, there it was in that portrait of Charles's first wife with their three children."

"Is that why you went so quiet when we drove in?"

"Yes, but the house I remember wasn't painted pink and there wasn't that big extension."

"Have you thought about why Charles was chosen to be in charge of your Trusts?"

"Didn't Edward say there had been something called a Curatel that looked after me until I came of age?"

William looked blank. "I think you'll have to ask Charles. I have no idea what that is."

"Hmm, I think that would be best in his office. I don't want to come face to face with that harpy of a wife. I might be tempted to slap her."

William chuckled. He did not think Melissa would stand a chance against such a seasoned player as Anne Cliffe. They turned towards the nearest set of steps.

"Lissie, didn't Daghorne French say these sea walls were also built by slave labour during the war?"

"Yes. Don't you find it horrible to know we're walking where people died?"

William nodded and wondered where her thoughts were going.

"They have an interesting theory about that so called Underground Hospital. I'm not a modern history specialist, but I feel sure they're right. However, it's going to be a difficult pill for the islanders to swallow despite it being so many years since the end of the war." Melissa's tone was thoughtful. "The evidence may well not be in the local files, closed or otherwise, which is why I think they should go to Germany."

They were paddling in a large pool of seawater trapped behind a bank of sand when the tide had retreated.

"William, what do you think of Ffrench and his friend?"

"You mean Scott's reference to my father?"

Melissa nodded. "I wondered just how he knew him?"

"There are all sorts of rumours about Tobias. Mum hinted at something brewing at the moment, but she didn't tell me what she'd heard. The sort of practices it's rumoured Tobias indulges in isn't my idea of entertainment."

Melissa looked perplexed.

"I think in your world, Lissie, the story tellers refer to it as Greek love."

"Oh!"

"It's not that he's gay, but we know he's a sadist. Combine that with his sexuality, it all begins to get a bit sordid."

"William, do you really think he's caught up with Lansbury?"

"Mother's certain they've been lovers since university."

Melissa considered this apparent contradiction of Tobias's relationship with the solicitor and his sexual proclivities and wondered whether Lansbury was a masochist.

The sun was hot and the water of the lagoon warm.

"He must have been surprised by your mother's pregnancy."

"He's always been a remote and odd figure in my life. My stepfather was a lovely man and he's the one I think of as my father. You might find this strange, but I've some idea of what you mean by not being able to relate to certain things other people take for granted."

"You said your stepfather **was** a lovely man."

"He died last year."

"Oh William, I'm sorry."

William stopped and took her hand.

"Come here Lissie." He pulled her toward him and, softly and tentatively, kissed her.

"*Just relax*" Melissa's inner voice whispered. She thought she could hear bells and was overcome with all sorts of fuzzy feelings.

Today was turning out to be extremely interesting.

The sleeping Melissa looked as innocent as a child; her hair was spread across the pillow. William lifted a strand and kissed it. She murmured in her sleep. Outside, the sky was only just getting light.

Suddenly his life was as upside down as hers. At first he had thought of her as the little sister he had never had, or perhaps a close cousin. This second definition made him feel slightly better about the events of the previous evening.

Originally Edward had wanted to be the one to introduce her to the Trustees. Then the old man had suggested that William do that instead.

Would Lissie regret going to bed with him? Had he been a clumsy oaf and ruined what had been a lovely friendship?

Melissa rolled towards him and put out a hesitant hand to see if he were there. He slipped his hand into hers and their fingers entwined. Her eyes were still shut.

"Good morning" he whispered softly.

"Hmmm . . ." she snuggled closer.

Charles Cliffe sat at his desk and contemplated his morning. Yesterday had been a disaster. He had never meant to slap her; his intention was that Anne just leave his study, but she had packed her bags and gone. Suzie Sampson did not know where and had suggested Charles was well rid of her. Charles was sure the Jersey glitterati already knew that Anne had left him.

The one person he had to ensure was happy was Melissa Carlisle. The alternative was to resign and retire. Having looked after her finances for all these years he wanted to see them through to their conclusion. He reached for the phone.

"William?"

"Pass the coffee."

"Please!" She handed him the cafetiére. "I was wondering what to do about Charles."

"I'd wait until he gets in touch."

"Do you still think I should continue with Charles's firm?"

William nodded, concentrating on his breakfast. "It's his expertise you want, not his wife's."

"I don't want anything to do with her ever again. Suzie Sampson's different." Melissa's thoughts drifted to Hetty's study and the neat ranks of notebooks. William watched her face.

"Lissie, how about we catch tonight's ferry?"

"Am I that transparent?"

"I bet you were thinking about what's in Hetty's diaries?" William touched her hand and held it.

"I am that transparent." Her emotions were in turmoil. How were you supposed to behave towards your lover the morning after you had made love for the first time? Studying the diaries would be a safe haven.

"OK, we have a choice." William was already checking ferry availability on his phone. "We can go overnight to Portsmouth, but will have to take our chance at getting a cabin, or it looks as if we can get on the faster afternoon hydrofoil to Weymouth."

"In other words we can sit up all night, or we can be back in the cottage in a few hours." As if on queue, her mobile rang.

"Charles, good morning." Melissa did not sound surprised. "Yes, thank you." Pause. "No, that would have been lovely, except we're booked on this afternoon's hydrofoil." Pause. "Oh no Charles, not at all. I would love to see you again. However, William has to get back to the office." Pause. "Thank you again for Friday. Bye."

William laughed. "What have we given up?"

"Lunch! Is City life all lunches and parties?"

"No, some of us do actually do some work, but in a sense, you're right. Technology might be all very well, but some things are still better achieved face-to-face."

"Well then, you'd better book those tickets home."

William parked under the carport next to Melissa's car. The Old Manor House was bathed in the golden light of the setting sun.

"Hey, wait,"

Melissa turned to face him, her hand on the large iron key she had just turned to unlock the door. William swept her up.

"What do you think you're doing?" she laughed, wrapping her arms around his neck.

"Carrying you over the threshold!"

"William, you're such a hopeless romantic, put me down!"

"Mrs P, is there room for two more?"

"William, you scared the life outta me! I thought you weren't due back 'til next Sunday?"

"Well, Jersey's a small place and we'd seen enough."

"Don't just stand there like a couple of bookends, set another couple of places." Mrs Podger put more bacon, sausages and tomatoes in the frying pan.

"Did you enjoy yourselves?"

"Mrs P, it was an education. It felt really strange knowing we were on British soil, but being where Hitler had left an indelible stamp. I wondered what it might have been like during the war."

"And I suppose you were wondering if I'd been around then?" Mrs Podger clipped the back of William's head with her hand. "Despite all your education young man, it seems arithmetic isn't one of your strong points!"

"Well done, William. That was as diplomatic as a brick! Mrs P, do you think Edward would be able to tell us?"

"Be able to tell you what?" Edward and Betty entered, both ready for breakfast. "What're you two doing back early?"

"Jersey's shown us all it has to offer Uncle Edward."

Edward sat at his place at the head of the table. "Well you look as if you've seen the sun. Tell me, how is Charles Cliffe?"

"He's well. Was he one of the people on my Curatel?"

Edward nodded. "Let me see, from what I remember, there was Charles plus several lawyers who appointed Hetty as your guardian and together they looked after your financial affairs." Edward paused, "The last time I saw Charles was the Christmas I stayed with your grandfather."

"Was Hetty still in Jersey then?"

"Yes, she'd just finished painting Charles's portrait."

"That's now in his study. I found it quite bizarre seeing Hetty's work on a complete stranger's wall."

"That Christmas was quite riotous. You were only small, but even so, we were all invited to Charles's father's place, a great Edwardian mansion with a view over St Aubin's Bay."

"Gramps, we were there yesterday." William interrupted.

Edward's reminiscences were cementing more bricks back into Melissa's wall of childhood.

"I'm surprised Charles is still working"

"Uncle Edward, he's only in his fifties, so why would he retire?"

"He always said he wanted to retire early and sail round the world."

"Well, Charles Cliffe is, from what I see, far too entrenched in the Jersey banking fraternity for him to retire, plus he has a very high maintenance wife!"

"Yes, I gather he married his secretary a couple of years after his first wife died. I never met the second wife. Anyhow, you had a good time?"

"Yes thanks, I even found my paternal grandfather, but it's nice to be home. I want to look at the contents of some deed boxes I was given and try and marry them up with Hetty's diaries."

"Excellent, well, I'm off to my study to read the newspaper. Glad to have you both home." Edward patted William's shoulder and kissed Melissa's cheek before disappearing to study his copy of The Times.

"Lissie, we'd better get on with our research."

Mrs Podger was clearing away the last of the breakfast things.

"Well, if you two are going to be busy all day then I suggest you come back 'ere for supper. It's nothing special, but it'll save you 'aving to cook."

"Thanks, Mrs P. We'll see you at seven." William gave the portly woman a hug. "Where would we be without you?"

"Get off with you, William. The pair of you look as if you've not eaten a square meal in at least a week!" Mrs Podger made to flick her tea towel at him. "'ere, Melissa, you take this tin. It's some 'ome made flapjacks."

Melissa laid Hetty's diaries for 1984 on the dining table. The diary entry for Christmas described Charles's house, who was there and confirmed Edward's statement that everyone had had a riotous time. Hetty described Suzie Sampson as Lady LaDiDa because evidently the more the wine flowed, the more she kept saying *you know what it's like darling, ladida!* Even Melissa's own behaviour had been noted. She had kicked up an awful fuss after being told she could not take the rocking horse home.

It was reassuring to know that her recurring dreams were based on real events. Perhaps now she knew about it, the rocking horse would go away. She tidied up the documents and put them back on their shelf before lifting the unopened second Carlisle box on to the table and snipping the seal.

One of the envelopes was stiffened and contained a modern heraldic roll of honour. The legend told that Hugh Carlisle was honoured for having attempted to escape the Nazis for which he had received a twelve-month prison sentence, then there were a lot of signatures, which Melissa assumed were his fellow escapees. A photograph of eight smiling men holding a Union Jack was in the same envelope and the names written on the back were among the signatures on the political prisoners honour roll. This photograph was dated 9th May 1945 - the day the islands were liberated.

Hetty's diaries revealed that Hugh Carlisle had survived the war, but had died tragically young at the age of fifty-four. They also revealed that his wife, Melissa corrected herself, her paternal grandmother had drunk herself to death.

Melissa opened the book she had bought about the Occupation to the pages describing events on the island after June 1944. The last commandant had been a dyed in the wool Nazi, determined to remain in his post until the 'final victory'. D Day had effectively cut the islands off from any communication with the outside world. Melissa sat back acutely aware that isolation from France had meant that the German supplies lines had been cut so everyone had been starving, but perhaps the islands' isolation had saved her grandfather's life. Edward could probably tell her more about the end of the war and she wrote down some questions to ask him.

William stood up and stretched. He was analysing how aspects of European legislation might be interpreted when the Government's proposed new planning regulations were eventually challenged in the courts. It did not appear that much thought had been given to this angle and he was more convinced that this was deliberate. He detested professional politicians and thought that many of them prostituted their public duty for personal gain. Working quietly for the public good seemed to be a concept that had long since disappeared.

"Wuff, wuff" Betty ran in through the open door making her strange coughing bark and stood barking at them.

"Betty, come here." William bent to picked up the little dachshund, but she avoided his grasp and continued to bark at them.

The phone rang. Melissa answered it.

"Oh my God!" Melissa dropped the receiver. "William, something's happened to Edward."

William grabbed the nearest set of car keys and Melissa grabbed Betty. He pointed the key fob at the cars and the VW lights flashed.

The car bounced down the drive as he floored the accelerator.

"William! Mind my axle!"

They abandoned the car outside New Manor and ran through to the study.

Mrs Podger was in tears: Mr Podger was on the phone.

Edward was in his chair.

William went to his grandfather. The old man's eyes were open and he was cold.

"He's dead." William whispered.

"The ambulance is on its way." Mr Podger stated quietly. William knelt at his grandfather's feet; Betty waddled up to him and licked his hand.

Melissa stood frozen to the spot.

Mrs Podger blew her nose.

"I suggest we all go to the kitchen and wait." William finally muttered.

A short time later they heard sirens. William let the paramedics into the study; then the police arrived.

"Mr de Braose, there will have to be a post mortem."

The words were chilling. Edward had seemed in great spirits at breakfast, so what had happened between then and . . .

Melissa thought about what came after the 'and'. The French windows were open so anyone could have come into the study, but there was no sign of violence.

"Miss Carlisle," the policewoman interrupted her thoughts.

"I'm sorry, it's all so sudden." Melissa's self-control broke. The policewoman waited until Melissa pulled herself together.

"Miss Carlisle, we'll be in touch should we need any further information. In the meantime, please ensure people stay out of the study."

Melissa nodded. "I'll lock the study door and shut the French windows from the outside."

"We've already closed those. If you could just stop anyone entering the study."

There was a noise in the corridor and the policewoman opened the door. William made to go through it.

"Mr de Braose, I would stay in here. They're just removing the body."

"NO!" William tore his hair; Melissa threw her arms around him and he sobbed against her.

Mr Podger picked up his copy of The Sun newspaper.

"Minister's Son Dies in Gay Sex Romp. The Honourable Tobias de Braose was among those arrested on suspicion of murder . . ."

"Oh my God" Mrs Podger gasped. "and Edward 'ad been so 'appy, too."

Melissa sat, completely stunned by the lurid details.

"When the police were called to a multimillion pound penthouse in Docklands following a complaint about noise, John Day, son of the Minister for Cultural Affairs, was found dead tied over a table in a compromising position."

"My bloody father, I'll kill him . . ." William stormed out. Melissa went to follow.

"Melissa, give 'im a bit of space." Mrs Podger moved like an automaton round her kitchen finally putting a plate of sandwiches on the table. Melissa and Mr Podger sat in silence until Mrs Podger sat down.

"Melissa," she whispered, "I always knew Tobias was a baddun' 'cept I didn't think even 'e would go as far as murder."

"Mrs P, I don't know what to say."

"Have your sandwich, dear. I 'ate to see good food going to waste."

"More's the point Melly, who's going to tell Tobias 'e's killed 'is father?"

"Mr P, don't say that."

Mr Podger raised his eyebrows in question. "Why not? I bet it was the shock of reading this what killed Lord Edward."

William returned to the kitchen, breathless from running.

"Come 'ere, William." Mrs Podger enfolded him in her motherly embrace. "I've made some beef sandwiches, so sit you down and eat something."

William smiled a sad remnant of a smile.

"I know it had to happen Lissie, but why now?"

"Mr Tewksbury, William de Braose here." William had the phone on loudspeaker. "I thought you'd like to know that the PM shows" there was a slight pause, "that Gramps died of a massive heart attack." William's voice betrayed no emotion. "Have you spoken to Tobias?"

"He's on bail at the moment. That's all I've managed to glean so far."

"Frankly, Mr Tewksbury, I don't care whether he goes to hell as long as I don't have to have anything to do with him."

"William, whether you like it or not, he's now the thirteenth Earl and there's the question of Edward's will."

"Gramps is hardly cold and you're already talking about wills!"

"Since the coroner's satisfied there's no foul play, the funeral can go ahead, and you know we have to abide by Edward's last wishes regarding the funeral, which you also know are contained in his will."

"Mr Tewksbury, just don't ask me to arrange it. Just let me know when it is."

"Are you sure you don't want to be involved?"

"I don't want to be part of Tobias getting everyone to jump to his beck and call."

Melissa winced at the anger in William's voice. She regretted not having been involved in the arrangements for Hetty's funeral.

There was a long pause and a heavy sigh before Mr Tewksbury spoke again. "William, Tobias has inferred he may sell New Manor."

"WHAT!"

"I thought it better you hear it from me than anyone else, but you should be prepared in case it's not an idle threat. Your grandfather left the entire contents of the house to you."

William sat holding his head in his hands. "Thanks Mr Tewksbury. I appreciate you telling me."

"Can I arrange the funeral for 5th July in the family chapel?"

"Yes."

"Is Melissa with you?"

"I'm here." Melissa piped up.

"I thought you should know that Lansbury has now been charged with intent to defraud. He too is on bail and may be at the funeral."

"No – this just gets worse. Isn't there some way we can prevent him from coming?"

"Probably not."

William stood at the open doorway looking over the park. "Mr Tewksbury, you will be there won't you?"

"Indeed, William. Perry and I, and our respective spouses, will be with you."

"Thank you. Have you asked Mrs Podger to organise the wake?" This time it was Melissa who spoke.

"No. Tobias gave instructions that's to be at The Dragon's Arms."

William looked up to heaven and bit his lip. "Well, it does mean Mrs P won't have to take orders from Tobias. That would really stick in her throat! We'll see you on the fifth." William broke the connection.

"Come here, Lissie." He held out his arms and she wrapped hers round his waist laying her head on his chest. "Gramps was so convinced my father would preserve the estate. Let's go and see if Mrs P has the kettle on. I want to enjoy the house while we still can."

Generations of de Braose men and women looked down from the hall walls.

"Lissie, we've looked after this land for five hundred years."

"Four hundred and seventy one to be precise."

"That's a hell of a long time and now my father's thinking of selling everything to some nameless rich tosser who wants a big house. I can't bear it!"

William pointed at a man dressed as a cavalier. "My namesake, the 3rd Earl, fought at the King's side in the Civil War."

Melissa could see the family resemblance. This William hung half way up the stairs next to Hetty's portrait of David in his RAF uniform.

"And before you ask, yes it's a Van Dyck. Bloody hell, we've nurtured this land and the people on it for centuries. It's not something to be sold!"

He pointed to another de Braose dressed in modern army uniform. "That's my great grandfather."

"He was at the Somme."

"I wouldn't be here if it weren't for your great grandfather."

"Edward looks terribly sad." Melissa thought Hetty's portrait of the 12th Earl wore a sombre expression.

They drifted from room to room.

"Do you think the Podger's know about Tobias's plans?" Melissa asked very quietly.

"No. I think Tewksbury was giving me the heads up ahead of the funeral. They're going to be devastated, but it will take some time for probate to be granted so I don't think we should say anything until there's something definite. Let's go back to your cottage. I want something stronger than tea!"

Realising the insistent banging Melissa could hear was not caused by the little men bashing the inside of her skull with their large hammers. Her head hurt and her mouth felt dreadful. She had fractured memories of a wild alcohol fuelled night of passion. A distraught Mrs Podger stood pounding her fist against the stubbornly closed oak door.

"Mrs P, what's the matter?" Melissa tied the kimono securely and pushed her hair back off her face.

"Oh, Melissa," the older woman stumbled inside and plonked herself at the dining table, sobbing. "I can't believe 'e's done what 'e's done."

"Mrs P, you're not making much sense." Melissa filled the kettle. William appeared wearing nothing but a towel wrapped around his waist.

"Morning Mrs P, what's the problem?"

"It's your father!"

William groaned. He too had the hangover from hell.

"Mrs P, sit down and take it slowly. Lissie, do we have any juice?" She handed him a large glass of orange juice and ice.

"First thing this morning I 'ad a knock on the door and got given this!" Mrs Podger sobbed, thrusting a folded piece of paper at William.

"Mr & Mrs Podger, you are to vacate the property known as The New Manor. You have twenty-four hours from the morning of 28th June to vacate your rooms after which time you will be evicted from the premises, the locks to the house will be changed and you will be denied entrance to my property.
Dated 27th June: Signed Tobias de Braose, 13th Earl of Poultney."

"Fucking Hell! Sorry Mrs P." William apologised, "Lissie, chuck me my phone!" He dialled Mr Tewksbury's home number.

"Mr Tewksbury, my father has given the Podgers twenty-four hours to get out. Can we stop him?"

"Technically he can't do anything until probate's been granted! However, as usual he's ignoring the rules."

"What are the other terms of Gramps's will?"

"You get the contents and the shares in the farm, Tobias gets the house and the park."

"Does he know I've inherited the contents?"

"Yes."

"Damn! I bet he's going to try and grab what he can before we can take a probate inventory. Thanks Mr Tewksbury."

William dialled again.

"Tobias de Braose, as the Podger's solicitor I'm notifying you that you are not authorised to remove anything from the property known as The New Manor until such time as probate has been granted and the Executors are in a position to dispose of the Estate."

Melissa watch William's jaw stiffen. He terminated the call.

"Mrs P, where's Mr P?" he asked.

"'E doesn't know yet, 'e's out on the farm with Neil."

"Well, we're going to need all the help we can muster if we're to empty the house."

"Mrs Podger, you must stay here with me, er, us!" Melissa handed them both mugs of tea.

William dialled again. "Neil, good morning. I need your help. My father's evicting the Podgers and I think he's going to try and grab my inheritance! We need to strip New Manor of its contents and store them somewhere today. Is there any room in any of the barns?" Pause. "Good, and if you can round up some more help, then that would be even better. See you up at there as soon as possible."

"Come Mrs Podger, we have work to do. Tobias isn't going to get the better of us." He kissed Melissa. "Good morning, Rabbit!" he whispered: Melissa blushed.

Neil mustered several tractors with trailers and drivers and a small army of helpers. Within twelve hours the contents of the eleven bedrooms, the attic, the ballroom, dining room, library, hall, Edward's study and the cellars had been inventoried and stored either in the great barn on the farm, or in the case of the books, paintings and Edward's wine cellar, in the studio at The Old Manor House.

By late afternoon Mr & Mrs Podger were installed in Melissa's spare room and Betty had taken up permanent residence on the sofa. The cat and kittens were in their basket and, for the moment, the kittens were fast asleep. Timmy, the big tomcat, stalked into the house and curled up on Hetty's armchair.

"Well my dears, I can't believe we've done it." Mrs Podger was surveying everyone who had given up what time they could and worked so hard to empty New Manor. Now they were all gathered in the garden of The Old Manor House.

William stood on a chair and banged the table with a spoon to get everybody's attention.

"As you know the title and New Manor has now passed to my father. You have all heard how he has evicted Mr & Mrs P from the home they've known and loved with only twenty-four hours notice. Thank you all from the bottom of my heart for your help in saving their belongings and my inheritance. I would like to say a very special thank you to Mrs P who, despite losing the kitchen she has known all her life, has produced a feast." Everybody clapped and cheered. "What you've all achieved is a miracle of logistics. Thank you. It couldn't have been done without you."

"Melissa, over the years Tobias 'as made a lot of enemies. Then again, I don't suppose 'e cares a damn!" Mrs Podger said.

"I've been thinking about what William said about his father planning to sell the Estate and I think we need to make sure we have every possible bombshell to lob at whoever might buy it." Neil was enjoying a well-earned beer.

"How do you mean, Neil?" Melissa agreed with his idea of being prepared, but wondered what it was he had in mind.

"Gill reminded me that her friend Pat David is one of the worlds leading botanists. She thought we should ask her to do a botanical survey of the estate while we still can."

"That's a good point, Neil." William leant back in his chair.

"Why?" Melissa asked.

"Provided it's done now, Tobias can't complain about someone walking all over the estate since probate hasn't been granted, which means that technically it's still Edward's property." William paused. Melissa saw him swallow and look away, his expression one of anger and grief mixed with tears of frustration. "Are you suggesting a full ecological survey?" he asked eventually.

Neil nodded. "We have to protect the organic status farm and if Tobias does sell the estate it might be a good idea to know exactly what the rest of the estate has in the way of either red list or endangered species while we have the chance, and in particular make sure what we have living in the farm boundary hedges."

William nodded, thankful Neil was thinking ahead. He was too angry to think straight. A full ecology survey would be costly, but it made sense to do it now.

"OK, Neil." William sighed and looked across to where he could see some of the estate deer grazing. "I can't believe it's come to this."

"Hello Mum." William kissed a tall middle-aged woman on both cheeks. "this is Melissa, Hetty's great niece."

"Melissa, you are so like Hetty, it's uncanny."

"I can't believe how everything has happened in such a short time." Melissa could not remember this woman who must have been at Hetty's funeral. She was regretting having hidden away in the kitchen at Hetty's wake.

"I shall miss Edward very much and I'm sure you will too." Rosemary murmured.

"Mother, do you think my father is ever going to turn up?" They were standing outside the family chapel waiting for the chief mourner, who had so far failed to appear.

"I have no idea, darling, but I wouldn't wait much longer." Rosemary kissed her son again and went to take her place in the chapel.

Mr Tewksbury appeared with the vicar, both of them were looking at their watches and shaking their heads.

"William, it's your decision. We have not had a phone call to say what's delaying your father."

William nodded. "We can't keep everyone waiting any longer. Come Lissie, take my arm."

The pallbearers started their slow march up the aisle. In the absence of the 13th Earl, William took his place in the front pew with Melissa. Melissa was quietly relieved not to have to come face to face with Douglas Lansbury.

William took her hand as Edward's coffin was laid beneath the chapel floor. Tears slipped down Melissa's cheeks as she said a final goodbye to the gentle old man.

William stood and shook hands with the many mourners inviting them back to The Old Manor House. Melissa had felt the pub was not somewhere Edward had known and had insisted on hosting some refreshment for everyone – except Tobias.

"Dr Carlisle?" A tall man in a dark suit accosted her.

"Yes." She expected him to murmur the usual platitudes, but instead he handed her an envelope and walked away.

"What's that Melissa?" Mrs Podger asked. Mr Podger was idly deadheading the rose bushes and dropping them in a neat pile.

Melissa could not believe what she was reading. Tobias de Braose was giving her notice to quit! It was so ridiculous she burst out laughing.

She handed the letter to Mrs P.

"'e can't do that, can 'e?"

"Clearly Lansbury hasn't told him I've owned The Old Manor since I was eighteen! After this I need a cuppa."

Mr Tewksbury was among those who had come back to The Old Manor. Melissa handed him the letter. Like Melissa he roared with laughter.

"Do you want me to reply?"

"You mean in legal speak for sex and travel? Yes please!" The elderly solicitor's eyebrows shot up. "Oh, I'm sorry Mr Tewksbury, I've shocked you."

"Understandable under the circumstances, Melissa. How strong do you want me to be?"

"I leave that to you."

"Well, clearly the battle lines are drawn. Despite it probably taking some months for us to get everything together in order to apply for probate, don't be surprised if you see various people being shown round the estate."

"Why?"

"Melissa, Tobias has used some pretty dirty tricks to get New Manor empty, so it's my thinking he already has a buyer."

"Mr Tewksbury, it may just be coincidence, but William and I were not due back from Jersey until the 29th June."

"Melissa, it was probably the shock of seeing Tobias's name on the front page of the paper that brought on Edward's heart attack, so you would have been back here as soon as you could anyway."

"I suppose you're right, but it does seem very coincidental."

29ᵀᴴ DECEMBER

An icy blast of wind had greeted Melissa as she stepped down from the 'plane at Edinburgh airport. William had texted to say he was stuck in traffic so she was waiting just inside the terminal building, watching a traffic warden patrolling outside. The uniformed predator was slapping parking tickets on the windscreens of those stupid enough to leave their vehicles unattended, the fine high enough to take a significant bite out of any wallet. The odd flake of snow was being whipped by the wind and the leaden grey sky suggested these odd flakes were a hint of what was to come.

Several minutes passed until a blue Range Rover with the de Braose crest on the doors drew up and William jumped out.

"Lissie!" He enfolded her in a bear hug. "It's so good to see you. Welcome to Scotland."

"Thank you." She was suddenly overwhelmed with shyness. She had declined his invitation to come north for Christmas as she felt she could not leave Mr & Mrs Podger for their first Christmas after being turfed out of New Manor. William had made it very clear where he was going to spend Christmas and New Year so she had not suggested he might want to join them.

"How far is it to William's lair?" she asked. The snow was threatening as they drove over the Firth road bridge.

"If we hit the rush hour through Perth it might take us a bit longer, but we should be there by tea-time."

"I had no idea you were so far out of Edinburgh." It struck her that William's property might not be quite as she had imagined. "The trouble with you Sassenachs is that you think civilisation ceases at Hadrian's Wall."

"Doesn't it?" she teased. "Shakespeare's descriptions of murder and betrayal have left us English convinced you're all savages."

"Ah, the Scottish play! That all took place a lot further north from where we're going. We're really quite civilised – we only toss cabers at each other now."

The clouds lifted sufficiently for Melissa to be able to see the snow dusted hills.

"It's beautifully wild up here." The emptiness of the Scottish countryside was a stark contrast to the well-manicured fields of southern

England. There were no ancient hedgerows defining field boundaries, but instead, open countryside with high hills and dry-stone walls.

"The hill farmers are finding it hard going with these cold winters."

"Isn't there any government help?"

"It's difficult to get many of them to understand that there are various national and EU grants they can claim, but they're an incredibly proud lot and feel they're failing if they accept what they think of as hand-outs."

"Oh dear. So are you persuading them?"

"It's been a hard slog, but once a couple of them had received the money and realised there was help with the paperwork, it's word of mouth and more and more of the local farmers are asking if we can give them a hand."

"So you really are the local laird!"

William turned off on to a smaller road. Melissa noted road signs that said Frenich, Foss, Daloist and Cremorne.

"My mother loves New Year and she's really looking forward to seeing you again."

Melissa had had not given New Year much further thought other than to take some Scottish dancing lessons.

The road followed the banks of a river, weaving in and out of woodland. The clouds had thickened again and the snow that had threatened all the way from Edinburgh was beginning to fall properly. Under the trees the road was clear, but out of their shelter the road was beginning to whiten. They crossed a bridge guarded by a grey granite gatehouse. A welcoming golden glow shone from the windows and someone inside pulled the curtains across just as they drove past. A sign declared this was the Cremorne Estate.

"Not much further now, Lissie."

William's idea of not much further was a mile long drive through mixed woodland to a huge Victorian gothic house set back from a loch.

"Welcome to Cremorne; welcome to the Highlands."

"William it's beautiful." It was nothing like what she had expected.

Two black labradors, a Jack Russell and four spaniels shot out of the front door, all barking furiously, followed by Rosemary trying to call them to order.

"Melissa, how lovely to see you." Rosemary kissed her on both cheeks. "Come inside quickly."

In the hall the various portraits of the de Braose ancestors, who had previously hung in the hall at New Manor, greeted her from their new places on the oak panelled walls. It might have been fanciful, but she thought Edward seemed pleased to see her.

"It's nice to be here, Mrs Bell."

"Melissa, please don't be so formal. Come, tea is laid out in the drawing room. William shot off without having any lunch and I bet you didn't have anything on the plane?"

Melissa murmured something about refusing a plastic sandwich and wondered, not for the first time, why the de Braoses always wanted to eat the minute they met up.

"Give the girl a chance, Mother. I'll take Melissa to her room so she can get her bearings."

The oak staircase wound round the perimeter of the hall forming a minstrel's gallery over the huge space below. She looked down and could see wooden double doors leading off the hall into various rooms. William led her down a corridor, round a corner, up several steps and she wondered if there was a map so she could find her way around.

"Here we are." William opened a door on to a large room dominated by a four-poster bed. "I thought you'd like a view of the loch." He put went over to window. "Look, you can just make out the mountains through the snow."

"It's beautiful." Through the gathering gloom Melissa could just make out a large expanse of water with high shadowy shapes beyond, which, she realised, were the mountains. She felt the wildness of the highlands seeping into her psyche.

"This is all thanks to my great, great, grandfather marrying an American heiress to save the estate from bankruptcy."

"Welcome to Cremorne, Lissie." He squeezed her tight.

"William, Melissa." Rosemary's voice floated up from the hall. "Tea's getting cold."

"Well done, Mother!" he murmured. "Ever the perfect sense of timing!"

"William, I wouldn't want her to get the wrong idea."

"I'm not going to get much of an opportunity to have you to myself."

171

"What do you mean?"

"This year's Hogmanay celebrations have sort of got out of hand!"

"Is the do here?"

"Of course – every year since I can't remember when! Provided the weather isn't too unkind, Charles is coming and I've asked Neil and Gill. Then there's an old school friend of mine, plus his wife, child and nanny and Lord Dunbar and his wife, who always come to the Ball and stay over. They'll arrive in time for lunch on the 31st, plus my other neighbours the Ross's and the McKinlays. They'll be here in time for tea. Not to mention those who end up dancing through the night."

Melissa groaned.

"How many're coming who won't be staying?"

"I think there's going to be about a hundred. I'd better warn you that you'll be under scrutiny as this is the first time I've been accompanied by anyone other than mother."

"Oh, thanks, Clunk-head. You could've warned me!" She bashed him on the chest, but William just held her closer.

"I thought that if I did, you wouldn't have come."

Melissa thought he was probably right.

"Come on," he said reluctantly, "otherwise Mother will be up here and you've still got your coat on."

"I suppose your mother walking in on us naked would be ok?"

William's answer was to kiss her nose.

Downstairs the curtains were closed against the storm.

"Do you shoot, Melissa? Or will you be beating?" Rosemary asked as she poured the tea.

"Oh, er, Rosemary, I've never done either. When am I expected to do this?"

"Provided the weather isn't horrendous, the Estate usually has a New Year's Day shoot." Rosemary handed Melissa a delicate bone china cup and saucer. "Help yourself to milk or lemon dear."

"If this snow keeps up I wonder if anyone will make it." Melissa suggested.

"Lissie, it takes a lot more than a bit of snow to keep people away from the Cremorne Ball. Everyone will get here – they always do!" William sounded positively exhilarated at the thought of his guests having to overcome the challenges set by the weather.

"William, do you think I'll have a chance to have a talk with Charles?" Melissa asked.

William nodded while munching a scone with jam and cream. Melissa had tried to speak to her Jersey Trustee several times, but so far their telephone calls had crossed and they had never managed to speak.

"Charles will want some indication of what you want to do before February. Have you come to any conclusions?" William poured himself another cup of tea.

"Charles who, William?" Rosemary asked. William had not provided her with a detailed list of guests and she was curious to know why her son was inviting anyone to do with Melissa."

"Charles Cliffe. We met him in Jersey and he invited us to the Bankers Ball, so I thought I'd return the compliment and get him up here for New Year."

"Good lord, William. I haven't seen Charles Cliffe since," she paused. "Since I was living in Hetty's flat and he was doing his banking exams. Hetty and Edward were incredibly generous to me. If it hadn't been for them I have no idea what I'd've done. My father didn't even know I'd got married, let alone given him a grandson." Rosemary said.

"Charles and my father were close friends and he's been looking after my financial affairs since I was little." Melissa explained.

Clearly the marriage between The Honourable Tobias de Braose and Miss Rosemary Wright was something neither had been proud of, but Melissa managed to keep her surprise hidden.

"How did you tell your parents?"

"I didn't, Hetty did."

William sat and listened with half an ear to his mother's reminiscences. Hetty's diaries had prompted a long conversation with his mother about the break up of her marriage and his admiration for Hetty de Braose had grown.

The phone could be heard ringing in the hall. Melissa wondered why neither of them went to answer it.

"Melissa," Rosemary paused. "William and I were rummaging in the cellar earlier and we came across a painting." She turned, "where did you put it, darling?"

William retrieved a large canvas from behind Rosemary's chair. He swivelled it so Melissa could see Hetty and David standing together with two young boys seated on the ground who she recognised as Edward and her own grandfather.

"Wow, how come the four of them were painted together?"

"I've not idea. The signature's Helier Lander's, who, according to Google, was a Jersey artist who came to London in the early 20th century and made his name as a society portraitist," Rosemary told her, "but as to your question, I have no idea."

"So the Jersey connection starts way before my grandfather went there then." Melissa mused.

"When was David shot down, Lissie?" William asked. He was taking a closer look at the man standing behind the two boys.

"24th August, 1940."

"Right, so this must have been painted sometime in the mid to late1930s. Edward looks as if he can't be more than about twelve." William looked at Melissa and then at the painting, as did Rosemary.

"According to the various birth certificates my grandfather was born in 1928 and here he looks about ten. I think Edward said he was born in 1926, which would give us a probable date of 1938. Was Lander alive then?" Melissa asked.

"He painted the Duke & Duchess of Windsor and the abdication was in 1936, so that narrows the time frame." Rosemary was enjoying relaying the fruits of her research. "Melissa, stand next to William will you."

Melissa did as she was told.

"Now both of you, stand next to the painting." Rosemary rummaged in her handbag and pulled out her phone. William propped the painting on the mantelpiece and they stood where Rosemary directed. William slipped his arm around Melissa's waist just as David had his around Hetty.

"Well that's extraordinary!" Rosemary stood looking at her screen. "Look." She handed them her phone. Melissa gasped: William laughed.

"William, you can't leave it mouldering in the cellar." Rosemary said firmly.

There was a soft knock and a woman stuck her head round the door. "William," she paused her attention diverted by the painting. "Gosh, is that a portrait you've had done?"

William shook his head. "No, Megan, Mum and I found it in the cellar." William introduced the newcomer as his estate manager.

"I've heard a lot about you Dr Carlisle. Is the woman a relation?" Megan asked as she shook hands.

"Please, call me Melissa and yes, it's my great aunt and she's standing next to William's great uncle."

"Ah, that explains the similarities, but it's uncanny how alike you both are to both of them. Who are the two boys?"

"Look carefully, Megan." Rosemary said.

Megan shook her head in puzzlement. "The one on the right looks vaguely like Lord Edward."

"It is and the other is Melissa's grandfather." Rosemary explained.

"What's the connection?" Megan asked.

"We think it was painted in or around 1938 so my great aunt would have been eighteen and great uncle David twenty two. They were married in 1939." Melissa explained.

"But you didn't come in for that, did you dear?" Rosemary prompted.

"Er no. William, that was your friend Angus on the phone. He sends his apologies, but he won't be coming because he doesn't want to risk the weather."

"Thanks Megan."

"I can understand his caution. His baby is only ten weeks old and it's a long drive." Rosemary replied. Melissa thought she looked slightly relieved. "However, we'd better make sure all the beds are made up, just in case we have more staying over after the festivities than we thought."

Melissa was amused by how Rosemary was making sure that everyone in the room knew who was ostensibly in charge of the New Year's arrangements. Megan smiled, nodded and disappeared.

"That's a bother!" William muttered to himself. "If you'll excuse me, I'll go and see if Megan has any problems looming for Hogmanay." William first kissed his mother and then Melissa, whispering in her ear. "See you shortly, Rabbit."

Melissa was still examining the painting and seemed not to have heard.

For an instant Rosemary wondered whether William's interest in Melissa was more to do with her millions than love. Clearly being an academic meant not being a follower of fashion and, if she were perfectly honest, Rosemary considered a generous description of Melissa's style would be 'comfortable'. With a face and figure like hers it was a shame the girl did not make the most of herself. From the little she had gleaned from William and the Internet, Rosemary wondered what it was her son saw in someone as studious as this beautiful redhead. She hoped he was not going to abuse Hetty's memory by feigning love, just for the sake of money.

William had also told her that HM Revenue & Customs had accepted a Canaletto painting of Venice in lieu of inheritance tax and had then snarled and raged about one of the family paintings having to be used to cover the death duties. She appreciated why a deal was done with the tax authorities using the family art collection to pay the inheritance tax. Tobias's insistence the Canaletto was given in lieu of inheritance tax was clearly another spiteful twist designed to irritate his son. During all the time she had known him, Tobias had made no secret that he hated everything Edward had held so dear and the Canaletto had been one of Edward's favourite paintings. Even Mr Tewksbury had said this was a really good outcome.

Rosemary understood exactly why Tobias was being difficult. Tobias had had to wait until his father's death until he came into any of the de Braose assets, whereas William had been given the Cremorne Estate, half the farm and some exquisite objects d'art years ago.

"Rosemary." Melissa interrupted the older woman's thoughts.

"Yes dear."

"Do you live in Scotland?" Melissa asked, making polite conversation.

"Oh no. My late husband loved Wales, so we bought a place there, but I have a little house in Belgravia. When William was very little, Edward used to invite us up here for August and then, when William was older, he would often spend time the summer here and we would go touring in Europe."

"William told me how very fond he was of your late husband."

Rosemary nodded. It had been a very happy twenty-seven years. "Sometimes I think Edward wished he'd been his son."

"From what I've read in Hetty's diaries I think everyone wished that." Melissa knew she was speaking out of turn.

"Sometimes, Melissa, when we are young we do stupid things and Tobias was mine."

"I didn't mean to imply anything . . ."

Rosemary waved away any apologies. "Back in '79 student life was not so different to now. Like most under graduates we stayed up late and went to riotous parties. Somehow Tobias and I ended up in bed and William was the result. I've often wondered whether I was some sort of bet, especially now Tobias's sexual preferences are all over the front of the newspapers."

"Yet he did the honourable thing." Melissa said.

"If I'm brutally honest I have wondered if our sexual blunder meant he had a means of securing an heir for the de Braose name without having to admit he was gay. Even if he hadn't had an ulterior motive, we came from such different backgrounds our marriage would never have worked. I wanted love, marriage and a home. Tobias wanted what Tobias wanted and what that was, he never told me."

Finding Rosemary happy to talk, Melissa continued with her questions. "Forgive me for saying this Rosemary, but Hetty's diaries show he was a sadist from an early age. Did you have no idea?"

"I knew he was selfish and thought I could change him except it was apparent from the very beginning that he wanted us to live separate existences. If I asked if we could do things together as a family, he would fly into a rage and it wasn't too soon before he gave me a slap. Edward and Hetty literally saved mine and William's lives and, thanks to Edward, I finished my education."

There was something chilling hearing the story from the person who had lived it.

"After I married I didn't see much of Hetty because I had a new husband and you had come to live with her, but she was often in my thoughts and wrote to me now and again asking how we were getting on. Eventually she painted a lovely portrait of my late husband."

"Edward told me you were at UCL."

"Yes, I studied History."

Melissa nodded. History, William and a mutual loathing of Tobias were three things uniting the two women.

"I hope mother isn't giving you a hard time, Lissie." They were lying in bed and William was playing with her hair. She had opened the curtains so they could see the stars glittering against the black expanse of space. Now the bedroom was filled with moonlight reflected off the virgin snow.

"No, not at all. She's very protective of Cremorne isn't she?"

"She has lots of happy memories here She's also having to adjust to not being the focus of attention this year."

"Oh, why not?"

"Because you are."

"William, I don't want to upset your mother, and I'm not sure I want to be the centre of attention."

"Since I became laird of Cremorne mother has been my partner for the New Year's Ball. Anyway Lissie, we have better things to do in the middle of the night than talk about my mother. Come here."

Melissa woke to find herself alone. She lay and thought about the festivities to come. If she had known there would be all sorts of pomp and circumstance she would not have reminded William of his invitation. He had said it was a strictly 'by invitation' event, assuring her she would find this ball a striking contrast to the ball in the summer.

William's disappearance from her bed in the early hours underlined how he preferred to keep up appearances on his own turf. She was quite happy to play second fiddle and let Rosemary play the 'hostess'. She thought it was far too soon for her to be seen as William's partner. People would make all sorts of assumptions and she was not sure she wanted that. The local lady doctor had advised her about contraception, which had made her realise how lucky she had been that William had been sensible. He was experienced in ways she had only read about. Melissa did not like to think about his being with other girls.

After showering and dressing, she found her way to the kitchen.

"Hi." Megan smiled warmly. "Breakfast?"

"That would be great."

"William's out with the tractors clearing the drive," Megan handed Melissa a mug of tea. "and Rosemary never gets out of bed before ten."

"Megan, how much snow fell?"

"Down here we have about eight inches. The top drive often gets covered in drifts and so it'll be thick up there. Of course, under the trees it will be fine, but the forecast is for snow showers and very cold temperatures for the next couple of weeks."

Melissa buttered some toast and spread it with Marmite. The Jack Russell who had been asleep in its bed came and sat looking up at her pleadingly. Melissa bent down and gave it a morsel of toast.

"Och, that's done it, she won't leave you alone now."

The little dog was turning quick circles in its eagerness to grab a bit more toast, jumping up with all four legs high off the ground as if it had springs in its paws. Melissa laughed with delight.

"Who's the acrobat then?"

"This is Lulu." At the sound of her name, Lulu sat and cocked her head to one side. "Do you have a dog, Melissa?"

"Sort of. Betty was Lord Edward's and when Tobias kicked the Podgers out she came with them and we all live in The Old Manor House. Betty's devoted to Mr Podger and follows him everywhere."

"That's a bit like how I got Lulu who came with the decorator, but stayed after he'd finished."

Melissa looked puzzled. She did not like to think the little dog had been abandoned.

"What I should have said was that the decorator was working here and brought Lulu everyday because his wife and Lulu didn't get on. Anyhow, he'd gone home one evening to find all his stuff in black bin liners on the street and the locks changed. So to cut a long story short, he had to find a place to live and his landlady wouldn't allow pets so Lulu is now part of the Cremorne menagerie."

Megan sat down to drink her coffee and Lulu jumped up on her knee. "As you can see, she's made herself very much at home." Megan gave the little dog a hug. "Haven't you pet?" Lulu licked the back of Megan's hand as if to say 'thank you.'

"She's very pretty." Melissa compared Lulu and her own story and wondered if the little dog somehow knew how similar they were. It was an absurd thought.

"Lulu clearly likes you as she hasn't tried to nip your ankles. She's not allowed into the big house when we're entertaining paying guests because she can be a bit temperamental, but my office is too cold today."

Melissa bent forward and stroked the dog's head. Lulu tipped her head back exposing her neck for tickling. "Megan, if there's anything I can do to help I'd be glad to lend a hand."

"I've got to go into Pitlochry, so you can come with me if you want?"

"Do you have any idea when William's other guests are due?"

"I believe they're expected before tea." Megan replied, "Come on, the car's just outside."

The two women and Lulu piled into the Range Rover and they set off over the crisp blanket of snow covering the drive.

The mountains looked like giants lying under lumpy white duvets. Melissa thought the view might be considered a visual cliché except the sheer beauty of the white against the blue of the sky was breath-taking. The cleared snow was piled into high banks on either side of the road as they came out of the shelter of the trees.

"Look, there are the tractors." Megan slowed down and wound down the window.

"Morning girls." William called from the warmth of his cab. "Megan, can you check on the band and see if Gordon is definitely able to make it."

"OK, William. By the way, I've got us more grit on the promise of an invite. I'm told it'll be delivered later this morning."

"Thank you Megan. Morning, Lissie." William blew her a kiss. "I'll see you both later."

Melissa blushed, not used to an overt display of affection in front of strangers.

"I believe Rosemary's hoping you can help her wrap the New Year's gifts for the ladies." Megan said.

Now they were waiting at the junction for a gap in the local traffic.

"Good, I was beginning to think I was going to have to sit and twiddle my thumbs in a ladylike fashion. This is all a bit foreign to me, Megan."

"It's not at all formal if that's what you're thinking, especially after the various toasts. Yes, we all wear long dresses and the men wear highland dress or dinner jackets, but that's where the formality ends. I hope you've bought some comfortable dancing shoes."

"I took some dancing lessons so I wouldn't be too much of an embarrassment." Megan's confirmation of William's statement that the ball was not going to be a formal event was reassuring.

"Oh well done. I can't dance for toffee, but I manage to struggle through the eightsome reels! Rosemary throws herself into the whole thing, but by midnight no one gives a hoot about how to do what step, then William goes first footing so a dark man, with a lump of coal and a bottle of Scotch brings good luck across the threshold. Have you never had a Scottish New Year?"

"No, the closest I've come to anything like this was a ball in the summer."

"Well there's nothing so funny as the morning after – you should have a camera handy. We Scot's know how to party and we always have more than a good few still standing for breakfast, but the casualties are hilarious. We've had to oust people from under the billiard table before now! We usually throw them in a Land Rover and take them home after they've sobered up a bit."

The trip into Pitlochry took a couple of hours. Megan seemed to know everyone. Some said how they were looking forward to the event and everyone wished each other Happy New Year. Finally, with the back of the SUV packed to the gunnels with cardboard boxes and carrier bags, they set off for Cremorne.

A sleek Mercedes with Jersey number plates turned left just ahead of them.

"That'll be Charles Cliffe?" Melissa was pleased the weather had not delayed him.

"He'd have a bother getting to the house in that car if we hadn't cleared the snow." Megan changed down a gear. "If you look behind, there's a Range Rover, which, if I'm not much mistaken, has the de Braose crest on the doors."

"That'll be Neil and Gill. Megan, can we go in through the kitchen?"

"Nay bother, Melissa. Any reason why?"

"I don't want to tread on Rosemary's toes and William seems to be making a big fuss of me being here."

Megan nodded. William had talked of no one else except Dr Melissa Carlisle from the time he arrived, until he had gone to pick her up.

"Megan, do you know if Edward ever let Cremorne out to film companies?"

"Oh, yes. He needed some serious cash to rewire the place so he approached the film and TV world to see if they wanted somewhere for filming, and the rest is history. William is very much like his grandfather in that he sees every one on the estate as part of a large family."

"I like that idea."

"Come on, Melissa. Let's get this stuff into the house. I need a coffee."

The kitchen was a hive of industry where Megan's husband, Peter, was preparing lunch. Including Megan and her husband, Melissa counted off eight for lunch, but was sure there were more staff who also needed feeding. The quiet solitude of The Old Manor was safe, but Mellisa found she was enjoying the bustling atmosphere of Cremorne.

"Ah, there you are, Lissie." William poked his head around the kitchen door. "Peter, any chance of coffee for seven in the drawing room?" he turned to Melissa. "Lissie, Charles has brought a surprise guest."

"You will be nine for lunch and dinner then, William?" Peter asked. William nodded and, taking Melissa's hand, they left the cosy comfort of the kitchen.

"Melissa, how lovely to see you." Suzie rushed up to Melissa and kissed her on both cheeks.

Charles greeted her warmly. "Lovely to see you, Melissa."

"Isn't Cremorne absolutely beautiful?" Suzie exclaimed. "After the snow last night I did wonder whether we'd manage to get here."

Clouds were beginning to bubble up over the mountains as another weather front moved in.

"Neil, Gill, welcome to Cremorne." William greeted his farm manager and his wife as they entered the sitting room. Coffee was served and Melissa sat observing the complicated social quadrille that was establishing the hierarchy of the newcomers. The academic world was so completely different. Rarely did they discuss the stock market or the economic climate and never mundane chitchat that Melissa thought was best described as 'vacant noise'.

Charles perched himself on the arm of the sofa next to her.

"Melissa, you're looking well." Charles sipped his coffee. Anne Cliffe's absence loomed over them. "Before you ask, Anne and I are separated."

"Oh!" Melissa replied, not knowing how to respond to his statement.

"Now we are tidying up the loose ends." Charles appeared to regard Anne as if she were a pair of old shoes that had outlasted their wearability.

"Charles, I'm sorry to hear that" was the best Melissa could muster.

"There are times when you have to withdraw for the greater good. If Anne and I had continued together it could have become very messy. This way, everyone benefits."

Melissa nodded; she had no wish to know the detailed ins and outs of his private life.

"Now you two," Rosemary and Suzie came across and Charles stood up. "I hope you aren't talking shop?" Rosemary said. Suzie slipped her arm through Charles's and Melissa noticed the large diamond on her left hand. Clearly Charles had wasted no time in finding someone to fill Anne's shoes.

The rest of the day passed with Cremorne staff preparing the house for the ball. The library was out of bounds, as was the ballroom. Despite the bustle around her, Melissa was bored. Rosemary and Suzie seemed to chatter endlessly about absolutely nothing. William had warned her that he was going to be busy and had disappeared.

Charles sat reading the Financial Times.

"Charles, would it be possible to have a few minutes of your time."

"No time like the present. What's on your mind?"

"Actually, it's to do with the De Braose Farm. William wants me to be a director, but I don't think I'm up to the job."

Charles looked at her, curious to know what she might suggest.

"If Tobias is going to sell New Manor it's bound to have an impact on both my land and the farm, so the farm will need someone with a lot of experience and I wondered if you could be a director instead of me."

"Very flattering, Melissa, but I've no idea about farming."

"But you do know about finance and economics and I would be hopeless."

"What about Neil? He's been manager for a very long time."

"Yes, but his expertise is the actual day to day management. I think the farm needs someone with a bigger view of the world and I recognise that certainly isn't me.."

"Would you suggest Neil comes on the board too?"

Melissa considered this for a minute. "So it would be the three of you?"

"I thing it should be you and William and Neil, if you are adamant, me. That way you can learn the ropes and when you think you're ready, you can boot me off."

Melissa considered this idea for a moment.

"I wondered if you've heard anything on the banking grapevine about Tobias, other than what's in the papers?" she asked, satisfied with the suggested compromise.

184

Charles chuckled. "The gutter press have come up with some interesting stories about that party, but it will all be speculation. I did hear that Douglas Lansbury has pleaded guilty and is to be sentenced shortly."

"Yes, Mr Tewksbury told me. Do you think he'll be sent to prison?"

"That depends on whether there are any violent people coming up for sentencing and how full the prisons are."

Melissa looked perplexed. "What do you mean?"

"I should think Lansbury pleaded guilty in the hope he will avoid being put away."

"Will he ever be able to practise as a solicitor again?" Melissa was surprised that a sentence might be dictated by who else might be sentenced elsewhere in the justice system.

"On no!"

"But you think he'll definitely go to prison?"

Charles folded his newspaper and leant forward. "Absolutely, yes. The judge will make an example of him in order to send a message to anyone else thinking they might try something similar. Now, have you given any thought to what you want to happen to the Trusts after your thirtieth birthday?"

"Yes." Melissa sighed, relieved Lansbury was probably going to prison. However, Charles now needed an answer regarding her trusts. "Is there anyway things can stay as they are?"

"There's no reason why we can't continue to look after your financial affairs and keep them tax efficient."

"I'm ill equipped for all this high finance and I suppose, if I'm honest, I don't want to do it."

The banker found her honesty refreshing, if a trifle naïve. "What's your attitude towards risk?"

"None!"

"You don't have an attitude? Or you don't like risk?"

"The latter. Hetty drummed it into me that debt must be avoided at all costs. Any mistakes I make could cost people their jobs and I don't want that responsibility. I don't need a huge income either, except I would like some money to convert Hetty's studio into somewhere for the Podger's to call their own and put a glass building over the swimming pool so I can swim all year round."

"Have you done any costings?" Charles wondered how anyone could be so disinterested in managing their money.

"I've a couple of quotes for the studio conversion and I've asked Mr Tewksbury how much Edward was paying the Podger's. I want to make sure they aren't out of pocket."

"What if they want to take a job elsewhere? Would you replace them?"

"Oh, I hadn't thought of that." She blushed, ashamed she had assumed the Podger's would be staying. "I haven't asked them."

"A fundamental question, Melissa, that needs to be clarified."

"But assuming they do stay, I think it would be nice for them to have somewhere they can get away from me because, at the moment, I'm very conscious that they don't have a place of their own. They had a separate flat in New Manor."

"We've received the assets of the English trust and sorted all the paperwork with the English tax authorities. Do you have any special instructions?"

Melissa winced. "Are you dreadfully expensive?"

Charles laughed. "Melissa, that depends on what you want me to do. You will have to give me some form of instruction. I assume you can read a set of accounts?"

"The basics – the finer points of accountancy I leave to the professionals, but on the whole I prefer black ink to red!"

"Come in." Melissa mumbled as she pulled the sweater over her head then straightened her hair. She had not had to twiddle her thumbs after her conversation with Charles and had spent the rest of the afternoon helping Megan. She had helped mend the net that would be filled with balloons to be released at midnight. They had tramped out in the snow and set up the torches on either side of the drive, then tweaked the Christmas decorations where they had begun to look a bit sad.

Later she had managed to slip into the library and after some searching had found an Edwardian book called "*Etiquette of Good Society*" by Lady Colin Campbell. It was full of helpful hints on what to wear when attending country house weekends, weddings, special celebrations and how to tip the servants. The knock on her bedroom door came again. "Come in." she called, a little irritated by the intrusion.

The knock came for the third time.

"Come in!" Melissa pulled opened the heavy oak door. "Oh, Gill."

"Sorry to bother you, Melissa. I wanted to know what you were wearing for dinner as I've not got a clue."

"Gill, I'm planning on going down like this. Why?" Melissa was wearing a polo neck sweater and jeans.

"This is the first time Neil and I . . ."

Melissa handed her the little book. "You can either read this, or we go in search of William and ask him, but I'm wearing what I'm standing in."

Gill flipped the pages. "It all looks a bit Downton Abbey to me."

"Right! Let's find William. If we have to dress for dinner every night, then I'm stuckered as I've only got jeans, sweaters and a long dress for tomorrow."

They found William in the kitchen enjoying a glass of wine.

"Hello you two. Gill, have you met our chef, Peter." They shook hands and Peter poured two more glasses of. Melissa smiled her thanks, sipped the wine and turned to William.

"William." She said determinedly.

"Yes, Lissie!" his voice had a whimsical lilt.

"Are we expected to dress for dinner?" She expected a simple yes or no.

"If it's all the same to you, I'd prefer not to have to see my mother naked!"

"Seriously William." Gill snapped. "Neil is sweating on having to wear a bow tie for tomorrow night. He'll die if he has to tie it more than once!"

"Who gave you the idea we were dressing for dinner?" William looked at both of them, puzzled by the sudden outbreak of fashion angst. "I told you, the only time we have any formality is to welcome in the New Year." He looked at Melissa and slipped his arms around Melissa's waist. "Where did the pair of you get the idea we were tarting ourselves up every night?"

"Your mother didn't exactly say so, but she certainly hinted."

"Well, she might change, but . . . "

"I wondered where everybody'd got to." Charles came into the kitchen interrupting William's instructions on the Cremorne dress code.

Peter handed a glass of wine to the newcomer.

"Cheers." Charles raised his glass. "William, Suzie wants to know what to wear for dinner?"

They all burst out laughing.

"What has my mother been saying?" William asked. "Charles, I'm staying as I am, but if Suzie and mother want to dress up like Christmas trees, that's fine, but diamonds and beans on toast are a bit surreal, even for Cremorne!"

"Och, thanks William! I've slaved over a hot stove for those beans all afternoon!" Peter finished his wine. "Now, if it's all the same to you, I need to get the bread toasted and those beans finished, so take your drinks and get out of my kitchen all of you!"

31ˢᵀ DECEMBER

Hetty's 1950's pine green taffeta ball gown rustled as Melissa moved to stand in front of the cheval mirror. Should she wear the pearls, or her grandmother's diamonds and emeralds. The book of etiquette told her that single women wore pearls. Unfortunately no explanation was given as to why, but she decided to go with tradition and opted for a triple string of creamy white pearls with matching earrings.

Her thick mane of red hair was swept back off her face and a wide belt accentuated her tiny waist.

"OK Carlisle, time to make an entrance." She told herself as she shut the bedroom door behind her.

"Should auld acquaintance be forgot . . ."

"Happy New Year, Dr Carlisle." They were standing under the mistletoe. "Here's wishing you a very happy year to come."

"You too, Mr de Braose. Thank you for asking me to Cremorne. It's been wonderful."

"I hope you'll come again – often."

2012

William felt sick as he read the email from Mr Tewskbury telling him that New Manor had been sold. The email also said that there were rumours that the new owners were proposing to develop the estate as a golf club.

The combined acreage of the park and the farm formed a very large chunk of the Sussex landscape, which, up until now, had been free from pesticides, herbicides and anything else unnatural for many years. The increasing interest in the organic movement meant the farm had become an education centre for farmers wanting to follow the de Braose way of farming. If the rumours were true and the park became a golf course then the impact of having a species poor acreage being sprayed regularly with herbicides and pesticides could prove disastrous for the status of the farm, not to mention the surrounding countryside. He hoped Melissa would understand the probable long-term ecological impact on the farm and on her land. He picked up his phone.

Melissa was sitting up in bed opening envelopes when her phone rang. There were birthday cards from the Podgers, Charles and Suzie, William and two envelopes with typed addresses.

"Happy Birthday, Birthday Girl."

"Thanks William. However, I feel ancient and 'orrible."

"What about a birthday dinner in town tonight?" William blew kisses down the phone.

"Where and what time?"

"How about I meet you in the American Bar at the Savoy at 7 and we take it from there?"

"That sounds fun."

"I'll see you at seven, Rabbit." Will blew more kisses down the phone before ringing off.

Melissa lay back on the pillows wondering what one wore to somewhere like the American Bar. There were lots of Hetty's vintage outfits in the wardrobe so perhaps she could wear one of those.

A thirtieth birthday was supposed to be a very special date, so she told herself she was going to indulge without limits.

Her mobile rang again, this time it was Neil.

"Morning Melissa. Gill and I forgot to put your birthday card in the post, so happy birthday."

"Thanks Neil, and thank Gill too." She tucked the phone under her chin, opened one of the two typed envelopes and scanned the contents.

"Oh hell!"

Thoughts of cocktails at the Savoy disappeared.

"What's the problem?"

"Neil, I've got a letter from the buyers' lawyers and they say I haven't got a right of access over their land!"

"Have you got the deeds?"

"Somewhere in the study, but if it's true, it means I can't get off the Estate."

"Drive round the lake and through the back entrance to the farm for now."

"I did that once before. My car won't take that sort of bumping around. She's far too old!"

"You can borrow one of the farm four-by-fours if you want."

"Neil, that's very kind."

"I'm sure there's a solution, Melissa."

"Thanks, Neil."

Melissa threw on her kimono and rushed out to the kitchen.

"Mrs P," she called. "Mrs P, we've got a problem."

"Mr P's taking me down to the village. Is there anything special you want?" Mrs Podger was buttoning up her coat.

"It's going to be a bit tricky. Is Mr P in the car because if he is, he'd better come in."

Melissa went into the study and found the deeds while Mrs Podger retrieved her husband.

"Happy Birthday, Melly."

"Mr P, that's awfully kind of you, but birthday celebrations are going to have to wait. We've got a rather large problem." She sat down and examined the deeds. Her heart sank. There was no mention of a right of way over any of the estate between her property and the main road.

"That's ridiculous. How do they think you're supposed to get off the Estate?"

"Mrs P, I'll ask Mr Tewksbury, in the meantime Neil suggested we use the track that links us with the back of the farm."

Melissa dialled Messrs Tewksbury, Mather & Grange only to be told Mr Tewksbury was in a meeting, but he would return her call as soon as he was free.

"What do we do until then? 'e might not be free for hours and I've got shopping to do." Mrs Podger sat down and huffed her indignation.

"We wait. Let's hope Mr Tewksbury has the answer."

Her phone rang. The screen showed 'Call'. Taking a deep breath she answered it.

"Melissa Carlisle."

"Good morning, Dr Carlisle. I'm Paul Jones and I represent the buyers of New Manor."

"I received your letter this morning." Melissa's tone was very clipped.

"My clients are happy to discuss a mutually beneficial solution to this small problem."

"Your letter was quite succinct, but I don't seem to remember any proposals regarding any solution."

"My clients would be very happy to meet you, say, later today?"

"I'm sorry Mr Jones, today is out of the question."

"Dr Carlisle, you are aware that if you intend leaving your property you will be committing an act of trespass."

Melissa nearly told him where to go.

"Yes Mr Jones." She flipped the phone off.

"What's the matter, Pet?" Mrs Podger asked.

Melissa outlined what had been said, "and what's worse, he sounded as if he's watching us."

"Oh, Melissa, what are we going to do?"

"Mrs P, I've no idea and until I talk to Mr Tewksbury, or William, I can't see any remedy. However, we can at least get out via the farm."

"But why are they doing this?"

Melissa gazed out of the window trying to think why.

"I have no idea."

Melissa opened the second typed envelope. It was from the Council.

"Well, I suppose that's more positive." She flipped the letter onto the table. "We've got permission to enclose the pool and convert the studio."

The phone rang again.

"Birthday greetings, Melissa. How does it feel to have reached the great age of thirty?"

"Thanks Mr Tewksbury, but I don't feel very birthday like."

"I got a rather garbled message saying you're being besieged by the new owners."

"I got a letter this morning, followed by a phone call just now from a Mr Paul Jones of Nesbitt & Green telling me I haven't got the right to drive from here to the road."

"Have you got a copy of the deeds?"

"I have. Furthermore, Jones told me that if I did drive across the estate I would be committing an act of trespass."

"What else did he want?"

"He suggested I met with him and the new owners later today. That was when he implied they would sue me for trespass."

"Have you spoken to William?"

"Yes, but before I'd opened Jones's letter so he doesn't know. My car's far too old to go bouncing over the cart track to the farm."

"For god's sake, Melissa, go out and buy yourself a new car! It's not as if you can't afford it, and don't meet with Jones or anyone from Nesbitt & Co. without me with you."

"What do you think they want?"

"To make you a really stupid offer!"

"Well they can go hang!"

"Come to the office tomorrow. I've got some of the original de Braose documents and I'm sure these will show you have nothing to worry about. In the meantime, either talk to Neil about buying you a car that can deal with any terrain, or if he's busy, I'm sure William will have some ideas."

"Thanks Mr Tewksbury, what time shall I come over?"

"Any time you like. You're probably far more capable of deciphering the hand written charters than I am. Some of them date from the sixteenth century."

"Didn't they all go to the buyers?"

"No. I didn't see they had a right to the original Tudor charters and indentures as these are now well out of date and, in my opinion, more rightly part of the de Braose family documents."

"I'll be at your office tomorrow, Mr Tewksbury."

Melissa sat back feeling relieved by Mr Tewksbury's suggestion, but peeved he thought she was incapable of doing something as simple as buying a car

"Mr P. Can you run me to the station, please? I'm going up to the flat and stuff Mr Jones, we'll go down the drive."

The original charter was dated 1539 and signed by Henricus Octavus Rex. It described the land and buildings as a priory previously owned by the Augustinians and now transferred to William de Braose, 1st Earl of Poultney. It was a beautiful document written in a clear early sixteenth century hand on fine parchment and in very good condition.

A second document detailed more land bought in 1543 and included a map showing the original buildings and the tracks over the land. Melissa recognised the new addition as the area of woodland to the north of New Manor known as Monk's Wood and Monk's Field.

There were more purchases of land over the centuries that meant the Estate had become the biggest in the south of England until the farm was separated off.

"Melissa, have you found anything?" Mr Tewksbury sat down at the table.

"I'm not sure, but I'm curious about this map." She handed him the 1543 document.

"I think we should compare it to an up to date ordnance survey map, Melissa."

A few minutes later they were spreading out a large modern map of the area.

"Look, here's the de Braose Estate and . . ." Mr Tewksbury stood up and smiled, "Melissa, I'm going to enjoy telling Nesbitt & Green just what they can do with their threats of trespass."

Melissa was still studying the new map. "I can't see what you mean."

"Look" the elderly solicitor traced his finger across the modern map. "By the way Mr Jones wants to meet this afternoon."

Melissa continued to compare 1543 document with the modern map, but was unable to see what had pleased her solicitor..

"How does this affect my right of way."

"Melissa, how about I tell you over lunch?"

"Only if the clock isn't ticking!"

"Oh I think we can make it part of our costs so Nesbitt & Green will eventually foot the bill!"

4.30 PM

"So you see Mr Jones, my client won't be committing any act of trespass."

Mr Jones had looked very uncomfortable as Mr Tewksbury outlined the various elements contained in the ancient documents.

"Miss Carlisle . . ."

"**Dr** Carlisle." Melissa stressed her title.

"I'm sorry, my apologies. Dr Carlisle, my clients have authorised me to offer you two hundred and fifty thousand for your property."

Melissa did not know whether to hit him, or laugh. Instead, she said. "Jones, get out."

"Mr Jones, I believe my client is saying we shall see you in Court." Mr Tewksbury rose and ushered the man out of his office.

Closing the door, Mr Tewksbury leant against it and sighed. "It seems there are none so blind as those that will not see!"

"In the light of all prevailing evidence, even I can see that only either the very stupid or the incredibly arrogant would consider pursuing this claim. As for their derisory offer, well . . ."

"Melissa, their arrogance knows no bounds. I'm afraid we will be in Court very soon."

196

2ND APRIL

"William, I've heard that the buyers of New Manor are definitely applying for planning permission for a golf course on 285 acres of the park."

"When did you hear?" William could hear pent up anger in Melissa's voice.

"I received the letter from the Council this morning."

"Lissie, can you get hold of Neil. We're going to have to put our heads together to make a decent objection."

"Also Nesbitt & Green have upped their offer to seven hundred and fifty thousand. Bastards! They're going to develop New Manor into a Country Club, health spa as well as a golf course." Her mobile rang. It was Neil. "I'm just on the phone to William – and I need to talk to you: hang on." She switched phones. "William, bye."

"Neil, have you had a letter from a firm of solicitors called Nesbitt & Green, or the Council?"

"Er no, I wondered if we could talk about dates for the next farm meeting. I'm sitting in a tractor at the moment."

"Well, you need to hear this."

Melissa read him Council's letter.

"This is a disaster. Golf courses are sprayed with all sorts of crap and, with wind drift, that's going to bugger up the farm's organic status."

"What do you think we should do?" she asked.

"Right now I'll get hold of a photographer friend of mine and send him over to you to photograph everything on your land and as much of the Estate as you can get to."

"OK, what's his name?"

"Fynne Duffe. He and his brother Patrick are totally dedicated to the organic movement."

LATER

"Melissa, there's a man here who says he's here to photograph the garden." Mrs Podger called out.

"Mrs P, I'll just be a minute." Melissa was in her study reading up on herbicides. She looked at herself in the mirror and dragged a brush through her hair before emerging to meet the photographer.

"Mr Duffe, welcome to The Old Manor."

"Dr Carlisle, you have a beautiful place."

"Thank you. I hope your photographs will help us stop this ridiculous planning application."

"Ah, the Country Club project. Neil told me. What sort of images are you after?" Fynne Duffe removed his lens cover and took a few random shots of Melissa, the Podgers and the kitchen.

"Without actually going on to any of the land, can we take photographs of what the land is like now so we have a set of decent photographs to file with our objections to this whole sordid idea?" Melissa suggested.

Fynne nodded and continued to click away.

"Everyone will say I'm objecting because of where I live, but I can't see how anyone with half a brain will think this development is a good idea."

"So what're their actual plans?" the photographer looked down his viewfinder.

"Here's their letter. I believe the plans are just outline at the moment. According to the application they're going to change the name to Priory Chase and develop the park as a golf course!"

"It's not the house you're worried about, then?"

"Mr Duffe, houses can be rebuilt, besides New Manor is Grade One listed."

"Do you think there's another agenda?"

Melissa was finding his soft Irish brogue hypnotic. "What do you mean?"

"Well, oi'm a bit surproised that anyone would want to invest in a golf course in this economic climate."

"From what I've seen on their website it's intended for a very exclusive membership of five hundred members paying up to two hundred and fifty thousand pounds a piece. Personally I can't see why anyone would want to pay that sort of money just to play golf!"

"That makes one hundred and twenty foive million reasons to build a golf course!"

"Grief, Mr Duffe, that's a huge amount of money. Surely it can't cost that much."

"Melissa, Mr Edward did say the house could do with a bit of sprucing up." Mrs Podger added.

"Even so, Mrs P, it's not going to cost millions even though it is listed."

"Tell me Dr Carlisle, what's your particular speciality?" Fynne Duffe asked.

"I'm an historian."

Melissa's statement confirmed the photographer's first impression that was she was naïve when it came to commercial motives.

"They've put a lot of detail on the Web." The Irishman sat examining the photographs he had taken in the past few minutes. "How many economically viable golf courses are there that you know of?" Duffe asked.

Mrs Podger was listening intently. "Not that many" she replied.

"Quoite so, Mrs Podger."

"Mr Duffe, are you suggesting there's a deliberate plan for this development to fail?" The idea that anyone would deliberately go through the fuss and expense of a venture for it to fail struck Melissa as bizarre. "With what object?"

"Dr Carlisle, just how many luxury houses do you think would fit on to some two hundred plus acres of beautiful English countryside?"

"Oh no!" Mrs Podger gasped.

Melissa wished William or Neil were here.

"Why would anyone go to all the expense, or even want, to do this sort of thing?" she asked.

"Well, there's a lot of money that needs, how can oi put this, well let's just say, there's a lot of doirty money in the world that would benefit from a bit of washing."

Melissa nodded, hoping she looked as if she understood him.

"What type of development do you think it would be?" Mrs Podger asked.

"It's not so much as how many, but what proice, so fifty or so five acre plots each with a luxury house at between five and ten million pounds plus apiece, you're talking some serious money."

"But the whole of this estate would be compromised." The enormity of the figures was making Melissa's brain ache. "Why would anyone want to set up that sort of plan?"

"I can think of several drug barons and oligarchs who might want to legitimise their cash."

"Mr Duffe, can we just take these photographs before you depress me any further." Melissa's heart sank.

"Dr Carlisle, they probably wouldn't want to live here all the toime. It would be a way of toirning their ill gotten gains from being a bit on the grubby soide, into something that was sparkling whoite. Oi call it the Persil effect." Despite what he was saying, she found Fynne Duffe's soft Irish brogue comforting.

"What's that?"

"Melissa pet, years ago there was a TV advert for a washing powder with the slogan *'Persil washes whiter, and it shows'*, but you're too young to know that." Mrs Podger explained. "Now, if it's all the same to you I need to clean this room, so why don't the pair of you get off and take those photographs."

Melissa took Fynne along the boundaries. They could see men with theodolites and poles marching about taking measurements of the park.

"What do you suppose they're doing, Mr Duffe?"

"Well, if it's a kosher golf course, they'll be plotting how the land loiys so the designer can then sculpt each hole. On the other hand, their measurements could equally be used for measuring plots for houses."

"But we don't know that and the letter says golf course, so until we're told otherwise, we have to accept what's been put to the Council. William is the one you should talk to about all of this."

"William?"

"William de Braose. Your photographs will form a key component of our objections."

"It's a good thing cameras don't recognise boundaries. Do you want me to photograph those guys doing the measuring?"

Melissa was depressed. "Why would anyone build a golf course if they wanted to build luxury houses?"

"Dr Carlisle, all over the country golf courses are failing and then, because they are what used to be called brown field soites, they are land roipe for housing because, unloike proper industrial brown field soites, golf courses don't require an expensive clean-up before building can start. Plus the government's happy because they want the economy to be back in the black as soon as possible and they want construction to lead the way."

"But you have no evidence."

"To be true, but unfortunately I've seen too much of loife not to be touched by just a little bit of cynicism. The sort of profits we are looking at would warrant a primary investment to fail."

"Ugh – that' so depressing! Let's hope you're not correct!"

"Dr Carlisle, have they made you a ludicrous offer for your house?"

"How did you know?"

Fynne Duffe smiled, thinking she was a lovely looking woman, but for all her academic prowess, she was just 'plain thick' in the ways of the world.

"It stands to reason and oi bet they did it the minute they got their hands on the deeds."

"Well I'm not budging. However, please photograph my boundaries just in case they try and take a nip and tuck here and there of what isn't theirs. I suppose I'd better get my own surveyors to detail the boundaries because the only things we have are a series of boundary stones buried deep in the hedges."

Fynne photographed all the ecologically sensitive areas and broad vistas of the surrounding countryside showing how the park sat in the surrounding land.

"Have you known Neil long?"

"To be sure, we go back to school days. You have dormoice on your land, don't you?"

"Yes and Roman snails. Neil's the one with the licences to move them so these bastards either need to get their own licence or get Neil to do it. I've a copy of the ecological survey we've had done in my office, if you want to read it."

"Oi don't expect they'll take much notice of a couple of snails except when the building inspector comes to call."

"That's illegal!"

"Come on Dr Carlisle, these sort of people don't care about wildloife or endangered species, so fluffy dormoice and a few rare snails aren't going to stop 'em."

"I believe there might be archaeological remains, so I'm going to see if I can get a geophysics survey done of my land. My late great aunt's diaries suggest there may be something Roman up here."

"Is there any other evidence for that?"

"No, but it's worth seeing if her diary entry has legs."

"Archaeological evidence is all very good as supporting evidence, but you need to look at the bigger picture and found your objections on what harm this will do to the surroinding area, visually, ecologically and envoironmentally.

Melissa looked at him questioningly.

"Look, Dr Carlisle, the whole of this landscape has taken thousands of years of nibbling by generations of animals grazing it, to become what it is today. It's not something that can be put back in an instant should the bulldozers move in."

"Oh, I see what you mean. I hadn't thought of looking outside the park boundaries."

"And, from our conversation this morning, Oi don't think Neil has thought further than the effect on the farm. Oi've been photographing this county for years and the whole area around here is rare chalk grassland that won't benefit from a monoculture being dumped roight in the middle of it."

"Tell me why golf courses are so bad."

"They scrape off the top soil, then sculpt the various obstacles for the men with silly sticks to knock a toiny ball into an equally toiny hole. The land will then be planted with carefully selected grasses that are manicured, sprayed, cut and tortured to within an inch of their existence."

"So all the cowslips will disappear?"

The photographer nodded. "And everything else getting in the way of the designer, so you can kiss goodboi to any wild flora that might benefit bees, butterflies etc."

"We're surrounded by golf courses. I can think of at least eight in the immediate area. Do you really think the council will grant them permission?"

"Who knows? It depends on how much local objection there is."

"Well, Mrs Podger say this development won't be popular in the village, but what do you mean about the gullibility of the councillors."

Fynne Duffe shook his head. "In moi experience, those who stand for public office are far too fond of hearing their own voices and most of them're control freaks desperate to wield power all in the guoise of working for the public good. Add a bit of glamour with the promise of free rounds of golf at an exclusive club and anything's possible. Oi leave the technical arguments to me brother, Patrick, who spends his time arguing against the more ridiculous aspects of EU legislation. I just provide the photographs for those challenging any of these greedy bastards."

"You don't have a very good opinion of government do you? You're talking corruption, Mr Duffe. By the way, I'm Melissa, to my friends."

"If oi'm going to call you Melissa, then oi'm Fynne."

Back at the house they found Neil sitting talking with the Podgers.

"Neil, good to see you again." The two men shook hands. "While oi was going round with Melissa, she told me you had an envoironmental survey done before the property was sold. The one the developers will have commissioned won't be worth the paper it's written on. Melissa pointed out the Roman snails and told me about the dormoice. If you want moi opinion, you'd be bonkers if ya didn't take a closer look at Monks Wood and Field while you've got the chance."

"What do you mean, got the chance?"

"Well, it's going to take some time for the designer to come up with his ideas, so oi doin't t'ink there's going to be many people about for the next few weeks, which will give us toime to get a further survey done on those specific places."

Melissa opened her mouth to speak, but Neil interrupted her. "I agree Fynne. The developers won't want to hear anything that will prejudice their planning application, so the more evidence we get the better."

"Wouldn't it be unprofessional for the developer's surveyors to produce something that is biased in their favour?"

Fynne looked at Melissa over his mug. "My gut feeling is you would be mad not to take advantage of this lull, but it's your choice."

Melissa looked at Neil for guidance.

"Do you have someone in mind, Fynne." Neil asked.

"I do. Pat David. She's a gooden, if a little feisty, and she's had great experience in court."

"Pat did our last survey and you're right, she's certainly is feisty."

"Well then, that's all roight. Oi don't need to panic about your not having really good ecological and botanical knowledge of what's here!"

After lunch Melissa gave Fynne her copy of the survey to study, then disappeared into her study to make a few phone calls and emerged some time later.

"I rang one of my old professors who gave me the number of the college geophysics department. They're coming next week to complete a survey over my land and any part of the estate that we, or rather they, don't get thrown off. If Hetty's diaries are correct, perhaps we can supply some archaeological reasons to run alongside the ecological arguments."

"Archaeology won't stop them unless you come up with something loike the Fishbourne mosaic, but it moight help to show this is an ancient landscape that desoives respect and preservation."

"Fynne, are you always so gloomy, or do you have to work at it?" Melissa quipped.

"Lookin' on the sad soide means that human nature never surproises me."

"According to Hetty's 1937 diary she and David found pieces of Roman pottery just south of where the pond is."

"Were these ever oidentified?" Fynne asked.

"Again, according to the diary, the British Museum said they were very high class Samian ware."

"Being this hoigh up moight mean you've got a villa." The Irishman speculated, "or perhaps even a temple."

"Oh, that would be exciting. Fancy that, Melissa, a Roman villa right next to The Old Manor." Mrs Podger's original mood was lifting.

"Let's not get ahead of ourselves, Fynne. A few pieces of high class pottery do not a Roman villa make!" Melissa cautioned.

"No, but on the speculation that something important moight be something up here will generate a great deal of publicity."

"Fynne's right, Melissa. People are potty about local history and this would be a great way of starting a campaign against the golf course immediately. The ecology will need careful handling because it is not so immediate. Having something obvious like a geophysics survey done now will capture local imaginations and they will want to know the outcome." Neil brightened at the idea of such immediate events to start a campaign.

"Melissa pet, I think it's a brilliant idea." Mrs Podger could see that Melissa was unhappy. "We can put the archaeologists up here and

204

I'm very happy to sell cake and refreshment for those what want to come and view what's going. The proceeds could all go to a campaign fund."

"Hang on Mrs P. The professors might not want an audience; and we'll look stupid if we find absolutely nothing?"

"It will give us the opportunity to drum up local support so we'd be mad not to get this into the papers." Neil countered. It felt good they were planning something positive.

"OK, I hear what you say, but only if we run the idea of using the professors as publicity past them first." Melissa sat down at the table. "And, Mrs P, we don't know how many archaeologists there will be so I think we limit who stays in the house to the leader of the dig, the rest can camp. By the way, did anyone ring while we were out?"

"Yes m'dear." Mrs Podger. "Mr Tewksbury said to tell you you're in Court next week."

Melissa sat next to Mr Tewksbury at one end of the front bench of Court No 3 of the County Court. Mr Jones of Nesbitt & Green sat further along the same bench next to a tall, slim man with a shaved head. Melissa realised he had to be Nesbitt & Green's client because he was wearing an expensive bespoke tailored suit.

"I'm surprised anyone's turned up. The company's registered offshore and most of their investors are offshore companies too." Mr Tewksbury whispered in her ear.

"Give me what you've found so far and I'll ask Charles Cliffe if he can find out anything more."

"I doubt he'll be able to tell you much." Mr Tewksbury said. "The whole point of taking companies offshore is so the shareholders can remain anonymous."

"Our Irish photographer reckons that all information is available, provided the price is right." Melissa said.

The door behind the Judge's seat opened.

"All rise." The clerk of the court commanded. The Judge took his seat and they all sat down again.

Mr Jones stood and presented his case on behalf of Kuckelimat Baquecks Development Ltd. relating how Dr Carlisle had refused to acknowledge various notices regarding infringement of his client's property rights and had consistently and determinedly continued to trespass over the land in such a way as to prejudice the future plans to develop the park and house. Having presented video footage as evidence he then sat down.

Mr Tewksbury rose. "Your Honour, the property known as The Old Manor was given to my client in 1999 by the late Esther de Braose. Lady de Braose had owned the property since the death of her husband, The Honourable David de Braose, who was shot down in the Battle of Britain on 24th August, 1940."

Melissa liked the way Mr Tewksbury was establishing provenance.

"I suggest that not only was there a right of way established by usage over sixty years by the late Lady de Braose, but also by Dr Carlisle who was gifted the property some twelve years ago and has lived at the property since she was four years old." Mr Tewksbury paused a moment.

"There is further evidence that this claim is spurious. If I can ask your Lordship to consider Exhibit A."

District Judge Pearce extracted the photocopies of Exhibit A from the papers in front of him.

Mr Tewksbury picked up the original 16th century charters. "Examination of documents dating back to the acquisition of the original land in 1539 and signed by Henry VIII demonstrates there are a considerable number of public footpaths across this parkland. Examination of this original map attached to this document shows that the track that now forms the drive to both the main house and Dr Carlisle's property, was developed by the 1st Earl of Poultney in the 16th century. There is a translation of the original Latin attached for ease of reading."

Melissa supressed a smile as Mr Jones's companion flipped his copy to read the translation.

Mr Tewksbury continued: "On the attached Ordnance Survey map (Exhibit B, your Lordship) this track can be seen to continue across the land to the de Braose Farm on the one side of the original boundaries of the Estate, over the main road and up over the South Downs on the other, which identifies it as part of an ancient right of way."

The Judge peered at the documents marked exhibit A, and compared them with the modern map. There was considerable shuffling and whispering at the other end of the front bench.

"Have you anything further to add Mr Tewksbury?" the Judge asked.

"I would like it known that these documents were shown to Mr Jones at the initial meeting with my client and he was given a copy set at that time. However, he has continued with this claim despite having been provided with the evidence now before the Court." Mr Tewksbury sat down.

The Judge leaned back in his chair and looked at the two men seated at the opposite end of the bench.

"Mr Jones, it's abundantly clear that there is not one, but several, rights of way across what you are now calling Priory Chase, formally known as New Manor. From the video evidence presented regarding the alleged continued trespass by Dr Carlisle, it is evident that she and her two companions rarely use the drive. The log you presented shows these three individuals pass over this access an average of eight times a week."

The judge paused to write something. Melissa found the tension unbearable.

"Initially I wondered whether you were going to attempt to establish that the driveway was, in your opinion, a ransom strip as defined by the 1960s precedent. From an examination of these documents, and especially those dating from the 16th century, it is evident that what you call the driveway, and claim is exclusive to the owners of New Manor, is part of an ancient right of way widened by the first earl when he first purchased the property in 1539. It is apparent from this early documentation that The Old Manor would have a right of access, in perpetuity, over the driveway created by the 1st Earl of Poultney. Either your client enjoys wasting the Court's time or has money to burn."

The judge banged his gavel: Melissa jumped.

"I find in favour of the Defendant, with a further ruling regarding maintenance of the public right of way that forms the driveway to both the houses previously called New Manor and The Old Manor House. In view of the fact that The Old Manor is a residential dwelling and will, therefore, not have the same level of traffic to and from the said property, I am setting out that any and all costs for repair or maintenance of the driveway to be born wholly by the company Kuckelimat Baquecks Ltd. Costs for this action to be borne wholly by Kuckelimat Baquecks Ltd." The District Judge banged his gavel.

Everyone rose as the judge left the Court.

"Don't think you've won, Dr Carlisle." The bald headed man who had been sitting next to Mr Jones snarled at Melissa as they left the courtroom

"Are you threatening my client, Mr er . . . I didn't quite catch your name." Mr Tewksbury stepped in front of Melissa.

"de Braose." Tobias walked away, his steel tipped heels clicking loudly on the marble floor.

"Well there's a turn up for the books."

"Mr Tewksbury didn't you recognise him?"

"Melissa, the last time I saw Tobias he had a thick head of hair and was holding a teddy bear! I think you need to chivvy up Charles Cliffe to see what he can find out about that development company."

The geophysicists were strapped into their equipment and walking up and down across the grass in front of The Old Manor.

"Lissie, which one is your professor?" William asked.

"None of them, Clunkhead. These are the archaeologists from Merton College. They will be revealing the results of their latest survey later this afternoon."

"I see Mr P's well in with the man with the digger."

"He's buttering him up so we can dig the new hedges. Neil's got me some container grown plants that can go in now along the edge of the driveway."

"Why?" William asked.

"I want to make an in and out entry just to press the point I have a right of way." Melissa announced. "Could tell me how we can make these hedges part of the whole farm concept?"

"The original farm hedges date from Anglo Saxon times. Do you want the same plants?"

Melissa nodded. "Anything to give the dormice sanctuary."

"You'll be doing more than giving the dormice somewhere to nest. There're lots of other species that'll benefit including a butterfly that lays a single egg in the crux of the thorn of the blackthorn."

"You two look as if you're hatching something." Neil came over to where they were standing."

"Lissie was telling me about the new hedge at the front."

"Yeh, I think it's a great idea. I've got some container grown oaks that can form stand alone trees and a couple of blackthorns we can put in across the front. We can lay the hazel and hawthorn whips later."

"What about adding some crab apples, elderflowers and damsons?" William suggested.

"Sounds like future Springs will be very pretty. You can make sloe gin and hedgerow jam." Neil added.

"Don't look at me for doing anything domestic. That's Mrs P's province!"

"I'll second that, but you do make a great salad Lissie." William teased. "Tewksbury did a great job on KB's claim of trespass. My father must be spitting feathers. I'd've paid good money to've seen his face when he was awarded costs AND maintenance. Are you going to send him the bill for the hedge?"

"No! The hedge is on my land. Since I've got the pair of you here, I think you should know that Charles is doing some delving to find out exactly who's behind Kuckelimat thingamajig!"

"How do we find out whether Tobias still has an interest?" Neil wondered just how the new Earl was involved.

"We can't if the park is an asset of an offshore company. However, I'm sure someone somewhere must know something." William said.

"Fynne said much the same, provided the price was right." Melissa's spirits sank at the thought of fighting faceless companies all based in places far away.

"Talking of Fynne, he's coming over later. He's suggested we keep a photographic diary of everything that happens here and what they're doing on the park." Neil's tone was buoyant.

"How were the cows when they were moved off the cowslip field?" William was sorry he had missed so much.

"It was a very sad day. They seemed reluctant to leave." Neil replied.

"Fynne took some great shots." Melissa added. "There's a particular one of five of the herd walking straight towards his camera, looking very determined. We've had it printed as a postcard."

"Excellent. What about doing a video of the dig to get people walking up the driveway?" William suggested.

"William, this is my home!" Melissa whinged. "Would you mind if we give the archaeologists time to see if there're any results before turning the whole site into a public performance." Melissa turned to Neil. "There's a barbeque tonight if you and Gill are free. The professors are going to tell us what the geophysicists have found."

"Thanks, Melissa. We'll see you later." Neil walked away.

"Lissie, there's clearly something here because why else would they be bringing in a battalion of students and set up this army style camp."

"You'll just have to wait, like the rest of us." The news was more than she had hoped and was unable to supress grinning from ear to ear.

"Lissie Carlisle, you know something don't you?"

"No, no, it's just as much a mystery to me, as it is to you."

210

William picked her up and twirled her round, "If you don't tell me, I'll dump you in the pond."

"If you try, de Braose, you're coming in with me!"

Mrs Podger watched them from the kitchen, glad to see them both so happy.

"Hetty, I can't believe it's a whole year since you left us." She said to herself. "Is there anything you can do to stop this golf course from where you are?"

JUST BEFORE MIDNIGHT

"Well, Dr Carlisle, it seems as if you're living on top of a mass of archaeology. Did you know about that rectangular structure in the middle of the front lawn?" William was lying in bed watching Melissa brush her hair.

"Prof London reckons it may be the Saxon Minster I found mentioned in the Domesday Book, but I'm much more interested in the echoes from south of the pond."

"Why?"

"That's near where I think Hetty and David found those bits of Roman pottery she wrote about in her diary. The echo is incredibly strong and clear, so there's definitely something there. More to the point, it stretches into the park!"

"Ha! Are you going to notify KB Ltd.?" William asked.

"And tell them we've been trespassing? I don't think so! Well, not yet." She climbed into bed and wondered whether she was the only one who had remembered it was the anniversary of Hetty's death. Despite the hustle and bustle all around the cottage and William lying next to her, she felt very alone. William put his arm around her and pulled her close.

"Rabbit, I haven't forgotten. Hetty meant a lot to me too."

The first layers of the dig had produced some Roman, medieval and Tudor pottery. The first trench in the lawn in front of the house had revealed stone foundations set on a south east/north west alignment so the Professors had increased it by a further three metres. The enlarged trench contained a broken stone cross and just outside the walls there were three stone kist burials. Now she had agreed to revealing the whole of what was certainly the Saxon minster referred to in the Domesday Book.

On one side of the incident tent artists were drawing the cleaned artefacts and then passing them down to where they were photographed, placed in labelled plastic bags and boxed. On the other were six computers on a long trestle table where all the finds were being entered into a database.

Mrs Podger was increasing her knowledge with bribes of home made cakes, while Melissa was becoming more and more reclusive and spent much of the time hidden away in her study. She was beginning to resent the intrusion of all these people into the peace and quiet of her home, but if there was any chance of defeating the planning application, she had no choice but to endure their presence.

Now she was hidden away examining the de Braose Book of Hours. There was a full-page illumination for each month and the one for June showed a large house set in a summer landscape.

"Oh my god!" She picked up her magnifying glass and looked more closely at the image. "I wonder?" She picked up her phone and dialled.

"Fynne, sorry to bother you, but do you have a photo of the front of New Manor anywhere, with an oak tree?" Pause "OK, but there's no oak tree. If you could send me that image anyway, I'd be grateful."

Five minutes later she was staring at the two images side by side on the screen. She wondered whether this was another Book of Hours than the one shown in the family accounts.

A knock on the study door interrupted her thoughts and Melissa quickly put her notepad over the Book of Hours.

"Melissa dear, why are you hiding away from everyone?" Mrs Podger gave her a mug of tea.

"Mrs P I'm feeling besieged."

"Oh that's interesting." Mrs Podger looked closely at the computer screen. "Is that a painting of New Manor?"

"Mrs Podger, you won't say anything."

"Of course not, my pet, but why?"

"Not even to William. I need to do a lot more research on this."

"It doesn't look like something Hetty painted?"

Melissa laughed. "Oh no, this is much older than the twentieth century. Look." Melissa lifted the notepad and showed her the original painting.

"Oh my, this looks ever so old."

"It is. Edward gave the book to me last year when." Melissa picked up a piece of paper covered with typing and handed it to Mrs Podger. "Here's a transcript of a document I found in Kew that says Henry VIII visited here in 1542."

Mrs Podger leaned forward looking closer at the image on the screen. "You can hardly see those figures in the original, but on the screen . . ." Mrs Podger stood up. "How do you know who painted it?"

"That's the problem, it's incredibly difficult to tell. Melissa peered at the computer screen and zoomed in closer on the house. "See, I'm sure that's New Manor with the king planting an oak sapling in the lawn at the front of the house."

"Well that tiny image looks just like those portraits of King 'enry in the 'istory books. I remember my art teacher telling me that 'ans 'olbein 'ad come over from Germany and been the first one paint a recognisable portrait of the king." Mrs Podger continued.

"Quite." Melissa sounded slightly distracted. "However, Edward told me he'd found a reference to the Bening family being paid for an illuminated Book of Hours in the 1511 accounts, which means that there are possibly two Books of Hours, unless the first was sold or lost, but to find it I need to look at the de Braose accounts and they're all in Scotland!"

"Is this the sort of thing you spent your time studying?"

"Yes, Mrs P. I know it's not everybody's cup of tea, but I find it fascinating."

"Melissa, I'm glad that someone's looking after our 'istory because otherwise we'd all be mindless chumps believing everything we're told on television or in the newspapers."

Melissa chuckled, warmed by Mrs Podger's loyalty. "Not everyone would agree with you. Lots of people think people like me are over-indulged eggheads."

"Well, I know there was a shrine here when New Manor was a monastery."

"Really, Mrs P! If that was the case then this might be the 1511 Hours."

"Why do you think that?"

"Everybody knows how Henry was desperate to have a son and heir and he divorced Katharine of Aragon, but it's often forgotten that she'd given birth to a son in 1511. Perhaps this image shows Henry visiting the shrine and planting that oak as a symbol of the continuation of the Tudor dynasty."

"Well I never! To think we had Good King Hal here at New Manor, before it was New Manor!"

"It's only speculation, but it is possible. I want to see those accounts and check there isn't another Book of Hours lurking in the de Braose library. However the accounts and the library are now in Scotland. Do you think William would mind?

"You won't go before the 21st will you?"

"No, Mrs P."

"It's been an 'ectic twelve months and I don't think it's going to get much better if the new owners do get planning permission."

"This be could all be academic because it hasn't gone before the Planning Committee yet."

"Somehow I feel we are going to 'ave quite a fight on our hands. Now, do you remember back in 1987 and the night of the hurricane?"

Melissa looked perplexed. "What are you getting at?"

"Well, an old oak in front of the house was blown down in the gale and I think that tree was about five hundred years old."

"I'd quite forgotten about that." Melissa thought for a minute. "Didn't Edward have it made into something?"

"The refectory table and six chairs William now 'as up in Scotland and that small oak table in the summer 'ouse here came from that tree."

"I remember the estate trees looking like matchsticks thrown on the ground."

Much later in the afternoon Melissa and William were standing on a wooden platform covered by a tent.

"This mosaic floor looks incredible. Gramps would have been fascinated by this."

Melissa nodded. "You should have been here the morning they discovered it."

"What happened?"

"One of the students was scraping away after the digger had taken off the top layer and not far underneath she came across some pieces of blue coloured tesserae, then she found a bit of glass mosaic with gold in it. Prof London watched as she scraped away very carefully and then helped her widen the area as she exposed the first complete pattern."

"So it was just like on TV?"

Melissa nodded. "The whole dig came to a stop as she and the Professor exposed more and more of the floor. Fynne stood and videoed the whole thing."

"So our Irish photographer has recorded it, has he?" William was jealous he had missed the excitement.

"Yes, he's been filming the dig most days."

"Brilliant. I spoke with Pat David the other day. She said there's some interesting botany on Monk's Field near the woodland on the ridge. I knew that field was special, but Pat says this particular ancient calcareous grassland should be preserved at all costs."

"When you say ancient, how old do you actually mean?"

"Six thousand years or so. I looked on the developer's website and tried to work out where the various holes and bunkers would be and I think they're planning to put at least a couple of holes on Monk's Field, if not more."

The survey news was exciting William far more than the archaeology. The survey would give him concrete arguments to counter the planning application, but the archaeology was still important as part of their objections even though all these important finds were on her land. It was clear there was an important Roman building that ran into the park and the discovery of the high-class mosaic suggested this could cause the developers a big headache.

"William, do you remember the archive boxes you took up to Scotland?"

"Yes." William wondered what Melissa wanted with them.

"Any chance I can go up and catalogue them?"

"Don't you want to be around to see what else they turn up?"

"I feel as if I'm being held hostage by all these bodies and now we've discovered the mosaic I don't want loads of reporters poking their noses into me, or my life."

"Lissie, I've been thinking. If we get the whole publicity campaign off the ground now, we might be able to sabotage KB's plans from the start. Do you know if Fynne has done anything about creating the website?"

"Oh yes, he was showing it to me earlier this week. He wants you to give it the go ahead to go live and we've got a slideshow that will be in the farm shop showing what it was like when the cows were here and the various rare species that are very specific to this type of grassland."

"You're beginning to sound like an ecologist."

"Don't tease. Fynne's been telling me that we'll lose all the cowslips and the harebells and the all the other plants that make this park so special. He says I'll get the so called 'benefit' of their sprays across the garden because of wind drift."

"Do you want to go to Cremorne is to get away from all of this?" William waved his arm in the general direction of the dig.

"Oh, yes, the boxes. They're important because they have all the accounts since the 1st Earl bought the estate, but we have no idea what else is in them. I can catalogue the contents and transcribe any documents I come across. Who knows what I might find?"

"I'll let Megan know you're coming, but it does mean I won't be able to drop in to see you."

"Scotland's not the end of the world, William."

"Cremorne takes some getting to, once you get past Edinburgh."

"I'm not completely incompetent! You forget, I've driven all over Europe."

"Melissa." Megan stood outside the door of the cottage by the edge of the loch. There was no reply. "Melissa."

Lulu, the Jack Russell, sniffed the doorstep; Megan tried the door, found it unlocked and stepped inside.

"Melissa?"

Lulu sniffed around before making herself comfortable on the sofa. The table was covered in neat piles of paper and Melissa's laptop. Megan looked at the stacks of boxes and wondered how on earth anyone found wading through old documents interesting.

"Morning, Megan." Melissa stood in the doorway drying herself with a towel.

"You haven't been swimming have you?"

"Every morning for the past five weeks. Would you like a coffee?" Melissa wrapped herself in her bathrobe then filled the kettle.

"I came up to let you know that we've got twelve guns coming up tomorrow for the 12th, and wondered if you fancied joining us for dinner at the big house?" said Megan.

"Ah, The Glorious Twelfth." Melissa paused. "Does this mean I have to get done up like a stuffed turkey?"

Megan laughed. "Only if you're planning on being shot like a grouse!" Megan paused, "I would really value you being with us."

Melissa made them both a coffee and sat down on a wooden dining chair.

"OK, I'll be there, puffed and polished like a prize poodle – are you sure you don't want me to wear a tiara?"

Megan laughed. "No the American's are coming next week, so you could break it out then."

Melissa laughed. "Since I've only got my jeans, then I'll be best in the kitchen; and there's no need to be polite about what I'm doing, I've been cataloguing all the documents brought up from New Manor."

"Did you find anything interesting?"

"I did and I wondered if there were any other files hidden away here?"

Megan chuckled. "We have a whole cellar full, plus stuff in the attic. It's all a right mess so it would be great if you sorted it out."

"Just show me what it is you want me to look at. If you give me five minutes, I'll come back with you now."

They left footprints on the dusty steps as they climbed the stairs to the tower room. The views across the loch and the mountains beyond were breath taking. Looking the other way, you could see all the way up the tree-lined drive to the gatehouse. The peaceful hills where the grouse spent their lives hidden in the heather until the Glorious Twelfth, were bathed in sunlight. Melissa wondered what was glorious about this sort of managed carnage, but William had explained that if the moors were not managed the birds would have died out years ago.

He had admitted said that without the fishing, stalking, shooting, weddings and corporate events, the Cremorne estate would not survive. Edward had passed it to him knowing he would look after the people who relied on Cremorne for their livelihood. Over the past six years William had made the estate somewhere exclusive to escape to so now it was a very upmarket boutique hotel and the most repeated comment in the visitors' book was that it was like being invited into someone's home.

Lulu padded about stirring up little dust devils that made her snort and snuffle.

"Melissa, here're the paintings we brought up from the cellar. However, there are more down there, but I can't spare anyone to haul them up here until Monday."

"About how many?"

"Och, I haven't a clue. I only found them a few weeks ago. It was seeing that portrait of your great aunt and her husband at New Year that made me look."

"So the cellar is pretty chaotic?"

"If you could knock that chaos into some sort of order, it would give me somewhere I could use for storage."

"OK, but I'll have to give this room a good vacuum first."

"There's no electricity up here. I'll get the broom."

"Do you have a long extension lead as it really would be better if we could suck this dust up." Melissa was surprised by the lack of electricity in the tower.

"I'll see what we can do." Megan left leaving Melissa contemplating the stack of paintings propped against the wall. There were various other wooden boxes and trunks, an old wardrobe, a table and a chair. If she were to catalogue everything and look at things closely, it would require a more intense light.

Melissa was engrossed in examining a stack of the larger framed paintings.

"Peter's just about to go into town," Megan announced.

"Oh Megan, you gave me such a fright!"

"Have you found anything interesting?" Megan was intrigued that anyone could be so completely absorbed in these dusty old-fashioned paintings in the same way as she had been amused about the mountains of paper Melissa had catalogued.

"It's difficult to see what these are until I've cleaned off the dust, but there are some interesting frames."

"As I was saying, Peter is going into Pitlochry and I've asked him to get another extension lead if you're going to be using this one. There's a socket just by the door on the landing so we're in business."

"Megan, is William aware of these paintings?"

"I think he knows there're here, but as far as I know he's never even looked at them. When he comes up here it's either a quick visit on estate business or he's out on the moor with the gillies and the guests."

"Just out of interest, how much does it cost for a weekend's shooting?"

"It's done on the number of guns so for the three days shooting it'll be sixty thousand for a twelve gun party."

"Blimey, that's a lot of dosh for a weekend's play"

"Most of the City boys don't know one end of a gun from another so the gillies have to make sure they don't shoot each other, or one of us."

"So the birds are really quite safe?" Melissa thought the whole idea distasteful. "Do you get many Americans?"

"Oh yes, and they can usually shoot properly, plus they're willing to pay well for the privilege of hunting on an old estate. More recently we've been getting very rich Russians too and quite often they bring their own evening entertainment! Some of those girls really take the biscuit!"

"How bizarre. I think I'll hide in the attic this weekend. On second thoughts, I think I'll pass on the invitation for dinner tomorrow."

"Oh, don't do that, Melissa. I need some moral support. I have absolutely no idea what's going to turn up with these guys."

"Are you saying this could be Chav City tomorrow night?" Melissa was amused by Megan's need for an ally.

"Aye, you may need to break out the diamonds on Saturday just so you don't look out of place! As a tempter, the reason Peter's gone to the village is to pick up the first of the Cremorne salmon from the smokery so it'll be home caught smoked salmon for starters. I know you don't like the fresh stuff."

"Sounds delicious, but you've got a lot on your hands so I'll be OK sorting this room out."

"Oh no, the beds are done so today is really quite quiet. I'll walk Lulu after lunch to make sure she's not getting bored and it'll be quicker if we both tackle this room."

Soon the tower room was vacuumed, dusted and polished. The table was moved to the south window and a lamp had been found.

"Now Megan, let's take a look at that big picture over there." Melissa pointed to a very large frame propped facing the wall. It was at about eight foot high and five foot across.

"Why this one, Melissa?"

"It's all on its own so I can tell myself I've done a whole wall and I need help turning it round!"

"So this cataloguing stuff isn't all that absorbing, then?"

"Not when it's a project this large."

They pulled the painting upright and away from the wall.

"Hold it there a minute, Megan. I'm just going to give it a quick dust." Melissa flicked the duster gently over the surface.

The painting was heavy and they propped it against the closed door before standing back to take a look at it.

"No wonder this is up here. Who'd want to have a picture of someone being ripped to shreds by dogs." Megan bent to look a bit more closely at the painting.

"Oh my god!" Melissa whispered to herself.

"Why's he dressed up as a stag, Melissa?" Megan turned to hear Melissa's reply. "You OK, hen? You've gone a white as a sheet."

"Megan, I feel sick."

"It'll be all that dust. I'll open a window."

"No, no, it's not the dust."

"Well, I know the picture's a bit gory, but I didn't think it was enough to make anyone feel ill."

Melissa bent closer, moistened the duster with some spit and cleaned the very top corner of the canvas. "Megan, it's nothing to do with the subject matter." She was looking very intently at the brushwork. "Do you have any idea who the artist is?"

220

"No, and I hope you aren't going to suggest we drag it downstairs and hang it on the wall for the guests to ogle."

"On the contrary."

They heard footsteps on the stairs.

"Wait! Don't open the door." Melissa called. Whoever it was stopped.

Melissa manoeuvred the painting so the door could open. "OK. You can come in now."

"I wondered where you two had got to." William gingerly pushed the door ajar.

"William!" Melissa wanted to contemplate this painting for a bit longer.

"It's the Twelfth so I have to be here." He was miffed his appearance was not being greeted with more enthusiasm.

Melissa realised she should have known he would be up for the most important date in the shooting calendar.

"I'll go if you aren't pleased to see me."

"No William, I didn't mean that." Melissa stretched out one arm, the other still holding the large painting upright. William stepped into her one armed embrace and kissed her hello.

"Let's go downstairs, Rabbit."

The painting was returned to face the wall; a closer examination would have to wait until the Laird was out on the moors.

Melissa and William were sitting outside the croft watching the sun change the colour of the heather clad mountains.

"Charles has booked this weekend so he could entertain some senior City people."

"Are they bringing their mistresses?" she asked, curious to see if the weekend was an excuse for hunting of a different sort.

"Some of them might request privacy if anyone phones asking for them."

"Don't they have mobiles?" Melissa thought this request was weird.

"We guys can be just as devious as you women and it may be their legitimate partners phoning us to check on them. Once we had a private detective turn up asking for a specific er . . .," William paused trying to find the right description.

"Lady?" Melissa suggested.

"That will suffice!" he chuckled.

"What will they think I am?"

William thought for a minute. "Do you care what they think?"

"I'm not sure. I'm glad Charles is coming. Do you know any of the others?"

"Charles has given us a list, but I don't know any of them." Melissa's question gave him food for thought. He had never given a thought about any of the women who came with the guns. Some reappeared on subsequent years, others were never seen again.

"William, what can we do to stop KB?"

"We'll fight them all the way through the Courts to Europe if necessary."

Melissa looked at the mountaintops now bathed with a rich golden light; the shadows lower down the slopes were deep purple.

"It's beautiful here, William. How do you ever bear to leave it?"

"Cremorne has a magic to it, but until my father is stopped from destroying New Manor's parkland I won't be able to rest."

"What happens if KB do get permission?"

"Melissa, the idea is not only flawed, it's downright rotten. Pat's latest survey is dynamite. I had a meeting yesterday and I think it will clinch a refusal. There's no way the Planning Officers will recommend permission be granted."

"But . . ."

"Rabbit, let's not talk about New Manor tonight."

"Glad to see you've finally woken up, Clunkhead." Melissa stood dripping water on the doorstep. "Have you made tea?"

"Good morning, Rabbit. How far did you swim?" He threw her a towel.

"Only to the island and back."

William poured boiling water into the teapot.

"I'm picking up the guns from Edinburgh airport at one. Do you want to drive the other car?"

Melissa wrapped another towel round her head.

"No. They'll ask all sorts of questions I'm not qualified to answer."

"Just thought I'd ask. You will be at the big house for dinner, won't you?"

"You don't mind me not driving to Edinburgh, do you? I've only just got the tower room clear of dust and still need to look at what's propped against the wall. Megan says there's a whole cellar full. You never know, I might turn up a Gainsborough or something."

"That would be handy as these legal fights are always expensive." William handed a steaming mug to her.

The cost of fighting KB Ltd had not crossed Melissa's mind.

"But don't worry, Rabbit. Even though the new building regs are no longer as comprehensive as they once were, thanks to a lot of lobbying there's a lot more protection for the countryside in the NPPF than were in the original document, plus the Government have made much about how they are dedicated to protecting the greenbelt. The Council won't allow a load of greedy rich people to have a golf club for their exclusive use."

"Watch it, Clunkhead. Some might call us fat cats. Particularly me, and since my house is right in the middle of the park I'm sure there'll be shouts of nimbyism."

"Lissie, it would be great if you did come up with something, but I'm sure my illustrious ancestors sold off anything valuable years ago. Are you sure you don't want to join the shoot?"

"I'm better off listing old documents as I haven't a clue what to do."

"You will be at dinner though?"

"Peter's cooking is way better than mine, unless you want to escape and come here?"

"Come here, Rabbit. I don't want to lose any minute I might have you to myself, especially if you aren't going to be on the hill with me."

Despite the late arrival of the Jersey flight, the various guests assembled in the drawing room at six for pre-dinner drinks.

"Melissa, how lovely to see you. William told me you were here cataloguing the family archive." Charles Cliffe kissed her on both cheeks.

"Charles, to be more accurate, I was cataloguing everything that came up from New Manor until yesterday. I've only just started on the stuff at Cremorne." Melissa sipped her champagne. "How's Suzie?"

"She sends her love and is currently in London. She hates shooting and since I hate shopping, it's the perfect solution."

"How's Peregrine's research into the Underground Hospital coming along?"

"He and Scott are in Germany rooting around in the archives, so no doubt he'll be in touch if he finds anything. They asked to be remembered to you"

"Charles, I've been thinking about the fight we might have with the developers of New Manor."

"Yes, William told me they're applying for planning permission."

Melissa chewed her lip, thinking. "Since I have a substantial stake in the farm and my house is right in the middle of the park, is there any way I can underwrite the legal costs without William knowing?"

"Why would you want to be anonymous?"

"William's very traditional and I thought that if the people behind Kuckelimat Baquecks can hide behind offshore companies, then perhaps I could be anonymous too."

"If permission is granted and you fight it, the costs could be substantial."

"Charles, I have a ridiculous income that I don't spend. The farm belongs to both of us and I don't contribute to the farm in any tangible way, so by providing the money to cover the legal costs means I have made some contribution."

"I think you should tell William."

"Why?"

"Male pride."

224

"That's precisely the reason I don't want to say anything."

"I suggest you put it to him in the same way you proposed your idea to me. It makes sense and he knows you can afford it." Charles patted her shoulder. "Melissa, the privilege of wealth means you can afford to underwrite the legal costs, but hopefully it won't come to that."

"That's the point, Charles. It's all changed with the NPPF."

"The what?" the banker looked perplexed.

"The National Planning Policy Framework. Basically the government has ripped up the existing planning regulations and 'simplified' them, so heaven knows what will happen. William doesn't think permission will be granted, but I'm not so sure. Fynne Duffe is fairly despondent about the whole thing and feels we're going to have a fight on our hands. Fynne reckons the costs could run into hundreds of thousands of pounds and the farm can't carry that sort of expense. I don't think William could either, not without mortgaging Cremorne; but I can."

"I still think you should tell William what you want to do."

"Charles, thank you. I'll think about what you said, but for the moment, if we need it, please make any donation anonymously."

"We've read the various objections and heard Mr de Braose's concerns. The archaeological evidence supplied from the dig on the land owned by Dr Carlisle has demonstrated the importance of this land as a place of habitation over the past two millennia."

William squeezed Melissa's hand.

"It is possible the whole area is of archaeological importance." The chairperson continued.

Melissa felt her spirits rise, pleased the archaeology appeared to have swayed the Planning Committee.

"Now I ask the Committee to vote."

Melissa held her breath: six votes against and six votes for. She could not believe how anyone would vote to destroy such a beautiful place.

"I see I have the casting vote," Councillor Pilkington paused, "I have considered the Planning Officers' recommendation that this application be denied. However, I believe this application would be of considerable benefit to the area so, provided a wider geophysics survey is undertaken to establish whether there are further archaeological remains present, outline planning permission is granted."

Horrified gasps rippled through the public gallery. Melissa burst into tears, William clenched his fists. Neil and Gill held each other's hands. Mr Podger leapt to his feet and shook his fist at the Chair.

"You fossilised old trout, you've known this Estate since you was a child. What backhanders 'ave you taken so you can sit there and ignore the recommendations of your own Planning Officers, not to mention ignoring all our objections? Do you really think this golf course is going to be any good for any of us? Do you?"

"Mr Podger, sit down. You aren't helping by calling anyone names." Gill tugged on his sleeve and he sat down.

"No, I know, but at least I feel better Gill!"

"Why?" Melissa asked, hoping someone would give her an explanation.

"Time for a council of war. I suggest we adjourn, Lissie." William squeezed her hand. "Don't worry, there's a long way to go yet before the bulldozers come in."

"Jones offered a stupid amount for The Old Manor and when I turned him down, he said I'd be sorry."

"You didn't tell me he'd threatened you."

"What's this, have I missed something? It's your bloody father again, isn't it William?" Neil was gritting his teeth in fury.

"No – it was the solicitor acting for Kuckelimat Baquecks."

"What sort of a name is that?" Gill asked no one in particular.

Outside the Council chamber there was the buzz of sympathetic voices asking what could be done to stop this development.

As they walked down the stairs William looked at the number of people thronging the foyer of the Council building and clapped his hands to get everybody's attention.

"Ladies and Gentlemen, thank you all for your support. If you have any ideas, or would like to join our campaign to fight this application, please contact the de Braose farm. So please, let us have your ideas."

There were murmurs and nods of approval.

"What sort of a name is Kuckelimat Baquecks anyway?" A voice echoed Gill's question.

"Sounds foreign to me" someone else replied. "I bet it's one of them oligarchs what's bought it."

"Well?" Mrs Podger was standing in the doorway. "What 'appened? From the expressions on your faces I'd say it didn't go well."

"No. Despite the Planning Officers recommending no, the Councillors were split and the Chair went against accepting their recommendation, so permission was granted by a casting vote. But the public gallery was full and there's a lot of support for us."

"Mr P called the Chair a fossilised old trout!" Melissa said.

"Oh well, I'm not surprised if that's what they decided! Any fool could see we don't need another golf course? The county's awash with 'em!"

"Quite so, Mrs P. We are going to put up a fight, but right now I think we all need a stiff drink!"

"Right," William said loudly. "I've registered The Campaign for New Manor Ltd with Companies House as a company limited by guarantee and so far Melissa and I are directors, but I'd like you, Neil and Gill, to join us. Fynne's put together a press campaign to take advantage of local public feeling and to attract more support through social media."

"What are we going to do?" Gill asked.

"First we apply for this planning application to be called in by the Secretary of State and it will, hopefully, then be subject to a Judicial Review. I've already set up a bank account for donations."

"Can we join too?" Mrs Podger asked.

"Mrs P, I'm so sorry. You've lived here far longer than any of us and here I am ignoring you."

"Mr P and I were 'oping you wouldn't mind us being part of anything you're doing to fight the developers."

"Until we've gone as far as we can we'll need all the help we can get. Do you want to be a Director?" William leant forward and took her hand realising he had made a big blunder by not including the faithful Podgers.

"Oh no, William. We just want our voice heard, but I do want to be involved in some way and I know Mr P does too." Her husband nodded his agreement.

"What else did your barrister chum say?" Neil asked.

"He reckons we have a more than good chance if we can get a Judicial Review."

"How do we get that?" Melissa and Gill chorused.

"We need to get as many local people as possible to write to the Secretary of State. That's where we can use the Farm shop for distributing leaflets and addresses, plus we must use social media to get our campaign recognised by other protest groups. If we can get all those who were at the planning meeting to put pen to paper, then we will be doing well."

"But don't we need grounds for a review?" Gill asked.

William nodded. "I'm convinced the planning process was compromised. I know the NPPF is untried and open to interpretation, but, if you read it, there are major protections for greenbelt and of course, the European regulations for the protection of the various specific sites with red list species have to be followed. As we know, our 'esteemed'

Planning Committee have ignored everything the Planning officers put in their report, including ignoring their own local environmental management plan, not to mention any European legislation."

"Are you thinking the Committee were nobbled?" Mr Podger was a man of few words, but voiced what everyone else was thinking.

"When it's a hung vote it's usual for the Chair to vote with the planning officers' recommendation and, as we all know, that didn't happen." William replied.

"I went to the developer's publicity evening up at the house, not that they wanted to let me in because I clearly wasn't the sort of person they want. Our money's just as good as anyone else's, but I got their message." Mrs Podger told everyone as she put a plate of cheese straws in the middle of the table.

"You never told me!" Mr Podger poured himself some cider.

"I don't have to tell you everything, Mr Podger."

"I thought about going, but couldn't bear the thought of seeing New Manor full of a bunch of greedy tosspots." Melissa said.

"Well, they've already got the electricians in and the majority of the re-wire is done. The proposed interior scheme is, I have to admit, quite nice."

"There are very strict regulations regarding a Grade One listed house, so I hope none of the Tudor panelling is going to be compromised, or any of the original plaster ceilings." William asked.

"One of the spokesman said they were abiding by all the Grade One regulations."

"What else did you find out?" This time it was Gill who spoke up.

"I got the impression that investors weren't exactly flocking to sign up and 'and over large cheques. I 'eard several posh people saying they thought the scheme was ill advised."

Melissa's heart sank. "William, if the whole golf course idea fails, will they be able to go for permission to build houses all over the park?"

"No."

"Why not?" Melissa asked.

"Because the estate lies within the greenbelt." William replied.

"The Planning Officers' recommendation was no, plus the Council's own local plan says that no more golf courses are to be built, so what guarantees are there that the Councillors won't vote for what's not supposed to happen, yet again?" Mr Podger asked, pouring himself another glass of cider.

"Because they can't."

"You seem very certain of that, William, but I agree with Mr Podger." Neil gazed into his beer.

"What happens next?" Melissa asked.

"Is there room for another one?" Fynne asked from the door. "Oi thought oi'd come and tell you what oi've been up to." He reached across the table and poured himself a glass of wine. "The website is getting a lot of hits. Oi've also been talking to the local CPRE man who wants to meet you tomorrow, William, you being the solicitor an' all. All the history stuff was fantastic, Melissa, but despoite all the objections by the locals, the various big NGOs and various local bigwigs, this Council seems to've been bedazzled boi the PR put out by this shower of greedy wankers."

Fynne surveyed the despondent group sitting round the table.

"So far you've all played it boi the book, but KB Ltd don't understand level playing fields or gentlemanly behaviour, so you're going to have to get tuff." His Irish tones were noticeably stronger than normal.

"I hear what you say, Fynne," William replied. "However, I think we should continue playing with a straight bat, so we are going for a JR through the usual channels."

"Well, dat's all very well, William, but a Review takes toime and I bet you the developers will crack on as soon as they can, which is a shame as there're the hoibernatin' dormoice and, if I'm not mistaken, Melissa is particularly fond of the little bloighters. Oi've looked at the plans the designer submitted and they intend to rip out some of the old hedges next to the public footpaths so unless you can produce some evidence of dormoice nesting in these, they're going to be the foirst thing to go."

Melissa sat comparing the tough, craggy features of the photographer, who looked as if he was chiselled from the land he photographed, against William's face. Fynne's face was tanned and weather-beaten, whereas William had classical, well-proportioned features. They were a complete contrast in looks, temperament and talent, and both were dedicated to the campaign.

230

"But I'm sure they're in the survey and dormice are red listed, so they can't." Melissa paused. "Can they?"

"Take a look for yourselves," Fynne rolled a copy of the outline plan on the table, "the hedges either side of the footpath just past the gatehouse halfway to the road are not included on the desoign for the golf course and, I hate to say this, they're not mentioned in **any** of the surveys oither." Fynne sipped his beer and waited for someone to say something.

"They've got to submit an action plan and the Council are obliged to let us, or rather Melissa, know when various things are happening." William said.

"Has anyone done a search to find out who the shareholders in KB Ltd are?" Neil asked.

"All I've been able to find are a bevvy of offshore companies." William replied.

"Where are these companies registered?" This time it was Gill. Melissa sat and listened carefully.

"There's a holding company for KB Ltd registered in Jersey, and there are shareholding companies registered in the Caymans, Isle of Man and the Bahamas." William outlined what he had found out.

"So can we find out who these people are?" Melissa asked.

"Melissa, unfortunately we will only know if someone breaks client confidentiality, which will cost them their job, reputation and possibly more."

"That's very depressing William, not to say cowardly!"

"If you want moi opinion, Oi tink you should keep an oi on the Council's website to see when the Action Plan is submitted, but the good news is that it's coming up to Christmas so nothing much is going to happen until the Spring. But don't think KB are going to aboide by the rules, because they aren't."

"Thanks, Fynne. Ever the optimist!" Melissa said.

William stood up, determined to lighten the mood.

"Well, folks, the New Year promises a fight, so we have a couple of weeks to get ourselves fit enough to take these people on." However, I do have some good news."

Everyone looked at William.

"The campaign has received an anonymous donation of two hundred and fifty thousand pounds. This is fantastic as it means we can employ the best legal minds for the fight ahead."

"Do you have any idea who it might be?" Gill asked.

William shook his head. "All I know is that I received two hundred and fifty thousand pounds into the campaign account and an email saying that if we needed more, then to apply to the email address given."

"How did they know how to make the payment?"

"The details for donations are on the website and as Fynne said, the website is getting lots of hits

It struck Melissa as ironic that she was behaving in the same way as KB Ltd.

William knew the next few months would be tough for those at The Old Manor House, but if Melissa came up to Cremorne at least he could make Christmas and New Year fun and, more importantly, remove her from Fynne's company.

2013

"Happy 31st birthday, Lissie." William's voice sounded very distant.

"You sound as if you're at the bottom of a treacle well. Where are you?" Melissa looked at the bedside clock.

"Unfortunately, my darling, I'm on my way to Brussels. Couldn't tell you before because I didn't know myself. I'll be back at the weekend."

"I had hoped we could have dinner, but since you're clearly busy elsewhere, I'll spend my birthday on my own!" This was the second time he had disappeared without telling her. She was beginning to feel that the Honourable William de Braose was taking her for granted.

"Lissie, I'll make it up to you at the weekend, I promise, but it was a last minute decision and the client wants their hand held."

"OK, OK," Waves of nausea were engulfing her. "I'll see you on Saturday. Don't be late!" She broke the connection and just made it to the bathroom before throwing up.

"Melissa, Happy Birthday." Mrs Podger entered carrying a tray laden with a birthday breakfast and a pile of post. Melissa climbed back into bed feeling very sorry for herself.

"Was that William on the phone, dear? I forgot to tell you he telephoned yesterday to say he wouldn't be able to make it down today. He's said he's off to Europe."

"Yes it was. Mrs P I wished I'd known as I've just been beastly to him."

"I'm sorry my pet, I should 'ave told you earlier. Ring 'im back; I'm sure 'e'll understand."

"Mrs P, William can wait. I think I've got a bug. Thank you for the lovely thought of breakfast, but I'm not sure I'm able to think about eating."

"What on earth are you talking about?"

"I've just been sick and I feel dreadful."

Mrs Podger felt Melissa's forehead. It was not clammy and did not feel hot.

"Well you've eaten just the same as us. Try a cup of tea and some dry toast."

Melissa nodded, preferring to curl up and hope the world would go away.

"Mrs P I'll try some tea, but I think I'm going to stay in bed."

"Alright my ducks, but moping won't do you any good. Far better to be up and doing, than lying around like a sick dog."

"Thanks Mrs P." Melissa lay curled up, waiting for the nausea to stop. Betty scrabbled at the duvet asking to be allowed up on the bed.

"Oh Betty, nothing seems to be going right!" Melissa picked up the little dog who made herself comfortable under the duvet so her nose poked out. "This is all getting rather horrid." Betty woofed softly in agreement then snuggled closer. "Now Betty, what do you suppose we have in the post?" Melissa slit the envelopes with a knife and started with the typed envelopes first. One of them was the Action Plan for the commencement of the building of the golf course.

"Oh pooh! Life just gets worse! I hope William comes home soon. He'll know what to do!"

"Neil, why do they have to spray the fields and why do they have to rip up the park to make a golf course?"

"I don't know anything except what I've discovered on the web, but their designer is supposed to have won awards and be environmentally sensitive."

"Have you seen that bloody fence and those poxy trees right on my boundary. Very soon I'm not going to be able to see Chanctonbury Ring."

Neil looked at the map where red lines defined where the various holes were planned.

"Melissa, have you got a copy of the latest survey handy?"

"Yes and I've got the one submitted by KB. I emailed a copy to William, but I don't suppose he's had time to look at it yet." Melissa stood up and paced up and down. "What I hate is not having someone to shout at."

Neil laughed. "Why not print off a photo of Tobias and throw darts at him?"

"Neil, don't you find all this offshore stuff a bit sinister?"

"In that you can't see a target?"

Melissa nodded.

"Unfortunately Melissa, today's battles aren't as simple as the ones back in the Middle Ages. I know William's going to be talking about the environmental aspects of the campaign with Pat in Brussels."

Melissa's stomach knotted. Why had William failed to mention that Dr David was also in Brussels? She tried to concentrate on what Neil was saying.

"See here, Melissa. There are a hundred and eight species listed on Monk's Field and most of them are endangered. There is a symbiotic relationship between red ants, a specific plant and the Large Blue Butterfly, which was long thought extinct in this part of the world. Doc David has discovered that Monk's Field has a colony of the ants, the necessary flora and what's more, to clinch it, yesterday someone came into the farm shop with photos they took last year of emerging Large Blue butterflies. Evidently, several butterflies have been sighted by other local enthusiasts and I'm promised their digital photos to add to our survey."

"So, if this butterfly was thought extinct, does this mean we can slap something legal on the developers to protect the field?"

Neil nodded. "William will know exactly what to do."

"Well, I don't pretend to understand half of what's being said in the various legal arguments, but even I can see there is a vast difference between their survey and ours. Do you think we will get a Judicial Review?"

"We can but hope. Are you all right, Melissa?"

"I just can't seem to throw off this bug." Melissa nodded. A wave of nausea hit her out of the blue.

"Perhaps you should see the doctor?"

"Mrs P suggested the same."

"Did William say when he was coming back?" Neil asked.

Melissa looked at her watch. "In about three hours time."

LATER

"How was your trip?" They were lying in bed.

"Rabbit, come here. It was OK. We presented a paper at the conference and it seemed to be well received."

"I thought you said the client needed their hand held."

"I was working on behalf of a client, yes, at a conference. I thought I told you?"

"Did you have a look at KB's survey?"

"I did. I've given it to Pat."

"Oh, was Pat with you?"

"Yes. I thought I told you?"

Melissa felt as if her heart was bursting out of her chest.

"Lissie, my darling," he paused, "I'm not going to be able to come down quite so often for the next couple of months. The vast difference between the two surveys shows exactly how KB are withholding information that might prejudice their case."

Melissa listened to him ramble on about how she was important for watching what was happening in the park and could she keep a daily log of what, who and where things were being done.

"Mrs Podger is probably better at all of this, William. Have you had a minute to look at my report of what you have at Cremorne?"

William fell silent.

"I'm sorry, Melissa. I haven't." He replied, deciding honesty was the best policy.

Melissa rolled over, trying hard not to cry.

236

"Rabbit, what's the matter?"

"I spent weeks listing every single piece of paper and every item in every box that came up from New Manor. Then going through your cellars and listing every single painting and document, their relevance and importance and you haven't even had the grace to read the Executive Summary."

William looked suitably abashed. "I thought you'd tell me if there was anything of importance."

"William, admit it, you weren't interested. You haven't even said thank you!"

"I'm sorry."

"No, you're not. You're so used to being Laird, you take everything around you for granted – including me!"

"Rabbit, what's got into you?"

"Got into ME? Suddenly it's my problem! I'm the one who's going to have bulldozers right next to me and visitors traipsing all over my garden looking at your new archaeological visitor centre. I put months of work into cataloguing and authenticating various documents and making suggestions regarding the conservation of some of the paintings and you don't even say thank you; and you ask what's got into me! William de Braose, do you know how hurtful that is?"

"I've said I'm sorry, Rabbit."

"And that's another thing. Why do you keep calling me Rabbit? My name is Melissa. Calling me Rabbit is as if I'm some construction of your own fantasy!"

"Well, I'm sorry if my pet name for you causes you problems." William was out of bed and dressing. "Pet names are a sign of affection. However, you don't seem to want me about, so I'll bugger off until you've cooled down."

His hand was already on the door. Melissa got out of bed and wrapped herself in the kimono.

"And what's more, William, perhaps a little more honesty about who you were with in Brussels with would have been nice."

"So that's what this is really about. Pat and I are colleagues, nothing more."

"You're so engrossed in all the stuff that makes you look the big City lawyer you haven't had the grace to even look at the work I've done for you."

"You're being ridiculous, Melissa. I told you, Pat and I are colleagues."

"You talk about your other colleagues, but you failed to tell me about Pat. What am I to think?"

"Melissa, you're being irrational."

"Don't tell me what I'm being – get out." Melissa screamed and picked up his car keys and throw them at him. "Go and see Pat. I'm sure you'll be very happy together."

"For Christ's sake, Lissie. Stop it."

"Stop what" she shouted. "I suppose I'm supposed to ignore it whenever you decide you need a week away with someone else."

"I give up. I'm too tired to argue. I'm going back to London and I'll call you when you've calmed down." William slammed the door behind him.

She heard him reverse his car and drive away far too fast.

Back in bed, she sobbed herself to sleep.

"Dr Carlisle, can you tell me the date of your last period?"

"Er, 10th December, why?"

"Your symptoms suggest you are pregnant."

"Pardon?"

"You seemed surprised. We can do a test now and have the results in a few minutes."

Several minutes later Melissa watched a blue cross appear in the positive box.

"This must be a mistake."

"From your records I see you missed your last appointment for your contraception jab." Dr Bell turned the computer screen so Melissa could see the No Show entry. "Dr Carlisle, I take it this is an unplanned pregnancy."

Melissa nodded. "I need time to think."

"If you wish to terminate . . ."

"Oh no, its not that. I can't believe I've been so stupid as to miss my appointment. What date was it?"

"You were booked in on 31st August."

"I was in Scotland."

Melissa was grateful the doctor was presenting her with facts, not raised eyebrows or tut-tutting.

"If you leave a termination too long you will have to go through a full labour. On the other hand, we can arrange for you to talk to an adoption agency if you want to continue with the pregnancy, but don't wish to keep the baby."

"No. NO! I couldn't do that." She paused and looked at the woman opposite her. "Doctor, I can more than afford to bring up a child on my own. What I might do is to take a prolonged holiday. If I were to go away, would you be able to let any practice I registered with have a copy of my notes. It wouldn't be forever; just a few months."

"Provided you let us know who and where, I can't see a problem." Dr Bell leant back in her chair. "I've signed up to the Campaign, by the way. The thought of a golf course on the park is awful."

"Oh thank you. I'm told the developers are going to spray the land adjacent to mine starting the 24th March and, in light of my condition, I don't fancy being about with all that chemical in the air."

"I completely understand. Where are you thinking of going?"

"I'm not sure, but possibly the Channel Islands."

"Well, just let me know the name and address of the medical practice and I will forward your notes on to them."

Melissa rose to leave. "Thank you, doctor. I was beginning to think my feeling as rough as I do was something terminal."

"You should begin to feel better within a couple of weeks as the first three months is when the hormones are going wild, but they will settle down soon. Just do everything as normal, but avoid alcohol and any unpasteurised cheeses."

"Thank you."

Outside Melissa sat in her car. What would Mrs Podger think? She had not commented on William's absence, but she had given Melissa a long hard look.

She dialled Neil's number. "Hi, Neil. I've decided leave the battle in yours and William's more than capable hands."

"Melissa, you're vital to the campaign. Why the sudden change of heart?"

"It's not a change of heart, it's more a case of not being able to stand seeing the bulldozers rip the park apart. I'll be at the end of a phone, so it's not as if I'm not contactable."

"OK, but where're you going?"

"Tomorrow." Melissa pretended she had mis-heard him.

"Blimey, that's quick. Have you seen William?"

"Yes – he's gone back to London."

"Will you be at the Board Meeting on the 24th March."

"Neil, you don't need me there. Charles will be over and you all know I've no idea about farming or finance, so Charles can use my vote as he sees fit."

"Where are you going?"

This time there was no getting away from Neil's question.

"I'm needing some space, so I'd prefer not to say."

"Have you two had a row?"

"Bye Neil. I'll give you a ring." She clicked the off switch on the phone and checked her voice mails: nothing from William. She dialled again.

"Hi Suzie, it's Melissa."

"Melissa, how lovely to hear from you."

Melissa paused, wondering how to phrase her next question.

"Suzie, the developers are about to move in and make my life a misery so I've decided to take a long holiday while William fights them through the Courts."

"Are you coming to the island?"

"Yes, and I wondered if you could help me find somewhere to rent for about a year."

"Darling, come and stay with Charles and me.   When do you want to come."

"Tomorrow?"

"Gosh, just time enough to make up your bed."

"Thank you, Suzie."

Melissa drove up the drive slowly and parked in the garage. She felt as if she were putting the car to bed.

"Well, Melissa. What did the doctor say?" Mrs Podger wore her worried look.

"She thinks I need a break, so I've decided to go to take a holiday."

"Melissa," Mrs Podger paused, not wanting to appear intrusive, but wanting to know why William was not at home. "Melissa, have you and William 'ad words?"

Melissa clenched her jaw in a vain attempt to stop bursting into tears.

"Oh, Mrs P, we had a terrible row and he's gone."

Mrs Podger put her arms around the younger woman's shoulders. Melissa cried as if her heart would break. "And I've just discovered I'm pregnant!"

"Oh my, Oh Melissa 'Ow did that 'appen? Oh sorry, that's a stupid thing to say." Mrs Podger was visibly shaken. "There, there my dear. I'm sure it's just a lover's tiff."

Melissa sniffed loudly and blew her nose. "He doesn't know and I don't want him to either, Mrs P. You've got to swear to keep my secret."

"You're going to Jersey to have the babe, then?" Mrs Podger made a random guess about where Melissa might be going.

Melissa nodded. "I've already spoken to Suzie Sampson and she says I can stay with them for a bit, but I need some time on my own."

"Do you love William?"

This question brought on another flood of tears. "But he doesn't love me. He's not been around much so it's obvious he's found someone else, so I'm going away to work out what I want to do with the rest of my life." She sobbed.

Mrs Podger was not sure of the logic of Melissa's plan, but agreed a holiday might be a good idea. She promised she would not breathe a word of where Melissa was, or why, to anyone, but pointed out that she would have to tell Mr Podger something.

"I'm relying on you both to look after The Old Manor. William doesn't have to put up with the bulldozers or the pesticides on his boundaries day after day. I couldn't bear seeing the land being torn apart. He wanted me to take pictures and keep a daily log of what's going to happen."

"Well I'll do that. If it means we 'ave more ammunition for our fight, I'll keep a daily dairy. When did you say they're starting work?"

"24th March." Melissa's sobs were lessening.

"'Ow are you getting to Jersey?" Mrs Podger's practicality exerted itself over her shock at Melissa's news.

"I'm going to fly. Do you think Mr P would run me to the airport tomorrow?"

"Book your flight, then we'll sort out 'ow you get to the airport."

"Suzie, do you think you could help me find a property to rent?"

"Well, darling, after our conversation yesterday I spoke with Charles and he tells me that one of your own is about to become vacant."

Melissa sighed with relief.

"Charles didn't tell you which one, did he?"

"I believe it's your grandfather's house out at St Ouen's. Daghorne Ffrench's bringing your property files over and he seemed to think there was quite a lot of furniture in store."

"That would make life so much easier if that is the case."

"You might want to buy your own bed. He said the house has been let for the past five years to one a hedge fund manager while he found a suitable house to buy."

"It took him five years?" Melissa was surprised by the length of time taken to find something that appealed to his tastes. "He must be incredibly fussy."

"He found the property relatively quickly, but it needed a considerable amount of renovation and I believe he's had to employ people from Germany. I've been told the kitchen is something to die for! He's only down the road from you, so perhaps you might manage a wee peeky sneaky view at some time." Melissa was amused by Suzie's curiosity about something as mundane as a kitchen. "And I can give you the number of a great decorator, if you want one." Suzie continued.

Despite her emotional life being in turmoil Melissa felt comforted by Suzie's interest in helping her make a home.

"'Ello William. Are you all right, my ducks. You're looking a little peeky."

"Mrs P she's driving me insane. Lissie won't answer my text or emails and now she isn't here." William paced up and down like a caged lion.

"I'll make you a cup of tea." Mrs Podger noted he had several days beard growth and looked as if he had not slept.

"Did she tell you we've had a row?"

Mrs Podger handed him a mug of tea and put a plate of biscuits and his favourite fruitcake on the table. "Yes, she did."

"It's my fault. Did she tell you I hadn't looked at her report on the cataloguing she did up at Cremorne?" Mrs Podger nodded. "And has she told you what's in it?"

"William pet, it pains me to see you both so upset."

"So where is she?" William threw himself on the sofa and lay looking at the ceiling.

"I don't know." Mrs Podger was not looking at her.

"Has she just taken off?"

"She 'as and asked me to keep a daily diary of everything that 'appens when the developers move in."

"I've been a fool and now even you don't know where she is."

"'Ave you now looked at that report she did for you?" Mrs Podger noted William had not touched the biscuits or his favourite cake.

"I have. It's comprehensive and beautifully presented. I'm so ashamed that I didn't even look at the summary." A tear trickled down his cheek. "Mrs P, what do I do?"

"First of all I suggest you get a good night's sleep. I know there're some clean clothes of yours in the wardrobe so why don't you 'ave a good long soak before supper and then get a good night's sleep."

"Won't Lissie be furious if I stay?"

"What Melissa doesn't know won't 'urt 'er and the bed's made up."

"Did she say how long she's going to be away?"

"William, Melissa can't live with the bulldozers on her doorstep, so she says she's taken 'erself off to try and clear her mind."

"That sounds as if she's going to be away for the duration."

"Yes, she did say that she would be away for as long as it takes. 'Owever, if you want my opinion she's gone away to lick her wounds from your tiff. Don't give up on 'er, just give 'er time."

"She's the reason I'm doing this."

"But did you tell her that?"

"No. I assumed she knew."

"William, faint 'eart never won fair lady, so you 'ad better make sure KB Ltd are stopped. At 'eart, she's a country mouse wanting to be left in peace and quiet."

"Do you think she'll be in touch?" William was grasping at the hope that Melissa had not disappeared forever. "And what if I fail? What if we don't get a JR and the golf course goes ahead, what then? Will she come home after course is built?"

"I don't know, and I don't think Melissa knows either, but if she's in touch then I will tell 'er you've been down. Do you want me to give 'er a message?"

"Can you tell her I'm sorry?"

"I think that's better coming from you. Now William, go and 'ave that hot bath. Supper will be about an 'our. Mr Podger will be pleased to see you. We've both been that worried about the pair of you."

William got up and gave her a big hug. "Mrs P, will it all be OK? Will she forgive me?"

"William, I 'ope so, but both of you need to do a lot of thinking about what you want from each other."

Mrs & Mrs Podger, William, Charles, Neil and Gill watched as the sprayers started rolling across the parkland right next to the fence separating KB's land from Melissa's ten acres.

"How soon do you think we'll get news of whether or not we'll get our judicial review?" Neil asked.

"Hopefully, soon. If not I've got a senior member of Chambers looking at whether or not the Council have broken planning law and before you ask, it's going to take time."

"If you ask me, and so far nobody 'as, this Council is as corrupt a bunch of bastards as ever there was." Mr Podger sniffed his contempt. "This'll be the last time this land will be covered in cowslips. Bloody travesty! It's about time they were put out of office."

"Well, Mr Podger, that's the longest speech you've made since our marriage vows!" Mrs Podger announced.

"And I'll 'ave a lot more to say when those bulldozers start!" Mr Podger turned and stomped back to the house.

"I don't think I've ever seen 'im this angry." Mrs Podger sighed. "I'll go and make us some coffee before you 'ave your Board meeting."

"Mrs Podger," Charles walked beside the despondent woman. The others stood watching the sprayers. "Here's a letter from Melissa. I have to say I'm a bit surprised by her behaviour." Mrs Podger took the envelope and slid it into her pocket.

"Melissa never 'ad what you might call normal teenage years, so 'as never had the rough and tough tumbles of the 'eart. 'owever, she's completely misread William."

"Do you think the situation's irretrievable?"

"Well, that depends on a lot of things and most of all, what 'appens 'ere. Any'ow, 'as she found a place to live?"

"Yes, and I'm sure it's all that in the letter."

JERSEY

"Thank you so much for all your help, Suzie. I wouldn't have known where to start."

There had been all sorts of boxes in storage with books, pictures, pieces of furniture, lamps, cutlery, crockery and various knick-knacks. There had been some lovely very dusty antique pieces that had been restored with some elbow grease and polish.

Suzie had marshalled a veritable army of decorators, carpet fitters and removal men with the efficiency of a sergeant major and now the two women were standing in Melissa's newly painted Jersey home.

"Did you know Peregrine and Scott have asked me to translate the documents they photographed in Berlin?"

"Charles is worried about what you and the boys will unearth. There's still a lot of ill feeling about the Occupation and he doesn't want it to affect the bank in any way. You know what people are like; they can take offense at the most odd things."

"Yes, but I haven't started translating yet, so the whole thing is hypothetical."

"Have you heard anything from Mrs Podger?"

Melissa went very quiet. "They started spraying today. This year the cowslips won't bloom and they've already ripped out the hedges where I know there were hibernating dormice, but unfortunately our, and their, ecologists failed to survey them. At some point the developers realised the hedges belonged to them and ripped them out before we could object. Those hedges had been there since Anglo Saxon times and in one afternoon they were gone to make way for a stupid golf course."

"Oh Melissa, that's awful."

"But there's another reason I want to be away." Suzie waited for Melissa to continue. "Will you promise to keep a secret?"

"Yes, of course."

"I'm pregnant."

"I suppose, from your sudden departure from England, William doesn't know?" Suzie raised an eyebrow, whether in question or surprise Melissa was not sure.

"Please Suzie, don't say anything. I want to have my child here, away from everything that's going on in the UK."

"I take it you and William aren't talking then."

Melissa shook her head. "The official story is I'm in Europe doing some research. Mrs P is sworn to secrecy as I don't want him knowing anything about the baby."

"Will you tell Charles or do you want me to?"

"He might be my financial advisor, but he was also my father's best friend and the nearest thing my baby will have to a grandfather other than Mr P, so I will tell him. I just didn't want to do it the minute I arrived on the island."

"He'll be back from the board meeting later and hopefully with some news about the JR."

"The lawyers don't seem to realise the need for speed."

"The Old Manor is in good hands with the Podgers so you just concentrate on having a baby." Suzie considered that if Charles was to be a surrogate grandfather that would make her a surrogate grandmother.

"Suzie, will you come with me for my first scan?"

"Well I never thought I'd see the inside of an ante-natal clinic again."

"Thanks for coming with me, Suzie. I've no idea what this is all about except that today we could find out what sex my baby is."

"Do you want to know?"

Melissa thought for a minute. She wondered whether the fluttering in her stomach was wind or the baby moving.

"Dr Carlisle?" A nurse stood in the doorway and looked around the waiting room.

Melissa and Suzie were shown into an examination room where a white-coated middle-aged woman stood up and held out her hand.

"Good morning. I'm Dr Godwin. Tell me Dr Carlisle, are you a medical doctor or a proper one?"

"I'm a medieval art historian, Dr Godwin, so useless at anything medical."

Dr Godwin smiled at Melissa's diplomatic reply. "If you'd like to hop up on the bed we'll have a scan of baby."

Melissa rolled up her jumper and wiggled her jeans down past her hips. Dr Godwin picked up a large plastic bottle;

"Now this jelly is quite cold." She warned, depositing a dollop of blue goo on Melissa's stomach. Melissa's sharp intake of breath indicated just how cold the blue gel was. Black and white squiggles were appearing and disappearing on the screen as Dr Godwin passed the rollerball of the sensor over Melissa's stomach.

"From your notes I see you're approximately sixteen weeks." Dr Godwin continued rolling the sensor across Melissa's abdomen.

Suzie bent forward for a closer look.

"This is so much better than when I was pregnant and the doctor had an ear trumpet to my tummy." Suzie declared, watching the screen and wondering how anyone could understand any of the squiggles.

"Diagnostics are so much easier with ultrasound. It's used in all sorts of medical . . ." Dr Godwin paused and rolled the sensor back across Melissa's stomach more slowly this time.

"Is anything wrong?" Melissa's voice trembled.

"No," Dr Godwin flipped the sensor across to the other side, then back again. Suzie held Melissa's hand, bracing them both against bad news.

"Dr Carlisle, you're carrying twins."

LONDON

"The application for an injunction against the continued development at Priory Chase is granted. Work is to cease immediately. Furthermore, in view of the importance of this case the request for a Judicial Review is granted." The judge's gavel came down with a bang.

"All Rise." The clerk commanded as the judge left the court.

William tried hard not to smirk unlike their barrister, Richard Berwick QC, who was grinning from ear to ear.

"Richard, well done; thank you. Round one to us." William extended his hand to the bewigged barrister.

"The opposition doesn't look too happy. Is that your father?" Berwick asked.

William did not turn round.

"It is, but it appears he's taking a back seat here."

"Who's the front man then?"

"I haven't a clue, we're still working on trying to find out just who's invested in KB."

Richard Berwick snorted with amusement. "Good luck finding that out. Any closer to finding out who your anonymous donor is?"

"Nope. Can't trace a bank account or the email."

The barrister raised an eyebrow. "They must have money to burn, or be really dedicated to the campaign."

"At the moment I'm just glad they haven't asked for it back. I'm dreading your bill for today's appearance."

"De Braose, when we win it won't be costing you anything."

"I just wish Lissie were here." William muttered softly.

"Who?"

"Sorry Richard, Melissa Carlisle is one of my fellow campaign directors. She's owns fifty per cent of the farm and The Old Manor House in the middle of the park is hers."

"OK, so she's got a vested interest in this case."

"KB gave her notice to quit, which was daft since she owns the property outright. Then, when they found that wasn't going to work, they made her a ludicrously low offer, which she refused. Then they tried to argue she didn't have a right of way to the road."

Richard wondered why someone with so much at stake had taken herself off.

"Come on, Richard." William continued. "I owe you lunch."

Outside the Courtroom the two opposing barristers nodded to each other. William heard the unknown KB representative on his phone.

"Yes, you heard me moron; stop work. I don't care if you are in the middle of digging out a bunker! The man paused. "Are you incapable of following a simple instruction? If you don't stop, we're in contempt of Court so unless you want to pay the fine yourself, STOP WORK NOW, DICKHEAD!"

"Perhaps you'd like to get hold of someone to make sure they're not waiting until the end of the day." Richard suggested, but William was already dialling.

"Neil, can you take a trip up to where KB's men are and make sure they've stopped work." He paused. "Yes, we've been granted an injunction and it is to be implemented immediately. Can you ask Gill to email Charles and Lissie to let them know, oh and don't forget the Podgers." William turned back to his barrister and they made their way out to The Strand.

"Richard, when do think we'll get notification of the hearing?"

"In view of the injunction, I don't think it'll be long. KB will probably ask for it to be expedited. Any news about the company set up?"

"All we've been able to find out is that a whole load of offshore companies have invested in this caper."

"That's a bother, William! I'm interested in who's going to be representing the Council. You and KB have deep pockets and the JR will be against the Council who have to use public funds."

"Well, let's wait and see. Who do you think KB will appoint?"

"I would've thought they'll probably try and get hold of George Nigra. He and I cross swords regularly."

"So, the battle of the legal Titans will continue with the fight for New Manor?"

"You could put it that way William, if you were cynically minded!"

"It's good news about the injunction." Charles sat down in his favourite chair. "I understand the hearing could well be listed within the next eight weeks and all work has stopped."

"Charles, that's brilliant. I have to confess I haven't checked my emails." Melissa had accepted Suzie's invitation for supper. "What convinced the judge?"

"Those digital photos of the large blue butterfly taken last year had the GPS, date and time on them, which was irrefutable evidence. Evidently Berwick was magnificent in the way he explained to the judge just how this butterfly was so important. Now work has stopped, will you be returning to England?" Charles asked.

"No, Charles. The truth is, I'm taking some time out to sort my head out. I'm pregnant."

Charles took his time considering his reply. "I take it William doesn't know?"

"No. I don't want him to feel honour bound in any way and I'm more than financially able to afford to look after my babies."

"Babies!" Charles was not sure he believed his ears. Suzie put a large bowl of salad down in the middle of the table.

"Yes dear, she's having twins."

Suzie's matter of fact attitude helped Charles recover from his initial shock.

"But you don't need to go through with this pregnancy, Melissa."

"Charles, what if Rosemary had taken that route? There would be no William; and Hetty didn't have to take me in and bring me up; I could have gone into care, so there was never any possibility of a termination."

"Have you two had a tiff?"

Melissa took a deep breath and told him about Pat David.

"Have you asked William about her?"

"I didn't need to. He took her to Brussels for a conference. She's an ecologist and understands his world far better than I do, plus she knows all about rare species. I only know about researching old manuscripts. If William had looked at my catalogue of what he's got up at Cremorne, he might not be doing what he's doing now."

"What do you mean?" Suzie asked.

"If William had taken the time to read it he would have known he has the means to fight the development without me. However, since he clearly hasn't been interested enough to look at what I spent all last summer cataloguing, I asked Charles to put some funds into the campaign anonymously so the best possible legal brains could be hired."

"Sorry, Melissa, you've lost me."

"I believe he has an unknown version of Titian's Diana and Actaeon in the tower,"

"What?" Charles was astounded. Suzie just listened.

"Plus, when I was rummaging around in the cellar and opening all sorts of boxes and suitcases, I came across a portrait on vellum which needs very specific research."

"But you must have some idea of who it it's by or of?" Charles asked.

"I am not sure, and it needs the relevant artistic authority look at it, but there is some very significant handwriting on the reverse of the sheet."

"Melissa, you can't sit there and not tell us. We promise we won't tell anyone. Anyhow, who do I know in the art world?" Suzie was intrigued.

"Suzie's right, Melissa. How can I help if you don't tell me?" Charles was racking his brains to think which artist might have 'significant handwriting'.

"If I tell you, and you tell William, then he will know I'm here."

"William doesn't have to fight this application," Charles added, "and there are ways and means of asking him about the result of the cataloguing you were doing up at Cremorne last August. In case you've forgotten, I was there too!"

"I know he doesn't have to continue the fight, but he will because of the farm. He believes passionately in the organic movement and the sprays used on golf courses means the farm might well become contaminated by wind drift."

"Melissa, who do **you** think this vellum thingy is by, and what's so significant about the handwriting?" Suzie's curiosity was getting the better of her.

"I'm not sure. I took photos of it and sent it to my prof. He wants to see the original, but he thinks I may have found a sketch of da Vinci's 'Lady with the Ermine', with da Vinci's notes on the back. He was left-handed and wrote backwards. But you mustn't say anything, Suzie. It's such an important find if it is, and we don't want anyone trying to steal it; and William doesn't even know he's got it."

Her revelation left her two hosts speechless.

"Don't worry darling. We won't." Suzie promised.

"That he's fighting KB for you hasn't crossed your mind?"

"Charles, if William were doing it for me, why did he take another woman away to a conference over a weekend?"

"But Pat David is an internationally renowned ecologist."

"It was my birthday and he didn't even send me a card."

LATER

"Suzie, I get the feeling Melissa looks on me as a surrogate father?"

"She said as much earlier, but I'm not sure I'm ready to be a grandmother!"

"Do you think there's any merit in William and Pat?"

"I don't know. Perhaps Melissa is being overly hormonal, but if I'd made as significant find as an unknown Titian, let alone a da Vinci, in your attic and you admitted you'd never even looked at the results of the work I'd spent weeks doing for you, I'd be very peeved. If you then capped that by forgetting my birthday and going off to Europe with another woman without telling me, I might decide to rethink our relationship."

"Does Mrs P know?" Charles wondered.

"We should respect Melissa's wishes and not say anything about her being here to anyone. How do you feel about being a grandfather again?"

"Old!"

Melissa took her time getting up from her desk. Her early morning nausea had virtually stopped, just as the doctor had predicted and she was beginning to feel more human. She had just finished translating the set of documents Peregrine and Scott had unearthed in Berlin and she reached for the telephone.

"Good morning, Peregrine."

Peregrine Daghorne Ffrench smiled at hearing her voice.

"Good morning, Melissa. What can I do for you?"

"It's more what I have done for you. I've finished translating all the German stuff."

"Anything of interest?"

"Perhaps you and Scott might like to come for supper and I'll give you the transcript."

"How about we pick up a takeaway?" The thought of one of Melissa's salads on a cold, wet April evening was not Peregrine's idea of a cosy supper.

"OK – could you make it Thai, with lots of chillies?"

"Yep. We'll be up about eight."

The past few days had passed in a flash. Melissa mused how the daffodils would be out at The Old Manor, but here they were already over. Melissa took her secateurs and went into the garden to tidy up the dead heads. She could not remember what Hetty had told her about what to do after daffodils had flowered. YouTube had all sorts of differing suggestions and videos of what to do. The leaves flopped everywhere and looked messy so she folded them over in and twisted an elastic band round each bunch.

The garden had rose beds and a large lawn and Melissa pruned some of the bushes for some time before deciding she did not know enough to get the roses under control and certainly did not have the energy to push a lawnmower up and down. She hoped Suzie could recommend a reliable gardener.

Her house was situated in the middle of the greenbelt of the northwest of the island. There was a cluster of small shops within walking distance, but the main benefit was it was quiet.

Mrs P was keeping her informed by email of everything that was happened back at The Old Manor House. Evidently the Visitor Centre was attracting lots of visitors and the campaign was gathering strength. The local press were doing a diary on the dig, with pictures of new finds and details of how to become involved in this great new local find. Mr & Mrs Podger were as important to William as they were to her and she thought it odd Mrs P never mentioned him.

Seeing Fynne's photos of the scraped landscape made her cry, so she had not opened anything from him that had an attachment. She recognised she was sticking her head in the sand, but it was too painful viewing his woeful images of destruction even though work had stopped.

She had read Pat David's comprehensive report on Monks' Field and Wood. Despite the SSI status of this part of the estate, William did not trust KB to respect anything contained in any regulation and it was Dr David's report that had got them the injunction.

Her mobile rang. It was Neil.

"Melissa, I'm glad I've caught you. I thought I should let you know that we've had to allow limited work on the park."

"Oh no! Why?"

"William said that it was too high a risk to keep the injunction over the whole park as it could blow the costs through the roof, but the injunction still holds for Monk's Wood and Field so the large blue butterfly is safe."

"Any news when the Review will be heard?"

"William's trying to find out and the minute we know, I'll let you know."

"Neil, you were lucky to get me on my phone, so email's probably best."

"OK, will be in touch. Bye."

Melissa wondered how much more damage would be done to the greater acreage of the park before the High Court got to grips with the review.

The letterbox flipped noisily. A large white envelope lay on the doormat. There was no stamp, just a typed label with 'M Carlisle'. Melissa took the envelope into the kitchen and slit it open. There were several sheets of neatly printed information. At first she wondered what she was reading then realised the pages listed the names of the individual shareholders of Kuckelimat Baquecks Ltd and its holding company. These were not only the shareholders, but also the directors of the Jersey companies and every single company in each offshore haven.

She sat at the kitchen table considering the information in front of her. The name Dryden Developers Ltd jumped out at her. According to this list, the company was wholly owned by DD Holdings (Jersey) Ltd and the principal shareholders of the holding company were Julian and Barbara Pilkington. Dryden Developers had tendered for enclosing the swimming pool at The Old Manor, but Melissa had thought their price too high. She did not think her not accepting that estimate was likely to have had anything to do with KB Ltd. and the development of New Manor.

Melissa wondered how they fitted in to the jigsaw. Like Hetty, she found the pursuit for money for its own sake, weird. The irony of that thought made her laugh. Perhaps she should ask Peregrine what her current income was. The costs for running both The Old Manor and the house here were not huge. She thought being filthy rich made being miserable a lot more comfortable than if you were stony broke, and being rich meant she would be able to concentrate on bringing up her babies.

Babies! Two little lives growing together. She looked at the photo of the scan and could just make out the two spines. Dr Godwin had asked if she had wanted to know the sex of each child, but she had opted for an old fashioned surprise. She rubbed her tummy wondering how large it would become.

Her attention returned to the papers on the table. How was she going to get this information to William?

Peregrine and Scott arrived with the promised takeaway full of chillies. They plied her with questions as to what she thought about their research.

"I'm impressed. Were you aware of the way the Nazis interpreted Hitler's *Mein Kampf* when they got into power?"

"Yes. It became a bloodbath within a matter of months of the first executions, with Heydrich and Himmler ordering the Einsatzgruppen to eradicate the Jews completely." Scott piled rice into his bowl.

"Well, here you are." She handed them each a copy of her translation of their photographed documents. She picked at her supper while the two men poured over her text.

"NO!" Peregrine and Scott reached the end of the translation at the same time. "I can't believe it! We've done it."

"Yes. It might not be an architectural blueprint, however you have found the original orders from Reinhardt Heydrich, countersigned by Heinrich Himmler, to develop the islands as the ultimate death camp for eradicating all those who were deemed imperfect. The later correspondence between Himmler and Eichmann is not only mind blowing, it's the sort of historical discovery that historians dream of, but you should consider whether the world is ready for this information. Even though it's nearly seventy years since the end of the war, it's still within living memory. You should give it considerable thought before publishing anything. However, it's a great piece of research."

"Melissa, there's an irony here."

"How so, Peregrine?"

"Today's the anniversary of Hitler's suicide."

They continued to debate their theories and it was a couple of hours before she produced her anonymous sheaf of papers.

"Do you know if anyone's going to London?"

"Why?"

Melissa handed over the lists.

"Bloody hell!" Scott could not believe his eyes.

"Good grief. Someone wants to see this development crash and burn." Peregrine was astounded by the breach of confidentiality.

"Who do you think it might be?" Melissa asked.

"Well it's neither of us! You say it was just pushed through the letter box."

Melisa nodded. "Do you think it's kosher?"

"Without researching the companies, I can't say and even then I'd have to shoot you if I did." Peregrine told her.

"I suggest you let William have it." Scott suggested.

"If I send it to him the envelope will have a Jersey stamp and I don't want him to know where I am."

The two men exchanged looks.

"At some point you will have to talk."

"But not yet." Melissa was quite emphatic.

"How long do you think the JR will take?"

"Scott, I don't know, but I've got other things on my mind and I'd rather stay out of the limelight. I've got a lot of thinking to do, especially if the JR goes against us and the development goes ahead. I want to try living here and see how much I miss The Old Manor.

"Charles says the developers are scraping back the topsoil and sculpting the landscape on the less sensitive areas of the estate." Peregrine replied.

"Mrs Podger said the same thing and added that it looked like a moonscape. I can't believe William has allowed any part of the injunction to be lifted." Melissa added.

"When do you think you'll get a date for a hearing?"

Melissa shrugged her shoulders.

"Well, whatever's happening in the UK, we really appreciate having you here." Scott patted the pile of carefully typed pages in front of him.

"Melissa, I've got to fly to the City tomorrow" Peregrine offered. "I could post the envelope there. That way it would have a London postcode and no one would connect the information leak with the island."

6TH JUNE

ROYAL COURTS OF JUSTICE, LONDON

From her position up near the judge, Mrs Podger was able to see every face in the public gallery as well as the barristers and the court officials.

William looked up at her and winked; she smiled encouragement. Fynne Duffe and Pat David were sat two rows behind. Fynne's photos were a major part of the Campaign's submission, as was Dr David's analysis of KB Ltd.'s environmental survey.

The authoritarian atmosphere inside the Royal Courts of Justice was overwhelming. From the outside they looked incredibly old, but a quick search on the Internet had revealed that they were actually Victorian. It did not matter who had built them, Mrs Podger thought were very splendid and a suitable icon of British justice. The wood panelled courtroom reminded her of the library at New Manor.

"All rise." The murmurings ceased and everyone stood. The judge entered and took his seat.

William and their barrister sat at the front bench to the Judge's right; the Council team was seated opposite the judge with an elderly barrister sitting next to two of the Council Planning Officers. The substantial legal team of Kuckelimat Baquecks Ltd. were to the left. Neil had shown Mrs Podger photographs of the barristers so she recognised their man, Richard Berwick and George Nigra who was representing KB Ltd. Both men oozed success and their wigs and gowns were crisp, in contrast to the Council's barrister whose battered wig looked as if he had sat on it and his gown looked as if it had been slept in.

The judge was a very dapper man and his red robes underlined his authority. Mrs Podger wondered how the barristers could spend two days arguing what, in her opinion, was a very clear-cut case. William had tried to explain that it was a challenge of the process, not the detail, of the way planning permission had been granted. Mrs Podger thought this sounded like legal semantics.

William resembled a younger, thinner version of Lord Edward and, despite William's hair needing a trim, she thought he was very much the young aristocrat.

The door at the back of the public gallery opened and Tobias slipped on to the rear bench. There was a clear family resemblance between him and William, despite Tobias being as bald as an egg.

Mr P hated London and had used the excuse that someone had to keep an eye on The Visitor Centre to make sure no one came into Melly's garden. Mrs Podger was taking careful note of what happened so she could tell him later.

Mr Justice St Claire cleared his throat and addressed the court.

"As I understand it, this case concerns a conflict between private developers and public campaigners. The interested party, Kuckelimat Baquecks Ltd., seek planning permission to develop an exclusive private golf with clubhouse facilities and health spa in the South Downs. The campaigners, The Campaign for New Manor Ltd., wish to prevent such a development in an area of protected landscape of national importance. Am I correct?"

Richard Berwick, the Council's barrister and George Nigra all stood and confirmed that this was so.

"Very well then. Mr Berwick, I understand you are acting for the Claimant. Proceed." The judge waved his hand and the occupants of the courtroom waited with baited breath.

Berwick addressed the bench.

"My Lord, the estate totals approximately 475 acres. It comprises a main house, originally known as New Manor, but now called Priory Chase, together with substantial outbuildings all set in parkland and semi-natural ancient woodland. The whole estate is within the South Downs area of outstanding natural beauty. Twenty acres are areas of great landscape value, which we understand, are to be considered shortly for inclusion within the AONB. The Estate includes a fifty acre field of uncultivated chalk grassland known as the 'Monk's Field', which is a UK Priority Biodiversity Action Plan Habitat and has the designation criteria of a site of special scientific interest. Monk's Field (on which it is proposed to put 6 golf holes) abuts an adjacent EU classified special area of conservation, which is another triple S I. This total area lies adjacent to the de Braose Farm, a substantial organic farm of 1000 hectares."

"Mr Berwick, for sake of clarification if you are going to use acronyms I take it AONB is area of outstanding natural beauty and you will be referring to an area of great landscape value in a similar short form?"

"Yes my Lord. The area of great landscape value will be referred to as the AGLV."

Judge St Claire wrote a note. "Thank you Mr Berwick. Continue."

"Kuckelimat Baquecks Ltd. applied for planning permission to develop New Manor and the surrounding estate into an exclusive clubhouse and spa complex together with an 18-hole golf course. The application was lodged under cover of a letter dated 18th September. The application sought planning permission in the following terms:

The use of New Manor and its existing associated buildings as an exclusive clubhouse health club and spa: provision of an 18 hole golf course, practice facilities, clubhouse, car park, maintenance facility and swimming pool.

Kuckelimat Baquecks Ltd also applied for listed building consent to make alterations to New Manor, a Grade One listed building, to make it suitable for use as a clubhouse. They submitted detailed evidence including reports from architects, golf course designers and various environmental, water and other technical consultants. The total cost of the scheme was estimated to be in the region of between £40 and £60 million.

The proposal requires a departure from the Council's Local Plan and Core Strategy."

"Mr Berwick, similar to the various acronyms used to described the surrounding land, would it be easier to refer to the interested party as KB Ltd?" The judge asked.

"Thank you, my lord, it would."

"In which case, please do so." The judge then looked at the interested party's barrister and asked. "If anyone can furnish the Court with an explanation of the name of this interested party at some point, I would be extremely grateful." He waved his hand for Berwick to continue.

"Thank you my Lord. The planning and environmental designations and policies affecting the application site are legion. They can be conveniently summarised as follows:

The whole site lies within the South Downs AONB. This is a national designation, which confers the highest level of protection in relation to landscape and scenic beauty. The site is adjacent to another triple S I, which is a special area of conservation, of both English and European importance for nature conservation. There is an eight hundred metre buffer zone associated with this SAC, which covers much of the southern half of the site. The site includes Monk's Wood and from our

262

own ecological survey, undertaken before probate was granted, we have identified that this area houses three red list species and a number of species on the amber list.

Monk's Field comprises chalk grassland which is a habitat identified as a biodiversity action plan priority habitat and is considered to meet the requirements for designation as a site of national conservation interest. The application site falls within a biodiversity opportunity area. Last year the large blue butterfly, thought to be extinct in Britain, was sighted emerging from a chrysalis. Digital photographic evidence is included showing GPS, date and time. The presence of the endangered large blue is of major importance. From this discovery alone, it is evident that this is a site requiring close protection.

A significant part of the parkland comprises areas of archaeological importance and includes designated archaeological sites.

The building of New Manor is described as a Grade I listed building and forms an important part of the nation's cultural heritage. The original part of the house dates from the twelfth century when it was an Augustinian priory and was listed in the Valor Ecclesiasticus as having an income of £500 per annum: the land and buildings were bought by the de Braose family in 1539. Monk's Wood and Field were acquired in 1543 with more acreage being acquired in the early seventeenth century. Development of the house took place during the Tudor, Jacobean, Georgian and Victorian eras and the building contains important architectural features from all of these periods.

On the subject of golf courses, there are eleven established golf courses in the immediate area. Recently a new course has been opened within a ten minute drive from the site in question. More generally, this part of the South Downs is very well served with golf courses. New Manor borders the counties of Sussex and Surrey and the combined number of golf courses in these two counties is in excess of two hundred and ten, many of which are of championship level. From the marketing information put out by KB Ltd, it is apparent that membership of this proposed golf course is for a moneyed elite with the number of members being limited to five hundred. It is alleged that membership of this club will be by secret ballot and will cost anything up to two hundred and fifty thousand pounds."

There was an audible intake of breath from people sitting in the public gallery.

The judge leaned forward. "Mr Nigra, is this so?"

Mr Nigra conferred briefly with the man sitting next to him then rose.

"I am told it is, my lord." The Judge scribbled some notes. Richard Berwick took a sip of water.

"Continue, Mr Berwick."

"Thank you, my lord. According to recognised standards of provision, there is no overriding need to accommodate further golf courses in the district. In considering proposals for new courses the protection of the district's Green Belt and countryside are considered to be of paramount importance. According to the Council's own local plan, applicants proposing new courses are required to demonstrate that there is a need for further facilities. New courses are likely to have an impact on the District's landscape because of their extensive size, formal appearance, considerable earth works and new buildings. Under their own local plan, the Council have a duty to ensure that proposals for golf courses do not reduce the distinctiveness and diversity of the local landscape.

Development of existing, and proposals for new, courses have to be considered against their impact on the landscape, any archaeological remains and historic estates; sites that are important for nature conservation and the extent to which any proposal makes a **positive** contribution to these interests. The Estate has a considerable number of bridleways and the main drive is itself a public right of way, as was proven recently in KB Ltd -v- Carlisle when it was shown that the main driveway has been part of an existing ancient bridleway that was widened by the first Earl during his initial development of the original monastery lands in the sixteenth century.

In advance of the relevant planning meeting of the Council's Development Control Committee, the Council's planning officers prepared a detailed report and an addendum report analysing the application in light of the national planning policy framework (NPPF). Their report recommended refusal of this application. The Executive Summary described the application as follows:

"The proposal is a substantial and complex application in a very sensitive location within land designated as Green Belt, being made up of Areas of Outstanding Natural Beauty, Sites of Special Scientific Interest, a Special Area of Conservation buffer zone

and an area of high archaeological potential. The site also falls within an Area of Great Landscape Value and includes Scheduled Ancient Monuments."

Within the planned development are serious breaches of adopted policies in the Council's core strategy, the local plan, The South Downs management plan and national guidance.

The planning officers recommended refusal of KB Ltd.'s application for planning permission was because the proposed golf course in this highly exposed and sensitive landscape would be *"seriously detrimental"* to the visual amenities of the locality; would fail *"to respect or enhance"* the landscape character and is contrary to the aims of Core Strategy Policies of the South Downs Management Plan.

The Council's Development Control Committee met in December to consider the matter. Council members objecting to the scheme proposed a motion that the planning officers' original recommendation of refusal should be supported and the application for planning permission be rejected. The motion to reject this application was eventually defeated by a majority of one vote, cast by the Chair. Permission was granted, subject to certain minor conditions.

My Lord, we challenge this planning permission on the following grounds:

Ground 1: breach of Green Belt policy requirements;

Ground 2: failure to demonstrate "need" for further golf facilities in breach of Policy;

Ground 3: breach of national and European policies on protected landscape;

Ground 4: failure to have regard to impact on European Protected Species of any of the various categories

Ground 5: failure to consider the optimum viable use of New Manor as a residential dwelling.

Ground 6: failure to give adequate reasons."

Having finished his opening speech, Richard Berwick sat down.

George Nigra stood up, flipped his gown back off his shoulders, placed his thumbs in his red braces and took a deep breath.

"My Lord, this challenge has no 'locus standi' because the Claimant, a private company limited by guarantee, was only formed after the grant of permission. The Claimant has never made any representations during the planning process itself. I further submit that it would not be unjust to refuse the claim since, by forming a limited company, the objectors are seeking to gain unfair costs protection."

Mrs Podger looked at William. She had no idea about what the barrister was talking about, but she could tell by the twitch in his cheek that William was furious.

"My Lord," George Nigra continued, "Mr de Braose has no other interest than sour grapes that his father has chosen to sell the family estate."

"Mr Nigra," the judge looked at the barrister over his glasses, "in my view it is KB Ltd's objection to the Claimant's standing that is artificial and unreal. Proof of active participation in the process of objection is not a sine qua non to standing, but merely strong evidence that such persons will ordinarily be regarded as aggrieved. Certain directors of the campaign, such as Dr Carlisle and Mr & Mrs Neil Hamon live in houses that once formed part of the greater part of the Estate, not to mention the concerns of the board of the De Braose Farm Ltd. represented by The Honourable Mr de Braose. These individuals can certainly be considered to be aggrieved as they live and work in the area and were actively involved in the objection process. It would not be unreasonable to consider Mr De Braose's interest as both a shareholder and director of the farm, which provides considerable employment in the area. Taking all this into consideration, there is nothing unfair or improper about a group of aggrieved individuals forming a limited company to bring a claim. Therefore, it is my opinion that The Campaign for New Manor Ltd has more than sufficient interest to bring a judicial review of this matter."

Mr Nigra sat down. The man next to Mrs Podger grunted something unintelligible under his breath and scribbled some notes in shorthand.

The Council's barrister stood and spent the next three quarters of an hour huffing and puffing and putting the various reasons as to why the Committee had decided to go against their own Planning Officer's recommendations.

"Poor bugger, he's having to defend the indefensible!" The man next to Mrs Podger muttered under his breath.

Mrs P looked at Neil and Gill. They were looking determined, but not unduly depressed. William was scribbling notes.

"Er, um," The standing barrister shuffled papers in front of him, "excuse me my Lord, I . . ."

George Nigra handed him a note.

"I believe the section in question is Section 1, my lord." The Council's barrister read out from the piece of paper in his hand.

The judge took a large sheaf of papers from the stack in front of him and everyone waited as he turned to the relevant clause and read it.

The judge questioned the Council's barrister, who continued to contradict himself and lose his place, so much so that both Berwick and Nigra both had to help him out on many occasions.

Finally the judge adjourned for lunch, telling the Court they would reconvene at 2 pm.

Mrs Podger watched Tobias and his companion slip out of the court ahead of everyone else. She then made her way outside the Court to where Neil, Fynne, Pat David and Gill, William and Richard Berwick were all waiting for her.

"Mrs P, who was in the public gallery?" William asked.

"Well, your father was at the back and someone came in who I assume was Douglas Lansbury, but I don't know what he looks like."

"I don't know whether he's out of jail yet, but it's not inconceivable. Who else?"

"Well, lots of people from the village were there and I think a journalist was sitting next to me as he was scribbling lots of notes and muttering under his breath."

"Was the gallery full then?" William asked.

"William, you couldn't have squeezed in another person if you'd tried."

William patted her shoulder and smiled sadly.

"Richard and I are going back to his Chambers, so I'll catch up with you after this afternoon's session."

Neil looked at his watch and suggested they try and grab a sandwich.

The hot blast of air as they emerged from the cool vaulted halls of the Royal Courts of Justice reminded them that it was June. Mrs Podger was feeling a little awed that all the months and months of discussion and arguments were culminating in the austere wood panelled courtroom.

"Neil, do you know what all that palaver about locus standi was all about?" she asked.

"Let's get something to eat first. William suggested a pub called Temple Bar." Neil steered both Mrs P and Gill across the zebra crossing.

Once settled with drinks and food Neil, Pat and Fynne looked up 'locus standi' on their phones.

"Wikipedia says "In law, standing or locus standi is the term for the ability of a party to demonstrate to the court sufficient connection to and harm from the law or action challenged to support that party's participation in the case." Pat quoted aloud.

"Hmm, so Nigra was trying to get the case thrown out on a technicality?" Mrs Podger was not impressed by the barrister's tactics.

"You can't blame him for trying, Mrs P." Gill was not sure why she was defending the barrister. "If the boot were on the other foot, you would've wanted your representative to do the same."

"Still doesn't make it right. When you've got to the High Court, that sort of trick seems wrong." Mrs Podger's opinion of KB's barrister was not improved by Gill's defence.

"Well, I think the judge's is on our side." Pat sipped her lemonade.

"It would be nice to think so, but just because he told Nigra to get back in his box doesn't mean he's already made up his mind." Neil warned.

"Well, if you want moy opinion" Fynne paused in case someone told him to shut up "I think he's playing a game and oi would put money on it that he's already come to his decision. He's far more aware of the various planning laws than we are and now he's seeing if the Council and KB are prepared to argue their cases properly."

"So you think Nigra is on the back foot?" Pat asked.

"You're the one who's usually in Court on this tiop of stuff, Pat, you tell me!"

"Fynne, I'm a scientist not a lawyer, neither am I a politician and this whole episode strikes me as highly political." The diminutive scientist folded her arms and scowled.

"How so?" Gill asked.

"These new planning regulations are a key part of the coalition's plan to kick start the economy by making the construction of new houses easier." Fynne sat back, nursing his pint. "The Chancellor wants the recovery led boi the construction industry so unemployment will drop, houses will be built and then, in moi opinion, he'll make a play to be PM on the back of his success. This is the foist serious challenge to these regulations."

"Do you believe the judge is just going through the motions and has had his orders from on high?"

"No, Mrs P. The judiciary proide themselves on being independent of government." Fynne sounded confident the judge would be maintaining judicial independence.

"Who's that chap sitting with Nigra. I thought it would have been Tobias." Pat asked.

"His face seems familiar, but I can't place it." Mrs Podger added.

"I know I've seen him in the farm shop." said Gill.

"It's a shame Melissa isn't here." Pat David voiced what was at the back of everybody's mind. "Does she even know the case is being heard?"

"She's had all the emails in just the same way as the other Directors." Neil said. "Mrs Podger have you heard from her? Charles said he hasn't heard a word."

Mrs Podger nearly choked hearing about Charles's deliberate lie and for a minute wondered whether Melissa really had taken herself off to Europe.

"No, I only know as much as you from the couple of phone calls I've had." This much was the truth, but Mrs Podger was very glad no one pressed her further. "Can anyone tell me what a CPR is?"

Everyone looked blank.

NOTTING HILL

Melissa opened the door to her London flat. Now she understood just how easy it was for those who lived on the island to commute into London. Anyone wanting to be in the City could be at their desk by 9 with no problem whatsoever, except perhaps for the cost. She gave herself a mental nudge reminding herself that bankers did not think about mundane things like the cost of airfares.

One of the twins wiggled and she rubbed her tummy. She was six months pregnant and felt huge. Melissa looked at the clock: it was lunchtime.

She was trying hard not to think about what William might think if she turned up at Court. Suzie had listened and been sympathetic to a point. Her voice of sanity had pointed out that since they were not married Melissa's behaviour looked intolerant and childish.

Melissa flung open the doors onto the little patio. Everything in the garden was burgeoning now the very long winter was finally over and the sun had returned. The beds needed weeding and the roses, honeysuckle and clematis were running riot over the brick walls. Reassuring sounds of London could be heard faintly. She started nipping off dead heads from the honeysuckle with her finger nails. Soon there was a pile of weeds, dead flowers and Melissa was trimming back the long shoots thrown out by the climbers.

Her phone buzzed in her pocket. It was a text from William thanking her for her good luck wishes and hoped she was well.

They must have adjourned for lunch, she thought and briefly considered telling him she was in London, but that would mean giving all sorts of explanations she was not ready to make.

ROYAL COURTS OF JUSTICE

The hearing was due to start at 10 am, but Melissa did not arrive at the High Court until it was well underway. She squeezed herself on to the end of the back row of the public gallery. The man next to her shuffled along as far as he could so she could sit down.

George Nigra was on his feet and being questioned by the Judge.

"Surely, Mr Nigra, it is not 'need' that is at the heart of this argument, but 'want'?"

Nigra put his hands on his hips. "On the contrary, Your Honour, by creating this exclusive spa and golf course we will be creating much needed employment in the area."

Mrs Podger watched Melissa enter. From the little she knew about pregnancy she thought Melissa was large for six months gone. Perhaps her dates were wrong. She switched her attention back to the front bench.

William looked pre-occupied. Mrs Podger willed him to turn around, but he remained concentrating on what the judge and Nigra were debating.

Five people separated Tobias from Melissa. You could not have got another body into that courtroom if you had tried.

The discussion about whether there was a 'need' for this development, or whether it was, as Judge St Claire considered, 'want' continued until one o'clock, but Melissa had slipped away before the judge adjourned for lunch.

She took herself down towards the river and sat in the little park. A man was taking instruction from his personal trainer and doing squat thrusts. She took out the salad she had bought and picked at it. Seeing William, even if it was just the back of his head, had given her the collywobbles. She had been aware of Mrs Podger watching her from her seat up near the judge. The judge had said everyone should return at two fifteen and she wondered how much longer he and Nigra would continue discussing the relative definitions of 'need', 'want' and 'desire'.

The twins were sitting on her bladder so she made her way back to the Courts and was thankful for the cool of the Victorian building.

There were deep recesses outside each courtroom so she took herself into the one outside Court 16 where it was unlikely she would be seen by anyone going into Court 15.

Melissa returned to pondering the tight definitions of 'need', 'want' and 'desire' that the judge appeared to be trying to get KB Ltd.'s barrister to agree. The judge was comparing Nigra's interpretation of 'need' to that of a spoilt child who demanded something of their parents by saying how they needed it, whereas in reality the child merely wanted it, or at best, desired it.

It seemed as if they were arguing another form of the medieval debate of how many angels danced on the head of a pin. The fine line between the intended meanings seemed obvious, but would that ensure the successful outcome of the JR?

The click of steel heel caps disturbed her thoughts; the last time she had heard these was at the County Court and she had no desire to come face to face with Tobias again. From the muted voices she realised he was accompanied by at least two others.

"What's the latest list of signups?" She heard him ask. There was a rustle and Melissa imagined papers being handed across. "Damn. There are no more since the last big event. The bank will be on our backs if we don't get some money in soon. What about the PR push the other night? What happened there?"

"Well, the report from Hong Kong was that potential investors wanted to have more details before any of them committed to even registering any interest." Another voice reported.

"There was an email from the bank asking the same question." One of the other men said.

More footsteps could be heard approaching.

"Ah, John. What did you make of this morning's session?"

Melissa strained to hear the reply.

"I think this judge isn't a golfer!"

"Yes, very funny. However, if it all goes tits up, we're going to have some very angry people wanting their money back." The unknown man said.

"We'll cross that bridge should we need to." The voice was accented and Melissa wondered exactly who he was.

"George said he's not confident and we've only got this afternoon to make our pitch." The newcomer continued.

"Well tell him to pull some rabbit out of his legal hat. I've no wish to lose two and a half mill!"

"If we lose this JR it'll be more than your initial investment you'll be losing, Tobias. What about the long term plan for the housing?"

"Dryden, when will you learn to keep your fucking mouth shut!" Tobias's voice had dropped to a hiss.

Melissa felt sick. Fynne had been. She sat remembering the night she and William had watched the deer come down to the lake to drink. Her hand rested on her stomach and one of the babies moved. If KB won her babies would never know the beauty of the estate. She managed to stifle a sob.

More voices could be heard in the distance and the steel heel taps clicked again as Tobias walked away. Presumably the other men had gone with him. She decided to wait some more minutes until everyone had gone back into Court before she slipped into the back row. She strained to hear the door close behind the gaggle of people she could hear waiting outside the court; she checked her watch. 14.20. She stood up and left the relative safety of her recess.

"Melissa?"

She froze. There was no escaping Mrs Podger. The older woman was sat in the recess outside Court 15. She patted the stone bench inviting Melissa to sit next to her.

"Pet, I'm glad you're here. I was beginning to think you'd abandoned us."

Melissa sat down and Mrs Podger took her hand in hers.

"Mrs P, do you think we have a chance?"

"William's done a grand job and our man is brilliant."

"Mrs P, Fynne was right. I've just overhead Tobias and someone called John Dryden talking just before the court reconvened."

"What do you mean?"

"The long term plan **is** to build houses on the estate."

"Oh my!" the older woman exclaimed, the news confirming her own worst fears. William needed to know about it, but that could wait until later; Mrs Podger wanted to know about Melissa.

"Don't worry. I'll find some way of telling William, but what about you? Are you sure your dates are right?"

"Yes, everything is fine. The doctor says that it's because I'm so tiny I look so big, but the baby's fine." Melissa kept the information that it was babies, plural, to herself.

Mrs Podger patted Melissa's hand. "When are you going to tell William? He has a right to know"

"I don't want him to think he has to do the honourable thing. Do you know why he's continuing with the JR? He didn't have to."

"Melissa pet, once William starts something, he sees it through. 'E tells me this is a really important judgement as it will affect planning decisions right across the country."

"That's what he told me right at the beginning. William calls it a developers' charter. William has always said that the PM was hoping that if the electorate could see the economy improving and the housing market booming, then there won't need to be a coalition after the next election. Mrs P, if the Conservatives get back in with a working majority the whole of the countryside will disappear under concrete. What happened to them being the stewards of the land and looking after it?"

"I know. This lot of little boys haven't a clue, and that's not just the PM and his cronies. None of them in Westminster would know one end of a tractor from another if they were dumped in the middle of a farmyard. William knows what 'e's doing and 'e knows it's going to be a tough fight. The Press are loving it because they see all this Courtroom stuff as son versus father. Everything about Tobias, Lansbury and that MP's son 'as been back in the papers."

"Has he been down to see you?"

Mrs Podger sighed. "Mr P and I have been over to Neil and Gill's to discuss the case with him and the others."

"So he hasn't been to The Old Manor?"

"Why would he? You're not there."

Mrs Podger's news confirmed that William did not have time to think about her.

"Has Mr P done the stuff in the garden we talked about?"

"Yes. 'E's also put in a couple of bee'ives at the front of the house." Mrs Podger paused. "Are you going back to the island tonight?"

"Yes." Melissa paused. Now that she had seen Mrs Podger and told her about the overheard conversation, she wanted to get away. She had much to think about, especially since William was clearly not thinking about her at all.

Mrs Podger put her arm around Melissa's shoulders.

"Come home, pet."

274

"Not yet, Mrs P." Melissa leaned against her. It would be so easy to go back to The Old Manor with the Podgers, but that would mean facing lots of questions and then there was the horrible scraped landscape where the cowslips had once bloomed. She could not bear living next to that. "I don't want to run into anyone, so I think I'll creep away to the airport."

Mrs Podger wanted to hug her all afternoon.

"Do you want me to paint the bedroom next to yours pink or blue?"

"Oh, Mrs P, what a lovely thought. What about pale yellow?"

"Do you want me to get a cot too?"

Melissa nodded.

"Mrs P," Melissa hesitated, "I suppose you'll have to tell him how you know about the houses."

"Don't you worry pet. I'll make sure he knows about what Tobias and his chums were saying, but your secret's safe with me. Are you sure you want to creep away?"

Melissa nodded and kissed the older woman's soft cheek that smelled of face powder. It reminded her how Mrs P had always been there, with Hetty, to welcome her home or to wave her goodbye. She also had to think about whether she wanted to live back at The Old Manor if William was not going to be part of their lives.

"It's hot and if I go now I can be back in Jersey by early evening." Melissa stood and rubbed the small of her back. "I'll text you when I'm home."

Mrs Podger was painting round the nursery window as William drove up. She watched as the car roof unfolded itself and re-set itself as a roof. She replaced the paint lid and went to wash her brush so was standing at the sink as William came through the door.

"Mrs P?" William paused at the door, conscious that he had not been at The Old Manor for a very long time.

"William, 'ow lovely to see you. You got my text then?"

He nodded.

"Sit down and I'll make you a cuppa."

"She didn't stay then?"

Mrs Podger busied herself filling the kettle. "I was surprised to see her myself! And before you ask, she didn't tell me where she was going."

William leaned back and looked at the ceiling. He stuck his hands in his jeans pockets and leaned back, swinging on the back legs of the chair.

"Did she tell you what she found at Cremorne?"

"No dear. What was it?"

"What did she tell you about Scotland?"

"Don't be silly, William. Melissa never discusses 'er work." She poured them both tea and cut some cake. "'elp yourself, William."

He bit into the dense, moist cake realising just how much he missed Mrs Podger's cooking.

"Well, suffice it to say that if I'd taken more notice of what Melissa had done for me, we could probably have been spared all this legal stuff and Melissa and you would not be being besieged by these bastards!"

Mrs Podger sat down opposite him, sipped her tea and waited for him to continue. She thought he had lost weight.

"William, what's a CPR?"

"Are you asking about something to do with the campaign or first aid?"

"William, what do you think?" Mrs Podger. "I've seen enough television 'ospital programmes to know 'ow to do that sort of CPR!"

"OK! OK!" William held his hands up in mock surrender. "I think you mean a CPO which is a Costs Protection Order, which limits the amount the campaign might have to pay in the event of us losing. If we do lose, it will still be a substantial amount."

"When do you expect the judge to tell us his decision?"

"I have no idea. We'll be asked to review his judgement before it's handed down publicly."

"Does that mean you'll be able to tell us the minute you know?"

William shook his head. "No. He gives us the draft so we can proof it, but I would be in contempt of court if I told anyone other than the directors."

"Will you text Melissa when you can?"

"We had a meeting of the Farm companies this afternoon and Charles asked if I'd heard anything from her." He looked up, "I had hoped she was in Jersey, but if Charles doesn't know where she is, she can't be, can she?"

"Are you just doing this for Melissa?" Mrs P asked.

"Mostly, but also for Edward. He drilled it into me that the de Braose's have a duty to this land. We are merely custodians; we don't have the right to destroy it."

"Since it's Friday, William, do you want to stay for supper and 'ave a night away from London?"

The old house had enfolded him in her embrace and he realised he wanted to absorb that peace.

"I'm sure there's nothing going on in London that won't wait 'til Monday." Mrs Podger poured them both another cup. "I 'ope the judge 'urries up with his decision."

"Charles tells me that there's a very similar situation to New Manor going on Jersey."

"In what way?"

"Developers were granted permission in turn a derelict holiday camp into a twenty eight unit luxury housing estate and this is right in the middle of Jersey's seabird protection zone. There's been a campaign to save the site since the camp closed in 2000 and the island's First Minister has tried to have the site made subject to a CPO. . ."

"William, why would they make a costs protection order?"

"Sorry Mrs P. In this instance it's a Compulsory Purchase Order."

"Why would anyone want to do that?"

"Because the First Minister wanted to stop any development and sell the land to the Jersey National Trust for the benefit of the islanders. The whole of the holiday camp is next to it is our equivalent of an AONB."

Mrs Podger looked puzzled.

"Sorry Mrs P. An Area of Outstanding Natural Beauty, like the South Downs. Last year, after a three-day debate in the Jersey States it all went horribly wrong. One of the spokespeople for the JNT – sorry! Jersey National Trust said, and I quote" William swiped the screen on his phone, *"We are saddened that the majority of States members could not step out of the box and actually repair some of the recent damage that has been inflected on this once beautiful land."*

"Sounds as if the developers are a chip off the KB bloc."

"The fight hasn't ended. The head of the Council for the Protection of Jersey Heritage wrote asking for the public enquiry to be revisited."

"Why?"

"Evidently the original survey was flawed, which is very much like the survey put forward by KB in their planning application. And the similarities don't stop there because the island's First Minister lost the vote for the States of Jersey to slap a CPO on the site by one vote."

"Well I never."

"The developers are arguing that the valuation of four million pounds was inaccurate and the site value is closer to fourteen million. Their scheme is for twenty eight homes and they say they will return eighty per cent of the site to the wild."

"You're right. It sounds just like what we've been fighting 'ere!"

"Quite so. However, eighty per cent of nothing is still nothing! That housing development will not benefit anyone with less than several million to their name. Anyhow, everyone's waiting for the result of the latest challenge by the Parish Council, who've waded into the fray."

The rumble of heavy machinery woke him at 7 am. No wonder Melissa was staying away, the whole fabric of the house was shaking. Mr Podger had warned him they were working a five and a half day week.

"Mrs P!" Mr Podger came into the kitchen moving as fast as he could manage. "Mrs P, all the diggers and trucks are being parked up and the men are all getting out."

"What do you mean?" Mrs Podger had her hands in a bowl making pastry.

"You 'eard me! They've parked all their vehicles in the pound and are standing 'round talking!"

The phone rang.

"Mr P, you can see my 'ands are covered in flour. Pick it up!"

"The Old Manor." He announced.

"We won!" Neil shouted down the phone. There was a long pause as Mr Podger absorbed what had been said. "Mr P, are you there?"

"Yes, yes. Did I 'ear you properly, Neil?"

"Has anything happened on the estate?"

"I was just telling Mrs P that all the men 'ave parked up and are standing 'round talking."

Mrs Podger was trying to press her ear to the back of the phone. She snatched the handset.

"Is that you, William?"

"No, it's Neil. William's just phoned me from Court."

"Oh, Neil. Have we won?"

"Yes, Mrs P. We have."

Mrs Podger went and sat down outside listening to the silence. The background hum she had grown so used to had stopped: the vibration from the movement of the heavy plant machinery had stopped.

She could hear birdsong.

Mr Podger handed his wife the phone.

"Tell Melly she can come 'ome."

"Mr P," she paused, "what if there's an appeal?"

Mr Podger looked long at his wife. "Is there something you're not telling me?"

"I have no idea what you're talking about, Mr P!" She hurriedly dialled Melissa's mobile number.

"Are you seeing Melissa today, darling." Charles dolloped a spoonful of marmalade on to his toast.

"Yes. She's got a check up, then we thought we'd have lunch somewhere. Why?"

"William's going to be in my office at 10."

"Why?"

Charles finished his coffee before standing up, picking up his car keys and kissing Suzie's cheek.

"Charles, you can't disappear without telling me what you want me to do."

"Well, if you want you can tell Melissa."

"Can I tell her why he's over?"

Charles looked at her and raised an eyebrow. "You know I can't tell you that!"

"OK! Banker's confidentiality and all that. Just tell me where you're going for lunch so I know where to avoid, or is that a secret too?"

"No. William said he's back to London on the lunchtime flight."

"So perhaps Melissa already knows he's coming?"

"You'll have to find that out."

"Charles, you won't say anything about the twins, will you?"

"You're asking a banker to keep a secret! Well I never!"

CHARLES'S OFFICE

"Charles, I can't thank you enough for seeing me this morning. Just one more thing, I must tell you that as I got off the 'plane I received a text saying our Council has been granted leave to appeal."

Charles raised his eyebrows. "Do you think they have a chance?"

"No, but then the judge said there was no leave to appeal and now an Appeal Judge has overturned that ruling, so who's to know what's in the mind of the judiciary."

"Is there any money left in the pot?"

William nodded. "There's been a great response with money is being dropped into the Farm Shop buckets and coming through the link on the website."

"What about the Podgers?"

William gave a wry smile. "The Old Manor is only hearing the sound of the birds and the hum of Mr P's bees, but if the appeal is upheld

280

the bulldozers will be back." William hesitated. "Charles, I know you can't tell me about Melissa's business, but you, of all people, might know where she is."

The wily banker smiled. "Did you know Jersey's got it's own New Manor campaign?" He knew this would divert William's attention.

"Yes, but I've not kept up with how things are going."

"That campaign has many similarities to ours."

"Jersey's lucky enough not to have to dance to the English NPPF, so how are the campaigners doing?"

Charles drew a deep breath. "Like much of what has happened with New Manor, the developers have deep pockets and tried to stop a last ditch effort by the parish council to get the whole case reviewed."

"Did they succeed, or did the great god Mammon win out?"

Charles nodded. "Thankfully, the States of Jersey finally saw sense."

"I get the feeling you weren't too keen on what was happening."

"No. The proposed development is in an exceedingly beautiful part of the island bang next door to an area of heathland, with rare green lizards and bird nesting sites. There was a huge public protest. Public appeal managed to raise £3.75m, which was just shy of the original valuation, but since 2000, the value has risen so it is now approximately half of the agreed current value."

"Considering the land values over here, seven and a half mill sounds quite low."

"Yes, at one point the developers tried to up their valuation to fourteen, but eventually the agreed price was about seven and the States matched what had been raised by public subscription."

"That sounds quite a coup for the people of Jersey."

"Absolutely, so now the dust is settling, the plan is to demolish the buildings and return the whole site back to the wild."

"That's brilliant, but I hope they leave any existing wild areas alone, if there are any. Those will have been like it since the last Ice Age, so fiddling with thousands of years of nature has to be carefully managed."

"Oh yes, everyone who knows about these things is involved and I have faith in the people at the top, who are very keen to make sure it will be returned to what it was before the 1960s, and what has managed to survive that development will be left alone."

"Charles, this is great news."

"Even a fool could see this was a vanity project. The developers seemed to believe that anything they put forward would go through on the nod. On the couple of occasions their applications didn't, the developers appealed and every time, permission was granted with very little amendment. The island has changed out of all recognition since I was a child. It's an anthill with building everywhere. If you want to have any idea of how the island was, you have to watch old episodes of Bergerac. This time the islanders revolted because I believe they've had enough of unscrupulous developers building yet another luxury development on one of the island's beauty spots."

"Were KB Ltd. involved?"

"Not that I know of." Charles paused and poured them both more coffee before continuing his monologue.

"Being involved in the New Manor campaign showed me that there's more to life than money, so I joined the fight here to save the Plemont site for future generations." He paused for a moment. "William, I've come to hate all this jiggery pokery with over-fed, over-rich, greedy people hiding behind faceless offshore corporate entities. As you well know, business depends on trust, and off shore corporate anonymity doesn't do much to engender this!

The original idea behind the islanders raising their own taxes was so they could fund their own militia for the defence of the islands. With modern technology being able to move funds around the world at the push of a button it makes it all too easy for tax haven status to be abused, wherever they're based, not just here. And likewise, modern warfare technology would make any island militia ineffective within a matter of minutes. What we need is a complete overhaul of the global finance industry, but both you and I know that will require considerable international co-operation, which we also know isn't going to happen in the foreseeable future."

"You sound as if you're contemplating retirement!"

"I wish I could, but I can't afford to – just yet. My divorce cost me more than she deserved, so I have some coffers to replenish and new ladies don't come cheap!"

William laughed. Suzie Sampson was not the sort of woman who would be content living on beans on toast or in a tent.

"Charles, I know Melissa is incredibly fond of both you and Suzie so I had hoped you would pass on the news about the appeal. If she is in touch, will you tell her I miss her dreadfully."

"William if she is in touch I'll pass on the news, but you'll have to tell her how you feel, yourself."

William looked at his watch. "Grief! I need to dash or I'll miss the flight. I'm off to a meeting in the wilds of nowhere later today and the flight connections are very tight." He stood and held out his hand. "Thank you."

"If you want my advice William, talk to Mrs Podger."

MIDNIGHT

"Mr Cliffe?"

Charles had been woken out of a deep sleep by the ringing of his bedside phone. "Yes? Who's calling?" He leaned over and switched on the bedside light.

"Dr Godwin. Melissa's waters have broken and she's asking if your wife could come and be with her."

"We'll be right there. Thank you." Charles put the phone back on its cradle and leapt out of bed.

"Suzie, get up. We're about to be grandparents!"

At 5.30 am on 2nd September, Melissa was delivered of a boy and a girl.

LATER

"Do you have names for them?" Charles asked.

Melissa was lying back against the pillows.

"Edward William David Alistair Charles and Esther Victoria Susannah Rosemary."

Charles was flattered by the inclusion of his own name.

"Edward and Hetty for short." Melissa finished.

Suzie sniffed, finding she was enjoying her new role of surrogate grandmother. She was thankful the two babies had been born safely. They were a little early, but all was well.

"Melissa, try and get some sleep. I'll ring Mrs P and tell her the news. Do you want her to come over?" Suzie asked.

Melissa nodded sleepily. No one had told her just how sick she would feel after giving birth.

Charles closed the door quietly and he and Suzie walked to the lift.

"Melissa looks just like Victoria did." Suzie said.

Charles nodded in agreement. "Do you remember how Alistair looked?"

Suzie chuckled. "Like a rabbit caught in the headlights."

"Well, old girl, since our old chums aren't here, little Edward & Hetty will have to make do with us as 'in loco grand-parentis'."

Mrs Podger arrived later that day and fluttered about like a protective hen.

"My, my Melissa, little Hetty has your nose."

"Charles says she's got my eyes. He got a bit misty eyed and I think he was thinking about my mother."

"And young Edward looks just like . . ." Mrs Podger paused.

"William – I know Mrs P and before you ask, he's got William's blue eyes." Melissa turned and looked out of the window. "Mrs P, what did you tell Mr Podger?"

"Melissa, all this secrecy is ridiculous. William thinks the world of you. He's told me!"

"Mrs P, I promise I'll tell him very soon." Melissa did not believe her. If he cared that much he would have been in touch.

"Mr Podger is here too, so he can drive me around, but don't worry. The Old Manor is in good hands. Gill and Neil have moved in to look after the house and Betty."

Melissa heaved herself upright, shocked to think her secret was out.

"Don't worry, pet. I told them we had to go to Wales as my sister's girl needed some help."

Melissa lay and looked at the ceiling, forcing back tears.

"Can Mr P come in and say hello?" Mrs Podger asked softly.

Melissa did not say anything, tears slid down her cheek. More than anything she wanted William.

Mr Podger came and stood looking down at Edward & Hetty lying in their clear basinets, swaddled in brushed cotton wraps. They were awake and appeared to be taking in everything about them.

The sister stuck her head around the door .

"Mrs Carlisle, Dr Godwin says she'll be along in about ten minutes to see you."

Melissa smiled weakly at the sister. Her breasts hurt. The Podgers were fussing and cooing over the two babies. Melissa swung her legs over the side of the bed, stood up, swayed and fainted.

"Melissa." She was aware of someone calling her name, but it was far away. "Melissa!"

She felt so cold.

A brightly lit tunnel opened and she zoomed towards a single point. It was like a closed helter-skelter and she shot out of the bottom onto a white beach where Hetty, Edward and another man were enjoying an evening drink. Her sudden appearance startled them and Hetty jumped up.

"Melissa, what are you doing here?"

Melissa looked at her and Edward, then looked at the other man realising it was David de Braose.

"Where am I?"

Before any of them could reply she sensed another presence and turned towards another man who held out his hand to help her up and she looked into the gentlest eyes she had ever seen.

"Melissa, you shouldn't be here. You have things to do." He helped her to her feet, then the scene began to circle and she was sucked back up the tunnel.

"Her blood pressure's 50 over 10." A distant voice sounded relieved.

"Keep up the fluids and give her another unit of A neg. She should be OK now." Another voice replied.

Melissa felt as if she were floating in a warm sea.

MUCH LATER

Melissa opened her eyes and lifted her arm to push her hair away from her face, but the back of her hand had drips and tubes attached to it, which in turn, were attached to a bag three quarters full of clear fluid and another half empty bag of blood.

"What happened?"

"Mrs Carlisle you're fine now." The nurse told her.

"Where're Edward and Hetty?"

"They're in the nursery."

"Please, I want to see my babies."

Dr Godwin entered. "You gave us all a bit of a scare there, Melissa. How're you feeling?"

Melissa smiled, "Much better. What happened?"

"You had a post delivery complication, but you'll be as right as rain in a couple of days."

"Why the blood?"

"You've had a haemorrhage so we've given you a transfusion."

"Oh!" Melissa wondered whether her experience was a delusion caused by her lack of blood.

"I want to see my babies and I want to go home."

Dr Godwin thought for a minute.

"You'll have to eat properly, otherwise you won't be doing either them, or yourself, any good."

Melissa nodded. "What's on the menu?"

"Anything particular you fancy?" Dr Godwin smiled.

"Smoked salmon, avocado and fresh raspberries, but preferably not on the same plate."

"Would you settle for soup and a tuna sandwich?"

Melissa nodded. Despite the tubes and transfusions, she was feeling considerably better and very hungry.

Ten minutes later the door opened and her new family were wheeled in; at the same time the soup and sandwich arrived. Edward wrinkled his little nose as if anticipating sampling the soup. Melissa did not know what to do first, eat or give them both a cuddle.

"Eat first, Mrs Carlisle" the nurse ordered, anticipating her thought. "otherwise you won't have the strength to look after these two." The woman smiled at her. It was not often someone gave birth to twins in their maternity unit.

"Thank you." Melissa was glad someone was telling her what to do since her brain was still mushy.

"Don't worry, Mrs Carlisle, just take your time."

Melissa ate her soup and sandwiches and took out her mobile.

Melissa's House, St Ouen's

"Mrs P, this has gone on long enough! We very early lost her! Either you ring William, or I do."

Mrs Podger sighed.   Her husband was right.   She dialled William's mobile.

CHARLES & SUZIE'S HOUSE

"I know I promised I wouldn't say anything, Suzie, but William has a right to know. Supposing she'd died? How would you explain that we had all been in cahoots and not said a word. It's wrong."

"Charles, it should be Melissa making this call, not you!"

"She's had months to contact him and it's going to be difficult enough to explain how we all kept schtumm about where she was." Charles hit speed dial. "Damn!   Voicemail!"

It was as if The Old Manor had been picked up and transported to Melissa's quiet corner of the island. Mrs Podger had taken charge of the house and Mr Podger had the garden under control.

There was knock on the door.

"Well, Mr P, I'm not going to open it at this time of night!" Mrs Podger looked meaningfully at her husband over her knitting. Mr Podger went to the door.

"William!" It was drizzling and a fine net of glistening dewdrops lay over William's hair and shoulders. "Come in."

"Thank you, Mr P."

Mrs Podger bustled forward, distinctly flustered at William's sudden arrival. They all stood looking at each other, no-one knowing what to say or do.

"You'd better come into the kitchen, young man. You look as if you 'aven't eaten for a week!"

Mrs Podger busied herself preparing a meal.

"Mrs P, I've been out in the middle of nowhere so I couldn't make it any sooner"

"Where've you been?" Mr Podger asked. He shut the door to keep any noise from upstairs.

"In a plain of mud volcanoes in Kazakhstan."

Mrs Podger handed William a plate of cold meats, pickles, cheese and French bread. "That sounds pretty remote!"

"Mrs P, I've had a text from Melissa saying she's been an idiot; and voicemails from you and Charles saying I had to get to Jersey a.s.a.p. What's going on?"

Mr Podger looked at his wife. Mrs Podger bought herself some time by filling the kettle and getting mugs out of the cupboard.

"I think Melissa needs to tell you that."

"Is she out?"

"No, she's asleep." Mrs Podger paused. "You say she sent you a text."

William already had his mouth was full of food. Mr Podger accepted a mug of tea. "Any cake, Mrs P?" If he was going to have to suffer a long night of explanations he wanted to fortify himself with a piece of one of his wife's chocolate cakes.

"Yes. I got here as soon as possible." William replied.

"What did she say?" Mr Podger asked, wondering just how much William knew.

William flicked through his text messages and handed his phone to the older man.

'*William, I've been an idiot. I'm in Jersey. Mx*' Mr Podger handed the phone to his wife.

"That's a bit brief."

"I've been travelling ever since I got her text. Is she in trouble?" William asked.

"I think you'd better ask her yourself."

William gulped down his tea and stood up. "Mrs P, you know what I've been through. I don't care what's happened, I just want to see her."

"Follow me."

Mrs Podger led William upstairs and opened the door to the nursery.

"William, don't be cross with her."

William looked at the two babies, one in pink and the other in a blue sleep suit, lying asleep together in a cot.

"Why, Mrs P? Why didn't she want me to know?" Hetty opened her eyes and looked at him.

Mrs Podger watched as William reached down to stroke his daughter's cheek and Hetty rewarded him with a hiccup.

"Well youngster, where's your mother?"

Melissa's bedroom door was closed.

William put his hand on Mrs Podger's hand and stopped her knocking.

"William," she paused, lost for words.

"It's OK Mrs P. I just want to see her."

Downstairs the Podgers looked at each other.

"Well, Mrs P, that's a turn up for the books. Did you know Melissa 'ad finally seen sense?"

"No, but she did promise she was going to contact 'im. Do you think I did the right thing letting 'im into 'er room?"

"You saw the text and both of them 'ave poured their hearts out to you, so only you know the answer to that one."

Mrs Podger cut herself a slice of cake.

"True, but even so . . ." she let her unvoiced thought hang in the air.

"Do you know when she texted our William?"

"No, but at least they're talking."

UPSTAIRS

William turned the door handle and let himself into her bedroom. Melissa had fallen asleep with the light on and her book had dropped to the floor. He bent to kiss her forehead; Melissa woke with a start, sat bolt upright smacking her head into William's face.

"Ow!" William stepped back clutching his bruised mouth: Melissa clasped her forehead.

"William!" Melissa burst into tears.

"Melissa, . . ."

William handed her the tissue box.

"I thought you were bored with me." She wiped her eyes and blew her nose.

"Why didn't you tell me?"

"I didn't want you to feel as if you **had** to do the honourable thing."

"WHAT! That's absurd, didn't you think I had a right to know?"

"That I'd been stupid!"

"What do you mean?"

"I forgot my doctor's appointment for the contraceptive jab."

"Because you forget to go the quack you take a unilateral decision to disappear out of my life! Didn't you think I had a right to know I was going to be a father?" William's anger was rising at what he saw as Melissa's deliberate actions to keep him away from his children.

"The first I know about anything is a garbled text from you, then voicemails and texts from Suzie, Mrs P, Charles and, believe it or not, Mr P, telling me you've nearly died and I need to get here double quick."

"What?"

"Yes – how do you think they feel? How dare you make them complicit in keeping me away from MY children. What if you **had** died?"

"Well I didn't and it wasn't that serious."

"Not that serious! Do you know what happened?"

"No!"

"Evidently you got out of bed and haemorrhaged all over the floor."

"Oh!"

"I suppose flat-lining was all part of your plan. Do you have ANY idea how touch and go it was?"

Melissa sniffed again and blew her nose. "Who told you?"

"Charles." He paused remembering the conversation he had had with the Jersey banker just as he had been boarding a flight from Kyzlorda.

"I suppose they are my son and daughter!" William paced up and down.

"How dare you accuse me of going off behind your back especially when I'm not the one who's been playing away." She shouted.

"How dare you! What about all your flirting with Fynne."

"So why did you go to Brussels with another woman?"

"What are you talking about? There is no other woman!"

"So who were you with in Brussels with then?"

"When?"

"The conference that was so important you missed my birthday."

"The meeting back in February?"

"You told me you had gone to Brussels with Pat!"

"Melissa Carlisle, you really are stupid at times! I was in Brussels with Patrick Duffe. He's an internationally respected environmentalist who was giving an important paper on the global effects of climate change. Patrick Duffe is an environmentalist; Pat David is an ECOLOGIST."

"Environmentalist/ecologist – they're all the same! Why didn't you say Pat was a him?"

"For all your academic prowess, I'm surprised you didn't find out more about who I'd gone away with before jumping to conclusions and making unilateral decisions. There's a world of difference between ecologists and environmentalists. It may have escaped your notice, but Patrick's a man's name notwithstanding that Pat David is engaged to be married."

"Who to?"

"Fynne!"

"Oh!" Rain pattered on the window matching her mood.

"Did it ever occur to you that I might want to be a father?"

"I didn't think you wanted . . ."

"You make all the decisions and don't even have the courtesy to let me to know that I'm going to be a father!"

"Yes." She shouted back. "If that's what you want to hear, then yes."

"So why text me and wish me luck in court? If you really wanted me out of your life, why do that?" He paced up and down the room. Frustrated he had missed her pregnancy and the birth.

Melissa sat looking at nothing.

"Didn't Mrs P tell you I'd been to see her?" William asked. He pushed his hair off his forehead.

Melissa shook her head. "No. Didn't she tell you about the emails we exchanged?

Both of them appreciated how Mrs Podger had managed to tread the delicate path of being confidante to them both

"William, I asked her to tell you I'd been at the hearing."

"Yes and she passed on the details of the conversation you'd heard between Tobias and his cronies." William sat down on the bed. "Rabbit, what if you'd died? Did you really think I didn't care?"

"I wanted to talk to you, but . . ." the stupidity of her behaviour was overwhelming. "William, I'm sorry." Melissa reached out her hand to him. "Will you forgive me.?"

His use of her nickname told her he already he had, but she wanted to hear him say it.

"Rabbit, the next time you get one of your daft notions would you please talk to me."

"William, I'm not a mind reader and you never talk to me about your work, so the only Pat I know is our Pat." She paused. "Do you want to meet your family?"

Edward was still holding Hetty's hand.

"Rabbit, I just don't get it. Why did you not tell me?"

"I didn't want history to repeat itself." Hetty whimpered in her sleep Her brother pulled his hand from hers and stuffed his thumb into his mouth. "I didn't want you doing anything you felt you were being forced into."

Melissa bent down and lifted her sleeping daughter into her father's arms. "Hetty is seven minutes younger than her brother."

Hetty yawned.

292

"She's so tiny." William was mesmerised. Hetty opened her eyes, took one look at her father and yelled. The look of fear that crossed William's face was comical.

"She's hungry. You take Edward."

Father and son regarded each other with a considered seriousness. Hetty sucked Melissa's breast as if it was going to be the last meal she was ever going to be offered.

"He's got Gramps's eyes." William said after a few minutes, "and I think his ears are like my mother's." Edward sucked his thumb and continued to consider the strange man holding him. "My first name's Edward too. Mother used my second name so people didn't get confused between Gramps and me."

"I want to call him Edward William David Alistair Charles and Hetty, Esther Susannah Victoria Rosemary."

"Well young Edward, what do you think of your Daddy? Do I meet with your approval?" William's was only half listening to her.

Melissa put her daughter up to her shoulder and gently rubbed her back; Hetty let out an unladylike fart.

"Melissa, I wish I'd been there."

Melissa woke early next morning and got out of bed and found William in the nursery.

"Come here, Rabbit." William laid his arm round her shoulders and hugged her. "Don't ever leave me again."

"I've never asked anyone about what happened in the hospital. Did I really flat-line?"

"Suzie said it was touch and go."

Melissa thought about her strange experience with the tunnel and the man who had sent her back from the beach where Hetty, Edward and David had been sitting. Who was he and why had he said it was not her time yet?

"I don't want to come back to The Old Manor just yet."

"The bulldozers have stopped working."

"I know, but there's still the appeal and what if we lose?"

"We can't, Lissie. If we do it will give any developer carte blanche to come up with any hair-brained scheme they like. The England we know and love will disappear under concrete."

"William, will you tell your mother she's a granny. She's the only real one they have."

William lifted Edward high above his head. "Well, little man, I believe I've got a phone call to make. Do you want to help me ring you Granny?"

Edward looked down at his father and dribbled.

Rosemary's delight was tinged with sadness as she watched her son lying on the rug next to both his children.

"Melissa, thank you for not taking the easy option."

"Rosemary, you too could have made that decision, but you didn't. If you had, then there wouldn't be a William."

Rosemary reached across and squeezed Melissa's hand.

"Thank you, all the same."

"Lord de Braose, I have a Mrs Rosemary Bell for you." The efficient receptionist spoke into the receiver.

"Put her through."

"No my lord, she's here, in reception."

Tobias sighed. "Do you know what she wants?"

"She said it was personal."

"Oh, all right! Show her up."

Tobias's wondered what his ex-wife wanted: they had not spoken in years.

Rosemary was shown into the palatial glass walled office on the forty ninth floor of Canary Tower.

"To what do I owe this pleasure." Tobias did not rise and indicated she take the seat on the other side of his desk. Rosemary remained standing.

"I shan't take up any more of your valuable time than is necessary, Tobias. However, I thought you should know you're a grandfather."

"Pardon?"

"You are the grandfather of twins. A boy, Edward William David Alistair Charles and a girl, Esther Susannah Rosemary Victoria. Born 1ˢᵗ September. Mother and children are both well." She turned and made towards the door.

"Stop!"

Rosemary froze. That tone, so long forgotten, made her stomach churn. She turned. Tobias was standing, leaning forward resting his fingers on the top of his desk. His complexion was an unhealthy grey overlaid with a sheen of perspiration.

"Who's the mother?" he whispered.

"Hetty Lavering's great niece." Rosemary waited for him to respond. Tobias looked down. It appeared he was unable to stand without support. For the first time in their relationship, Rosemary realised she was in control.

"Goodbye, Grandpa." Rosemary turned and left Tobias looking as if he had been hit with a brick.

As the door closed behind his ex-wife, Tobias sat down. He spun his chair round, looking with unseeing eyes across south-east London.

A "Happy Birthday, Daddy" banner hung across the fireplace in Melissa's dining room. The table was set and delicious smells were coming from the kitchen.

"Rosemary, how many years is it since you were first in this room?"

"Oh Charles, you made me jump." She was so lost in her thoughts, Rosemary had not heard him enter.

"The first time was when William was a baby and I came over and stayed with David and Pat. Hetty was living with them then."

Charles chuckled and sipped his aperitif.

"I remember that Christmas. Victoria and Alistair were soon to be parents and you all came for drinks at my father's place on Christmas morning."

"William was just a toddler. Your father still had your nanny living with him and, thanks to her, I had a wonderful Christmas."

"Dear Nanny Truman." Charles smiled at their shared memory. "Now look at us!"

"I haven't told William, but I went and saw Tobias."

"That was generous of you, not to mention brave."

"Strangely enough it was curiously liberating."

Charles waited. Rosemary gathered her thoughts.

"He seemed to shrink: it was as if I'd hit him."

"Did he say anything?"

It was Rosemary's turn to chuckle. "Come on, Charles. I don't think the possibility that he would ever be a grandfather had ever crossed his mind." She paused. "He turned quite grey."

"Have you heard from him since?"

"No. I doubt I ever will." She finished her glass of champagne. "Has William told you the appeal date is set for the 20th January?"

"Yes. I'm coming to London for it. I gather Melissa is quite adamant about staying here until it's all settled."

"Yes, she told me she won't go back to The Old Manor until the earthmovers have gone for good." Rosemary looked into her empty champagne flute. "Charles, do you think KB've got a chance in overturning the judge's decision?"

"Between you and me, yes. William says the judiciary take great pride in demonstrating they're independent of governmental pressure, but

I've been around far too long to agree with him. This is a direct challenge to the Chancellor's economic strategy so, in my opinion, because the NPPF is key to the recovery, this challenge has to fail otherwise it could bring down the government."

2014

Rain was falling relentlessly as Charles and William crossed The Strand to the Royal Courts of Justice.

"We're listed for one of the courts right at the back, but we can get to it via the front entrance."

"Sounds good to me, William. I can't believe this weather. It seems to have been raining for months."

"You were lucky to get into City airport this morning."

"It was a hairy flight, but I'm told the weather'll improve before tomorrow. Do you think . . ." KB's barrister, George Nigra was just putting his briefcase into the X-ray security machine. "Isn't he a bit late?" Charles whispered.

"Perhaps something's wrong with his trains, but I think Richard would have said something when I met him for breakfast. He and George both come in on the Chiltern line." William glanced at his watch. "We'd better get a bend on otherwise we'll be late too. Will you sit on the front bench with me and Berwick?"

"Be glad to."

Inside Court 69 Rosemary was seated with Neil, Gill, Pat David and Fynne on a side bench.

"Where do you think William is?" Rosemary asked.

"He was meeting Charles for a quick coffee. More to the point, where are the legal teams? According to the clock, we should be underway in about 2 minutes and I'd have thought . . ." Neil stopped. The door opened and William and Charles entered. William turned and smiled at the campaign supporters.

"Neil," Gill elbowed her husband in the ribs. "the rows at the back of the are still empty. Where do you think KB's lot've got to?"

"Oi'd 've thought they would've been 'ere to make sure their man did 'is stuff." Fynne's Irish brogue cut in.

"Is Berwick going to bring up all the stuff about KB ignoring the LEMP?" Pat David asked.

"What's a LEMP?" Rosemary asked. The others seemed to know exactly what she was talking about.

"It's the Council's own local environment management plan and is supposed to protect the countryside from inappropriate development."

Pat's brief explanation did little to enlighten Rosemary as to why it would be included now. She thought it seemed a bit late to be introducing it at this stage.

The clock now showed 10.40.

Richard Berwick came in and, together with his bewigged lady pupil from Chambers, sat in the row behind William and Charles. They leaned forward and the four of them went into a huddled conversation.

Several minutes later George Nigra and his pupil took their places at the other end of the same bench together with the Council's barrister who sat all on his own as the buffer between the protagonists.

Nigra had his back to Rosemary and she felt an immediate and illogical dislike for the man. The roll of fat bulging over his collar revolted her. He adjusted his wig and she gave an involuntary shudder at the sight of his short, stubby fingers.

Richard Berwick leaned back and rested his elbow on the back of the bench. He was tall and slim. He had long elegant fingers; artistic hands that possibly caressed the ivory keys of a piano in order to unwind from the pressures of his day. Rosemary's imagination was carried away with her appraisal of their barrister.

"All rise." The Clerk of the Court intoned.

"That's KB's PR man," Gill nudged Rosemary gently and pointed to where a tubby little man had just taken up one of the empty seats near the door. "He's just like Mr Toad in Wind in the Willows?"

Rosemary supressed a giggle as three black robed judges entered and took their places then everyone sat down.

There was a lot of shuffling of papers and conferring between the three men before the lead judge spoke.

"The appeal by Kuckelimat Baquecks Ltd of the Judicial Review handed down on Thursday, 11th July by Mr Justice St Claire is adjourned." The three judges all stood; the Clerk of the Court stood; the barristers and the legal teams stood; everybody else stood: the judges left.

There was an immediate buzz of speculation. Mr Toad shot out of the door. All the campaign supporters pushed and shoved, eager to get to William to find out what had happened.

There was a knot of people in the corridor, but still no sign of KB Ltd.'s directors or any of the councillors. Mr Toad was nowhere to be seen and George Nigra and his pupil had disappeared. The Council's barrister was hurrying away as fast as his legs could carry him and William and Richard Berwick has also vanished.

Charles took Rosemary by the arm, "Come along my dear, let's lead the way and find somewhere quiet for a few minutes. We need to phone Melissa urgently."

Charles led the group to the back exit into Bell Yard. It was still raining and they all huddled in the shelter of the doorway. Charles took out his phone and dialled.

"Charles, what's happened?" Neil asked.

Charles held up his hand, "I don't want to have to repeat this more than once, so listen." They clustered forward. Charles could hear the phone at the other end ringing, then Mrs Podger's voice.

"Ah Mrs Podger,"

"Mr Charles, that was quick. Is it all over?"

"Er not exactly. Is Melissa there?"

Charles put the phone on speaker. They could hear Mrs Podger call and then the sound of footsteps.

"Charles, is everything all right?" Melissa asked.

"You may well have the Press on your doorstep. There have been some interesting developments and the judges have adjourned the hearing."

"Why?"

Charles smiled gleefully at his audience. "Evidently there were some arrests last night that will affect the whole case."

There was a loud intake of breath from the little gathering.

"Melissa, don't open the door to the Press or anyone. Phone Perry and tell him to come up to you now. If you do get bothered by journalists, he'll know how to deal with them." Charles cut the connection.

"Charles, what's happened?"

"Rosemary, William has more knowledge than me, but it's big."

"Where is William?"

"He and Berwick are putting together a press release to hold the journalists off for a bit." His phone rang again and there was a brief exchange of words before Charles cut the connection. "That was William. He wants us all back in the country and we're not to speak to anyone."

1700 HOURS

JERSEY

Edward was fast asleep in his mother's arms and Hetty was almost asleep within Mrs Podger's embrace.

The phone rang.

"Rabbit, open the champagne; you can all come home."

1800 HOURS

THE OLD MANOR

Charles, Rosemary, Neil, Gill, Pat and Fynne sat mesmerised as the BBC news announcer told how four Councillors of Sompting District Council and the MP for Ardur & Sompting, Sir Bernard Fordingley, had been arrested on suspicion of malfeasance in public office.

"Late this afternoon Tobias de Braose, the 13th Earl of Poultney, his partner, Douglas Lansbury and John Dryden, a Sussex builder, were arrested on suspicion of fraud and tax evasion."

Gill jumped up and down with joy. "Where's William? He should be here."

Neil picked her up and swung her round. "Is it really over?"

"I hate to throw a spanner in the works, but they've only been arrested." Charles announced, "but even so the police must have enough evidence to get this far."

"And they have." William announced from the doorway. "I've brought the champagne." He handed over a carrier-bag. "Veuve Clicquot; Gramps's favourite."

"William, what's happened?"

"In the summer I received a list of shareholders of the various offshore companies who've invested in KB Ltd. I've absolutely no idea who sent it, the postmark was EC2, but in short, it led to today's arrests."

"Was it you, Charles?" Fynne asked, popping a cork and filling glasses.

"No. William showed me the list and I don't know any of them."

"What do you think will happen next?" Gill asked.

"That depends." William smiled. "From our point of view, everything rests on whether the pleas are guilty or not. If not guilty, then there'll be a lengthy trial. We can only hope it won't be long before the next step. Thank you everyone."

Corks popped, glasses were filled and handed round to the ecstatic group.

"Whaw's like us?" he asked.

"Damn few" everyone replied. There was a pause because no one wanted to finish the toast they all associated with Edward.

"And they're all in this room." William finally said, raising his glass and drinking their health.

"Well almost." Charles corrected. "Melissa and the Podgers are with us in spirit, I'm sure."

THE OLD MANOR

"Rabbit, our babies have been shopping."

"That was extremely clever of them."

William handed her a beautifully wrapped box. "Thank you for the best two children ever born."

"Thank you." Melissa kissed him on the cheek.

"The pressie I couldn't wrap is the news that further charges of fraud are being brought against KB's directors.

"How?"

"It appears that all the paperwork they were putting out was bogus and the punters who did sign up have lost the lot."

"How many?"

"I believe some a hundred and twenty uber-rich foreigners were eager to part with £250k of their dosh to be able to say they owned part of an ancient family pile."

"Where did the money go?"

"Presumably some of it went into the work on the estate that's already been done."

"William, I'm so glad we came back to England. I love the Jersey house, but it's so much nicer to be back. The Old Manor seems happy to have us home."

"Lissie, I've decided to give up being a lawyer and concentrate on running the farm."

"What!"

"Yes. Neil hates doing the office stuff and with the Visitor Centre, the farm, plus Cremorne, I've got more than enough to keep me busy."

She threw her arms around his neck. "William, that's the best birthday present ever."

"I don't want my children to grow up with me as a distant father, nor do I want only to see you at weekends. Come here Rabbit I've not seen you all week!"

Mrs Podger stood at the sink looking out at the fence and the hedge. Two men were walking up and down examining the trees and the fence.

"I wonder who they are and, more to the point, what do they want." She mused to herself, undoing her apron and going outside.

"Can I help you, gentlemen?" She called as she approached the fence.

"No thanks. We're just checking boundaries."

Mrs Podger wanted to ask more, but they turned and walked away. It was nearly a year since the diggers had moved in. The piles of scrape were growing weeds and the vast areas of exposed chalk were still dramatic white scars on the parkland.

"Mrs P." Mrs Podger turned; Melissa was standing at the open door waving to her. Mrs Podger made her way back to the house thinking that perhaps Melissa needed help with the babies. They were a bright light on the horizon; two new little lives to carry on the de Braose name. She felt a moment of sadness. How she missed Mr Edward, but if David and Hetty had had children, William and Melissa would never have met and there would be no twins.

"Mrs Podger, William's on his way back from London and wants us to get the others here."

An hour later the key Campaign members were gathered together. Mr Podger had taken his seat next to the fire with Betty curled on his knee. There was a gabble as everyone speculated as to why they had been summoned.

William banged on the table and stood where the laptop microphones could pick up his voice. He had Skyped Charles so he heard the news at the same time as everyone else.

"Ladies and gentleman. I've just come from Southwark Crown Court."

"Why weren't we told there was going to be a hearing?" Neil called from the back of the room.

"Sh, Neil. Let William finish." Gill admonished her husband.

"Neil, yes, in hindsight perhaps you should have been told. I'm sorry."

"Hang on William. Did you say hearings, plural?" Melissa was listening intently.

He nodded. "This morning there was a plea hearing for those arrested on 20ᵗʰ January. All of them, except my father, pleaded guilty."

There were loud cheers.

"Did Tobias plead not guilty then" Pat asked.

"The charges against him were dropped because of lack of evidence. However, sentence will be handed down on the others next week."

There was a mass outburst of indignation because Tobias had walked free. William waved his arms for them to calm down.

"What're the Councillors charged with?" Pat asked.

"They and our esteemed MP are charged with malfeasance in public office, plus intention to commit fraud and evade paying tax."

"Bloody hell. I hope they get sent down for a really long time!" Mr Podger said. "Sorry to say this, William, but it's a shame Tobias's got off Scott free!"

"Mr P, I agree. No doubt he will 'resign' from his directorships."

"Seeing him sacked would be better." Fynne said.

"He's probably resigned already. He's guilty by association, even if it can't be proved in law." William suggested. "There's more. At lunchtime Richard Berwick and I were informed the Council have officially withdrawn their appeal so therefore the JR stands."

The joyous outburst was riotous.

In Jersey Suzie and Charles could hear the cheering muted by the Skype link.

"Charles, you didn't have anything to do providing evidence for this, did you?"

"No dear, I didn't."

Suzie raised an eyebrow as if to say she did not believe him.

"Really, darling, it was as big a surprise to me as it is to you." Charles blew her a kiss.

William and Melissa sat in the public gallery of Southwark Crown Court. The ex Member of Parliament for Ardur & Sompting was standing in the dock.

"William, it occurred to me there'll have to be a by-election since old what's his face over there is about to go down." Melissa whispered.

"It will certainly expose public feeling for this government, but before you ask, no, I don't want a career in politics. Just because I went to the same school as the PM doesn't mean I want to join him and his cronies."

They sat and listened as the sixty-five year old Sir Bernard Fordingley received twenty-five years for malfeasance in public office.

"He was lucky. He could have been given life." William said.

The councillors, including Julian and Barbara Pilkington, received fifteen years each for the same offence; John Dryden was given a further seven years for attempted tax evasion and fraud and Lansbury was handed a twenty year sentence.

"Do you think Lansbury was the brains behind the whole thing." Melissa whispered.

"Possibly, but I doubt it." William looked around the Court. "My father is conspicuous by his absence."

"It's a shame he isn't here to support his partner." Melissa squeezed William's hand.

"You're judging him by your own standards, Lissie. One of my father's more 'endearing' traits is his selfishness. He's probably taken himself off somewhere to get away from any Press attention. Come on, let's go home."

Lansbury was found hanging in his cell within a week of being sentenced.

"Mrs P, Charles says KB's bank has foreclosed and New Manor has already been sold." Melissa sat holding the phone as if it were a baton.

"Is this some sort of April Fool's joke!" Mrs Podger asked, thinking it was in rather poor taste if it were. "Did 'e tell you who the new owner is? It's only a couple of days since the KB lot were sent to prison!"

"No, no he didn't." Melissa drank her coffee. "I never thought it would happen so fast."

"The bank presumably wanted its money back so sold to the first person who covered the debt. Does 'e know who it is?"

"I didn't ask, but I suppose we can always do a search at the Land Registry, but if it's owned by a foreign company that won't tell us much."

"Melissa, the sooner our William stops is away from all that devious legal stuff, the better."

"I agree, Mrs P, but he doesn't want to leave the firm until he's finished his current workload."

"When does he think he'll be free?"

"I haven't a clue; my guess is not before Christmas."

"What the hell is that?" Melissa jumped out of bed and threw back the curtains. The house was shaking. "William, there're earth movers rumbling down the boundary." She grabbed the kimono.

"Rabbit, stop! I'll deal with them. You can't go shouting the odds in your jimjams!" William was already pulling on his jeans. "What's the time?" The clock showed 7.00 a.m. "It's too bloody early for a Saturday! I'll go and find out what it's all about."

Melissa and the Podgers watched as William gesticulated wildly at the driver of the bulldozer.

"Melissa, what do you suppose's 'appening?" Mrs Podger asked as William started walking back to the house. A loud bellow came from the nursery. "Sounds as if young Edward's awake. Mr Podger you make the tea." Mrs P re-tied her dressing gown cord and disappeared to the nursery.

"What's happening, William?"

William brushed his hair back of his face. "They've apologised for the early start and the good news is they're going to be pulling out the hedge and bringing down that eyesore of a fence. They've been given instructions to restore the park to exactly as it was before KB did their worst!"

"Eh, William, that's good news." Mr Podger poured boiling water into the teapot. Melissa realised she had never seen Mr Podger in his dressing gown until today.

"Mr P, it seems we really do have decent new neighbours. Have you told the bees about the change in ownership?"

"I 'ave, Melly. I tell 'em all the news of the estate. It might be an old wives tale, but I'm not prepared to lose 'em just because I think it's a load of old bunkum so I tell 'em everything."

"'ere William. It's all very well, but all that noise has woken Edward and he's very grumpy. You can soothe him for a bit." Mrs P handed the bawling baby to his father "When did they say they were coming back?"

Edward stopped crying and beamed at his father.

"They said it'll take them a couple of hours to rip out the trees and backfill the holes, so they asked if they could come back in an hour."

Melissa was smiling so broadly she felt as if her face was going to split. She stood at the kitchen window holding little Hetty.

"Hettybang, they're going to make the park all better so you will be able to see all the way to the Chanctonbury Ring. William, are they going to seed it with proper seed?"

"Yep, he told me they've been given orders to use local wild flower seed, and I've suggested they contact Neil for help in sourcing it."

"Might as well make some money out of someone. Good thing that someone's got their brain in gear. The honey harvest hasn't been up to its usual standard ever since your father sold up to those greedy bastards." Mr Podger might have sounded grumpy, but his happy expression gave him away. His beloved bees would once again have their favourite flowers to gather nectar from.

Melissa watched as the bulldozers dragged the fence away and dug out the trees. The long familiar wide vista over the South Downs was slowly reappearing. Lorries were dumping their loads of topsoil, which was then being pushed into the holes left by the removal of the trees. Soon the whole view would be open and flat with only the brown of the new soil to show something had been there. She sat rocking the double buggy. Hetty lay watching her mother; Edward was more interested in sucking his thumb and watching the clouds.

"Your Daddy says the new owners are going to make the whole park better." She told her children. "I wonder who they are?"

"Aye, pet. I do too. P'r'aps they'd let you use the family chapel to 'ave these two christened?" Mrs Podger handed Melissa a mug of tea as she gave her gentle reminder of what she believed was the next big event in the life of all those at The Old Manor House.

"What a good idea, but it seems a bit of a nerve since we haven't even met them."

"One thing I've learned is if you don't ask, you don't get."

"Mrs P, while we're on the subject of christening, I'd like to add your name to Hetty's."

"Oh, Melissa, that is sweet, but it's already there! I'm Susannah, like Mrs Sampson."

"Oh Mrs P, that's wonderful."

"When you were little I tried to suggest you called us Auntie Suzie and Uncle Godfrey, but 'etty wouldn't 'ave it."

"She was a bit odd like that."

"I suppose it stopped you getting all sorts of airs and graces, unlike some we know!"

"You mean Tobias?"

Mrs Podger nodded. "It's always infuriated Mr P 'ow Tobias called us both Podger as if we were some sort of flunkies."

"It makes you both sound like characters in a rather bad Victorian melodrama."

Mrs Podger sniffed disapprovingly. "That might be so, but the Podger's are an old Devon family. Tobias 'as delusions of grandeur way above 'is station. I think your great aunt 'ad the right idea."

"I didn't mean to offend, Mrs P. I'll get William to ask if we can use the chapel. He's been trying to invite himself into New Manor ever since it was sold, but the owners evidently live abroad and take an age to answer him."

"And if the weather is good, we can have tea 'ere on the terrace looking over the park without a tree or fence in sight to spoil the view, just like it's always been."

1ST JULY

Two large removal vans rumbled through the Estate gates, up the drive and turned off to New Manor, followed by the postman on his bike.

The postman cycled up to The Old Manor and handed Melissa a bundle of envelopes.

"'Morning, Dr Carlisle. I see the neighbours are moving in."

"Have you see anyone other than the man in the car, Spike?" Melissa asked. If anyone knew the identity of New Manor's new owners, he would.

"No, only 'im. They get all the usual rubbish from Sky, Virgin and the pizza delivery services, but very little else. If I 'ear anything interesting I'll let you know."

Melissa turned her attention to her post, which included a similar bundle of advertising blurb. There were a couple of envelopes addressed to 'The Occupier'.

"Well, they can all go out." Melissa dropped them into the recycle bin.

One envelope was addressed to her. The envelope was franked, but there was no company name. She took it into the study and slit it open.

"Dear Dr Carlisle," was written in ink. The letter continued:

"As sole executor of the Will of Tobias de Braose, 13th Earl of Poultney, I write to advise you that the infants, Edward William David Alistair Charles and Esther Susannah Rosemary Victoria Carlisle are the sole beneficiaries of his Will, executed on Tuesday, 21st October 2013. I attach a copy of the Will . . .

Melissa put the letter on her desk. Tobias was dead. William had said nothing, neither had Rosemary. It was bizarre.

She did a Google search, but that elicited nothing. She reached for the phone and dialled the telephone number at the top of the headed paper and listened as a male voice told her that Tobias had died of pancreatic cancer on 28th March. It had been his specific wish for no public announcements of his passing. His other wish was that his body be cremated and his ashes scattered to the four winds with no member of his family present. This had been done. Either he, or someone from the probate department, would be back in touch shortly.

She thanked him and sat back, shocked at the news.

Perhaps Mr Tewksbury could help.

"Melissa, leave it with me." Mr Tewksbury told her. "I'll get a copy of the death certificate and come back to you, but it might take a few days."

"Mr Tewksbury I don't think William knows."

"If the executors are doing this by the book, since William isn't a beneficiary they don't have a duty to inform him."

"He's away until the weekend and I'm not going to tell him over the phone. I'd appreciate having a copy of the death certificate just in case he doesn't believe it."

"I'll get the certified copy to you before the end of the week."

William sat looking at his father's death certificate.

"If I weren't holding a certified copy I wouldn't believe you." He picked up and re-read the letter addressed to Melissa. He then re-read Tobias's will.

"Have you seen this Mrs P?"

"No, William. It's the first I've heard about it. 'tis as big a shock to me as it is to you."

"Presumably mother doesn't know either." He looked at Melissa sitting opposite to him at the table.

"I shouldn't think so. Your father was quite explicit – no announcements and the twins are the sole beneficiaries."

"I'm going for a walk."

Melissa started to follow him.

"No, Lissie. I want some space."

Mr Podger was sat in his usual chair next to the fireplace. "I wish you'd told me, Melly. I've 'ad two swarms this week and I thought it were for no apparent reason."

"I did tell the bees, Mr P. I just couldn't tell you before I told William."

"No matter – I'm going to tell 'em again anyway, just in case they didn't 'ear you the first time."

Mr Podger's telling the bees about Tobias's death was completely illogical and irrational. Tobias had died in March; but Melissa was not going to argue.

William sat by the side of the lake remembering the night he and Melissa had watched the deer come down to drink. Was it really only three years ago? He took out his father's death certificate and looked at it yet again. He had difficulty recalling his father's face. The only photographs he knew of were of Tobias as a child and they were in Scotland. The only other references to the late Earl were Hetty's diary entries and now, this piece of paper. But that was it; no service, no gravestone. Even the ashes had been thrown to the winds. It was as if Tobias had never existed.

How had Tobias known about the twins? Melissa had not made any formal announcement of their birth. Rosemary was the only one who had any right to pass on this news. He would have liked to have been a witness to that meeting. Their meetings had been few and far between, but perhaps Rosemary had felt he had a right to know he was a grandfather.

Perhaps Tobias's death explained Lansbury's suicide. 29th March was the same day he and Melissa had sat in Southwark Crown Court listening to the sentences being passed on the fraudsters. William felt guilty he was unable to acknowledge he owed his very existence to Tobias. Now it was all over. A chapter of his life closed.

He sat leaning against an old oak, watching the fish rise and take the midges flitting just above the water. The gentle twittering of the birds and the soft sound of the summer breeze in the branches above lulled him into a restful, healing sleep.

For the moment the babies were asleep. Mr Podger was mowing the lawn on his new ride-on mower, which was the loudest noise anyone ever heard now the park had been restored. Fresh new growth of special meadow grasses and wild flowers now covered white wounds that had been inflicted on the parkland. The wounds may have disappeared, but it would take thousands of years before it returned to being the rare chalk grassland it once was, but the tiny harebells and the cowslips, as well as many other of New Manor's original wild flowers were blooming again.

Thanks to the injunction Monk's Wood and Field had remained untouched and the rare large blue butterflies had been sighted again. The re-appearance of these was grounds for rejoicing. The new hedges on Melissa's boundaries were all flourishing and the ones that had been ripped out by the developers had been re-planted. Roman snails were found every morning on the terraces of The Old Manor and another survey had discovered that the dormice were flourishing. The new hedges would, hopefully, eventually become homes for the endearing, sleepy rodents.

In the kitchen Mrs Podger was putting the finishing touches to her latest cake. She had spent hours creating an edible version of The Old Manor in a parkland setting, fashioning dormice, snails and a large blue butterfly out of sugar. In the garden caterers had set up a pop-up kitchen behind the marquee, which was all ready with tables, chairs and a dance floor. The band were doing sound checks and the archaeologists had just arrived and were setting up their tents so they would have somewhere to sleep after the festivities.

William and Melissa were grabbing a few minutes together by the lake.

"Do you remember the night we sat and watched the deer come down to drink?"

"You pointed out a badger, but I missed it."

"That's when I fell in love with you, Rabbit."

She leaned against him. "Why then?"

"I've no idea."

"Thanks Clunkhead, that's not very flattering."

"You appeared so much part of the land."

Melissa remembered how she thought how unlikely it was that someone like him would ever even look at her. She would forever regret having excluded him from the birth of their children.

"William, thank you for defeating KB."

"If we hadn't had that list of shareholders it could have been a different story."

"Perry and Scott tell me they've decided to publish their findings about the Underground Hospital as a novel."

"I think that's very wise. From what you've told me, I don't think the world is ready for that particular piece of information about the German occupation. Even so, a novel with their research at its core, will still be hard reading."

"Being fiction will soften the reality."

"What about you? Are you going to publish a book of stories?"

"What do you mean?"

"Rabbit, do you think I haven't heard you weaving tales of naughty gnomes causing all sorts of mayhem with twins called Tedward and Hettybang."

"Don't mock. There was a whole load of stuff in storage in Jersey and I found a box of sketchbooks full of Hetty's illustrations together with notebooks of stories in Daddy's handwriting, so I'm just telling our children stories their grandfather had written."

"Were you substituting their names for yours?"

Melissa nodded. "It's quite odd; it's as if Daddy's next to me. I can't remember hearing any of them, but they do seem familiar."

"Perhaps you should write the story of how New Manor nearly became a housing estate."

"So could you now you've decided to give up being a lawyer. By the way, I've been studying a full page illumination in the de Braose book of Hours which shows Henry VIII planting an oak tree in front of what I believe is now New Manor."

"The oak that blew down in '87 was about four hundred and fifty years old."

Melissa nodded. "There's a payment in the de Braose accounts for 1511 to the Bening workshop for a Book of Hours and that's the same year that Henry VIII's first son was born."

"But we didn't own it until 1539."

"Quite so, but when it was a monastery there was a shrine here, so I think the illumination was painted to commemorate the King's visit when he came to give thanks for the birth of his heir in 1511 and planted an oak as a symbol of the growth of the Tudor dynasty."

"Prince Edward wasn't born until much later!"

"There was an earlier prince born to Queen Katharine in 1511 who died within weeks of birth."

William thought for a minute and chuckled.

"Do you think the 1st Earl was here in 1511 and grabbed the chance to buy it when Cromwell dissolved the monasteries?"

"Yep, and I think he commissioned the Hours in memory of that pilgrimage in 1511, but what puzzles me is that we've never had any evidence of Simon Bening visiting England, until now."

"Lissie, it so nearly disappeared."

"I know." She whispered.

They sat enjoying their rare moment of peace and quiet together.

"William, I think I've worked out what KB's name was all about."

"Go on."

"Well, I went back to the idea that their end game was always that the land would be OK'd for a housing development."

"So tell me, what does Kuckelimat Baquecks stand for?"

"Let Us Make a Quick Buck."

William was not going to admit that he had been stumped.

"I think the judge had spotted it, made his decision and was just making KB go through the motions."

"It's possible Rabbit."

"Why do you think they went to appeal?"

"They had to."

"Do you think they'd've won if it had been heard?"

"Definitely! I think the appeal judges were under orders from on high because the Chancellor couldn't afford to have his new planning regulations torn to pieces at the first challenge. His whole plan for economic revival rests on the construction industry leading the way, which is why the JR would have been overturned."

Melissa was no longer surprised by the cavalier way those in power manipulated the system to their own ends.

"So how come the whole plan came crumbling down?"

318

"Because when it was investigated, that shareholder list showed how KB was a probable tax scam."

"I still don't follow."

"Because KB Ltd appeared to be a tax scam, Her Majesty's Revenue & Customs were the ones who led the first raids."

Melissa looked shocked.

"There were a series of dawn raids and the evidence the taxmen grabbed was gold dust. Initially, they were looking for anything that pointed to tax evasion, but not only did they turn up tax stuff, there was evidence that lead to the criminal charges of malfeasance and fraud."

"How?"

"The developer you heard briefing Lansbury and Tobias at the High Court was John Dryden, brother-in-law of Councillor Pilkington of casting vote fame. Evidently the Pilkingtons had a major shareholding in KB through another one of the offshore companies on that list and Councillor Pilkington was a director of Dryden's offshore holding company. When the police raided Dryden's home, they found he had made very detailed notes of meetings and telephone calls with Pilkington, Lansbury, Fordingley and a whole host of other local worthies."

"Why would Dryden record conversations?"

"They provided the key, and when the fraud team ploughed through everything they found in Dryden's study, they turned up details for payments made to Sir Brian. The thorough record keeping of our developer led to the discovery that Fordingley was a major investor in KB Ltd through a complex series of offshore companies based in the Cayman Islands. All the evidence was there, all dated and filed neatly away."

"That sounds more like a personality disorder!"

"No, I disagree. My nasty cynical mind tends to think it was more a case of having an insurance policy should their plan go belly up." William's

"So he wouldn't end up being the one carrying the can?"

"Exactly. If I were going to try to pull off something like this, I wouldn't trust anyone."

"So Dryden's cache of documents is why they all pleaded guilty?"

William nodded. "The evidence against them was so overwhelming there was no way they could defend their actions."

"Your father was never charged."

"He didn't feature. It was only Lansbury or Dryden's signatures on any document. The only concrete connection we have of Dryden, Lansbury and Tobias is your report of their conversation outside the Court." William paused for a minute. "The raid on Dryden showed there was a vast network of companies the defendants had been using to hide profits from other various scams they were into, but Tobias never featured in any of them."

"It wasn't just this golf course development then?"

William shook his head. "No, there were projects going back ten or so years."

"Do you think it was all Lansbury's brainchild?"

"No. He was the one who knew how to set it all up, but Tobias had the social and political connections. There were various offshore companies for various local developments and similar setups for some big developments in the City, all of which involved certain people with privileged information or position, including some of those who had invested in KB; then my father inherited New Manor and the concept of a failing spa and golf course providing prime land for a luxury residential development was irresistible."

"Do you think drug money was being laundered?"

"I don't know." William paused, "and frankly, I don't want to. There are some powerful people out there who think they are above the law and I'm sure there will be more revelations in the months to come." William threw a pebble into the lake and they watched the ripples moving out in a series of ever increasing concentric circles. The surface of the lake returned to normal with midges dancing above it. Melissa threw another pebble making more rings and contemplated how that list of shareholders dropped anonymously through her door had been like that pebble.

"Marry me, Lissie."

"Why?"

"Because I love you." William slipped a ring on to her finger "and I think I should make an honest woman of you."

"They're the Jersey diamonds!"

"They look so much better on your finger than in my pocket."

Melissa looked at her hand remembering how they had argued over these stones.

320

"Rabbit," William whispered, wondering whether she was admiring the ring before handing it back to him. "Would that be a yes?"

Melissa threw her arms around his neck. They were nose to nose.

"Since you're now the 14th Earl of Poultney, do you think we could we ask the new owners if we can use the chapel?"

William kissed her. "If we ask them now, we could announce the date tonight."

They walked across the front lawn of New Manor. The old oak front door stood open. Melissa stopped.

"Perhaps we should ring them first."

"Don't be silly, Rabbit. We're here and the door's open so we know somebody's finally home. Anyway, it's about time we introduced ourselves. You never know, perhaps they'll change their minds and come along tonight." He pulled her towards the house. "Come on."

Melissa stopped again on the porch. "Perhaps we should ring the bell."

"Oh for God's sake woman." William swept her up and carried her over the threshold.

"William, put me down! What will they think?"

The hall smelled of lavender and beeswax furniture polish.

"Welcome home, Lady de Braose." he whispered.

"What do you mean?"

William put her down on her feet. Melissa stood looking at all the de Braose portraits back in their rightful places. The 17th century William, resplendent in his cavalier uniform was in his old place at the foot of the stairs; the living William's own great grandfather wearing his army uniform was hung at the half landing.

"Have you sold Cremorne?"

William shook his head. "Never! Charles organised a bridging loan until the Titian was sold."

"So you **did** look at my inventories."

"Without them this wouldn't have been possible."

"But the da Vinci!"

"I know how you love it. It's still safe in it's box."

"Do you have your phone?" Melissa held out her hand. William gave her his handset; she dialled.

"Melissa. How can I help?" Charles wondered what was so important it could not wait until he and Suzie arrived for the party.

"Charles, I know I was going to have a dabble in the art market."
Melissa flicked the phone on to speaker.

"Yes, it's a very safe investment at the moment."

"I take it I'm not going to own the manuscript I told you about?"

Charles coughed and spluttered. Melissa smiled at a slightly puzzled William.

"William here, Charles. When you said you had an English investor interested in buying the Titian you were pretty evasive about the buyer."

Charles shifted down a gear and accelerated down the slip road on to the dual carriageway. The traffic ahead was relatively light.

"You and I had already had the conversation about my brokering a sale for the painting. When I told you I thought I might have found you a buyer, you were quite happy about their wish for anonymity, just as long as the painting wasn't going to leave the country."

In the car Suzie was looking daggers at Charles, a thousand questions forming in her head.

"So to keep my pride intact and the Titian in the family, you came up with the art investment idea for Melissa?"

"On the contrary William. I had advised her she had too much cash in her accounts. She vetoed the idea of playing the stock market or buying any more property. It was Melissa who wanted a little speculation in the art market. I looked at the options and investing in a Titian seemed the best option."

"Charles, the Rothschild Hours are just as safe a bet as a newly discovered Titian! More to the point, how come you never said New Manor was up for sale?"

"It never came on the open market."

"Charles Cliffe, you are a conniving, manipulating old banker! Where's the painting now?" Melissa asked.

"National Gallery, being restored. We've just got off the ferry so we're only about an hour away. We can discuss this then." The banker broke the connection not relishing the quizzing Suzie was about to subject him to between now and their arrival at The Old Manor House.

"Rabbit, do you think Charles really did send that shareholder list?"

"Whatever Charles did, he did for the best possible reasons and if he did send it, that's something he's not going to tell anyone. Does it matter who sent that list? What's important is that New Manor is back in the family. Anyway, who did you buy the estate off?"

"Charles brokered the whole deal. I gave him my power of attorney to act should New Manor come up for sale and gave him the Titian as collateral."

"That's ironic considering your advice to me when Lansbury tried to get me to sign a power of attorney?"

"Evidently the mortgagor was an English subsidiary of a Russian bank. Don't you think it's ironic that some of the sale money may form part of Tobias's estate, so will come back through the children."

"That's weird." Melissa thought about all the strange twists of the past three years.

"Rabbit, would you've bought the estate if it had come on the open market."

"You heard Charles, I'd already told him I didn't want anymore property.

"Somehow Lady de Braose, I'm not sure I totally believe you!" William hugged her. "Perhaps we should go and tell Mrs P she's got her old kitchen back."

Melissa looked up at Hetty's portrait of Edward. Perhaps it was a trick of the light, but it appeared as if the 12th Earl was smiling.

"Not yet, William. I want to enjoy New Manor welcoming us home for just a bit longer."

AUTHOR'S NOTE

This book was inspired by two specific fights to save our landscape from being destroyed; one in England, the other on the Channel Island of Jersey.

The South East of England has several hundred golf courses, many of which are struggling financially. The legal history of the fight to save an area of rare calcareous grassland that inspired the English element of this story is summed up on this website.

http://www.cherkleycampaign.co.uk/About.html. The campaigners won the Judicial Review, but unlike the outcome of the novel, the campaign lost when the local council went to appeal. The case was the first serious challenge to the English government's revised planning regulations, known as The National Planning Policy Framework (NPPF). The world's areas of chalk grassland are coming increasingly under pressure from population growth and pollution; they take thousands of years to develop and contain rare micro ecosystems. The destruction of this ancient, species rich, area of the Surrey landscape and its replacement with a limited selection of grasses, is a travesty. The golf course will be completed shortly.

The Pontin's Holiday Camp site is at Plemont in the northwest part of the island of Jersey. In 2014 the owners of the site finally agreed to sell this site to the National Trust of Jersey, thus ensuring the area will remain a place of beauty and a haven for wildlife for future generations. Local support was key and the islanders were photographed showing their support in a mass demonstration on one of the island's beautiful beaches. In July 2014 the States agreed to match the amount raised by the NTJ. The site was purchased and work started on the site. In June 2015 BBC's 'Countryfile' broadcast the progress of the re-wilding of the areas where the Pontin's buildings had once stood and Radio 4 featured the island in their programme, 'Open Country', in August 2015.

The National Trust of Jersey recently won the 'NGO Impact Award' from the Chartered Institute of Ecology and Environmental Management for their '*Love Plemont*' campaign. This important award acknowledges the Trust's hard work and dedication to preserving the island's natural and historical heritage. www.nationaltrust.je

Other Books by Melanie V Taylor

The Truth of the Line

In 1572, the good looking and talented Nicholas Hillyarde paints the first of many portraits of Elizabeth I, England's "Virgin Queen". His ability to capture the likeness of his patrons makes him famous and his skills are much sought after by the rich and powerful members of the Elizabethan Court. His loyalty to Elizabeth even leads him to becoming part of Sir Francis Walsingham's information network.

One day he is approached by a young man calling himself Arthur Southron who asks to be painted holding a lady's hand - a hand which descends from a cloud – and to include the puzzling motto: *"Attici Amoris Ergo"*. Hillyarde is intrigued by the familiarity of this young man's features.

A possible interpretation of this apparently nonsensical Latin inscription leads Hillyarde to believe he may have stumbled across a dark royal secret. If so, is there evidence hidden elsewhere?

Published by **www.MadeGlobal.com** in paperback, Kindle and audio format through Amazon.

The Walls of Truth

The year is 1945. Hitler's war in Europe is over, but for The Man and The Interrogator things have only just started.

The Interrogator sat behind a large desk, examining the features of The Man seated across from him, and smiled.

The Man did not react. He had no idea of where he was or how he had got here . . .

The identity of The Man may be obvious, but who is the Interrogator and where are they? That will be your choice.

My short story is a tribute to all those nations occupied by the Germans during WW2, those souls who lost their lives through Nazi persecution and all those who fought so we can enjoy the freedom we have today. I am proud that a copy of this novella has been accepted for inclusion in the Yad Vashem Holocaust Museum library in Jerusalem.

Published by **www.MadeGlobal.com** and is available as a paperback and in electronic format through Amazon.

Made in the USA
Charleston, SC
21 February 2016